HIS ACCIDENTAL COWBOY

A.M. ARTHUR

T0020024

carina
press

Recycling programs
for this product may
not exist in your area.

carina
press®

ISBN-13: 978-1-335-44869-9

His Accidental Cowboy

Copyright © 2023 by A.M. Arthur

For questions and comments about the quality of this book, please contact us at CustomerService@Harlequin.com.

Carina Press
22 Adelaide St. West, 41st Floor
Toronto, Ontario M5H 4E3, Canada
www.CarinaPress.com

Printed in U.S.A.

For Alissa,
I am forever grateful for your
keen editorial eye and generous insights.

HIS ACCIDENTAL COWBOY

Chapter One

Jackson Sumner leaned back in the old wooden chair, stretched his long legs out in front of him, and surveyed the pickings in the dim light of the Blue Tavern, his favorite out-of-the-way watering hole when he had a particular itch to scratch. An itch he used to get scratched by a friend who was now off the market for such things, so he was back to his hunting days. Looking for someone to fuck or to fuck him—he wasn't too picky tonight.

The Blue Tavern was a long drive from home, about thirty minutes if he sped and forty if he didn't, but it was worth the time and gas to sit in a small square space full of other gay, bi or gay-curious men who wouldn't pitch a fit if Jackson flirted. A few butch lesbians wandered the crowd, usually there to hustle some of the newbies at pool, but a lot fewer women came here in general.

Not a lot of people drove to a dive bar in the middle of nowhere, period, unless they were looking for something specific.

Jackson picked up his beer glass and sipped at the warming liquid. Most of the beer here came out of the tap lukewarm, which was almost a badge of pride for the place, but they offered free baskets of over-salted popcorn as long as you kept buying drinks. Great selling strategy since you needed beer to eat the stuff. He rested his jacketed arm on the edge of the small round table, having learned a long time ago to never put his bare skin on those tabletops. The familiar scents of beer, sweat and cigarette smoke filled the air—three things that were oddly comforting as a combination, considering his history.

Not a lot was churning in the waters tonight, though, which sucked. He'd come out for a reason, and while he wasn't above fucking someone he wasn't much attracted to, he wasn't in the mood for that. Sure, it had been a few months since his last fuck buddy had called things off, so he really shouldn't have still been hung up on the guy, but their arrangement had lasted for four years.

Hard to say goodbye to someone after so long, especially when said fuck buddy had always made Jackson feel seen and present in the sex they were having. But the guy had a boyfriend, and they were living together, and Jackson truly did wish them well. The people in his life were happy and that helped.

Helped on the lonely nights when he thought about walking into the wilderness surrounding the small towns of Claire County and not coming back.

Except Dog kept him firmly at home or at work. She was a mutt who'd wandered up to him one day out of the blue, hadn't gone away, and she'd never told him her name. So she was Dog, with her beautiful blue eyes and a bit of border collie that came out when she herded the cattle.

She was waiting at home for him right now, so he'd eventually go home to her. Scratch behind her floppy ears and go to sleep—with or without his own itch scratched.

A shadow fell over his table from the right. Jackson looked up at a stocky man with a full, trimmed beard, a red flannel shirt and a cigarette dangling from the same hand that somehow held a beer bottle by the neck. The dexterity was promising, but Jackson wasn't in the mood for a bear tonight.

"That chair over there looks lonely," the stranger said with a flirty smile. "Mind if I sit in it?"

Jackson relaxed his expression so his response came out more joking than annoyed. "Not at all, so long as you take it to another table."

He grunted and moved on. Jackson didn't watch to see where he went, more interested in a small commotion near the door. The bar was maybe two thousand square feet, including the bar space and closet-sized kitchen that spat out greasy wings and over-cheesed nachos, making it easy to see everything going on. No angry voices, so it wasn't a fight. The only thing that usually caught so much attention was fresh meat.

And fresh meat it was—or at least Jackson had never seen the guy before. At least as tall as him, a slender guy with curly red hair eased his way through the thin wall of men and took a spot at the short bar in front of Darlin', the place's only bartender. Jackson had no idea where Darlin' got his nickname, but he was sure to correct folks when they spelled or pronounced the *g*.

The hair intrigued him. Not many gingers lived around here, and even fewer guys sported those sort of long, thick ringlets that seemed more in place on one of Santa's elves than a guy in the middle of the Texas nowhere. The Blue Tavern was ninety minutes from the nearest big city, so the kid had come a long way for some cowboy thrills. At least he hadn't walked into Bullhorn's down in Daisy, or he'd have been laughed right out of the place.

A few guys seemed to try to buy him a drink that the redhead declined. He left the bar with a tall glass of something bubbly and clear, and Jackson got a better look at his face. Definitely young, so *kid* was an okay word. The dim light made it hard to tell if he had any freckles to go with that hair, and he seemed a touch uncertain where to go next. The joint had about twenty tables, most of which were empty, plus two pool tables, and one pinball machine in the corner by the bathrooms.

He zeroed in on Jackson, and something about that direct stare sent happy signals right to Jackson's dick. Jackson didn't usually go for tall, redheaded twinks, but something about this guy waltzing into the Tavern on a Monday night intrigued him. It was ballsy and bizarre, and Jackson wanted to know more. He tilted his head toward the kid in a slight nod.

The redhead threaded his way to Jackson's table and plunked down in the seat beside him. "Hey, man."

"Hey, yourself." Jackson didn't see any freckles, but his eyes were a pale shade of something. Sharp nose and cheekbones, definitely cute. He towered over Jackson's slouched posture, and Jackson had a feeling the kid had a few inches on him anyway. Of height, at least.

"Name's W-Wilson."

Of course it was. "Jackson." Wilson started to take off his fleece-lined flannel jacket. "I wouldn't do that. They clean the tables about twice a month, and I think the next scheduled time is tomorrow."

Wilson stared at him, as if unsure whether Jackson was joking or not. He left the jacket on and sipped his drink. "So you from around here?"

As lines went, that was about as lame as humanly possible, but it also made Jackson smile. Wilson was clearly out of his element right now, and there were too many guys lurking around, ready to make a snack out of him, for Jackson to scare the kid away. "No one's from around here, really. There ain't a town for ten miles. But if you're talkin' about Claire County, then I live here. Not from around here."

"Right. For the middle of nowhere, the bartender is really good at spotting a fake ID." A flush spread across his nose and cheeks, as if embarrassed he'd admitted to using one.

Jackson's gut tightened in a less pleasant way. "Tell me you're at least eighteen, or you can walk away from this table."

Wilson scowled. "I'm twenty, thank you. Just figured if I was traveling by myself, being a little older wouldn't hurt."

"Traveling alone, huh? On your way to where? I'd say college, but you're definitely goin' in the wrong direction for that."

"No, I'm out looking for work."

"Doing what?"

"Whatever. What do you do?"

"This and that. I have quite a variety of skills, depending on the situation." As true of his job as his skills in the bedroom. As a rustler out at Woods Ranch, Jackson did all sorts of chores, from mucking stalls and grooming the horses, to riding the lines and herding the cattle from one grazing pasture to another. As a man? He could probably show this kid a thing or twelve.

Wilson's dark red eyebrows raised. "You sound pretty sure of yourself."

"Gotta be around here." Jackson took a long drink from his warm beer. "Now, what kind of work is a pretty boy like you lookin' for out here in the sticks? Ain't got much need for modeling or car salesmen."

"You assume a lot about me."

"Prove me wrong, then." Jackson crossed his arms, enjoying the conversation now that he'd gotten the kid's temper up a bit. "You drove out of your way to get here, but you're underage, so it wasn't for a quiet drink, and no one comes here for a quiet drink, anyway. They come for one of two reasons."

"Which are?"

"Get drunk and sleep it off in the backroom because Darlin' has taken your car keys away from you." He tilted his head and smirked. "Or get drunk and go home with a guy you wanna fuck your brains out." When the blush across Wilson's nose and cheeks darkened, Jackson continued. "Since you already admitted you're traveling around lookin' for work, and there's no motel within forty miles, you're lookin' for someplace to crash for the night that isn't your car."

"So what if I am looking for a place to crash? I've done it before."

Something in the way Wilson's eyes flickered said that was a lie. "Besides, you don't know me. I can defend myself, and how do you know I don't have a gun under my jacket?"

"Because if you did, you wouldn't have just told me." Jackson abhorred guns, and the only reason he owned one was because he lived in an isolated spot away from the main roads. He'd only ever fired it to scare away an errant coyote, but strangers occasionally crept around the property. He saw the signs when he got home.

Wilson's mouth flopped open in an amusing, almost endearing way as he sought for a response. He was pretty cute when flustered, and while Jackson's dick was still interested, he didn't want to take advantage of someone who was trying so hard to appear tough but was pretty obviously clueless about a lot of things. Had he dropped fully formed from childhood into adulthood? A sheltered kid wandering unsupervised into a bar full of adults was a recipe for disaster.

A little concerned, Jackson sat up straighter and angled closer to him. "Look, are you in some kinda trouble? You a runaway?"

Wilson's steady gaze dropped to his lap.

Crap. "I'm not judging you, kid. Most of us in here got a story, and a lot of them ain't nothin' you'd want to hear around the family dinner table. But tricking out for a bed ain't safe, no matter how old or experienced you are."

"I just…" Wilson fiddled with his glass of what was either Sprite or club soda. "I needed to get out of my hometown. To find something else. Somewhere else."

"Trust me, I get that more than you know." Jackson's own past would probably scare the kid into going back home, but he didn't know Wilson's story. He might have legitimate reasons for running away, and it wasn't Jackson's job to question those reasons. Not without hearing more. "Don't take this as a come-on, because it ain't, but you wanna get out of here?"

He startled. "I thought you just said—"

"Not for sex, kid." Even if Wilson did push a lot of his buttons, Jackson needed to know more first. Wilson seemed both smart and clueless. "I can give you a safe place for the night in exchange for one hour of conversation. Honest conversation."

Wilson gazed at him, his intelligence shining in those pale eyes that seemed as curious as they were wary. "Does this hour start now or later?"

Jackson grinned. "It starts when we get back to my place."

"Okay then."

"Great. Just one question first."

"Shoot."

"Do you really have a gun? Because I don't like them."

Wilson shook his head. "No, I don't have a gun. You were right about me bluffing."

"Cool." Jackson drained the last of his beer and set the glass on the sticky table. "Then let's get outta here."

The kid followed Jackson in his own car, which gave him plenty of time to change his mind and drive away—especially when Jackson pulled off the main road to Weston and onto Diamondback Road. More a dusty, formerly paved track than a road now, it had a dead-end warning sign about a quarter-mile down. It had once been a through-road to a small town north, but about ten years ago a freak thunderstorm washed out a bridge no one had bothered to rebuild. The little town had a busier way in from another direction, and it had died out a few years back anyway.

Even after the dead-end sign, Wilson followed him.

Jackson had lucked into his digs and he knew it. They passed the remnants of a service station whose gas prices hadn't come up from seventy-two cents a gallon, and beyond that was the old Diamondback Motel. Six rooms, plus the office. The old neon sign had long ago been stripped, as had the vintage Coke machine by the office door. The property owner was adamant about not selling—Jackson had never asked why—but was tired of vandals and thieves picking over the place, so he'd enlisted Jackson's help.

Jackson got free run of the property as long as he kept it looking lived-in, deterred thieves, and kept things from falling into more disrepair. He had no idea if the owner thought he could renovate it, pass it on to his kids, or have it named a historical landmark, and he didn't care. It gave him seven rooms (he only used one), plenty of open space for Dog to run, and freedom from the rest of the world when he wasn't working.

The sun on his face, the wind in his hair, and wide-open spaces day and night? It was heaven on earth, and all he paid a month was the nominal electric bill, and the occasional sewer bill to have the tank pumped. What more could an ex-con ask for?

In the dark, the motel probably looked haunted, barely lit by the quarter moon and sky full of stars, but to Jackson it was home. He kept all the exterior room lights burning on dim bulbs, set on a timer so no one could sneak around in the dark, and he thought it gave the place a slightly less saggy look.

Jackson parked in front of room four. He'd chosen that one because it had the only working TV and VHS player, plus the cleanest bathroom, and he'd quickly become very popular at the county library as one of the few patrons who still checked out VHS movies on a weekly basis. The place didn't have cable or internet, so it was his only entertainment besides books and the radio that picked up two stations. He did all his necessary internet stuff on the ranch's Wi-Fi.

Wilson parked beside him and climbed out of the four-door blue sedan slowly, head swiveling, taking in everything. "Why do I feel like I just stepped into the first act of a horror movie that will end with me being stalked by cannibals intent on making me the centerpiece of tomorrow night's family supper?"

The earnest way he said that made Jackson laugh out loud—something he hadn't done in a long time. The sound roused familiar barking from inside his room.

"What's that?" Wilson asked, spinning in the direction of room four, both hands raised in an adorably defensive way.

"It's Dog. Don't worry, she won't bite."

"You have a dog?"

"Sure. Grab whatever stuff you need for the night and come on in. We can start our one-hour conversation."

"Yeah, okay."

Jackson unlocked his door and pushed it open. The sensor he'd installed to turn on a light when the door opened flashed to life. Dog yipped and jumped onto her back paws without bounding outside. "Hey, girl. Go whizz."

She darted outside, spared one soft bark for Wilson, then headed toward her favorite patch of spotty grass. The old parking lot had been mostly overtaken by grass and weeds, and Jackson tried to vary where he parked so he didn't leave an obvious spot behind. He had an office-sized water dispenser by the door that he traded bottles for about once a month, because he was home so infrequently. By the time Wilson took a tentative step inside—the poor guy tripped on the doorjamb—with a green duffel bag slung over one arm, Jackson had two plastic cups of water for them.

He whistled and Dog came in, then he shut the door with his foot. Wilson stood in the center of the room, probably trying to figure out which era the dated décor was from, with its diamond-pattern wallpaper, green shag rug that always smelled slightly of old beer, and gaudy gold chandelier in the center of the room. Jackson had added a few small touches, but he was a big fan of minimal living, so the bulk of his personal belongings consisted of clothes, toiletries, and the mouth harp he'd learned to play as a child.

"Here." Jackson held a cup out to Wilson. Dog sniffed at Wilson's feet, her shaggy tail wagging.

"Thanks." Wilson took the cup and sipped, keeping his body angled so he never gave Jackson his back.

Jackson didn't take a single ounce of offense as he pointed to the room's pair of chairs, upholstered in some sort of orange-and-brown floral pattern. "Have a seat. You can put your bag anywhere for now."

He did, dropping the duffel on the floor by his chair.

"How did you end up living in a motel? Are you squatting here? The place looks deserted."

"Not squatting. I've got permission from the owner to live here and chase off other potential squatters. Plenty of land for Dog and plenty of sky for me. No city noise or light pollution."

"No neighbors to hear you murder your victims?"

Jackson burst out laughing for the second time in Wilson's presence. "Yes, exactly. In the other five rooms, you'll find the bodies of all the other young men I've lured out here for sex, bondage, and asphyxiation."

Wilson's eyebrows jumped, but his expression was difficult to decipher. Not scared or shocked. Almost…curious? Jackson didn't want to scare the kid into running off into the wilderness, but this was their hour of conversation. Might as well get to know Wilson, and maybe see how well Wilson even knew himself.

"So you admit to an ulterior motive in bringing me here," Wilson said with a surprising touch of flirt in his voice. He sat with one ankle resting on his knee, posture relaxed, as if he'd known Jackson for a lot longer than an hour.

"Well, I was at the Tavern looking to get laid tonight and along came you. A tall, ginger drink of water with all the coordination of a newborn foal. I kind of wanna keep you safe until you can walk, as much as I wanna help you run as soon as possible."

If Wilson had flinched, angled his posture away from Jackson, or done anything besides lick his lips, Jackson would have backed down. But Wilson did lick his lips, while a new kind of heat flared in his eyes. The kid was definitely into him, and Jackson was definitely into Wilson. He had a kissable mouth and, from what Jackson could see behind those worn jeans, a very fuckable ass.

He was also a potential runaway, possibly coming out of a bad situation, and Jackson wasn't that guy. "How about you tell me what kinda work you're lookin' for?" Jackson said, cutting off the flirting before it went too far. "Maybe we've got something like it around here."

Wilson raised a single auburn eyebrow. "You really want to spend your hour with me talking? Seriously?"

"What?" Alarms rang in Jackson's head. "Kid, if you're some kinda rent boy, I wasn't out shopping for that tonight. You can take your skinny ass right back to the Tavern and find yourself another customer."

"Huh? Rent boy? I'm not a— Oh, the hour thing." He chuckled long and low, deeper than his light voice had any right to go, and no that did not ripple across Jackson's skin like a caress. "So not what I mean, old man."

"Old man?"

"Dude, you called me kid."

"You are a kid. I am not an old man." Even if he did feel like one some days, especially after three days camping out with the herd. His back didn't like the hard ground as much as it used to.

"I can see the gray hair and wrinkles."

"Yeah, well, I can see your attitude and arrogance, and it's gonna get you into trouble with the wrong person one day if you don't settle down a little bit. If we wanna clear the air here, I did bring you back to give you a safe place for the night in exchange for conversation, not sex. Am I attracted to you? Hell yes." He kind of wanted to know if Wilson's ass got as red as his face when smacked but he wasn't about to admit that.

Cue the kid racing for the foothills.

Instead, he said, "Am I gonna do anything about that tonight? No."

Wilson, the little devil, pouted. "Bummer. The reason

I came over to your table tonight was because you were the only guy in the bar not eyeing me like he wanted to tie me to the back of his motorcycle and steal off into the night with me. You were just…watching."

"I watch everyone. Like to know who's around, who's safe and who's not." A skill he'd picked up in prison and hadn't been able to shed, even fifteen years later. "Don't usually bring strangers back here for a one-night stand, and Dog seems to like you, though she likes everyone, so I guess you're okay."

"Wait, your dog's name is really Dog? Why?"

"She hasn't told me her name yet."

Wilson frowned. "Are you some kind of new-age hippie person who eats alfalfa sprouts and meditates and does downward dog into the sunrise?"

"Hardly." Jackson reached down to stroke the top of Dog's head. "She came to me and chose me, not the other way around. Doesn't seem right to name her."

"M'kay." Wilson uncrossed his legs and let them fall open, showing off his crotch. "So you really don't want me for anything other than conversation?"

"Want you? Yes." He knocked Wilson's nearest leg the other way, effectively closing off temptation. "Gonna do something about it? No. Don't care how many times in the past you've had to trick your way into a bed, it ain't happening tonight. You get a bed, just don't rip me off. Not that there's anything in room three for you to steal except stale sheets."

"I'm not staying with you?"

"Nope." Jackson stood and produced the right key from the dresser drawer and tossed it at Wilson. Wilson fumbled and it hit the floor with a clank. "Since it sounds like you don't wanna tell me anything about yourself tonight, why don't you go to bed. The water works just fine, so take a shower if you want. I have to get up early for work anyway."

"Oh." Wilson scooped up the key, then stood. He seemed disappointed for someone who'd come here with the expectation of being fucked, but that was probably because he hadn't gotten the payday he'd expected. The kid knew how to pick a mark out of a bar, and Jackson wouldn't be surprised if he heard the sedan's engine start in the next thirty minutes or less.

"Good luck, Wilson," Jackson said as he held open his room door. "Just leave your key in the empty planter outside when you go."

"Sure, thanks."

At the door, Wilson paused and looked slightly down at Jackson. His eyes swam with something a lot like regret, and Jackson didn't have time to ponder what exactly he regretted. Wilson brushed his lips lightly over Jackson's, just enough to spark a small flame deep in his gut. A flame that burned there long after Wilson left, shutting the door of room three behind him.

Jackson shut his own door and leaned against it, skin prickling with arousal and the awareness that a very hot young man was on the other side of their shared wall. But he wouldn't do it. As much as Wilson intrigued him and made his body ache for more than a five-minute chat, Jackson wouldn't be that person. He wouldn't take advantage of a young guy who appeared to be on a mission to find himself, and who was possibly running from something.

He wouldn't do to another kid what he'd allowed to be done to himself.

So he took a cold shower, and then tried very hard to sleep.

Chapter Two

"You have gotta be fucking with me," Jackson said.

The first words out of his boss's mouth that morning had him both stunned stupid and also not hugely surprised, but still. This was the second damned time in a year this had happened.

"Not fucking with you," Brand Woods replied. He stood just inside the break room in the main barn, having followed Jackson in there while Jackson put his lunch in the fridge. Brand was a straight shooter, always had been, and he never delivered bad news lightly.

"Alan broke his damned hand again? The same hand?"

"Yep."

Jackson snorted and eyeballed the coffee maker in the corner, positive his days were about to get a lot longer. He didn't guzzle the stuff like he used to but it kept him awake when he had to work extra shifts to make up for a lack of ranch hands. And he hadn't slept for shit last night anyway, too aware of Wilson only ten feet away. The independent ranching business wasn't what it used to be, and Woods Ranch had been struggling to find and keep good hands for the past couple of years.

They'd had good luck with hiring on Hugo Turner and Michael Pearce this past year, but one of their longtime hands, Alan Denning, was having his own string of bad

luck. He'd broken his left hand last spring and taken a leave
of absence, and now he'd apparently broken the same hand
again, leaving the ranch a man down.

Again.

They'd get through it like they always did, but right
after Christmas was a hard time for a lot of folks. Money
was tighter after holiday spending, and working at Woods
Ranch meant a commute, since they knew or had once
hired most of the capable hands in the county. And the
ranch's switch to all-organic, grass-fed beef had been a
risky one that turned off some folks from applying.

So far so good with the ranch's finances, though, thanks
to Brand's good business sense, and a side investment in
wind power, but God knew things could turn on a dime.
Especially for farmers of any sort. Hoof rot, Q fever, or
even a bad storm could hurt the herd and their combined
livelihood.

"How long's he out this time?" Jackson asked.

"About the same," Brand replied. "Eight weeks, give or
take. Maybe a little longer since it's the same hand. Trust
me, Alan's pissed off about this. I don't think I've ever
heard the man say *fuck* so many times in a three-minute
conversation."

"I don't blame him. He's a working man who likes to
work, same as me."

"Well, then do me a favor and don't break anything."

Jackson grinned. "Don't worry, boss, the last thing that
broke in this body was my heart, and no, it was not because you called off us fucking around last spring." His
teasing seemed to go over fine, because Brand smiled back
at him. He and Brand had begun fucking each other years
ago, about three months before Jackson was hired onto
the ranch by Brand's father, Wayne. The relationship had

continued in a casual way for ages, until Brand began a serious relationship with Hugo last summer.

Jackson had been jealous for about five minutes, and then he'd wished the pair well. He'd always known what he and Brand had was casual, because Brand had also been fucking a bartender named Ramie who worked at a local dive. All three of them had been very aware of the arrangement from the start so feelings didn't get hurt, and while Jackson was still friendly with Ramie, that was it.

"So does this mean we're hiring again?" Jackson asked, his brain skipping back around to Alan no longer being able to work. Even the worst of the busywork, like mucking stalls or tacking a horse, took both hands to do right.

"Yeah, and shockingly I had an application in my inbox this morning before I even posted the help-wanted memo. Young guy, only twenty, but his work experience looks decent. Not ranching specifically, but he says he knows horses and he's willing to relocate. I've got an interview with him later today."

Only twenty, just like Wilson. Hopefully this other kid had a bit more life experience under his belt.

"That's good," Jackson said. "I mean, between you, me, Hugo, Michael, and Rem, we can stretch the shifts for a while, but an extra pair of hands is always helpful."

"I know, especially with Dad stepping back."

Family patriarch and ranch owner Wayne Woods had been trying to scale back a bit in recent years, but still stepped in when they needed help. He was the kind of gracious, supportive family man Jackson genuinely wished his own adoptive father had been, and he was grateful to work here for this family. Even if Wayne didn't completely understand something, like Brand being bisexual and happy with Hugo, Wayne listened. He tried.

"Well, I was supposed to be out with Michael today," Jackson said. "He here yet?"

"He texted he was running a few minutes behind but should be here in a bit. His dad was having a slow morning."

"Got it."

Last year, Michael's father, Elmer Pearce, had suffered a stroke, and while Elmer was doing well, some days he required extra help to get started in the morning.

"I'll go get our horses tacked," Jackson said. "Good luck with your interview later."

"Gee, thanks." Brand winked on his way out of the break room. While Brand had an incredible mind for business and investing in things that would be profitable for the ranch, he wasn't the type of guy who'd ever manage a human resources department. But a handful of employees who were as dusty and used to the rustler life as himself? Good fit.

Dog was waiting for Jackson in the big barn's main corridor, her shaggy tail already wagging when she spotted him. "Ready for a new adventure, girl?" he asked.

Dog sneezed.

Jackson had his preferred horse, Juno, tacked and ready and No Name out of her stall when Michael and Rosco arrived. Jackson had been initially nervous about adding another dog to the ranch. Brand's own dog Brutus, while aging and still healing from an animal attack last spring, was still protective of the property, but he got along great with Dog. Rosco was an attentive pit bull mix who'd come back into Michael's life about two months ago and, after very careful introductions to both Brutus and Dog, was now welcome on the ranch. Rosco wasn't much of a herding dog, but he was gentle with the animals, and Jackson had never heard the dog growl.

"Your dad doing okay?" Jackson asked as Michael ambled down the barn to the tacking area, Rosco on his heels.

"Yeah, he's all right. Cold weather leaves him a little stiff in the morning, so sometimes he needs extra help to get going. Sorry to be late."

"The cattle don't care. Let's get out there."

"Sure, man."

Michael finished tacking No Name, and then they were out in the winter sunshine, running the fence line and making sure none of the herd had wandered off. At first, Jackson hadn't been sure what to make of Michael, who'd come to them after spending the past twenty years in the city, playing with computers. But he'd grown up in the ranching life and had acclimated quickly, and he'd also helped Brand completely update the ranch's website and social media. He might not be a lifer, but he was around for now and did the job.

Plus, Rosco was a pretty awesome dog.

Jackson also liked that Michael didn't try to fill the quiet with meaningless conversation for the sake of hearing his own voice. They rode, drank from their canteens, kept an eye on their dogs and the herd, and did their job with the minimum amount of words shared between them. Perfect morning for Jackson. Alan would have nattered on about whatever new TV show he'd watched the night before. Sometimes it was entertaining but Jackson had little interest in most television or movies. Life was hard enough, and he didn't need to spend his free time watching fictional people suffer, too. His supply of VHS tapes from the library was pretty limited, so he filled a lot of his free time reading.

After eating his cup of instant ramen soup and downing a sports drink, Jackson fed Dog her midday share of kibble. She got her regular meals in the morning and at night, but he always felt strange about eating in front of her without giving her something, too. Had since the day she wandered into his life and blinked those big blue eyes at him.

Eyes that said *dump the liquor and the pills instead of swallowing them.*

He had a few minutes left on his break, so he went to the main barn doors and leaned against the frame. Tilted his face up into the sunshine, grateful for it against his skin every single day, after spending far too much time without it.

Dust rose on the horizon, followed a minute or so later by the distant rumble of a car engine. Probably Brand's afternoon interview. Dog loped out of the barn and took a familiar position by his side. Up on the main house's porch, Brutus rose from his cushioned bed and stood by the steps, watchful over the family home. The old German shepherd still had some scars that would probably never go away, but he was loyal as hell and a good judge of people.

Way better than Jackson was.

A blue sedan eventually appeared on the dirt road that led to Woods Ranch from the main state road. An oddly familiar sedan. Curious and a little confused, Jackson hung around by the barn and watched the car circle to park near one of the ranch pickups. Brand appeared on the porch of the smaller bunkhouse situated between the main house and the barn. No one had used the bunkhouse for years until recently, because the Woods family hadn't employed the help to make it necessary. Then Hugo had needed a place to live last year. Hugo had cleaned it up, and now it was both Brand's office as ranch foreman and a shared living space for Hugo and Brand—getting the very-much-in-love pair a home of their own.

The car's driver-side door opened and a tall, lanky figure emerged. He wore a familiar uniform of jeans, a fleece-lined jacket, and boots. Way too familiar. Jackson took a few steps backward, deeper into the gloom of the barn, his heart kicking a bit. No fucking way was last night's... what? He hadn't been a hookup. Last night's bar save? No way was he here for an interview.

The guy also wore a knockoff Stetson, hiding his hair, and in the light of day the clothes almost made him look like someone playing a cowboy role on TV. The clothes were practical, sure, but something about it was almost comical to Jackson, and he couldn't figure out why. Not until the guy stumbled getting out of the car, and then Jackson knew. Even without seeing his face, the coat and car and tripping were enough.

As the interviewee approached Brand and the bunkhouse/office porch, he took off his hat to reveal a head of curly red hair. It glinted like fire in the sunlight, the tight curls a little unreal, and it was definitely his Wilson. When Wilson tripped on the one step up to the porch, Jackson snorted, both amused and a little angry. He had asked Wilson point-blank what kind of work he was looking for, and the whole time he'd had this interview lined up? Had the whole runaway thing been a lie, too?

Had he played Jackson for a free bed?

Annoyed and in no mood to make nice if Brand spotted him, Jackson stalked back into the barn. It was up to Brand to hire this guy or not, whatever. Hopefully Wilson didn't make it a habit of tripping up stairs. If he did, it was going to be a long winter.

For about five minutes of his life, Wyatt Gibson had wanted to be a spy. Granted, he'd only been seven years old and the urge came after he'd watched *Mr. & Mrs. Smith*, which made the life look insanely fun and glamorous. In reality, spying on other people was kind of boring, took a lot of time, and only got him spanked by his stepdad for reading his older stepsister's journal and tattling on her for smoking weed with her friends.

Early life lesson: smoking weed is fine; telling is bad.

The "telling is bad" lesson hit even harder about a year later after his stepbrother, Peter, did something epically stupid, and it had haunted their family ever since. Wyatt had learned quickly to keep things close to the chest. Not that he'd had a lot of adult life so far, since he'd just turned twenty last spring, but secrets ran deep in his family. So deep that he was in the middle of Bumfuck, Texas, on a hunt to find out about the other half of his birth family, because his mom had refused to tell him anything other than his sperm donor was a selfish prick who hadn't cared about Wyatt before he was born and wouldn't give a shit now.

If he hadn't stumbled over one of his late mother's old high school yearbooks in a dusty box in the attic two years ago, he wouldn't have even known where to start looking.

Now he was being interviewed for a job he wasn't qualified for, by the man who might be his biological father. Sometimes he really longed for the simple days of being a seven-year-old wannabe spy.

At least he'd gotten a little bit of subterfuge practice last night with some hayseed named Jackson, if that was even his real name. Wyatt had chosen the Blue Tavern because a bit of internet digging showed it was a local gay bar. A gay bar hundreds of miles from home that gave him a chance to explore something his stepfamily would shit themselves over if they knew about.

He'd thought finding a bed to sleep in, rather than shelling out for a seedy motel or sleeping in his car, would have been a nice bonus. Turned out he'd found both a seedy motel and a bed—albeit not a bed with a hot loner in a leather jacket. Wyatt had thought for sure the "run-away" obfuscation would win him some extra sympathy and it had—just not the kind he'd wanted. The grumpy-looking loner from the back of the bar had seemed like the exact type to take Wyatt somewhere and bang him. He had definitely taken Wyatt somewhere. The motel had scared him, then intrigued him, and the sexy teasing had revved his engine.

But Jackson had been too nice and kept his hands to himself all night, which had made Wyatt doubt his ability to size up people. He wouldn't make that mistake with Maybe Daddy.

Stumbling on the first step of the building he'd been told to go to by his potential new boss wasn't a good look, but he didn't mind being stared at. He'd always been kind of accident-prone, which probably came from always being oddly tall and gangly (not sure where that came from) and standing out for having very red hair (definitely from his late mom, who'd had almost identical ginger curls). He'd learned to take the teasing from a very young age and how to lean into it, so it felt more like he was being laughed near, rather than laughed directly at.

Mostly it helped assuage his ego while he learned how to make people take him seriously. Not only as a man who deserved to know his past, but also as a guy who was still exploring his attraction to other guys.

Thankfully, the man in front of him simply smiled at his bumbling and held out a hand. "You must be Wyatt Gibson. I'm Brand Woods." He spoke with a firm, lightly accented voice, but nothing about the man seemed familiar. Not his hair, his eyes, his chin, and he was even a few inches shorter than Wyatt. This guy was supposed to be his father?

Maybe the amateur detective work Wyatt had done to find this place had been wrong.

"Yeah. I mean, yes, sir, Wyatt Gibson." He started to reach out with his right hand to shake, realized he was holding his hat in that one, and switched it over fast. "Nice to meet you. You've got quite a spread out here."

"Thank you. It's been in the family for quite a long time. Please, come inside."

"Yes, sir."

He followed Brand into a large living space with a kitchen/dining area to the left and a kind of living room to the right, where another guy was stretched out on a sofa reading on a tablet. The other guy waved vaguely at them, but Brand didn't introduce them, so Wyatt just waved back. Brand led him into a room on the right, which was obviously an office. Desk, laptop, stacks of folders, one bookcase with not much on it. Sparser than he expected but what did Wyatt know about how a cattle ranch was run?

Nothing.

The one thing that did surprise him about the space was the three sets of bunk beds shoved into one corner. He'd never been great at keeping certain things off his face—something he was definitely still working on, because Brand chuckled. "This used to be the ranch bunkhouse, back when we were a much larger operation and had more hands. We dusted it off last year, so I could have office space that wasn't in the family home."

"Got it." Wyatt was curious about the guy hanging around outside the office. Maybe the other room was a fancy break area for the hands? That would be cool. "So the hands don't live on the ranch?"

"Only one, not including myself and my father." Something in Brand's eye twitched, and Wyatt wasn't sure what to make of it. "It's a specific arrangement."

"Cool. I mean, I'm sure I can figure out a place to stay. If you hire me, of course." He had no idea where, because the neighboring town of Weston didn't have any kind of apartment complex—he'd checked that out in advance—but before he worried too hard about that he needed to land the job. That was the whole point of coming here.

"Well, then let's get this interview started." Brand gestured at one of the two chairs opposite his desk, then sat in his desk chair. Tapped a key on his laptop. "According to your résumé, you've never worked on a ranch, but you have experience with horses. Can you tell me more about that?"

Wyatt was insanely proud of himself for not blushing, which was something he did a lot when caught in a subterfuge (another reason he might not make the best spy), but he'd practiced this. "My stepfather is a large-animal vet, so I grew up around horses, cattle, hogs, you name it."

"He took you with him to see his patients?"

"Not very often, unless the animal's owner was okay with it, but he also took in animals at the clinic, so I have a lot of experience with barn stuff. Mucking stalls and feeding and stuff." Constantly saying "stuff" was probably not impressing his potential boss, but coming here at all had been an impulsive decision, and he'd had less than twenty-four hours to learn everything he could on his phone.

He had to nail this and find out what he'd come here to find out, or he'd never get his stepfather's sneering "I told you so" out of his head. Never be able to face his maternal grandparents, who'd told him to forget the paternal side of his family.

"I see." Brand's expression was kind of passive, giving nothing away. "How about riding experience?"

"No formal training, sir."

"Have you ridden a horse before?"

"Yes, sir, twice."

"On a ranch? At your stepfather's clinic?"

Wyatt straightened his shoulders. No sense in lying about this, because he'd be found out the first time Brand asked him to mount a horse. "Once at the county fair, and another time when a traveling rodeo show came to town."

Brand's eyebrow twitched. "Can I assume this was in a corral and not open country?"

"Yes, sir, you can."

"Have you ever tacked a horse?"

"No, but I'm a fast learner. I can learn anything. I graduated high school at the top of my class, and I completed my associate's degree in three semesters instead of four because I had the credits."

He glanced at the computer. "An associate's in applied science. And you want to work on a cattle ranch? You could do a lot more with that degree in a bigger city."

"I could."

"But you came out here, all the way from Glasbury, with hardly any practical experience necessary for this work. Now, it is something we can teach you, if you're really interested in the life, and if this isn't some sort of postcollege freak-out where you're trying to find your place in life. I respect it if this is a rebellion of some kind, but I need someone serious about the job. This ranch is my life."

"It's not a freak-out, sir, I promise. My stepfather insisted all his kids get a degree of some kind, and then we could choose our own paths." That part was true. Here came the big lie, and Wyatt silently prayed he sold it. "I've been interested in the ranching and cowboy way of life for a long time, but my parents didn't like the idea. I didn't have any way of gaining the practical experience I'd need while I still lived at home, so I admit I'm coming to this pretty green."

"Wyatt, you're so green you're practically a leprechaun."

Wyatt still wasn't sure what to make of Brand. The cowboy wasn't dismissing Wyatt's lack of real experience outright, which kind of surprised him based on his stepfather's insistence that the entire Woods family had been a bunch of insulated, narcissistic rednecks who only thought about what was best for themselves. The fact that Brand was possibly considering hiring someone as green as Wyatt butted up against those insinuations.

"I know I don't have a lot of experience, sir," Wyatt said, "but I am a fast learner. And I'm willing to put in the work. If you've got textbooks, I'll read those. Videos you recommend that I can watch online. I just really want a chance to do this." *I really want a chance to see who you are and find out why you left me and my mother before I was even born.*

Brand held his gaze steadily for long enough that Wyatt wanted to squirm, but he managed to keep still and not blink, just as he'd done last night with Jackson. Something familiar seemed to lurk in Brand's eyes—eyes that started appearing similar to Wyatt's the more he looked at them, and in a way he kind of resented. Eyes that watched and calculated. Eyes that should be cold and wary but weren't.

Eyes that could also be warm and welcoming but weren't that, either.

"Tell you what, Wyatt," Brand finally said. "One of my men broke his hand last night, so he's off the roster for at least eight weeks. That leaves me in a small bind in terms of scheduling, because my father is supposed to be semi-retired. How about I offer you an eight-week trial run? I'll pair you with one of my other ranch hands so they can show you the ropes and teach you the skills you lack. At the end of those eight weeks, if you've proven yourself, I'll offer you a job. If not, then we'll part ways, and you'll have some experience under your belt for your next step down the road."

Wyatt's heart thumped against his ribs, and he fought to keep his smile even and professional, when he wanted to pump his fist into the air in triumph. "I think that sounds fair, Mr. Woods."

"You can call me Brand, everyone does. My father is Mr. Woods until he says otherwise."

"Of course, sir."

"I'll draw up an employment contract for you to look over. Hours vary and weekends are required, but I do my best to make sure everyone gets two days off a week, and I can work with specific requests. You obviously have your own transportation to and from the ranch. I suppose when you can start depends on how quickly you're able to relocate."

"All I need is a place live around here. Everything I have is in my car."

Brand's eyebrows went up, his face showing a different expression for the first time in the whole conversation. "You're kidding. May I ask why? Or is that none of my business?"

I packed up my whole life to come here so I could prove something to my stepfather and grandparents, and also to figure out if you're my biological father. And if you are, if you're the kind of person I want in my life.

"It's personal, sir," Wyatt said instead.

"I respect that, and I apologize if I overstepped."

"You didn't, but thank you."

"And if it helps pry my foot out of my mouth, I do have a lead on a place you could potentially rent while you're here in town."

Wyatt perked up. He'd been prepared to shell out for a motel for a few nights while he searched—or pick up another guy like he had last night, and maybe this time he'd get everything he wanted out of the encounter. This was better and, as Jackson had pointed out last night, a lot safer than tricking for a bed. Not that Wyatt had seen it that way, and he'd been genuinely offended Jackson thought he was a rent boy.

Not appropriate thoughts for this particular moment. "I'd appreciate the lead," he said.

"We have a neighbor a few miles from here named Elmer Pearce, and he has a trailer on his property he's rented to our workers in the past. The rent is reasonable, it's currently empty, and if you need any other reference for the place, Elmer's son Michael works here, too."

"Oh. Wow." A place close by, rented to him by someone who knew the Woods family. He couldn't have asked for better. "That's all the references I need. If Mister, um, I'm sorry?"

"Pearce."

"If Mr. Pearce agrees, I'd love to take it. My credit score isn't great, but I'll pass any kind of background check."

Brand chuckled, and the sound was too damned close to Wyatt's own laughter. "Don't worry about any of that stuff. Elmer never asks for it. He also keeps a shotgun on hooks above his front door." His smile helped Wyatt see the gentle teasing.

They discussed his salary, which Wyatt thought was fair considering he had very little experience. Wyatt did have a decent savings, though, so he'd be fine either way. He'd been planning to do something like this for the past two years, and had pinched every single penny while getting his degree at community college. Last night's stunt with Jackson had been less about not affording a motel room and more about the life experience he'd been hoping for.

Too bad he'd sold the runaway story too well and Jackson had been a decent guy.

"So do you officially accept?" Brand asked. "I can have you start as soon as tomorrow, if you want. We just need to do some paperwork."

"Yes, I accept." Wyatt stood so he could more easily shake Brand's hand, unofficially sealing the deal.

When Brand sat back in his own chair, he seemed more relaxed than ten seconds ago, as if he'd been nervous about this interview, too. Seemed weird for the ranch foreman, but beyond knowing the ranch had been down a hand, Wyatt had no idea what was going on in the man's personal life.

Yet.

The great thing about small towns was everyone knew everyone else's business. Wyatt just had to find out that business without being too obvious and making people suspicious. That would be the trick his entire time here: find out what he wanted to know, when he wanted to know it, and maybe confront Brand with what he suspected. If what he suspected was even true.

They completed the official hiring paperwork, which didn't bother Wyatt in the least. This was an official job, and he'd taken his stepfather's last name when Mom married him. And his former address was counties away from where Wyatt had been born. According to his mom's parents, his bio dad didn't know where Mom's family had moved after being rejected by Maybe Brand.

But Mom's parents also knew exactly who his bio dad was, and they'd both refused to tell him when he started asking at sixteen. If his stepfamily knew the secret, they never said anything. Wyatt had a right to know his past, damn it. Maybe this subterfuge wasn't the best way to go about finding the truth, but if Brand Woods really had coldly turned his back, who was to say he'd tell Wyatt the truth if Wyatt asked point-blank? He'd obviously given Wyatt up for a reason.

This was Wyatt's truth to know, and by God he'd find out. One way or another.

Chapter Three

The trailer at Elmer Pearce's was a bust for now, and that disappointed Brand a bit because he'd promised it to his new hire. But it also wasn't Elmer's fault.

After finishing the formal stuff, Brand had decided to give Wyatt a quick tour of the barn and surrounding property. Michael and Jackson were still out in the pastures, but he did manage to track down Hugo in the garage. He'd been tooling around with one of their old tractors, hoping to get it running for the upcoming local farm consignment auction. Dad had finally agreed to let go of some of the unused things on the ranch (Dad hated the word *declutter*), and Hugo liked to keep busy on his days off.

Brand smiled at the sight of his boyfriend with his butt in the air and head under the tractor, unable to help himself from admiring that taut ass even after all these months. "Hey, Hugo, get your hands off your wrench and come say hi to our newest recruit," he said, tossing out the innuendo on purpose.

Hugo scooted backward, wrench in hand and a streak of oil on one cheek. "Fuck off, boss, you like how I handle my wrench."

Yes, he did, but this was not the time or place to explore that. Brand waited for Hugo to stand and take a few steps toward them. "Wyatt Gibson, this is Hugo Turner. Wyatt, Hugo."

"Hey, man," Wyatt said in the same affable tone he'd had since he arrived. The guy seemed friendly enough, if a touch wary at times. But he was also in a new, unfamiliar environment. "Are you a mechanic?"

"He thinks he is."

Hugo laughed and shook Wyatt's hand. "Nah, I'm a rustler, but I've always liked to tinker with things. Keeps my mind active, plus you can learn almost anything online nowadays. Even how to fix a sixty-year-old tractor. It's nice to meet you, Wyatt. Welcome to Woods Ranch."

"Thank you, sir," Wyatt replied. "I'm glad to meet you, too, and I'm really glad Brand is giving me a chance to prove myself."

"Prove yourself?"

"I'm a bit of a greenhorn, but I'm a fast learner and really eager to do the job."

"In that case, Brand's a fair boss and a good teacher. You picked a great place to get started in the ranching life."

Brand hoped so. He'd been torn about hiring someone with almost zero experience, but the kid had a degree, sounded eager, and if he'd already packed his life into his car, he had everything to lose if he failed at this job. Giving him a chance had also lifted a bit of weight off Brand's shoulders.

Only immediate family knew, but Dad was scheduled to have hand surgery next week, so he'd be out of commission for a while. Even if all Wyatt could do was muck stalls and feed the horses for a few weeks, it would help them out immensely so the experienced hands could focus on the herd.

"I really look forward to getting started," Wyatt said with a cheerful grin.

"So who are you pairing him with?" Hugo asked Brand.

"Not sure yet," Brand replied. Truth. His best options were Hugo or Jackson, because Michael was still too new to the ranch. And Brand's younger brother, Rem, did not have the patience to teach someone with almost zero experience. "Besides, I've gotta get Wyatt settled over at Elmer's place first."

"Um, Michael didn't tell you?"

He bit back a groan, not liking Hugo's tone or the way his eyebrows scrunched; Brand knew those signs. "Tell me what?"

"That's a no, and I only know because Josiah told me, and I guess he assumed Michael would tell his boss."

Brand noticed the slightly glazed-over look in Wyatt's eyes. The kid was probably confused by all the names being tossed around and the interpersonal relationships on the ranch. He'd figure them out soon enough. "What's wrong with the trailer, Hugo?"

"It had an electrical fire last night in the kitchen. Elmer has someone coming out today to assess the cost of repairing it versus, you know, not. It's not like the trailer is vintage or anything he'd want to sink a lot of money into, but it's also not livable right now."

"Damn it." Brand remembered himself. "And that really sucks for Elmer. Is there anything we can do?"

Hugo shook his head. "You know Elmer's too proud to accept money, and if Michael didn't say anything, it's probably because his dad asked him not to. It's not like anyone expected Alan to break his hand again and for us to need a new hand this soon. Um, no pun intended."

"It sounds like Mr. Pearce is having a run of bad luck," Wyatt said. "May I ask a dumb question?"

"Ask away," Brand replied, his brain already whirring for a solution to their problem. He didn't like offering a new hire a place to stay and then having to go back on his word. Especially a kid who didn't seem to have much life experience.

"Well, that building where your office is? You mentioned it used to be the bunkhouse, and that another hand lived there because of a special arrangement. Sorry if I'm being rude, but there's no space for other hands to live there?"

Sweat prickled the back of Brand's neck. He glanced at Hugo, who shrugged with his eyebrows. While they didn't hide their relationship from the ranch staff or their families, it wasn't something they paraded around town.

Wyatt was going to find out anyway. "It used to be a bunkhouse for staff until last summer when Hugo needed a place to stay," Brand said, "so we cleared it out and fixed it up. He's the special arrangement."

Brand took a step closer to Hugo and brushed their fingers together without actually holding his hand. Brand was still working up to that around family, much less a new hire. "Then after we became an official couple, I moved in with him. The bunkhouse is our place."

Wyatt blinked once. His gaze drifted from Brand to Hugo, then back to Brand, and Brand watched for any sign of disgust or disapproval. He was ready to tear up the employment contract if Wyatt gave either of them shit, especially Hugo. Hugo had been bullied enough to last a lifetime.

"Oh, cool," Wyatt said. "Like I said, dumb question. I was just curious about the place, 'cuz it seemed like an easy solution to the problem. But totally cool, sir. Sirs?"

"Don't sir me," Hugo replied with a grin. "I'm an employee, same as you. I don't get special treatment while on the job."

Maybe when they were alone, but definitely not on the job.

"I can stay in a motel for a few days," Wyatt said, "and look around for a room to rent or something. I mean, I looked at the map on my phone, and there are a few towns around here. There has to be something."

"I hate for you to do that when I promised you a place," Brand said. A nebulous idea came to him, but damn he'd probably owe her later. "Listen, do you have an hour or two to hang here, Wyatt? You can keep Hugo company while he plays with the tractor, or chill on the bunkhouse porch. I need to run into town for a bit."

"I have absolutely nowhere to be for the rest of the day." He pulled a cell out of his pocket. "Actually, I'll probably wait in my car. I need to charge my phone before it dies."

"You can use the charger in our place," Hugo said. "I need to take a break and get something to drink anyway. I worked through lunch."

"Great." Brand checked his pocket for his own phone; he kept his truck keys in the cab out of habit and in case someone needed to use it in a hurry. "I'll be back soon."

Twenty minutes later, Brand strode into the Roost, a local dive bar he favored because of its cheap burgers and even cheaper beer. Plus, his best friend Rachel Marie "Ramie" Edwards bartended there. A petite woman with long black hair, a curvy figure she loved to show off with tight tops, and the kind of "don't give me shit because I'll serve it right back tenfold" attitude he loved, she stood behind the Roost's bar drying a glass with a towel.

Her eyebrows lifted when she spotted him. "Playing hooky on a workday, boss?"

"Not exactly." Brand rested his elbows on the bar rail, leaned in, and flashed her his most charming smile. "I have a favor to ask, and I think it'll help us both out. When's your next break?"

* * *

The only reason Wyatt had been able to keep his surprise at the "it's our place" confession was because of his family's obsession with keeping secrets. He'd long ago perfected his Calm Face, his Mildly Surprised Face, and his I'm So Happy, But Not Really Face. Maybe he couldn't always control his body or stop from tripping over his own big feet, but he could definitely control his face in most situations and not trip over his expressions.

His Maybe Daddy was gay? How was that possible? Okay, dumb thought, because it wasn't as though he'd never heard of such a thing before; he simply hadn't expected it from his own old man. The blunt way Brand had admitted to the relationship, though, added a small ounce of respect to what little Brand had already earned by the simple fact he was Wyatt's boss. The statement about Hugo being an employee on the clock with no special treatment? Yeah, time would tell on that one.

Wasn't there a reason people were told not to work with their significant other?

Wyatt had downplayed the whole conversation to give himself time to absorb the news. The last thing he wanted was for either of those guys to think he was homophobic, especially if he wanted to befriend them and learn more about Brand. Hell, Wyatt had no room to judge them when he wasn't even sure of his own sexuality, and wasn't that exactly why he'd tried to pick up Jackson last night?

Too bad his need to try out his acting skills had gotten in the way and fucked up what could have been a great learning experience.

The way Jackson had talked about "sex, bondage, and asphyxiation" still made him shiver sometimes. Not the asphyxiation part, because no thank you. It had been his tone of voice. The subtle purr and promise.

His jeans got a bit uncomfortable, and Wyatt bit the inside of his cheek as he followed Hugo toward the bunkhouse. He didn't care that Hugo and Brand were gay. He'd had gay classmates in high school and college, and one brief encounter with a guy at a party had shaken Wyatt's previous assumption that he himself was straight. Even if it hadn't, Wyatt wasn't some sheltered asshole from the sticks; he just hadn't expected to find it out about his possible bio dad.

Was that why Brand had left Wyatt's mom, signed over his rights, and refused to be part of their lives? He banged a girl, figured out it wasn't for him, and didn't want anything to do with them? From everything Wyatt's grandparents had told him about that time in his mother's life, it was entirely possible. Maybe Mom had just been a sexual experiment gone wrong.

Too many questions and no answers yet. About both his past and his own sexuality.

Hugo opened the bunkhouse door, and Wyatt took a few extra moments this time to really take in the place. The small details like the shelf with framed pictures and a TV mounted on the wall in the living area. What looked like embroidered throw pillows on the couch. Two pairs of sneakers on a mat by the door, and hooks on the wall above for keys and coats. He could see now that a couple lived here, rather than just a bunch of cowboys.

"Charger's over here." Hugo lifted a cord plugged in near the dining table and chairs. A small round table with three metal chairs that looked like they been stylish thirty years before Wyatt was born.

"Thanks, man." Wyatt's phone was still half-charged, which was actually fine for a few more hours. Charging it had been an excuse to sit alone and do a bit more research about the names he'd learned today (particularly Hugo

Turner and Elmer Pearce), but maybe he could get some information directly from the horse's mouth. So to speak.

He sat in one of the chairs and plugged in the charger, pretending to fiddle with his phone for a few seconds. "Hey, do you think it's okay if I get the Wi-Fi name and password?"

"Don't see why not, since Brand hired you. Hold on, Brand keeps it written down in his office." Hugo went into the office—apparently, he did get certain perks if he could go into the boss's office without permission—and came back a moment later with an index card. "Here you go."

"Thanks." Might as well make conversation while he typed in the numbers. "So how long have you worked here?"

Hugo was washing his hands in the utility sink by a mini-fridge and microwave. "It'll be a year next month. I actually grew up about ten miles from here and lived out of state for a long time before moving back." He shut off the water. "You want something to drink?"

"Sure, thanks." His phone connected and he pretended to type something else while observing Hugo. Hugo was good-looking in his own way and seemed nice enough. He moved comfortably through this space, delivering a bottle of water to Wyatt before getting something out of an upper cupboard. Wyatt also hadn't missed the polite way Hugo had changed the subject about his employment.

He latched on to that. "So where did you work before here? I'm guessing you got hired with a lot more experience than me."

"A lot more, yeah." Hugo unwrapped a protein bar and sat in the chair opposite him. "I left after I graduated high school and traveled around the state for a while, doing odd ranching jobs, before I landed at a working dude ranch in Northern California. I really enjoyed that job and the people there, but I had unfinished business here, so when a spot opened up at the ranch, I applied. Wayne Woods hired me pretty fast, and I moved back."

"And then in with the boss?"

Hugo's face went blank, and he held Wyatt's gaze with more intensity than he expected. "That didn't develop right away, and it's private. Between me and him. But I will stress that what Brand said is true. On the job, we are boss and employee. We don't take it to work. We do our best to keep it in here and at the family house. And if our arrangement is going to bother you, Brand needs to know right now."

"It doesn't bother me. My family isn't very gay-rights-friendly, but I don't share their views. It's part of the reason I needed to get away, find my own path."

Hugo tilted his head to one side but didn't press, thank God. "If you ever need to talk about directions on that path, I'm a good listener."

"Thanks, man." He was really starting to like Hugo and his quiet way of accepting things. It also made him wonder how much of Brand's distant past Hugo knew about and how many secrets Brand might be keeping from his boyfriend.

Do you know he might have given up a kid in high school? Do you?

"So you said you were pretty new to this life," Hugo said. "How new is that?"

Wyatt explained his story again, a bit more briefly this time, including some of his experience working with his stepfather, and the chance he had now to explore something new. He left enough meaning there so Hugo seemed to catch on he wasn't just talking about the ranching life, but also himself as a person. "Even if it doesn't work out, I'm really grateful to Brand for giving me a chance."

"Like I said before, Brand is a fair boss. None of us are rolling in cash, but no one gets into this life to get rich, not unless you're one of the huge cattle barons down near Corpus Christi, of which we definitely are not. Just a family operation trying to keep things going for the next generation."

"Speaking of, I'm curious how many siblings Brand has. You said it was a family op, but he only mentioned his father and one brother working here."

Hugo took a bite of his protein bar and chewed, possibly buying time to figure out how much to share. It was information Wyatt would learn at some point anyway, so why bother to hide it? "They are a family op, yeah. The youngest brother Rem works here. Brand's got one older brother who works in California, and two younger sisters who are both married with kids. I think Rem's on the roster tomorrow, and I'm sure you'll meet Leanne and Sage at some point. Wayne and Rose make it a point to introduce all the new hires to the family."

Interesting. Wyatt would get a chance to observe his Maybe Family in action sometime soon. The idea both intrigued and terrified him. And what if Brand really was his Maybe Daddy? Did that mean Wyatt could inherit a share of this ranch one day?

No, that was impossible, wasn't it? His grandparents said his bio dad signed away all legal rights to Wyatt, so did that mean Wyatt had no legal rights now? He probably should have looked in to that before he came here, but coming had been an impulsive decision he needed to live with and navigate now that he was here.

Besides his two left feet, impulsiveness was his other serious vice, and he needed to work on both before he did something to blow his cover.

"Hey, dude, you okay?" Hugo asked.

Wyatt blinked at him, surprised Hugo had finished his snack. How long had Wyatt been staring into space? "Sorry, yeah. That's cool, I'd like to meet the rest of the Woods family. And the other guys who work here, obviously."

"Obviously." He glanced at his phone. "They should be back from the line soon. Did Brand introduce you to the horses yet?"

"Yeah, we took a tour of the barn, saw the horses and the equipment. The section in the back is cool. What's calving season like?"

"It can be intense, for sure, up all night waiting for a heifer to give birth."

They talked for a while about the process of insemination, gestation, and preparing the barn for the impending spring births. Wyatt soaked in the information, genuinely fascinated by it. He'd enjoyed his biology classes and learning about reproduction and the miracle of life. "I've never seen a cow give birth, but I assisted my stepfather with a few horses," Wyatt said. "It's an amazing thing to watch."

"Yeah, it is."

A dog barked in the distance, and a deeper woof seemed to answer the call from the porch, probably the German shepherd who hadn't approached Wyatt when he first drove up. He'd forgotten to ask the big beast's name.

"I hope you like dogs," Hugo said with laughter in his voice, "because when Michael and Jackson are both working, we've got plenty around the ranch. Brutus lives here, and he's Brand's dog, but the other two come and go with their owners."

An odd chill wormed through Wyatt's gut. What were the fucking odds that the Jackson Hugo had just mentioned (who owned a dog!) was the same Jackson from last night? No way. Except his Jackson had hedged on what exactly he did for a living, and had only talked about doing this-and-that and odd jobs. He must have lost control of his expression, because Hugo leaned forward, his face a mask of concern. "You aren't afraid of dogs, are you?"

"No, I'm not." Wyatt worked to school his expression and his surprise. "Sorry, I'm fine. My stepfather was a vet, remember? I'm cool with most animals. Not a huge fan of snakes and lizards, but if it's got fur or feathers, I'm down."

"Great, sounds like they're coming in, so let's go meet your coworkers."

Yeah, let's prove there's more than one Jackson in this dusty county, please.

He left his phone on the table to complete charging—who knew what accommodations Brand had in mind or when they would pan out—and followed Hugo outside. He was getting a little tired of following people around, but that would be his new normal for a while as he learned the ropes of Woods Ranch and his job here.

Hugo led him toward the big red barn. In the distance, the sound of hoof beats drew Wyatt's attention to the western horizon. Two men on horses were heading in their direction, accompanied by two smaller specks that had to be a pair of dogs. They all moved at a canter, he was pretty sure, making headway without hurrying. Hugo stopped near the mouth of the barn, and they waited, squinting in the direction of the lowering sun.

That damned sun made it difficult for Wyatt to see the faces of the two men in the saddles. They were equally tall and broad, both wore hats, and Wyatt had stupidly left his own hat behind in the bunkhouse. Raising his hand to shade his eyes was tacky so he stood next to Hugo and tried not to squirm.

The dogs got there first. One was brown with a bit of pit bull in it, and the other was Dog, the pretty mutt he'd met last night. She loped right up to him, barked once, and jumped up, paws slamming into his gut. She wasn't a heavy dog, but Wyatt still stumbled backward a step, reaching to grab her shoulders and steady himself.

"Dog, get down." Hugo grabbed her collar and pulled her off. "Geez, mutt. She doesn't usually jump on strangers." The pit bull sniffed at Wyatt's boots. "And this one is Rosco. He's Michael's dog, and Dog is Jackson's dog, and yes, her name is Dog. Don't ask."

He wasn't about to ask but that was because Wyatt already knew. "Hello, pups."

Rosco's big eyes didn't seem to trust him, but he didn't bark or growl. Just wandered off and peed against the side of the barn.

"Hey, man, who's this?" a deep voice asked. It belonged to one of the cowboys. Both had dismounted at this point, and it only took Wyatt a brief glance up to recognize the one on his right as Jackson from last night.

Shit.

"Guys, this here is Wyatt Gibson," Hugo said. "Brand just hired him to fill in Alan's spot. Sort of."

"He's sort of hired like I was sort of hired?" The stranger took several long strides forward, leading his horse, his features easier to see up close and with less sun glare. "Michael Pearce."

"Nice to meet you," Wyatt said automatically. "I'm here on a trial basis to see if I can cut it."

"So, like I was sort of hired." Michael chuckled. "First piece of advice is don't look quite so intimidated or spooked, especially around the horses. They can sense fear same as other animals."

Wyatt wasn't spooked at all by the two hulking horses nearby but rather by the silent shadow behind Michael. "Good advice, thanks." He placed the name Michael to the son of the guy he was originally supposed to rent a trailer from. But Michael apparently hadn't told Brand about the fire, and Wyatt didn't want to stick his foot in anything right off the bat, so he kept silent.

"The quiet one behind me is Jackson Sumner. He's like one of those old mechanical toys. Usually, you gotta wind him up to make him talk to you."

Hugo laughed.

Jackson grunted and stepped forward, his expression blank. "Nice to meet you, *Wyatt*." Mercifully, that was all he said. Nothing about last night or the name lie Wyatt had told.

He tried to say thank you with his eyes as he shook both Michael's and Jackson's hands in turn. "It's great to be here. It was kind of Brand to give me this chance."

"Where is Brand, anyway?" Michael asked Hugo. "I need to talk to him about something when he's got a minute."

"If it's the thing Josiah texted me about this morning," Hugo said, "then he knows. He's actually out chasing up another living arrangement for Wyatt."

Michael grunted. "I'd tell you to stop texting my boyfriend but he needs more friends."

Wyatt took in the light exchanges, the puzzle pieces starting to fall into place. He'd been confused earlier listening to Hugo and Brand use so many different names, but relationships made more sense as he got another face to add to the mix. Michael was handsome in an almost prettyboy way that seemed less suited for a ranch and more for wining and dining folks in a big city. By contrast, Jackson was even more rugged and mysterious in his full cowboy getup, from the boots to the hat, and especially the way he seemed to be trying not to scowl at Wyatt.

That scowl was bizarrely sexy.

"What other arrangement?" Michael asked.

"No idea, he didn't say," Hugo replied. "Just asked Wyatt to hang out for an hour or two. He's already had a tour, so I've been trying not to bore him too much while he waits. You two done riding for the day?"

"Yeah, we're in for the afternoon."

"Awesome." Hugo flashed Wyatt a grin. "How about your first hands-on lesson in untacking and brushing down a horse? Jackson can show you how it's done."

"Uh…" Wyatt couldn't think of a good way to get out of a lesson he desperately needed, and why try? Cozying up to Jackson for a little while? Getting hands-on with him? "Okay, sure. Lead the way, Jackson."

Jackson did scowl this time. "Fine. Keep up, kid." He turned and led his horse toward the barn entrance. Wyatt took half a second to admire his departing backside, then hustled after him. His afternoon was about to get more interesting than he'd anticipated.

Chapter Four

"Down this way, *Wyatt*." Jackson was going to give himself away if he didn't stop stressing "Wilson's" real name, but he despised being lied to. He'd gotten a belly full of it from his adoptive parents, even more in prison, and enough from Cyrus to last him a fucking lifetime. Right now wasn't the time to lose his temper, though; he had a horse to take care of around a greenhorn, and the last thing he wanted to do was spook Juno.

Jackson led his horse down the wide aisle between stalls to the tacking area and looped Juno's reins around the rail. Wyatt followed at a respectable distance, hands folded behind his back like a student waiting to be scolded, and Jackson wanted to do more than scold him for lying. He wanted to bend Wyatt over his knee and spank the kid's ass bright red.

Not happening. Focus, idiot.

"When you're out riding the line, your horse is your best friend," Jackson said. "You need to bond with them, and the process of tacking and untacking them is part of that bonding. The horse has to trust you. How much ridin' you done?"

"Not much." Wyatt's voice tickled over his skin in a familiar way Jackson both liked and hated. He turned to face him, still annoyed Wyatt was taller than him and unsure why. "It's all been supervised, no range riding or anything like that."

"Can you at least mount the horse? You got the long legs for it, but you seem to have a bit of a problem stayin' on your feet."

"Yes, I can mount a horse."

"Fantastic. Show me." Jackson stepped closer to Juno's head and held on to the halter just in case Wyatt did something to startle her.

Wyatt stared at the saddle for a long moment, as if he could teleport himself onto it if he tried hard enough. Jackson waited, aware of Michael nearby untacking his own horse and watching them at the same time. Both their dogs were sniffing around the stalls, not paying their humans or the horses any attention. Jackson couldn't look away from the intriguing wannabe-cowboy who'd yet to mount the horse in front of him.

"Should we go outside to do this?" Wyatt asked.

He's stalling.

"Ceiling's plenty high in here," Jackson replied. "Show me what you got, Wilson."

Wyatt narrowed his eyes, the rebellious twenty-year-old in him rising to the challenge Jackson had purposely thrown down. He put his left foot in the stirrup, which should be at a good height for him since they were adjusted for Jackson, grabbed the pommel with one hand and the back of the saddle with the other. Not the best way but Jackson wasn't here to critique him yet. Just observe.

Jackson counted four bounces on Wyatt's right foot before he pushed off the ground. He managed to get his stomach across the saddle, lost his left foot's hold on the stirrup, and ended up sort of flopped across the saddle, long legs dangling. Michael snorted. Jackson covered his eyes with one hand and groaned.

Wyatt slid back down to his feet with a thump. "That, um, didn't work."

"Wanna answer my question again?" Jackson reached for the saddle strap, over this particular exercise. He had chores to do before clocking out for the day.

"Okay, I'm sorry. I can't mount a horse without a little help."

"Good. You need to remember one thing, and that's don't lie to us about what you know and what you can do. That's a fast ticket to a broken neck, kid." He pulled the saddle off and thrust it at Wyatt. "Hold this. Don't drop it."

"You aren't going to teach me to mount?" Wyatt's perfectly innocent tone poked at Jackson's temper—and the part of him that was still attracted to the guy, damn it.

Jackson fixed him with a cold glare, impressed that Wyatt didn't flinch or back down. "Not today." If there was a God, Brand would assign someone else to teach Wyatt everything he needed to know, and then Jackson could do his very best to avoid the tempting little brat.

Okay, not little. Very tall, very grown-up. Still a fucking brat.

"Watch what I'm doin'," Jackson snapped as he continued to untack Juno. He talked Wyatt through the steps as he did them, which was ass-backward to how he'd normally teach someone but this also wasn't an official lesson. Just him doing a favor for Hugo while they waited for the boss to get back.

He showed Wyatt where everything was stored in the tack room, then went over every single thing in the room. Every hook and shelf, where to find the saddle soap, rags, and other things. Michael came in once with his own stuff, and he gave Jackson a curious look but didn't offer up any commentary. Maybe Jackson was being a little anal about things, but he'd worked here longer than the other hands, and everything in the tack room had its place. Might as well get Wyatt used to the way things were done from the start.

Then he grabbed two brushes, took Wyatt back out to Juno, and showed him how he preferred to brush down his animal. They needed to ensure their horse was free of sweat and dirt and comfortable until the next time they took him or her out to ride. Jackson did his best to explain those things as they worked, concentrating on the sharp smell of horse and not the faint scent of Wyatt when he got too close. Some combination of shaving soap and deodorant that was both earthy and spicy, and way too appealing.

"When do we take the bridle off?" Wyatt asked.

Jackson inspected the horse's flank where Wyatt had been brushing her. "After she's in her stall. And it's a halter, not a bridle. The bridle uses a bit, and we don't usually use those unless the horses are around strangers or the public. They don't need them."

"Oh."

"You should have spent a few more hours on the internet before you interviewed, kid."

Wyatt bristled. "I'm not a kid."

"You're half my age. You'll always be a kid."

"Half? Yikes. You're old."

Jackson bit back a growl when he saw Wyatt's teasing smile. "Watch it. Let's get Juno into her stall and hope Brand is back with an idea on where to store you for the night."

"No more rooms left at the inn?"

He poked a finger into Wyatt's chest, not liking the way Wyatt's nostrils flared at that simple touch. "Listen, I don't know what part of last night's story was true, and I don't know what bullshit you spun to Brand today, but let's be clear here. You fuck him over, or you fuck over this ranch? I'll take care of it."

For a fraction of time, Wyatt's bravado cracked and a flash of vulnerability peeked through. It was gone in a blink, though, and Jackson had probably imagined it. "Loud and clear, boss," Wyatt said. "I'm not here to fuck anyone over, just to work. I wasn't lying when I said I was out here looking for work."

"You just forgot to mention you knew about this ranch." Jackson led Juno to her stall and showed Wyatt how to undo the halter now that she was safely put away. "There. Hang this up and we're done in here for now. Go find Hugo and leave me alone."

"You really sure that's what you want? Me to leave you alone?"

"Fuck yes, it is. I don't make friends with liars."

"I'm not a liar. I may have exaggerated a few bits of truth, but I didn't lie. Let me buy you a drink later and explain."

"You're underage. No thanks." Jackson stormed down the barn to the break room, Dog at his heels like she always was. He finished the last of his soda from lunch in three long gulps, not caring it was flat and cold enough to threaten a headache. Thankfully, Wyatt didn't follow him.

The little jerk was under his skin in less than twenty-four hours, and now he was going to work here. Jackson needed to get a handle on his emotions and his attraction, shove both down as far as they would go, and nail the lid on that shit. Yes, a part of him was curious why Wyatt had both lied about his name and "exaggerated" some of what he'd said last night, but Jackson was also done being other people's fool. The plain fact was Wyatt had lied to him, and he really should go straight to Brand with what he knew.

A truck engine roared outside. Jackson went to the break room's small window that looked out over the main yard. Brand was back, and he parked in his usual spot by the bunkhouse. Now was Jackson's chance. Take Brand into his office, admit to meeting "Wilson" last night at Blue Tavern, and blow up all of Wyatt's lies.

But Wyatt could have said something the moment he first saw Jackson, and he hadn't. Maybe Wyatt had been saving his own ass, even though Jackson couldn't see an angle for the kid. Wyatt could have told Hugo that Jackson picked him up, tried to seduce him, any number of things to paint himself as some sort of young victim. Not that Hugo would have believed such a thing, and even if he had, Brand wouldn't. Wyatt had kept his trap shut, though, and now Jackson really wanted to know why.

What was Wyatt's angle here? What did he hope to achieve? How much of what he'd said last night about being a runaway and trying to find himself had been true? Wyatt seemed willing to keep his mouth shut for now and play the role of the cowboy wannabe. And for the moment? Jackson was willing to keep his own mouth shut and play the familiar role of the silent, stoic cowboy who let nothing faze him.

He'd bide his time, because sooner or later Wyatt would fuck up. He'd do something, say something, let something slip, and Jackson would be there to pounce. Even if he didn't know what Wyatt's end game truly was here, Jackson's first loyalty was to the Woods family. He wouldn't let anyone fuck them over.

Period.

Chapter Five

Wyatt didn't take Jackson's abrupt dismissal personally. He more than deserved it after lying to Jackson last night about his name and his actual destination today. Although he technically hadn't lied about Woods Ranch being his destination, he'd just waffled on his response to where he was going and what kind of work he was looking for. Brand hadn't actually called him back to schedule the interview until this morning.

The timing had been stupidly perfect and further proof to Wyatt that packing up his life and coming here had been the right decision, impulsive as it was. If Brand had never called him back for an interview, he'd still planned to hang around Weston and learn what he could about Maybe Daddy. The fact that he'd been hired and Brand was going above and beyond to find him a place to stay? Exceeded expectations.

And was a little confusing. The guy was being extra kind for someone his grandparents warned him was a selfish asshole. Maybe twenty years did change people?

He'd find out for himself over the coming weeks. He'd also have a hell of a lot of fun flirting with Jackson, whose entire demeanor over the past hour or so had been a fascinating combination of "I hate you" and "I want to fuck you." Wyatt was definitely on board with exploring the latter; he just had to get on Jackson's good side again. Not an easy task when their relationship began with Wyatt being untruthful, but he never backed down from a challenge. His mother hadn't been the confrontational type, so maybe he got that from his father.

Asking Jackson out for a drink had been impulsive and dumb, but it had definitely gotten a reaction out of the older man. The much older man who lived in a defunct motel and had a dog named Dog. Add in the grumpy cowboy factor, the obvious hotness of the guy, and that scowl? Wyatt was obsessed. Ob. Sessed.

An obsession that would have to wait for a little while. After Jackson stormed out of the tack room—his coat hung a bit too low for Wyatt to properly admire his departure— Wyatt slowly made his way up the barn, taking his time peeking in at the horses again. He admired horses for their beauty, power and patience in dealing with their human riders. Maybe he couldn't mount one by himself yet, but he just needed practice.

And maybe a boost up by the ass from his favorite grumpy cowboy.

An engine outside stole his attention. Wyatt wandered to the mouth of the barn. Brand pulled up in front of the bunkhouse and parked his truck. The big German shepherd (the name started with a *B* but Wyatt had forgotten it) loped off the porch and went to meet his master. Hugo came out of the bunkhouse and did the same, greeting Brand with a sway of his hips that might have been a hug or kiss had they been in private. They seemed like an odd pair but also somehow matched.

Hugo said something, looked over at the barn, and beckoned Wyatt forward. He seemed amused by something, while Brand simply stared as Wyatt approached, no hint as to his mood after the run into town.

"I hear you're gonna need a bit of work," Brand said. "Kinda sorry I missed seeing you mount a horse like you were belly-flopping into a pool."

Hugo snorted, then covered his mouth with his hand.

"I need a bit of practice, sir," Wyatt replied, taking the knock on the chin in the good spirit it was meant. He probably had looked pretty funny sprawled over the saddle like that, legs dangling and ass in the air. In the air and pointed right in Jackson's direction. With his head facing the other way, Wyatt had no idea if Jackson had taken a moment to admire the goods, but he hoped he had.

"It's a learned skill for a lotta folks," Brand said. "Like anything else, some take to it fast and others need a little practice. But that's something we can worry about tomorrow. For now, let's get you settled in your new digs in town."

"My—where in town?"

"I both called in a favor and am doing a friend a favor. There's a real nice lady named Ramie Edwards who lives here in Weston. She bartends at the Roost and owns a little house her great-aunt left her a few years ago. But it's an old house and that winter storm we had come through last week did some roof damage, and the repairs are gonna cost her a pretty penny. She mentioned the other day she might take on a roommate for the extra cash to fix the roof, so I talked to her about you."

Wyatt started at Brand. A place in Weston, close to the ranch was ideal, obviously, but it sounded like this Ramie lady was also a friend of Brand's. Lucking into living with someone who knew the guy was almost too good to be true. "That sounds amazing. I'm pretty tidy and don't mind doing my share of chores and such."

"Make sure you do, because Ramie's a good friend and I promised I'd front her a security deposit for any damages."

"Damages beyond the roof?"

Brand's left eye twitched. "Yeah. Look, she's good people. Just think of her like a big sister with a whole lotta sarcasm and the occasional choice bit of wisdom."

This Ramie woman sounded a bit like his stepsister Lily. "I can do that. I really appreciate this. Not all bosses would put in the effort to make sure an employee, especially a brand-new one who chose to uproot his whole life, had a place to stay."

Brand glanced at Hugo, and Wyatt couldn't begin to guess the meaning behind their shared look. "Woods Ranch is a family business," Brand finally said. "We do our best to treat our employees like part of the family, which means making sure they got a place to stay and aren't sleeping in their cars. Ramie also agreed to the same eight weeks minimum that you'll be trying things out here. Not sayin' she'll kick you out if it doesn't work out here, just that you've got a spot for at least two months."

"I really appreciate that. If she's used to living alone I can't imagine she'll want a roommate indefinitely, but it's nice knowing I've got a place for a while. Thank you."

"Not a problem. Like I said, we're doing her a favor, too."

"I wish I could say I've got handyman experience and can help with her roof but I don't. I mean, I can use a drill if I have to but the last time I used a hammer, I ended up losing my thumbnail."

Brand finally cracked a smile. "Why does that not surprise me in the least? Rem was like that when he was a kid, always skinning a knee or cutting himself with the bread knife. You two should compare war stories one day."

"I'd like that." It amused Wyatt that Maybe Uncle Rem was accident-prone, too, and still worked full-time at the ranch. Maybe there was hope for Wyatt, as well.

"Great. Well, if you follow me, I'll take you to Ramie's house. She's working but said she'd take her break when we were ready to meet her."

"Cool."

Wyatt hoped for another Jackson sighting before he left for the day, but no luck. He followed Brand's pickup into Weston, taking care to observe the town like he had that morning. The homes and businesses and people on the sidewalks. Pretty typical small town. He'd driven through dozens on his way here, and if he ever found a thriving town without at least one church in it, he'd eat his over-priced cowboy hat.

Brand parked on a quiet, tree-lined street full of squat midcentury homes. Some had bikes and kid toys in the yards, and he spotted one car up on cinder blocks in a driveway. None of those things were in the yard of the house Brand approached. White with black shutters, grass in need of a cut, flowerbeds with nothing but mulch and a scraggly bush. Wyatt left his suitcase behind for now and followed Brand up the cement walkway.

Instead of knocking or making a phone call, Brand produced his own key and let them inside. "You have your own key?" Wyatt asked dumbly.

"Yeah, in case she needs me to do something for her."

Wyatt briefly wondered if Brand and Ramie had always been "just friends" or maybe something more, but Brand was with Hugo. Whatever, he'd get those details eventually, if he asked the right questions.

The front door opened into a tiny patch of linoleum that was the foyer, and beyond it was the living room. Beyond that was the kitchen, and a hallway to the right had a few doors, so probably the bathroom and bedrooms. The décor was "old cat lady meets single bartender" chic, with a mash-up of the same stuff he'd find in his grandparents' house and new technology. A flat-screen stood on top of a boxy TV set that had come straight out of the sixties.

"Who's her decorator?" Wyatt asked, his mouth acting on its own accord.

Brand snickered. "Ramie spent a few summers living here when she was a kid and once told me she has fond memories of the place. Didn't want to change it too much."

"Obviously." Not wanting to sound rude, he added, "It's cozy. Did the roof leak damage anything?"

"Just some boxes in the attic. Fortunately, it didn't leak through the attic floor, and she's got it patched for now, but it needs to get fixed right before spring. It rains the most around here in April and May."

"Got it."

"You heating the whole outdoors, Brand?" a sharp voice asked from behind them. A short, curvy woman with thick black hair and darkly lined eyes shut the front door and scowled past Wyatt at Brand.

"Sorry," Brand said. "We were taking a moment to admire your killer decorating skills."

The woman who had to be Ramie flipped him off, then turned a pleasant smile to Wyatt. "Hey there, you must be Wyatt. I'm Ramie."

"It's a pleasure, ma'am," Wyatt replied, with a polite nod of his head.

"Oh God, don't ma'am me, I'm not your mother, your teacher, or your boss. I also work more evenings than days, so we probably won't see a lot of each other. All I ask is you clean up after yourself. You cook? You do your own dishes. I've got a washer and dryer in the kitchen, and if you don't know how to use it, I'll show you. No parties without permission, and I don't care if you bring a girl over to fuck as long as you don't leave wet towels on the bathroom floor."

"I hardly know enough people yet for a party, but I appreciate the rules ma'—um, Ramie."

"Good. Brand over there is vouching for your character, but just in case you've got some hidden drug problem I don't know about, the pipes are plastic, the TV has a weird line at the top, and I don't have any jewelry that I didn't buy at a swap meet, so there's not much of value here to hock or pawn."

Wyatt gaped at her, at once appreciative of her blunt nature and slightly offended by the insinuations. "No drug problem, I promise. I've got a small savings, so I can pay up front for the remainder of this month."

"Great, we can talk about that stuff later. The rent's all-inclusive, so I won't be nickel-and-diming you for the electric or internet or whatever. Wi-Fi password is on a card by the TV and your room's this way." She marched down the hallway.

It took him a split second to kick it into gear and follow her. His room looked like a magazine page out of the 1970s with a hideous green-and-orange bedspread and matching curtains. The orange upholstered headboard was just as scary as the weird green carpet. It looked like a circus tent had vomited into the room. "Wow" was all he could manage.

Ramie laughed. "It's a bit much but Aunt Florence loved this room. It's where I stayed when I was a kid. If this arrangement becomes long-term I might let you change it, but we'll take it a week at a time, yeah?"

"Sure, yeah. But, um, tell me the mattress is at least from this century?"

"It is. So are the sheets. Might be a touch stale, though,

so you probably want to turn down the bed and let them air out a little. Haven't had anyone crash here in a while."

"Awesome, thanks. I guess this is a dumb question but do you mind if I put food in the fridge or a cupboard?"

"Don't mind at all. I'm not too particular about my food so help yourself to anything except my Cajun peanuts. If you are particular, feel free to label your stuff or claim a shelf or whatever."

Wyatt nodded, really liking Ramie already. She was very easygoing and had this big-sister vibe that he dug. Like she'd said before, she wasn't his mother and didn't seem to have much going on in the way of house rules beyond "don't leave a mess behind." He could deal with that. His stepfather had been a bit of a neat freak and had blown his top enough times over stupid shit like a tooth-paste smear in the bathroom sink that Wyatt knew how to keep a clean room.

Ramie showed him the bathroom, the linen closet, and the kitchen. It was a small, eat-in type with no real pan-try, just the cupboards and some sort of Ikea-style, build-it-yourself cabinet where she kept extra stuff like snacks, paper plates, and a slow cooker. At the end of the brief tour, she grabbed a bottled protein shake from the fridge. "Okay, I need to get back to work, you two." She included Brand, who'd hung back in the living room the whole time. "Wyatt, I'll see you later tonight if you're still awake. Brand, you mind giving him your key until I can get another copy made?"

"Sure, no problem," Brand replied.

"See you guys."

Wyatt made it to the front window in time to see her backing out of the short driveway in a battered Ford pickup that had seen way better days. Keys jangled and then Brand handed him one. "All yours," he said. "I'll get outta here and let you settle in. You remember the way to the grocery store in town?"

"Yeah, no problem." The town was small enough that he'd have to be a complete moron to actually get lost in it. Plus, if he was going to stock up, he'd use his phone to find the nearest Walmart for a cheaper, better selection. Not that he was going to tell Brand that. "Thanks again, man, I mean it."

"You're welcome. You ready to get your feet wet tomorrow?"

"Definitely."

"Good man. See you at eight thirty, then."

"Bright and early." Wyatt shook Brand's hand again before the older man left. Waited until Brand pulled away before collecting his own things from his car. Some of the personal stuff he left in the trunk—he was pretty sure car thieves were in short supply around Weston.

Time to settle into his hideous new room and prepare for his first day as a cowboy at Woods Ranch.

"What are you doing out here? It's freezing."

Brand wasn't surprised to hear Hugo's voice behind him. He'd heard the storm door creak open but not the louder squeak of the screen door, so he was still inside the relative warmth of the bunkhouse. Brand was sitting in one of the two folding lawn chairs he'd rescued from the garage a few weeks ago so he and Hugo had something to sit on if they felt the need to chill on the porch instead of inside.

Tonight, he'd wanted to be outside.

"Stewing in my big mood," Brand replied. He was warm enough in his coat and gloves, despite the winter chill of the night air. After the sweltering heat of summer he liked the temperature changes this time of year.

The screen door opened, and Brutus was the first to

make it to Brand's chair. While Brutus still reigned like a king from the family home's porch during the day, he'd gotten used to sleeping in the bunkhouse with Brand and Hugo. He put his furry chin on Brand's knee, and Brand rubbed the top of his head and behind his ears.

"What's this mood for?" Hugo asked as he eased into the other chair. The aluminum frame creaked a lot, and Brand was sure that one day the old chairs would collapse when one of them sat down.

"Just thinking about Dad a lot tonight. Not sure why."

"Well, he's going to have surgery next week, so that's kind of a big deal. You're allowed to worry about it. Especially after that cancer scare you told me about."

"Yeah." Watching his father deal with non-Hodgkin's lymphoma as the eldest sibling (at the time), on top of keeping the ranch going, had been insanely stressful for Brand. Next week's surgery was nowhere near as scary as cancer but it was a vivid reminder that his father was human. Fallible. Fragile.

"There's something else, though. I know you, Brand. Is it Wyatt?"

"A little, I guess." Something about the kid reminded him so much of his teenage years, and it freaked him out more than he wanted to admit. The awkwardness and ginger curls and his age…he saw Ginny in Wyatt, and he really didn't want to see an old girlfriend in a new employee. Especially an old girlfriend who'd taken a part of Brand with her when she and her family moved away.

"Are you worried hiring Wyatt was a bad decision?" Hugo asked. "Because of his inexperience?"

"Some, yeah. I'd be lying if I said no. He's adamant about wanting this life, so I'm gonna give him a chance. I just don't want the kid to get hurt, you know?"

"Oh, I know. I saw him try to mount Juno today, remember?"

"Lucky you." He bumped his knee against Hugo's. "I just hope I didn't impulsively hire him because I'm worried about Dad. What if someone better qualified applies tomorrow?"

"Then you look at your budget and figure out if you can afford them both. Plus, Wyatt's got an eight-week probation so if he doesn't work out you can fire him and find someone who's better. It's a stop-gap right now, Brand, just like that tarp on Ramie's roof. And who knows? Maybe Wyatt will surprise you and be really good with a little bit of training. Stranger things have happened."

"True. When did you get so optimistic?"

"Last year when I gave up a job I loved on a dude ranch to move back here and try to win your affections. And it worked, too. I got a job I love, a man I love, and a family who supports us both. May not be blood, but your family is everything to me. Just like you."

One of Hugo's main goals last year when he left California for Texas was to be with Brand, but another had been to try to reconnect with his mother. That hadn't gone well, and Hugo had no contact with his mom or stepdad, or the abusive older stepbrother currently cooling his heels in state prison for aggravated assault. The Woods family was Hugo's family now, exactly as he always should have been.

Brand leaned over and kissed Hugo gently on the mouth. "You're everything to me too, babe." Brutus whined softly, as if understanding their conversation, and Brand scratched his chin. "You too, pup. You three are my whole life."

"Your whole life that isn't devoted to this ranch, you mean." Hugo bumped his knee in return. "And that's not a criticism at all, you know that. Woods Ranch is your legacy, and you have put all of yourself into making it succeed despite the odds. And I'm with you, Brand, no matter what happens."

"Thanks. Sometimes I feel like I'm wandering around in the dark, and other days I can see everything so clearly. Today was one of those murky days, I think."

"Well, it did start out with bad news but I think it worked out. Honestly, I admire you for taking a chance on Wyatt. The kid's as likely to fall off a horse as successfully ride one, but he's passionate about this life. You just need to help him rein in that passion and use it in a way that won't get him hurt."

"I'll do my best. I was thinking of pairing him up with Jackson. He's been here the longest, been in the life for… hell, I don't even know how long. He grew up on a farm and has been ranching most of his adult life. There's a few years in there he never told me about, but he doesn't owe me his life story. We've all got secrets we don't like talking about."

Hugo quirked an eyebrow at him. "What secrets do you still have that I don't know about?"

Only one thing that Brand had buried so deeply in his memory he simply didn't talk about it anymore. There was no point, but one day he'd share it with Hugo. Probably. Nothing about the kid he'd never met affected their lives in the present. A kid he hoped was doing amazing things with their life. College or trade school or some other path, he didn't care as long as they were happy. Healthy. Safe.

"The secret of how I make my homemade chili taste so much better than yours," Brand teased.

"Okay, those are fighting words, Woods. You know my chili is superior."

"Am I gonna have to wrestle you into admitting mine's the best?"

"Yup." Hugo punched him lightly in the shoulder before sprinting back into the bunkhouse.

On a bark of genuine, amused laughter, Brand chased his boyfriend inside.

Chapter Six

Jackson genuinely thought his luck had turned in a positive direction these past few years. He'd worked at Woods Ranch without any issues or injuries, lucked into a cheap and private place to live with wide-open skies, and up until last summer had an easy way to scratch his itch when he wanted some physical relief.

Still having two out of three things was pretty damned good in his book. The third was why he'd been at Blue Tavern two nights ago, looking for somebody to fuck or fuck him. Brand had usually topped when they fucked around, so someone to fuck had been at the forefront of Jackson's mind, until "Wilson" invited himself into Jackson's personal space. And now he was ten kinds of glad he hadn't fucked the kid, or working with him would have been even more awkward than it was going to be.

No more fucking around with coworkers.

Well, no more fucking around in the carnal sense, anyway. He was still determined to figure out what Wyatt's game was. Using a fake name when you were hunting for a hookup wasn't unheard of (Jackson had never done it but to each his own), but Wyatt landing at Woods Ranch irritated him—and not just because the kid was still intensely fuckable and appealing.

He parked near the barn right at eight thirty, not at all

surprised to see Wyatt's car already there. He also spotted Rem's pickup next to Brand's. Dog leaped out of the cab and trotted up to the main house's porch to greet Brutus for the day. No Michael or Rosco, which left an uneasy feeling in his stomach. Not that he expected Brand to partner Wyatt up with Michael, since he'd only been back in the life for half a year. Hugo was his only hope.

Hoping to get started on his chore list unnoticed, Jackson slipped into the barn and stashed his lunch in the break room fridge. He turned and jumped, not expecting to see Rem and Wyatt standing in the doorway. "Dammit, Rem, you're gonna give me a heart attack," Jackson snapped. "Don't sneak around like a thief."

Rem scuffed his boots on the hard-packed earth. "Sorry, man, didn't mean to. Brand said you met Wyatt yesterday, so I guess I don't have to introduce you."

"Yeah, we met. You training him today?"

"Nope. Brand told me to tell you that you get to mentor him today. Tacking and riding, while I handle your other chores."

Jackson bit back a groan. "Yeah, fine. Where is Brand?"

"Finishing up breakfast with Hugo and our folks. Mom's making pulled pork sandwiches for lunch to officially welcome Wyatt to the ranch, so plan on taking your break at twelve thirty."

Rose Woods could cook the hell out of a pork shoulder, and she'd made the same lunch for Jackson the week he was first hired. "Okay." He turned his attention to Wyatt, who looked like he was trying to hide a smile or a smirk, Jackson wasn't sure. "Come on, greenhorn. Let's see if we can get your ass up on a horse the right way today."

"I look forward to the challenge," Wyatt replied, narrowing his eyes slightly.

Yeah, the kid was trouble in jeans and an oversized hat.

"Have fun," Rem called out as Jackson walked down the barn.

Jackson resisted the urge to flip him off. Rem wasn't technically his boss the way Brand was, but Rem was a Woods and his name was on the ranch. Better to resist his worst urges and play nice, even though the last thing he wanted to do was hang out with Wyatt all day. This was going to well and truly suck.

"Let's go," Jackson growled in Wyatt's general direction when the kid didn't immediately follow him. "I'll put you on Shirley Temple today. She's old, slow, and a little short, so you shouldn't have a problem getting on her."

"Whatever you think is best, boss," Wyatt replied with that annoying shit-eating grin. "I'm cool with starting slow. We can work up to the big, strong horses, no problem."

He waited next to Shirley Temple's stall for Wyatt to catch up with him, then poked Wyatt in the chest. "Look, you got off on the wrong fucking foot with me by lying the other night, so how about you concentrate and quit flirtin'. It ain't gonna work and I ain't interested."

Liar.

Wyatt's single quirked eyebrow didn't believe Jackson, either. "Okay, boss. Morning, Miss Temple. Looks like I'll be riding you today."

The paint mare stuck her head over the stall door and nickered at them. She was a favorite of the Woods grand-kids because of her gentle nature, and Jackson had watched them ride her around the corral on more than one occasion. Seeing the happy, joyful kids spending time with their parents and grandparents was too painful most of the time. He'd never be able to do a job like Colt did, working around families week in and week out. It made him extra grateful for the solitude of this ranch.

Jackson showed Wyatt how to attach the halter and lead

Shirley Temple to the tack area. She plodded along, Dog following behind her at an equally steady gait, probably curious what her master was up to. If only his sweet pup had a clue what sort of challenge today was going to be for her daddy.

"Get a brush and get started, just like yesterday," Jackson said.

"You aren't helping?"

"Not unless you fuck up. You say you're a quick learner? Prove it."

Wyatt took that as the challenge it was and got the brush. And he did a decent job brushing Shirley Temple down, pulling the brush down her neck, across her flanks, and down to her legs. Steady strokes with one hand while keeping his other on the horse as a grounding touch while he worked.

"Good," Jackson said. "Now the blanket. Get the gray one, it's a good fit for her."

"Yes, boss."

The use of "boss" was almost affectionate now, rather than snarky or challenging. Wyatt did a good job following his instructions on tightening the saddle and adjusting the stirrups. "There's always a little give," Jackson said when Wyatt seemed dubious over the saddle's ability to not go completely sideways on him. "You don't wanna squeeze the horse to death but you also don't wanna fall off."

"Right. Falling off is definitely bad."

"Definitely." After testing all the buckles, Jackson had Wyatt lead Shirley Temple out into the corral. He glanced around but they didn't have an obvious audience. "All right, kid, let's try mounting again."

"Okay." Wyatt got into position, determination overtaking all previous trepidation. "I watched a bunch of videos on my phone last night, so I think I got this."

"Then have at it."

Jackson took a few steps back and waited, arms crossed, and no, he did not briefly admire Wyatt's ass in those tight jeans. Nope. He was simply paying attention to his student so the guy didn't go tumbling, that was it. Wyatt braced, bounced, seemed to count to something in his head, and then he surprised the hell out of Jackson by hauling his long, lean body up into the saddle. It took him a minor struggle to get his right foot into the other stirrup but by God, he'd done it.

Jackson let out a low whistle that made Dog bark. "Nice job."

Wyatt pumped his fist into the air once. "Nailed it. Yes."

He hadn't completely nailed it but no sense in pissing in the kid's oatmeal first thing in the morning. A little practice and he'd definitely nail it. "Now try to dismount."

"Already?"

"Yep. We're gonna perfect each step at a time. You can't walk if you don't learn to crawl first, and you can't run without first learning to walk."

"Wise words, I guess. Who said them?"

"Dunno who said them first, but my old man used to say it when I first learned to ride. Then again, I was five years old, so I was still gettin' a handle on running without tripping over my own ankles and skinning a knee."

"You've been riding since you were five? Wow." Wyatt looked genuinely impressed by that.

Jackson shrugged. "Grew up on a working farm. All us kids were expected to pitch in from a young age to keep things goin'." And that was as far down Memory Lane as he wanted to travel today. His personal past was not up for discussion with Wyatt. "Same as all the Woods kids, I suspect. Brand's been riding since he could walk."

"Makes sense growing up on a farm or ranch." Wyatt petted the side of Shirley Temple's neck. "I grew up in what you'd probably think of as a big city, but compared to someplace like Amarillo or Houston, it's a small town. Just not much in the way of ranching or farms nearby. A few factories and a prison employed most everybody in the area. It wasn't a horrible place to grow up, but I wanted a different life. A life where I was free to be me." He gave Jackson a pointed stare. "You know?"

"I know. Come on, try a dismount. Opposite of mounting, just swing that right leg back over her rump and make sure you plant it firm on the ground before you let go of the pommel."

"Got it. I think."

Wyatt didn't quite have it and nearly fell over backward when his right foot hit the dirt. Jackson caught him under his armpits and kept him upright, and that brief contact should not have made his hands tingle the way it did. Nah, he was imagining it. He still took a long step backward once Wyatt righted himself.

"Thanks," Wyatt said. "That was kind of embarrassing."

"You'll get it, you just need to practice. Crawl before you walk, remember?"

"Yeah."

Now that Wyatt was back at eye level, Jackson was tempted to ask about Monday night and what all had been true about Wyatt's past and his reasons for being in Weston. But they were on the clock, Jackson had a greenhorn to train, and they didn't need the distraction. "All right," he said instead. "Again."

By the time lunch rolled around and Jackson called it quits for a while, Wyatt's entire body ached. All he'd done was spend the past three hours mounting and dismounting Shirley Temple, and eventually Jackson had given him a pair of gloves to wear. He was still going to have at least one blister on his left hand, though—he could feel it rising.

He also occasionally rode her at a slow walk around the corral. Wyatt really wanted to go faster on the mare, but Jackson was taking his damned time.

All this "crawling" was getting on Wyatt's damned nerves, but he didn't want to fuck things up by pushing to go faster. If this was Jackson's style of training newbies, Wyatt would suck it up and go slow. It gave him lots of time in the grumpy cowboy's proximity, even if he kept a constant arm's reach of space between them.

Wyatt had also pulled back on his flirting, not wanting to irritate Jackson into handing him over to Hugo or Michael for training. He liked Jackson and wanted to know more about the guy, but Jackson had seemed mad after revealing what little he had about his past growing up on a farm, so Wyatt didn't push. Jackson seemed like the type who was wholly professional on the job but knew how to kick back when he was off the clock.

He really wanted to be alone with Jackson again off the clock. Jackson was sexy as hell and Wyatt enjoyed getting under the older cowboy's skin. That scowl always went right to Wyatt's dick.

Meeting Maybe Uncle Rem this morning had been slightly tense on Wyatt's side, but Rem was high-strung, earnest, and a really nice guy. He spoke fondly of both his wife and little girl and promised to introduce them at some point in the near future. But when Jackson called for lunch, Wyatt's stomach twisted up tight. Today was lunch with the elder Woods couple, Wayne and Rose, his Maybe Grandparents.

Were they the awful, self-absorbed people his maternal grandparents had insisted they were? Had they mellowed in recent years? Was the whole lunch thing just an act so Wyatt did a good job and earned his keep, and it didn't matter if they actually liked him or not? Too many questions, and the only way to get answers was to make his feet carry him up to the main house.

Jackson went right into the break room, leaving Wyatt to traverse the wide yard by himself. He cast around for Hugo or Rem, or anyone else. Brutus was sitting on his big bed by the front door and he only raised his head at Wyatt. No barking or growling, hopefully sensing a friendly. Wyatt liked dogs well enough, even though he'd never been able to own one. He'd only been nine the first time his stepfather had made Wyatt witness him putting an elderly stray dog down, and it had almost been more than Wyatt could bear.

But he'd sucked it up so his stepfather didn't get angry later. Angry at Wyatt for being a "sissy" or a "child," or for "being gay" about putting a dog down.

Brutus yawned and rested his head on his massive front paws.

Wyatt took off his hat and knocked, unsure of the protocol here. A moment later, a brown-haired woman wearing a floral apron opened the door and smiled at him. Brand definitely favored her. "Good afternoon, ma'am," Wyatt said. "Um, Brand invited me to lunch?"

"Come on inside, you must be Wyatt," she replied, never losing that cheerful smile. "I'm Rose Woods, and yes, you're invited to lunch. I made pulled pork and coleslaw, so we've got sandwiches, iced tea, and there might even be a peach pie for dessert."

"That sounds wonderful, thank you." He followed her down a long hallway lined with family photos that he didn't have a lot of time to study, and into a wide, bright kitchen with a built-in breakfast nook. Brand and Hugo were already there, setting the table, and for one brief moment, Wyatt felt a bit like an alien on a new planet, unsure of himself or his place here with his Maybe Family.

Just ask him and get it over with!

He silenced his better angel and colluded with the devil on his shoulder who insisted Wyatt investigate this on his own. To keep his cover for as long as possible. If he gave away who he was and why he was here too soon, he might fail in his goal to get to know the real Brand Woods and family.

"So how did your first lesson with Jackson go?" Hugo asked.

"We crawled a lot." Off Hugo's confused look, Wyatt explained the metaphor that was the foundation of Jackson's teaching methods. "I appreciate the time he's taking, I really do. It can be tedious, but I want to learn how to do things right the first time. No sense in creating bad habits I'll have to break later."

"That's a wonderful way to look at your training," Rose said. "Jackson's been here a long time and he's helped many a new hand get used to the ranch."

"He's definitely got experience, and I'm grateful to learn from him. He isn't joining us for lunch?"

"I asked him," Brand said, "but he said he'd be fine with his sandwich."

"Guess the teacher needs a bit of a break from his student," Hugo joked. "You'll get sick of him at some point or another, too, Wyatt. Give it time."

Wyatt wasn't so sure about that, but he laughed along with the teasing. "I look forward to the challenge."

Wayne Woods joined them moments later, and Wyatt had another bizarre moment when he shook the eldest Woods's hand. His Maybe Grandfather was as kind and welcoming as Rose had been, and in some ways, the pair made him think of Mr. and Mrs. Claus, minus the white hair and red suits. They were just...nice, and it confused the hell out of Wyatt. He deflected that by concentrating on the delicious food and answering any questions lobbed his way as vaguely as possible. Rose was curious about the family he'd left behind, and after a few brief responses from Wyatt, Brand stepped in and redirected the conversation to the upcoming farm equipment auction.

Wyatt would never admit he was grateful for the save, or that it made him like Brand a little bit more. He needed to stay objective about every member of this family until he sussed out the truth.

At the end of the meal, he thanked Rose and Wayne several times for inviting him to lunch, and for their faith in his ability to live up to Brand's expectations. Rose walked him to the front door. "Welcome to the extended Woods family, Wyatt. I know you're still on a probationary period but you've got a fighting spirit."

"Thank you, ma'am."

"I look forward to seeing you around the ranch. And I know you're young, but don't let those older boys boss you around too much."

"I'll do my best." He was not allowed to like her as much as he wanted to, but she was warmer than either of his other grandmothers. More genuine in a way he couldn't explain.

Brutus barely raised his head when Wyatt crossed the porch and went down the steps to the yard. Dog trotted over from the bar and butted her head against his thigh, so he reached down to scratch behind her soft ears. Maybe getting into Dog's good graces would help endear him to her daddy.

Speaking of her daddy, Dog followed him into the barn. The break room was empty and so was the immediate interior of the barn. Curious, he went out to the corral. Jackson stood near the far fence with Shirley Temple, feeding her what looked like a carrot. Wyatt hadn't made any specific kind of noise, but Jackson still looked up. Right at him.

"You ready to get back to walking, now that you're done schmoozing the owners?" Jackson asked.

"Bring it on," Wyatt retorted. "I can finally mount the horse. Can I learn how to ride it now? And ride it in a way that evokes…pleasure for us both?"

Jackson's eyes narrowed. "You do anything that causes a horse pain, they'll buck you right into the dirt."

"Then I guess you better teach me to ride right, huh? Or walk, I guess? Since we're still in walking mode. Walk right? Walk the line?"

"You wanna walk the line, you better get yourself a good singing voice, Mr. Cash. Otherwise, get your ass up on Shirley Temple and we'll see what you can actually do for the rest of the day. Might be a little sore after ridin' for a few hours, but that's what ice packs are for."

"You some sort of pain-loving dom there, boss?"

His nostrils flared in an intensely sexy way. "Not much for pain, but I do like seeing things done right. Might even know a few good punishments for students who don't put in a proper effort."

"Punishments, huh? You know, when I was a kid there was always a rumor that the school principal kept a wooden paddle in his office for students who acted out. You got one of those?"

Jackson smirked at him. "Test me and you'll find out, kid."

"Promise?"

"Don't beg for somethin' you don't really want." His dark eyes stared hard into Wyatt's a beat, and the look made Wyatt's blood pulse. He definitely needed to get Jackson alone somewhere off this property. "Now get your skinny ass up on Shirley Temple. We got work to do."

"Yes, sir."

This was going to be so much fun.

* * *

His afternoon turned out to be a lot less fun than Wyatt had anticipated. After those first flirty moments postlunch, Jackson's sense of humor disappeared and he turned back into the strict teacher/coach. And not the fun kind of strict. After two hours up on Shirley Temple, walking her, learning voice and noise commands, and how to guide her properly with both reins and his heels, his ass hurt. A lot.

Instead of easing up, Jackson gave Shirley Temple a break and had Wyatt saddle up Cobblepot, a male horse with a bit more personality and a good hand taller than Shirley Temple (thanks to the internet, Wyatt already knew horses were measured in "hands" and not feet).

"Who came up with the name Cobblepot?" Wyatt asked as he tightened the saddle strap.

"I think Rem named this one." Jackson was leaning against the barn wall, watching and chewing on a piece of hay. The position was insanely hot but Wyatt was too busy tacking the horse right to properly ogle his teacher. "He liked her coloring with the white patches on black. Made him look like a penguin, so Rem named him after the Batman character."

"Penguin actually had a name?"

Jackson snorted. "Sometimes I forget how young you are."

Wyatt stuck his tongue out, but he was facing away and Jackson couldn't see it. "Whatever, man. I got life experience, it's just different than yours."

"I'll say." That had been under his breath but in the near-silent barn, Wyatt still heard it.

Once Cobblepot was squared away, Jackson attached a rope to his halter and led the horse into the corral. It took Wyatt a bit more effort to mount the taller horse but he managed without being too awkward about it. Jackson left them near the corral fence and moved to the center, still holding that rope.

"All right, we're gonna try a trot," Jackson said. "It's bumpier than a walk. Nudge him in the flank."

He did and Cobblepot surged forward, his walk wider than Shirley Temple's had been, and Wyatt did his best to roll with the motions. They did a full circle of the corral at a walk before Jackson said to nudge him again. Cobblepot sped up, and Wyatt's ass bounced uncomfortably in the saddle. He gripped the reins and pressed his feet harder against the stirrups, a little nervous about falling off now.

"Try to relax a little," Jackson said, "or you're gonna be stiff tomorrow. He ain't got nowhere to charge to, so don't worry about him galloping off with you astride him. Try to roll with him."

Wyatt did his best and gradually relaxed into a posture less likely to spontaneously sprain something. Jackson even nodded at him and offered a half smile, some kind of silent praise that he was doing better. After an hour of alternating between a trot and a walk, Wyatt wanted to cry for how much his body hurt, but he clung tightly to his pride and somehow did not groan in agony while climbing off Cobblepot.

"You did good today, kid," Jackson said. "It's about quittin' time, so why don't you go ahead and clock out for the day? I'll take care of Cobblepot."

He resisted the urge to hug Jackson. "You sure? I can do my part."

"I bet you can but I rode you pretty hard today, so I can have mercy."

If only he'd ridden me hard. Naked and without a horse involved.

"Thank you," Wyatt said, genuinely grateful to be done

for today. "I can't really say I had fun today, but I did learn a whole lot."

"Good. If Ramie's got any Epsom salts at home, a long soak in a hot tub will do your muscles a world of good."

"Thanks for the advice." A hot bath sounded like heaven, maybe with a cold six-pack to go along with it. Only the small grocery store in Weston didn't sell beer, and Wyatt was too exhausted to drive out to the convenience store on the highway. He'd just close his eyes and imagine he was drinking an ice-cold beer.

"See you tomorrow morning, kid."

"Hey, Jackson?"

"What?"

Wyatt bit his upper lip, then squared his shoulders. "Could you maybe not call me kid anymore? I know I'm only twenty and can't buy a beer without a fake ID yet, but I'm a grown man. Haven't felt like a kid in a long time."

Jackson held his gaze for a long moment before nodding. "Sure, I can respect that. Wyatt."

"Thank you. See you tomorrow."

"Yeah."

Wyatt left with a bit more bounce in his step than before, proud to have stood up for himself and for getting through his first day of training without having to wave a white flag in surrender. Jackson had been tough, but not cruelly so, and he'd shown a lot of restraint with Wyatt's teasing. He respected the older man a hell of a lot, both as a teacher and a future coworker.

He'd also enjoyed spending time with the Woods family over lunch, way more than he'd expected to. Nothing about the past two days on the ranch had gone the way he'd expected (other than being hired, of course) and, despite his exhausted, sore body, Wyatt was eager to see what tomorrow would bring.

Chapter Seven

For the second night in three consecutive days, Jackson found himself at a back table in Blue Tavern, eyeballing the offerings and not liking anything he saw. Anyone intriguing enough to bleach his brain of the mental image Wyatt had fed him that afternoon in the corral. An image of Wyatt bent over, hands braced on a mattress, jeans around his ankles while Jackson spanked his ass cherry-red.

An image that had threatened to give him wood multiple times today while he continued training Wyatt to be a decent cowboy and ranch hand.

Jackson wasn't into BDSM in general, despite having dabbled in the lifestyle briefly in his early twenties. He enjoyed certain things but definitely not others. He didn't want a boy or to be a daddy, and he didn't want to control another person in or out of the bedroom. Did he like being spanked? Yes, with the right person. Did he enjoy spanking others? Hell to the yes, again with the right person.

Was Wyatt the right person? Probably not, even though the kid's mouth knew how to write checks and suggest future possibilities. Wyatt was only twenty years old, still finding his place in the world, and no way was Jackson the right person to settle him down or introduce him to the kinkier side of sex.

Then again, Wyatt could have a kinky sexual history

that Jackson knew nothing about. But if Wyatt was on the hunt for some kind of older daddy to take him in hand, Jackson wasn't the guy. He'd never make that mistake again. Fantasies were safer for both of them.

A tall, slender frame moved in Jackson's peripheral vision, and he snapped his head up, stupidly hoping to catch a glimpse of Wyatt. But the man was blond, wore skintight leather pants, and a bit too much eye makeup for Jackson's taste. A bear of a man in a fringed suede jacket swooped in, and the pair moved off together.

Lucky them.

"Your beer looks a little low," a deep voice said. "How about a fresh one?"

A beer glass with a good head on it appeared next to Jackson's almost empty one, and he followed the tan hand that had put it there up to a smiling, bearded face. Not a thick bear beard, but neatly trimmed close to the skin and nothing on his upper lip. Past it was a pair of dark eyes crinkled at the corners, and light brown hair swept up in a fancy style that had probably taken quite a bit of product to keep that way.

Cute, appealing, with a slender body Jackson took a moment to appreciate. "Thanks," he said. And out of sheer politeness added, "Join me?"

"Thank you." He pulled out a chair and sat opposite Jackson, his own beer in one hand. No hat or leather jacket, just casual clothes, and his voice didn't have the familiar lilt of someone from around the area. "If I'm disturbing your solitude, tell me to buzz off. I just usually feel awkward drinking alone when I'm new to the area."

"The county or Texas in general?"

"What gave me away? The lack of boots and chaps?"

Jackson smiled. "Mostly the accent. Name's Jackson."

"First or last name?"

"Could be both. You got either?"

"I'm Drew Banner. Do I get extra points for having two names?"

Amused by Drew's easy sense of humor, Jackson said, "Sumner. Jackson Sumner."

"Nice to meet you."

They shook hands across the table like two men starting a business meeting. Jackson didn't feel a thing from the touch, and while Drew was easy enough on the eyes, he wasn't turning Jackson's crank at all. His hair wasn't red enough.

"So where are you from if not from Texas?" Jackson asked.

"Relocated to this area from Denver for my job. I'm still getting used to small-town life after growing up in or around a city. It's not easy to, ah, find folks with similar interests."

"True story. Makes this place pretty popular if you live within a fifty-mile radius. It's private and people mind their business."

"I see the appeal." Drew made a show of cruising Jackson, who'd remained in his comfortable, slightly slouched position. "To borrow on a tired cliché, do you come here often?"

"Once in a while. Depends on my mood. If I just want a beer, there's three bars a hell of a lot closer to where I live."

"Which is where?"

"Not too far, and not too near." He'd kicked back more than a few at the Roost after work, both alone and with his coworkers, but he almost never found a guy to take home there. It was a locals' place and not great for cruising, unless he wanted his night to end in a fistfight with drunken homophobes.

"A man of mystery. I don't suppose you're secretly a spy, Mr. Sumner? Jackson Sumner?"

"If I was a spy, would I tell you I was?" Jackson was enjoying the banter, even if the guy himself left Jackson cold in the attraction front. But Drew was a great distraction from his Wyatt problem. He sipped his new, much colder beer. "So what kind of job drew you away from the city and into our quiet little county?"

"Would you believe me if I said I'm a minister and am taking over from Pastor Ross at the Protestant church in Weston?"

Jackson blinked, uncertain if he believed Drew or not. But the guy seemed perfectly serious, and Jackson had certainly heard stranger things in his days. "You do realize you're in a gay bar, right, pastor?"

"A gay bar forty miles from town. My beliefs can co-exist with my sexuality. It isn't always easy, but it's worth it if I can change minds and help folks accept that gay is normal and we're all loved by God."

"I can understand wanting to do that but why pick a small town like Weston? Wouldn't you have a better audience for those teachings in a city church?"

"Probably, but Warren Ross is my great-uncle, and he asked me to step in when he retires at the end of the month. I don't have a lot of blood family who still talk to me but he does, so I couldn't say no."

"Good luck, then."

"I take it you aren't a churchgoer?"

"Nope. Can't really say I believe in God, either, but I respect other folks who need that comfort." As long as they didn't use that comfort to tell Jackson he was going to hell, or to shove their views down other people's throats, they could do what they wanted. Go to church, sing hymns, have holiday bake sales, whatever.

"So what do you do, Jackson? Really?"

Jackson gulped more of his beer. "I work on a cattle

ranch. Been farming or ranching in one place or another most of my life. Could say it's in the blood."

Drew grinned. "Then that makes you my first official Texas cowboy."

"Trust me, we aren't as sexy or interesting in real life, not like the movies show."

"I think I'd disagree about the sexy part."

The compliment sounded sincere but still fell flat for Jackson. He'd been uninterested in a fling with the guy before the pastor thing, and now Jackson was definitely off-board with anything happening between them. The guy deserved a sex life if he wanted one, but he wasn't for Jackson—especially not with Jackson's mind full of a gangly redhead whose tenacity at learning to properly ride a horse made him smile at his beer.

"Ah, I see," Drew said. "Getting over someone?"

Technically, he'd come here to get under someone, but that was unlikely to happen now. "Sort of. It's complicated and not a story for telling over a beer with a new acquaintance."

"Understood. Want me to leave you alone?"

"Yeah. Sorry. It was nice to meet you, and there's a good chance we'll run into each other again. Weston's not that big. And if you ever find yourself craving a cheap, greasy burger, check out the Roost some night."

"Thanks for the tip."

"Thanks for the beer."

"You're welcome. See you around, Sumner. Jackson Sumner."

Jackson laughed as Drew disappeared into the other side of the bar, then finished the beer. His attempt at a hookup had failed spectacularly, and even though it was only nine o'clock and still early, it was time to go home, down a few shots of whiskey, and go to bed.

Alone.

* * *

By Friday at quitting time there wasn't a part of Wyatt that didn't hurt, ache, or throb in some way or another, and it was all that sadist Jackson's fault. If an orgasm or two had come along with the pain, okay, he could deal. But this was all from horse riding, stall mucking, and learning how to tie proper knots (apparently learning to actually throw a rope and catch something was on the to-do list for next week's lessons).

Ramie, bless her, had a huge box of Epsom salt under the bathroom sink, and Wyatt had made liberal use of it the past two nights. He limped into the house a little after six, surprised to find her home. She was on the couch wrapped up in a knitted afghan, with a big mixing bowl of some sort of colorful sugary cereal it, and a baking show on TV.

"What the hell did Jackson make you do today?" she asked. "Roll around in cow manure and then dunk you in a water trough?"

"Feels like it." Wyatt eyeballed the other end of the couch but if he sat down, he wasn't getting up for a while and he needed a bath. Not just to relax, because he kind of stank. "I've never been worked so hard in my life. I feel more aching muscles than I ever knew existed and that's a fact."

"Then go take a soak. I'm eating cereal but I brought home a burger and fries someone ordered but never claimed."

"Cool, thanks." Even cold, a burger sounded like heaven on earth right now.

He trudged into the bathroom and in under five minutes—her water heater was some kind of new wall-unit thing and shockingly fast—slipped into hot, salted water. He closed his eyes and let different memories of Jackson float through his mind, especially that gorgeous scowl. The few times he'd smiled and praised Wyatt's performance. The perspiration dotting Jackson's upper lip after they'd mucked all the stalls together, and how much Wyatt had wanted to lick it off. Jackson's body heat, deodorant, scent of sweat, and every damned thing about the man that made Wyatt want to roll over and beg.

Thank God Wyatt had the day off tomorrow, not only to let his body heal a bit from its overexertion, but also get some distance from his sadist of a trainer. He hadn't complained, though, not a single time, and especially not to Brand. The last thing Wyatt wanted was to be assigned to someone else.

The cool water and his hungry stomach finally urged Wyatt out of the bathtub and into clean sweats. He found the foam container with the leftovers and didn't mind cold fries, so he munched on those while he washed ketchup off the meat patty, then nuked it for a bit. The bun, lettuce, and tomato were acceptable, so he reassembled the sandwich and took his dinner into the living room.

Ramie was still watching the baking competition show, and he tried to pay attention while he ate, but that stuff just wasn't his jam.

"You aren't working tonight?" Wyatt asked during a commercial break.

"Doing a half shift later tonight," she replied. "I was actually off but I'm covering part of it for a friend. Don't go in until eight."

"Oh, cool. I bet you get better tips on weekends."

"Most of the time, yeah, they're the most sought-after shifts, but the boss tries to rotate us so even the newbies get a good shift once in a while. You should stop in some night. Just don't ask for alcohol, because I know you're underage."

Wyatt snorted around a mouthful of his sandwich. "I'd

never get you into trouble by serving me. Is the Roost the best place in Weston to chill?"

"Pretty much, but I'm also biased. The boys usually come by a few nights a week but I haven't seen any of y'all from Woods Ranch gracing my bar this week."

"Really? I didn't know that."

"Which part?"

"Both, I guess. Is the Roost like a cowboy bar?"

"More like a dive bar that attracts cowboys from all around the area. Brand and Hugo still come around pretty regular, but I haven't seen Rem there as much. Then again, he and his wife having been trying for another baby for a long time, so I suspect they value any nights they have together minus little Susie."

Wyatt went through his mental file on Rem. Susie was his little girl. While both his sisters had multiple kids, Rem and Shelby only had one. "I can't imagine having a wife and kids, or really even wanting those things."

"Well, you're really a kid yourself, Wyatt. Not many people nowadays are craving those things at twenty. You've got too many other things to worry about."

"You're older." Off her cross look, Wyatt hurried on with his train of thought. "I just mean you don't have a husband and kids. Unless you're divorced or something, which isn't really my business."

She snagged one of his cold fries and popped it into her mouth. Chewed. "I'm not the marrying or motherly type. Relationships are complicated beyond reason for me, and I've never wanted kids. Not even when I was a kid myself, playing with dolls, and giggling with my girlfriends over the boys we thought we liked. I'd have been a terrible mother."

"People say not everyone is meant to be parent. Maybe you're just one of those and that's cool. I mean…" He took a calculated risk with his next statement. "My boss Brand is like almost forty or something, and he doesn't have kids."

"He's not forty, and you're right. Not everyone is meant to be a parent." Something odd flickered in her eyes, though, and Wyatt didn't know if it was about her own lack of kids, or if she knew something about Brand and his "lack" of kids. Or at least, lack of ones he hadn't sired, given away, and never bothered to claim. Like Wyatt.

Maybe.

"I guess being kid-adjacent isn't too bad," Wyatt hedged. "Like being an aunt or godmother or something. That way you can give the kid back to the parents after a little while of entertaining them."

Ramie laughed. "Yeah, if I had siblings of my own, I guess I could handle being the crazy spinster aunt who works at a bar and has ten cats. Although instead of cats I've got a cowboy-wannabe roommate. Then again, I might be able to get away with being the crazy aunt if Brand and Hugo stay serious and end up adopting."

Wyatt's brain stuttered for a few seconds. First, over the idea of Brand and Hugo being so serious they'd adopt a kid or more. Not that gay couples adopting was all that unusual nowadays, even if some states made it stupidly difficult, but it was still kind of a surreal thought about two guys he'd only known for a handful of days.

Second, over Brand and Ramie being so close he'd consider Ramie an aunt to any hypothetical kids Brand might or might not adopt.

Instead of going for the obvious, he said, "I didn't realize you and Hugo were such good friends."

"Oh, we're not. I mean, I like him a lot, and he's great with Brand. No, I've known Brand for a lot of years, and we were pretty close for a spell. Still are, which is why I trusted him enough to let you live here with no references and not even a phone interview. But for me personally? Being the crazy aunt is way better than being the actual parent."

"I hear you. And Brand is a really nice boss, so far. I haven't seen a lot of him since the day he hired me, but I guess he's busy running the ranch." The kid angle wasn't getting him anywhere, and fatigue was battling with Wyatt's need for information. "I didn't realize him and Hugo were serious enough to adopt. I mean, they live together and stuff, but... you know."

Ramie waved a hand in the air. "That was just me being hypothetical. Pretty sure Brand doesn't want kids at all, and I couldn't guess about Hugo. They haven't even been together a year, so this is just me babbling about stuff that will probably never happen. Call it PMS brain if you want."

"Okay." He wanted to keep pressing but he also didn't want to risk alienating Ramie if he pushed too far and got on her bad side. "So, uh, this burger is good. Guess I'll have to stop by the Roost some night for dinner and try stuff when it's fresh cooked."

"Definitely recommend hot off the grill or out of the fryer basket. Just don't ever expect fresh meat from the market, because the freezer is way bigger than the fridge. Just sayin'."

Wyatt chuckled. "Duly noted. Do I get a roommate discount?"

"Maybe on your first burger. Just don't test me by trying to order a beer."

"Promise. I'll save my fake ID for that bar way out on the highway in the middle of nowhere."

One black eyebrow went up. "Blue Tavern? What are you doing out there? You know what the place is, right?"

"I know. Knew before I went there the first time." He

held her gaze steadily, curious what she'd think about this bit of information. He hadn't explicitly said anything but she was smart. Really smart.

"Just be careful when you're there," Ramie finally said. "You're young, and I'd hate for something to happen to you." She winked. "I need your rent money to fix my damned roof."

"Better be careful, then."

Even without her saying it, Wyatt knew he had an ally in Ramie Edwards. The last thing he wanted to do was flirt with the wrong guy and put himself in harm's way. His one major goal right now was on track to being complete, and as much as he wanted a smoldering hot cowboy (preferably Jackson) to take him to bed for a long, blazing night of sex, he needed this more.

He needed to know what kind of man Brand was, who his family was, and if Wyatt had a snowball's chance in hell of being part of it.

Only time (and probably a DNA test) would tell for sure.

They watched TV together for another hour, until Wyatt's boredom with the baking show forced him out of there. He cleaned up the tiny mess he'd made in the kitchen, then took a glass of water into his room. Watched a bunch of online shit on his phone for a while, until a call interrupted his viewing of yet another video of cats doing stupid shit.

Jared.

He hadn't spoken to his best friend in over a week, not since their fight about Wyatt's determination to find his bio dad's family. Jared thought his entire plan was stupid, that he should just make a few phone calls, or better yet, forget the entire thing and live his life in the present. But Wyatt couldn't just forget it. He wanted—no, he deserved—answers about his past.

Mom had died of liver cancer because she hadn't been able to find a living or nonliving donor in time. Her parents hadn't been a match, and she had no siblings. Even on her deathbed, she wouldn't tell him who his father was. After she died, his grandparents had still adamantly refused to tell Wyatt, because it was "what she wanted." Yet another reason he'd been eager to leave his old life behind and get away from them.

And while Wyatt was in perfect health now, what if? What if he needed more extended family because of a genetic defect? And even if not, why shouldn't he know his own roots?

Why shouldn't he be able to control something in his life?

"Hello?" Wyatt said, answering the call with a rock of ice in his stomach.

"Hey, dude, how've you been?" Jared replied. "You just disappeared from town and I haven't seen you on social media all week."

"I've been a little busy." He stared at the ugly orange-and-brown curtains, positive the random shapes were actually eyeballs staring right back at him. "I told you where I was going and why. I got the job, by the way, if you care."

"Really? You don't know dick about ranching, dude, how'd you do that?"

"Right place, right time."

"So you meet your dad yet?"

"I interviewed with and was hired by Maybe Daddy, yeah. I have no idea what the fuck to make of him, though."

"How's that?"

"He's nice!" That had been a little loud. Wyatt glanced around his room but it wasn't like Ramie had him tapped or whatever. "I don't know, he's nice. After everything my grandparents said about him, it's weird. He's not this giant asshole who only cares about money and no one else. I want to like him, but at the same time he gave me up and abandoned my mom."

"Sounds like a shit spot you're in. So you're out in Weston, right?"

"Yeah, I told you that's where I was heading."

"Cool. So you remember last week when I told you to take that emergency roadside kit out of the car before you took it? You did that, right?"

Wyatt went through the two dozen things he'd tried to remember to do last week before he left with the car he'd shared with Jared. Jared had said he could take the car for this trip, no problem, and he vaguely remembered something about a roadside kit. "I don't think I did, but it's an emergency kit, dude. I'll Venmo you the money to buy a new one. I mean, I've got the car. What are you driving now, a bike?"

"It's not the car, I just…never mind. Are you staying at the ranch?"

"No, someplace in town." He'd known Jared since they were sixteen, and he was getting weird vibes off his oldest friend. And the only friend from Glasbury who knew Wyatt was gay. His self-preservation instincts were buzzing around his head like angry hornets. "Is something going on at home, because you don't sound right."

"Nah, dude, you just left town earlier than I expected. Thought maybe you could use a friend out there for a few days while you get situated and stuff."

"No, I'm fine. Brand did me a solid and got me a safe place to stay. With a girl bartender, actually. And one of the guys I work with is super-hot. He's the one teaching me."

"Just don't fuck around with the wrong guy and get yourself fired before you find out what you want to know."

"I'm being careful." So far. He didn't want to push Jackson too far, too fast and get reassigned to another cowboy. "You get a job yet?" Jared was in the middle of his third year of college but had lost one of his scholarships last semester, so money was a little tight. It was one of the reasons he'd let Wyatt take the car; Wyatt could afford to pay the insurance and loan, even though both were in Jared's name.

"Still looking, but with my class schedule it's hard. It's all fast food or supermarket stock boy or whatever."

"Dude, a job is a job. You can be pickier after you graduate."

"I guess. Anyway, I gotta go. I'll text you later or something."

"Yeah, okay. Later."

The call was as normal as it was bizarre. They usually texted each other more than they spoke on the phone, and he couldn't shake the feeling that something with Jared was off. Maybe it was stress over paying for college, maybe not. Either way, there wasn't anything Wyatt could do about it tonight, and he had the whole day off tomorrow.

He stuck his earbuds back in, turned on some music, and hoped he would dream about a certain rugged cowboy and his sexy scowl.

Chapter Eight

Jackson hadn't minded his schedule being rearranged so he'd be working the same days as Wyatt, since he had to train the kid, but he also wasn't used to having two days in a row off. An actual weekend to himself. Brand had done that to give Wyatt a break from the strenuous training. Jackson wasn't sure what to do with all his free time. By the end of the day Saturday, he was bored and antsy and pretty horny. Jerking off to porn hadn't helped much, and it was really hard to find redheads on free sites.

So he took his chances and went back to Blue Tavern Saturday night. The bar was packed for nine o'clock, music blared over the speakers, and a dozen or so guys were dancing in one corner of the room. Okay, so the dancing was basically grinding and clothes-on simulations of sex, but it was action that rarely happened during the week and way more interesting to observe than people standing around chatting.

"Don't usually see you here three times in a week," Darlin' said as he poured the draft Jackson ordered. "You on the hunt, sugar?"

"A little bit but I guess I'm picky," Jackson replied. "Hard to find new faces when the pool is so small."

"Don't I know it. Start a tab?"

"Yeah, thanks."

All the tables were being used, so Jackson took his beer and stood near the dance floor, admiring the goods on display in all their variety. A flash of auburn hair caught his attention, and he straightened. Tall, lean, and when the redhead turned in his direction, very definitely Wyatt. He wore skintight jeans and a black T-shirt, and danced in a way that was an all-too-familiar simulation of sex.

Irritation rippled across Jackson's skin, and his knuckles cried uncle from the grip he had on his beer glass. He glared at Wyatt, angry at himself for caring who Wyatt danced with, and so jealous of Wyatt's dance partner his head wanted to erupt in flames. Wyatt shouldn't be dancing with a guy in green flannel who was so much older, and especially not in such a suggestive way. He should be safely tucked under Jackson's arm where he belonged, sipping cola and being a lot more careful about who he let get close to him. To run their hands over his hips and rub against his taut ass.

Jackson swallowed back a growl and washed that down with several gulps of beer. Wyatt's behavior wasn't his to police but the kid was, well, a kid. And there were a lot of eyeballs on him older than Jackson's. Eyeballs he did not trust, and it wasn't because Jackson was attracted to Wyatt. Not at all. He just didn't want to show up for work on Monday and have an exhausted student to try to teach.

Yeah, that was it.

The music changed to another techno dance track, and in that brief space between leaving the old beat and finding the new, Wyatt looked up. Right at Jackson. His eyes widened briefly, before going half-lidded in a flirty, sensual way that put Jackson on red alert. The little shit couldn't have known Jackson would show up tonight, but he acted as if he had. As if he'd anticipated and planned accordingly.

Jackson held his gaze while Wyatt continued to dance,

ready to capture those eyes every time Wyatt opened and closed his or spun around, showing Wyatt he was paying attention to everything happening. And, he hoped, tele-graphing his displeasure with the way Wyatt was con-ducting himself. Or maybe not so much the "how" as the "who" because the who wasn't Jackson.

Another older guy moved in on Wyatt and Flannel Guy, making a sandwich of Wyatt that blocked their eye con-tact, and this time Jackson did growl. No one was nearby and the music was too loud for anyone to hear him, but it still grated on his nerves that he'd made the noise at all. Aggravated by his instinctive reactions, Jackson drained his beer, then went to the bar and ordered another. Darlin' gave him a curious look, as if he'd been observing Jack-son, then slid the draft to him.

Jackson drank half before he returned to his spot on the wall. Only now, Wyatt and the two guys weren't dancing. He looked around the crowded bar, seeking that familiar head of sun-fire curls. Nowhere. And that worried him. He put his beer down on the nearest table and wove his way toward the bathrooms. The alcove leading there had a dark corner people used to make out, but Wyatt wasn't in that corner. He checked the dude's room, but no dice.

Wyatt wasn't his friend, brother or kid, and Jackson had no real reason to take care of him, but he couldn't shake the instinct that something wasn't quite right. He headed back to the bar and asked Darlin' if he'd seen a tall skinny redhead.

"Yeah, saw him leaving a minute ago or so," Darlin' replied. "With Bernie and another guy I've seen, but don't know his name. The redhead a friend of yours?"

"Coworker, and young. Young and stupid." Jackson thrust a twenty at Darlin', which was more than enough to cover two beers and a tip, then charged outside Blue Tavern.

The parking lot was only lit by the few exterior lights on the side of the building. Jackson squinted into the gloom, eyes adjusting to the dimness faster than his ears did to the faint music now muffled by the bar's walls. His instinct to protect Wyatt battled with his desire to keep his distance from others. If the kid wanted to get tag-teamed by two older bears, that was his business. But Jackson needed to be sure.

He'd been unsure too many times, been taken advantage of as a young, desperate gay man with no good instincts of his own, and he didn't want that for Wyatt. He didn't want someone else to have those same regrets.

The Tavern had once been the main office of an old quarry that saw brisk business for about five years two decades ago, and the building butted up against a pile of rock, stone, and sand. Jackson went around the back of the wood building and spotted three figures. One seemed to be struggling against the firm holds of the other two, and the instant Jackson spotted flaming red hair, he charged.

He knocked Flannel Guy onto his ass with a solid body-check. Flannel Guy yelled the moment he crashed but Jackson turned his attention to the other guy smashing himself against Wyatt. He grabbed Guy Two by the shirt collar and sent him sailing into Flannel Guy, the pair of them rolling across the gravel, cussing and trying to figure out what was happening. Jackson towered over them, breath puffing in faint clouds of vapor in the cold air, arms straight by his sides.

"Who the fuck're you?" Guy Two snarled as he tried to get off Flannel Guy in a somewhat dignified manner and failed.

"Go away," Jackson said. "Both of you."

"Back off, I'm fine." Wyatt yanked on Jackson's left arm. The action left Wyatt off balance, though, and he started to stumble backward. Jackson grabbed him before he fell over. "Okay, not quite fine."

"Are you drunk?"

"I only had club soda."

"Was it salty?"

"Huh?"

"All right, kid, come with me. You need to sleep this off."

Wyatt plastered his hot, sweaty body right against Jackson's. "Sleep, huh? You got a bed big enough for two in that motel room?"

"I got room for us both to sleep without touchin', now calm down a minute." Flannel Guy came at him and Jackson took him out with a simple punch to the mouth. Jackson wasn't much for hitting guys who couldn't defend themselves, but Wyatt was his priority right now, not the rando who wanted to get into Wyatt's pants. "Stay down!"

Flannel and Two both hit the dirt on their threadbare jeans, and that didn't surprise Jackson at all. What made him want to laugh out loud was the way Wyatt's ass hit the ground at his growled order, as if Jackson was giving his dog a command.

"Not you," he said to Wyatt. "Let's go."

Wyatt struggled to get back to his feet, so Jackson hoisted him up with a hand under each armpit. He listed into Jackson again, and if the kid said he'd only ordered club soda, there was a good chance he'd been roofied. Just in case, Jackson fished out his phone and took a few quick snapshots of the other men, who both mumbled protests and tried to hide their faces.

"Who the fuck is this kid to you?" Two snarled.

"He's a friend and he's underage, jackwagon," Jackson retorted. "Stay away from him."

He pulled Wyatt toward the parking lot and his own pickup. Wyatt leaned heavily against him, seeming more out of it by the second. "Not underage," he said.

"To be served in a bar, you are. Plus, those guys are predatory assholes who might have drugged you."

"My hero."

"Come on, in, you." He got Wyatt situated in the cab and buckled him in. "We'll come back for your car in the morning."

"M'kay."

Wyatt was asleep by the time Jackson parked in front of his motel room, snoring away with his cheek pressed against the window. Jackson studied him in the dim light, unsettled by the protective instincts he had for Wyatt after knowing him for less than a week. Wyatt looked so young, his curls a cauldron of red fire, and Jackson hated knowing what might have happened tonight if he hadn't been paying attention. Maybe Wyatt had initially been into the dancing and groping, but by the time Jackson found him, he'd lost the ability to properly consent to anything, much less a threesome with two strangers.

It took a bit of doing, because Wyatt was taller than him, but Jackson managed to wrangle him into his room and sprawl him on the bed. Not wanting to overstep, Jackson pried off Wyatt's boots and belt, then tossed the bedspread over him once he was sure all limbs were in semicomfortable positions. He also left a cup of water on the bedside table next to two aspirin.

He didn't want to leave Wyatt alone, just in case he had a bad reaction to whatever he'd taken, so Jackson grabbed a bedspread from another room, changed into his flannel pants and a T-shirt, and settled into one of the sitting chairs to try to sleep.

* * *

Wyatt woke slowly, limbs sluggish, positive he'd gone to a fun party, gotten wasted on shots, and now had the worst hangover of his life. He blinked bleary eyes open and tried to remember where he'd crashed last night. The dated wallpaper was sort of familiar but he wasn't sure why. Then he heard a light snore nearby and looked to his left. He was alone in the bed, so who was—big guy in a chair. In a motel room.

His night at Blue Tavern came back in bits and pieces. Being horny, hoping to get laid, and then getting inspired when he spotted Jackson at a table. Humping the guys nearest him, hoping to get a reaction out of Jackson. Getting a little dizzy. Going outside for some fresh winter air.

Everything else was a blur.

His stomach heaved once but he didn't barf. He sat up carefully, wincing as the old mattress squealed beneath him.

Jackson woke with a start, his broad body almost too large for the chair he'd obviously slept in. "Ow, shit." He rubbed at the back of his neck, that familiar sexy scowl back in place. "You're awake."

"Yeah. How did I get to your place?" Wyatt did a quick systems check but his clothes were on and nothing felt sore besides his head and stomach. "Did we fuck?"

"No, we didn't fuck. Someone slipped you something at the Tavern last night, so I brought you here to sleep it off."

"Oh. You could have shared the bed with me."

"Didn't want you to wake up and freak out. You don't remember the fight outside?"

"Fight? I got into a fight?" He didn't feel like he'd been punched, but he was also still woozy and thirsty. He spotted a cup of water but couldn't muster the energy to reach for it.

"No, I got into a fight. You went out back with two guys intent on turning you into some kind of human sandwich filling, but you were out of it and not really aware, so I stopped them. Brought you here. I didn't touch you."

"I believe you." He trusted Jackson implicitly. "I can't believe someone drugged me. Ugh."

"You told me you only drank club soda, so yeah. I didn't report it to the bar manager yet, because I needed to ask you directly and while you were sober. Did you take anything last night before or after you got to the Tavern?"

"No. I mean, I smoked weed and did speed a few times in college, but I'm not really into that shit." Wyatt scrubbed both hands over his face. "I'm glad you were there last night, man. I mean it."

"I'm glad, too." Jackson finally had mercy, stood and handed Wyatt the water.

He sipped, glad to get the stickiness out of his mouth. "Thanks."

"No problem. Been taken advantage of a few times in my life, so I don't like letting it happen to other people if I can stop it. Do you want me to call the Tavern and report this? I took pictures of the guys who were mauling you."

"I don't know. Will you get in trouble?"

"Dunno. I did hit them first without them threatening me, so they could probably press charges for assault. Worth it, though, to keep you safe."

Wyatt's heart skipped happily. "Then I don't want to report it if you'll get in trouble. What if we left an anonymous message or something so they can keep an eye out for the behavior?"

"We can do that."

"Okay. Um, are you afraid of getting into trouble with the law? Because of your past?"

Jackson's eyes narrowed. "Not afraid but I'd rather avoid

police whenever possible. Don't have a great track record with them. You?"

"I got a speeding ticket once, but I've never been arrested."

"Keep it that way. Jail sucks but prison is worse."

As curious as Wyatt was about that statement, Jackson's expression clearly said to leave it alone. "You mind if I take a shower? I feel gross." And not just because of the possible roofie. Guys whose faces he didn't remember had been gropey last night and he wanted to wash the phantom hands away.

"Sure, help yourself. There's a few clean towels under the sink."

"Thanks." It took Wyatt a minute and a bit of mental pep talking, but he finally got up and stumbled into the bathroom. Even in the bad light, he looked pale and had dark smudges under his eyes. If he remembered having a good time last night he might not have minded the hangover quite so much. He inspected his neck but didn't see any hickeys so that was something.

The shower felt great. Jackson used basic Ivory soap, which fit what he knew about the older cowboy. He found the towels but no secret stash of dildos or other sex toys, just a box of condoms and bottle of lube. The discovery might have given Wyatt some fun ideas if he didn't still feel like he might barf if he moved too fast. He made a face at himself in the mirror. Here he was, naked in the motel room of a guy he was attracted to and his body wouldn't cooperate.

Fucking figures.

He also didn't want to take advantage of Jackson's kindness in saving his ass (probably very literally) last night. Wyatt could have woken up this morning in a very different situation.

He put his old clothes back on, glad they weren't too smelly from body odor or cigarette smoke, and finger-combed his wet hair to fluff his curls out a bit so they didn't dry in a big frizzy puff. He usually used a bit of styling gel to tame them but Jackson didn't even have hair spray, just toothpaste, a toothbrush, and deodorant. Very, very basic guy.

Jackson was doing something on his phone when Wyatt left the bathroom, and he looked up. "How's your stomach?"

"Okay."

"Feel up to getting breakfast before I drive you back to your car?"

"Sure." He might only order a dry pancake but it was more time with Jackson, and neither of them worked today. Thank fuck. "I'll pay. It's the least I can do."

"Okay."

Jackson collected their coats, and they headed for the truck. Instead of Weston, Jackson drove them to a truck stop on the main state road. It wasn't a huge one like the big travel plazas Wyatt had stopped at on his trip across the state, but it had a few pumps, a small diner, and a convenience store that looked like it needed a good clean.

A young woman with pink streaks in her blond hair seated them in a sticky booth by a window that overlooked the gas pumps. "Coffee to start, Jackson?" she asked.

"Yep, thanks."

Wyatt quirked an eyebrow and ordered a ginger ale. Once the waitress moved off to get their drinks, he leaned across the table. "First-name basis with the staff here? Favorite spot?"

"Don't always feel like eating at the diner in Weston, especially on my days off. This place is closer to the motel.

Probably did even better business with travelers when the motel was still running, but shit happens."

"True. Good food?"

"I like it. The cook here makes decent pancakes. They might be good for a queasy stomach. I'd stay away from the hash, though. It's usually yesterday's leftover home fries and meat of the day."

"Thanks for the tip."

When their waitress returned with their drinks, Wyatt ordered two pancakes with no syrup or butter, and no sides. Jackson got something called the Big Chief, but they lost their menus before Wyatt could investigate it. Whatever, he'd let Jackson eat. He wasn't the idiot who'd gotten himself drugged last night; he was the hero who'd swooped in and saved Wyatt's dumb ass.

Going to the Tavern alone had been stupid, and he said as much to Jackson.

Jackson shrugged. "Probably a little stupid, yeah, since you're still very new around here. And in a bar like that, where it's ninety-nine percent regulars and one percent newbies, it's easy to get in over your head. Especially when, I suspect, you don't have much gay bar experience under your belt."

"Not really, no. A lot of parties in college, but I didn't let myself get wasted too much because I was trying to graduate early. It's hard to take exams with a hangover." He glanced around, but no one was seated near them. "I'm not a total virgin or anything but it was all experimenting with guys my own age."

"Not a couple of old bears looking to get with fresh young meat?"

"Pretty much." Wyatt rested his forehead on the table. "God, I'm an idiot."

"You're twenty years old. Doing idiotic things comes

with the territory. Learning from those things is what's important. Until you've met more people, don't go out to strange bars alone."

He looked up, unable to stop a sexy smile. "Are you volunteering to be my chaperone?"

"Don't ask for something you don't really want." Something new and almost flirty danced in Jackson's eyes. "You're sex on two long legs and you know it, and if we didn't work together then I'd probably have been less of a gentleman this morning while you were in my motel room."

"No, you wouldn't have." Wyatt wasn't sure of his own certainty here, but he'd gotten a pretty good sense of who Jackson was this past week. "I could have been naked on your bed and begging you to fuck me this morning, and you wouldn't have done it. And not because of your amazing self-restraint, but because you care. You care what almost happened to me last night and you were being kind by taking me home, not taking home a potential lay."

Jackson stared at him for several long moments before reaching for the table's sugar container. "Guess you're right. And since we're bein' honest, I can understand you lying about your real name the night we first met. You were protectin' yourself. But how much of that runaway sob story was true?"

Wyatt sipped his ginger ale to bide more time and organize his thoughts. He'd been waiting for Jackson to bring up the name thing specifically, and it had taken longer than he'd thought it would. "You're right, the name lie was me protecting myself from a stranger. I had no reason to think I'd ever see you again, much less end up working and training with you. But you didn't really tell me much about yourself, either."

"True, and fair point. But I was also chattin' with a

stranger and don't tend to tell my life story to them over a beer."

"Okay, so we both obfuscated and withheld certain things. That doesn't make either of us a liar, and you have to admit we've got chemistry." Wyatt wished he had a prop a lot sexier than a glass of ginger ale, and that he wasn't as pale and washed out as he was from that roofie, but such was life. "You sure you don't want to tie me up for sex?"

Both of Jackson's eyebrows rose. "You mess with the bull, boy, you're gonna get the horns."

"Promise?"

Their food arrived way too fast for Wyatt's liking because it interrupted their banter, and it gave Jackson the perfect excuse to ignore him for a little while. The Big Chief breakfast was some combination of pancakes, sausages, home fries, and grease, and Wyatt leaned back in the booth to stay away from the smell while he ate his dry pancakes. They did help settle his stomach, just like Jackson had promised, so points for that.

It was the kind of diner where you still went up to the register to pay your bill. Once they were done and Jackson had downed his third mug of coffee, Wyatt took his debit card up to the front. Jackson hovered by the door, a toothpick in his mouth, and opened the door for Wyatt.

Back in the warmth and privacy of the truck cab, Wyatt said, "I feel a lot better, so if you want to take me back to your place I won't object. In fact, I will enthusiastically consent."

The simple fact that Jackson hesitated with the key hovering right by the ignition was all the answer Wyatt really needed. Jackson looked over at him, desire simmering in his dark eyes. He licked his lips and it was all Wyatt could do not to lean over and kiss the man. To finally sample the cowboy he'd been lusting over for a week.

"This is a really bad idea," Jackson said.

"Maybe. But we'll have a lot of fun proving it."

"If we do this, it stays off the ranch. No quickies in the hayloft, no kissing in the break room. Hear me?"

"I hear you." They were doing this. He was finally going to get with his sexy, scowly cowboy. Getting laid had not been on his to-do list when he came to Weston, but by God, he wasn't going to waste this chance. "Let's go, boss."

With a soft growl, Jackson started the truck.

Chapter Nine

This was such a bad idea, and Jackson had no idea where his brain had gone when he agreed to take Wyatt back to the motel. Part of his brain had dropped directly to his dick, that was for damned sure, because he was hard the entire drive. It did not help that Wyatt had inched as close as his seat belt allowed, and it made Jackson want to pull off onto the nearest deserted road and fuck the kid's brains out in the truck.

Or take him over his knee and spank Wyatt for being so fucking sexy, with those pouty lips and flyaway curls.

Bad. Idea.

But everything in him said it would be worth it.

As long as it was just one time; that was all it could be.

Wyatt practically vibrated in his seat by the time they got back to the motel. Jackson stalked right inside, jeans uncomfortably tight, trusting Wyatt to either change his mind and stay in the truck, or to follow him. He followed. As soon as Wyatt was inside, Jackson slammed the door shut and crowded Wyatt against it. Not easy with Wyatt's height, but Wyatt seemed to try to make himself smaller, deferring to Jackson and what he wanted.

Jackson wasn't entirely sure what he wanted, other than to get off with Wyatt. He crashed his mouth against Wyatt's in a fierce, dominating kiss. Showing him that no matter who fucked who this morning, Jackson was in charge. Wyatt relaxed against him, hands squeezing his hips, submitting perfectly to what Jackson wanted. Nice. He tasted like ginger ale and something uniquely Wyatt, and it was addictive. Like the finest scotch.

Wyatt showed a touch of spirit by licking into Jackson's mouth, not quite reversing the power of the kiss, but also not completely submitting to Jackson. He liked a challenge. Passive sex was unsatisfying now. No more rolling over and taking it; no more partners who did the same. Enthusiastic consent, as Wyatt said earlier, was a hell of a turn-on.

He allowed Wyatt to nudge him backward, and they each divested the other of their coats. Said coats landed wherever, as did boots when they separated long enough to yank them off. All that mattered was getting to skin-on-skin as fast as possible, and then they were wrestling together on the bed, first Wyatt on top and then Jackson. Over and over, they moved together, still kissing and groping, hard cocks rubbing, neither really trying to overpower the other. The struggle was the fun part.

While closely matched in height, Jackson still had a lot of muscle on Wyatt, so he eventually wrestled the younger man onto his stomach with Jackson straddling his bare ass, his cock riding that pretty, pale crease. Wyatt panted, face turned to the left, cheek blazing almost as red as his hair. Jackson liked seeing Wyatt overwrought and no longer so cocksure.

"Get a condom and fuck me," Wyatt said. "Please."

"You ever been fucked, spitfire?"

"No. But I want it. Please."

"Hmm." Jackson thrust his cock along Wyatt's crack, loving the idea of gloving up and shoving deep inside. Popping that cherry. But too many memories of uncomfortable fucks kept him grounded. Kept him in the moment and from losing his mind with this hot-headed twenty-year-old.

"Come on, boss, fuck me."

"Am fucking you, just in a different way. Slow down a little, Wyatt, there's lots of ways to have sex that aren't just sticking your dick in a hole."

"Yeah, but that's the kind of sex I want."

"You want me here?" Jackson shifted just enough to press the pad of his thumb over Wyatt's hot little hole. Not enough to breach him, not dry, but enough for him to really feel it. To know this wasn't a game and a dick was not small. Hell, a thumb wasn't all that small. "You want me inside you tonight, Wyatt?"

"I think so."

"Think?" He rolled Wyatt onto his back so they were having this conversation face-to-face. "You don't gotta do anything with me you're not sure about. We can try it the other way, too."

"Really? You like being fucked?" Wyatt asked. His genuine surprise was all kinds of endearing.

"When I trust the guy I'm with, yeah, I do."

"And you trust me?"

"Not sure I trust your skill level, but I do trust that if I tell you to do something or not do something, you'll listen to me."

It had taken Jackson a lot of years and the right partner to discover that, yeah, he actually did like being fucked. Being the guy who helped another figure out what he did and didn't like wasn't something he'd done before, but he would do his best to give the kid a great experience, no matter what.

"Can I touch you there?" Wyatt asked.

Jackson didn't have to ask where he meant. "Definitely."

With those long arms, Wyatt had no problem reaching

behind Jackson. Slender fingers slid over his ass cheek, toward his crease. Wyatt stared up at him, a little glassy-eyed, and rubbed against Jackson's entrance, a hard and steady stroke that heated Jackson's blood and drew a breathy moan from his lips.

Wyatt smiled. "Yeah?"

"Oh yeah. You think you got what it takes to fuck me, firebrand?"

"I think so."

The tiny crack in Wyatt's veneer of self-confidence was what fueled Jackson into rolling off Wyatt and onto his back. Legs splayed wide, hard cock against his own belly, ready for whatever Wyatt thought he had to give. "There's condoms and lube under the bathroom sink." Since he couldn't interpret the hesitation in Wyatt's expressive green eyes, Jackson added, "I'll talk you through it."

"Okay." Wyatt climbed off the bed, and Jackson admired the view of his departing backside. So pale like the rest of him, narrow cheeks flexing as he walked. He returned with the lube and the whole box of condoms, which made Jackson smile.

"Don't think we'll need them all."

"I know, I just, um." His upper cheeks stained pink. "I've never worn one and I might, you know, rip it or something."

Jackson sat up. "You're twenty years old and have never worn a rubber?"

He shrugged as he sat near Jackson's feet. "I've never done this with a guy. Never wore one for blow jobs. A guy I blew at a party once wore one, and it tasted awful."

"You never had sex with a girl?"

"One girl but she was on the pill and said she was allergic to latex. It was fine but nothing special. I was still figuring out I was gay but nervous to act on those feelings, you know?"

"Yeah, I know. Small-town boy, remember?"

"Right." He lifted his head and met Jackson's eyes. "Is it weird to be talking about this while totally naked?"

"Nah. It's never a bad thing to talk about stuff before the sex happens. Unless the whole point is for it to be an anonymous hookup, and while I'm fine with those when the mood strikes, getting to know someone can make the whole thing a lot more enjoyable for all parties involved."

"Makes sense." He wiggled his eyebrows. "Especially when you're about to nail your coworker?"

Jackson snorted laughter, liking that he could laugh in bed with Wyatt. "Yeah, especially when you're about to nail your coworker. You still wanna?"

"Hell yes. You still want to?"

"Fuck yes." He stroked his rock-hard cock. "You feel like sucking this before we get to the main event?"

With a devilish grin, Wyatt lunged up the bed and knelt between Jackson's spread legs. Took hold of his cock with one hand and lowered his head. Licked around the crown in a ticklish way before closing his lips over it. Jackson sighed and closed his eyes, wanting to savor the sensation of that hot mouth over his flesh. Wyatt had both enthusiasm and decent technique, and he wasn't shy about touching, licking, and sucking his dick while rolling Jackson's balls. He licked at the flesh between Jackson's cock and balls without actually sucking on his nuts, but that wasn't every guy's thing.

Jackson was very oral and eager to show Wyatt what that felt like. As his own orgasm built, Jackson floated on the sensations buzzing along his nerve endings, but everything got a bit too close. Then he grabbed Wyatt by the shoulders, hauled him up, and rolled them so Wyatt was

on his back. Wyatt yelped in surprise and then in utter
delight when Jackson took Wyatt's cock into his mouth.

He tasted like soap and spice and all the things Jackson
loved about giving head. He took Wyatt's cockhead into
the back of his throat and swallowed once. Wyatt cried
out, fingers digging into Jackson's shoulders, either to pull
him off or keep him there, Jackson didn't know or care. He
nibbled at the vein on the underside of Wyatt's cock from
tip to root, then nuzzled at his balls. Wyatt drew his legs
up higher, farther apart, giving Jackson plenty of room. He
licked Wyatt's fuzzy sac, enjoying the sharper taste here.
The way the skin grew tauter and his balls drew up. He
sucked on one, then the other, while a single finger rubbed
at Wyatt's taint. No lower, not unless Wyatt begged for it.

When Wyatt didn't beg, Jackson took his cock into his
mouth and held still, a firm pressure without moving his
tongue at all. He'd learned about cock warming a long time
ago, and it was a fun way to amp his partner up. Wyatt
tried to thrust, to move his hips sideways, and Jackson
held him still with both arms across his belly.

"Oh fuck, come on," Wyatt panted. "Let me move,
damn it."

Jackson laughed, and the sensation made Wyatt gasp.
"Jesus, you're killing me."

He'd barely scratched the surface of how far he could
edge a guy, but Wyatt was young and if he had a hair trig-
ger, Jackson wasn't getting fucked anytime soon. With a
long, hard suck, he pulled off Wyatt and squeezed the base
of his cock. "Lightweight."

"You're a sadist."

The hair on the back of Jackson's neck prickled and
not in the fun way. "No, I'm not. A true sadist would take
pleasure in causing you pain. I just like hearing you beg
for my touch. Positive touches, not painful ones."

"Okay." Wyatt's understanding reflected in his smile. "Sorry."

"It's okay. Talking about stuff is good, remember?"

"Yes."

"You ready to prep me?"

"Fuck, yes."

Grinning himself, Jackson moved to the side, still on his hands and knees, ass presented to Wyatt. Wyatt rolled around, making the bed bounce in an amusing way, and settled behind Jackson. His stomach tightened a bit but he shoved those old memories away, very much trusting Wyatt to stop if it hurt. It hadn't hurt in a long time, but the fear never went away.

The cap on the lube popped, and then a cold, wet finger rubbed against his hole. Jackson closed his eyes and re-laxed into the sensations, enjoying the careful way Wyatt pressed that first finger into him. "Holy shit, you're tight," Wyatt said. "Wow. Will this—?"

"It'll work." He pushed back, taking more of Wyatt's fin-ger. "In and out. Plenty of lube. I'll tell you when to try two."

"Okay."

Wyatt was so tentative that it endeared him to Jackson even more, while also frustrating him so he began to fuck himself in faster, harder thrusts until he knew. "Two now." The stretch and burn only lasted a handful of seconds, followed by a familiar, pleasant fullness inside that he'd missed. And as much as he'd love to feel four of Wyatt's fingers in his ass, he wanted dick a lot more.

"Get the condom on," Jackson said. "Now."

He missed Wyatt's fingers the moment they were gone, but he knew what was coming and craved it. Craved the pressure and slide and slam when the other guy really got going and pounded his ass. He listened to the crinkle of the wrapper and the sticky sound of Wyatt putting the condom on, kind of wanting to watch but also not wanting to make the kid self-conscious doing it for the first time.

Jackson was kind of honored to be the one guiding Wyatt through his first time. Experience often trumped eagerness when it came to significant things like sex.

The bed creaked and moved beneath him. Jackson breathed evenly, doing his best to relax his lower body as Wyatt scooted closer behind him. Smiled at the first press of Wyatt's glans to his hole. "Steady goes it," Jackson said. "Push. Trust me, I'll tell you if it hurts."

"I do trust you. Fuck. Okay." On a hard thrust that made Jackson gasp, Wyatt breached him. "Oh shit, was that too far?"

"No, just give me a sec to breathe. It's been a hot minute so I need to adjust. It ain't like porn where the bottom's prepped and ready for a hard fuck."

"Right, sorry."

"Don't apologize." Jackson angled his head and smiled. "Keep going, short thrusts. Feels good, trust me."

"Okay, good. I want this to feel good for you, too."

Everything about Wyatt's hesitations and concern turned Jackson on more than he thought possible, keeping him hard even though he often lost wood during penetration. And as Wyatt finally began to move inside him, Jackson closed his eyes and remembered everything he loved about this intimate act.

Wyatt was losing his damned mind in the very best way, and he never wanted to feel sane again. Not if the alternative was every nerve in his body singing an aria while his dick slipped deeper and deeper into Jackson Sumner's ass. A thickly muscled ass without a tan line on it, which suggested the guy sunbathed naked, and why not when he lived alone in an abandoned motel? Wyatt loved feeling the sun on his bare skin.

Bare skin currently pressed close to Jackson's as he draped himself over Jackson's back, one hand on his hip and the other on his shoulder, mostly to steady himself. His body was so alive with sensations, far beyond the ultimate pleasure surrounding his dick, that he thought he might fly off the bed and right into the sky.

Fucking a girl had been good. Fucking a dude? Mind-blowingly, amazingly perfect, and Wyatt could stay here forever.

Too bad his dick had other ideas. His hips snapped almost by themselves, and he shoved deeper into Jackson's ass. Even with the rubber, the heat around his cock was intense, almost painfully so.

"Oh yeah," Jackson moaned. "I'm good, go harder, Wyatt. Fuck me."

The panted demand broke the last of Wyatt's hesitation. All he could do was act on instinct and thrust. To chase his release and, he hoped, push Jackson toward his own. For all his lack of experience with sex, Wyatt didn't want to be a selfish lover, especially when he really liked the guy he was fucking.

He also selfishly wanted to see Jackson's face. This wasn't some anonymous encounter with a stranger. This was them. Wyatt and Jackson.

His whole body protested when Wyatt held the condom and pulled out. Jackson twisted his upper body around, both eyebrows arched in surprise. "No stamina, fire-brand?" he teased.

"Get on your back." Wyatt surprised himself with the forceful command. Jackson's eyes widened briefly, a kind of heat flaring in them, then he did as told. He rolled onto his back and raised both legs, holding them up and open with a hand behind each knee. Wyatt could just see Jackson's hole from here and he wanted back inside.

He leaned forward and planted his hands on the mattress on either side Jackson's head and kissed him. A hard press of lips Jackson returned in kind, and it told Wyatt everything he needed to know. Wyatt rocked his hips and Jackson grabbed him by the waist, allowing his legs to wrap around Wyatt. Heels dug into Wyatt's ass, urging him on. They moved together, Wyatt driving in and Jackson rising up to meet him, an imperfect rhythm that drove Wyatt toward the edge faster than he expected. He wanted this to last. With Jackson writhing below him, his solid body cradling him, demanding him, Wyatt felt freer than he ever had in his life.

Too soon his balls drew up tight and release colored the edges of his awareness. Wyatt thrust harder, deeper, wanting more of that perfect heat, more of everything. "So fucking close. Are you?"

"Hell yeah." Jackson grabbed his own dick and jerked himself. He threw his head back as he came, his ass squeezing impossibly tight around Wyatt's cock. His come splattered Wyatt's chest and belly, a slick heat that threw Wyatt over the edge. He thrust hard once, twice, three times, and then his own orgasm crested. Seemed to hover just out of reach, like a wave that couldn't quite hit shore. Then he crashed. His body broke apart and came back together in that moment, and all he knew was a constant flow of amazing pleasure washing through his entire being.

His hips jerked through the aftershocks, and he barely registered Jackson's deep pants. Wyatt was too far gone on endorphins from fucking a guy for the first time. A guy he liked a hell of a lot more than he should, considering he was a coworker. None of that mattered in this moment, though. Nope. All that mattered was dicks and come and orgasms and Jackson.

Jackson helped him pull out, then his bigger body rolled them so Jackson was on top of Wyatt like a broad, sweaty blanket. Wyatt wrapped his arms around Jackson's waist, unable to find the words for anything more demanding than a satisfied grunt as their slick, softening cocks continued to rub together.

"That was fucking awesome," Wyatt whispered when words finally came to him. "Wow."

"You were pretty wow yourself." Jackson stroked his fingers across Wyatt's shoulders and chest. "Pretty damned great for your first time."

"Yeah?" He licked the underside of Jackson's chin, because it was the only part of his face Wyatt could reach, loving the lightly salty taste. "Did we go long enough?"

"We went fine. Sex isn't always about stamina. Sometimes it's as simple as two good orgasms, and if that takes sixty minutes or sixty seconds, it's about the people involved. And I had a pretty great time." Jackson held him by the chin, his expression serious now. "Did you?"

"That's a stupid fucking question." He pressed his hips upward, wishing they were both still hard, but this was good, too. "I feel amazing."

"Me too. I had a fantastic time. Maybe more than's good for me."

He yanked his chin out of Jackson's hold. "Why's that?"

"Because we had sex today but tomorrow I'm still gonna be your supervisor."

Not wanting to think about that tonight because the afterglow was too amazing, Wyatt pulled on a terrible bit of humor. "You aren't going to use some cheesy line like you don't know how to quit me, are you?"

Jackson's belly laugh had the older man falling sideways

onto the bed, hooting like Wyatt had told a million-dollar joke. "No, not doing that. Got no use for quoting tragic movies, so if you try to use some 'king of the world' crap line on me, we're done."

"So we aren't done now? This wasn't just a one-off fuck?" The idea delighted Wyatt to no end. "Sweet. And I promise, no cheesy movie lines. I'm honestly not that great at them because I don't watch a lot of movies, especially the stuff people consider quotable classics. I like the stuff most guys have never heard of like small indies, foreign films, super-low-budget things. The more obscure the better."

Jackson sat up now that his laughing fit was over, legs crossed, hands clasped over his groin. "I don't watch many movies or shows in general, I guess. The movie lines I know are from other people sayin' 'em, me looking at 'em funny, and them having to explain. Although I did get your *Brokeback Mountain* reference all by myself. It's one of those pop culture things that's hard to completely miss unless you live in a hole."

"True." Wyatt adopted a horrifically comical Austrian accent. "I'll be back."

"Funny."

"I know, but I really will be back. Need to dump the rubber and get a washcloth."

"A washcloth?"

"Yeah." Wyatt gazed at him, confused by Jackson's surprised smile. "My best friend Jared said it's polite to help clean up the person you just fucked. Is that wrong?"

Jackson reached out and stroked a single finger across Wyatt's left cheekbone. "No, it's not wrong. It's actually very kind. Some guys fuck, dump, and go. But yeah, lube gets sticky and into uncomfortable places, so I'd appreciate the washcloth."

"Cool." Glad he hadn't fucked up or come across as a bumbling hayseed, Wyatt slid off the bed and stripped off the condom, careful not to let its contents drip on the vintage shag carpet on his walk into the bathroom.

A walk free of shame, and full of pure delight and eagerness to do this again soon.

Very, very soon if he had his way.

Chapter Ten

Jackson had imagined sex with Wyatt would be pretty great, based on their chemistry, but reality was so much better. Wyatt cleaning Jackson up turned into an erotic wrestling match that left Wyatt flat on his stomach while Jackson rubbed off on his back. Then Jackson relaxed next to him while Wyatt beat off, which was an erotic adventure of its own, because Wyatt had a bit of an exhibitionist streak. He stroked and played and tugged at his own balls, while making the most delicious faces at Jackson. Faces that made Jackson want to kiss him senseless, but he refrained in favor of watching the erotic show happening in front of him.

After Wyatt came, Jackson took great pleasure in licking him clean.

They lounged on the bed for a while with some movie playing on Wyatt's phone for background noise and chatted about nothing important, until Wyatt's stomach released a loud, amusing growl. Hungry himself, Jackson drove them back to the truck stop diner for lunch. A chicken club sandwich with no mayo for Jackson and a double cheeseburger, extra pickles, for Wyatt, whose stomach had apparently bounced back since this morning.

Jackson drove them back to the motel, but instead of stopping there, continued down the dead-end road to the washout. Water no longer ran in the dry gulch, which had once been a flooded creek that had taken out the bridge and sank part of the road on both sides, but there was something beautiful to Jackson about the way the sand had dried in waves that reminded him a bit of the rings of trees.

He backed up to the washout, just to the side of the road so they didn't have to stare at the ugly orange sign reading Road Closed, and they settled in the truck bed to eat. Both meals came with bags of generic potato chips, and Jackson set his aside for a snack later. The sandwich with its three pieces of bread and stacks of sliced chicken and bacon was more than enough. The truck's radio played some local station, which Wyatt had requested, and it amused Jackson to realize that Wyatt didn't like complete silence. He needed noise of some sort. A funny personal quirk Jackson liked knowing about the kid.

Not kid, he doesn't like being called a kid.

Wyatt might not want to be called a kid, but he sure made Jackson feel like an old man sometimes. He was literally half Jackson's age, and Jackson still wasn't entirely sure he trusted Wyatt. He had fun with Wyatt, for sure, and they shared intense sexual chemistry. But this was a fling, an infatuation and nothing more. It could never be more than sex.

Could it?

He watched Wyatt eat, amused when a blob of ketchup sat on the bottom edge of his lip and Wyatt didn't seem to notice for several more bites of his burger. For all that his life was about cattle, Jackson wasn't huge on red meat. He'd eat it when it was in front of him, of course, and every chance he got he talked up Woods Ranch beef. No reason to let his own food preferences hurt his employment, or the livelihoods of people he cared for and respected.

"I've never seen anything quite like this," Wyatt said after he'd finished his burger.

"Quite like what?" Jackson had finished eating first and was leaning to the side, his left arm braced on the wheel well. Purposely adopting a semisexy slouched position.

"This washout. The road just stops and when you look across the gulch, it starts again. Like someone up and decided to break these two sides of the creek apart because of a feud or something. They just cut ties to family because of their beliefs."

Jackson studied Wyatt's pensive profile, surprised by the deep statement from someone his age. And also curious if the "cut ties to family" remark was just about the Civil War, or if it also applied to Wyatt and his reasons for leaving his hometown. And what exactly those beliefs were.

"It does look like that a bit," Jackson replied. "I know it was nature that did it, but sometimes in life it feels like we blow up a bridge or cut ourselves off literally from other people. People who say they love us or who we're supposed to love. And sometimes blowing up those bridges is exactly what we're meant to do. What's best for us."

Wyatt wiped his mouth with a paper napkin. "You've got experience with that?"

"A lot of it, yeah." The only reason he said more was because Wyatt watched him with an open, curious look. Not the hungry gaze of someone looking for gossip or ammunition. "I was one of many kids adopted by a couple who couldn't have kids of their own. As little kids, our middle siblings helped take care of us, while the eldest kids worked the family farm. Our parents basically took in hired help and got tax credits for it. They didn't care about us, our emotions, or our well-being. As soon as I was old enough, I got out."

"Wow." Genuine misery crept across Wyatt's face. "I'm

sorry that happened to you. You have no idea who your biological parents are?"

"Nope. They gave me up when I was three, and I've got no clear memories of them. Records didn't say why, and I honestly don't care. I shoved that part of my life aside a long time ago and wanted to forget about it. Live in the moment and for the now. For Dog and my job, not people I'll never meet again. Well, except for maybe two of my adopted brothers. I keep in contact with Kirby and he keeps in contact with me and Donnie. None of us loved our parents. Most of us resented them, but they're both dead now so what's the point in holding on to old anger, right?"

"Right." Wyatt squeezed Jackson's thigh. "I'm sorry. I can't say I understand, because I had a good family growing up. My mom loved me, even if my stepfather could be pretty hard on me sometimes. I had grandparents and some extended family around. You grew up in the farm life and I didn't. Guess the only thing we really have in common, besides being born in Texas, is not knowing who our bio dads are." His face flushed bright red.

Jackson studied Wyatt, confused by both the admission and embarrassed reaction. Not knowing a biological parent wasn't anything to be ashamed of; they were part of an exclusive club of millions. And Wyatt had specifically mentioned not knowing his biological dad. "Your mother didn't know who he was?"

"She knew." He studied a broken potato chip, as if it held the answers he wanted. "She refused to say before she died, and my grandparents won't tell me. I know they know, but all they'll say is he was a selfish asshole who gave me up, signed away his rights, and that I'm better off not knowing who he is."

"But you don't agree?"

"Not really. I mean, even if he is this horrible person,

it's still my truth to know, right? It's my family history. My genetic history." He turned wide, curious eyes to Jackson. "Don't you ever worry if you get sick and need, like, blood or an organ or something, that you don't know who your parents are? Or siblings?"

"Sometimes but not much, no. That's why blood banks and transplant lists exist. I can't spend my life planning for the worst to happen or I won't be able to live my life in the moment, and that's how I prefer to live it."

Wyatt waggled his eyebrows. "I dunno, if you really lived in the moment it wouldn't have taken a full week for us to finally fuck."

"Last week was different. I thought you were some vulnerable runaway who wasn't sure what he wanted." Jackson deliberately gave Wyatt's lean body a once-over. "I was very wrong about those things and I'm glad we waited until I was sure."

"So am I. I like you, Jackson, and I'm not trying to take advantage of you, I promise. I also don't regret a single thing we've done this morning."

"Neither do I. But I meant what I said. This thing we're doin', fuckin' around, it stays off the ranch. When we're workin', we're workin'. I owe the Woods family too much to take advantage of them."

"I hear you and I get it, swear." Wyatt scooted to the edge of the truck bed and let his legs dangle over the tailgate. "Can you tell me more about this brother you still talk to?"

"I guess." Jackson moved to sit beside him. A chilly breeze had picked up but the sun kept him perfectly warm in his denim jacket. "His name's Kirby. He's a few years younger and lives in Nebraska. Because of the age difference, I was one of the kids taking care of the youngers while our elders worked the farm. We just clicked as friends and he was the only person there, girl or boy, who really felt like a sibling. When I was eighteen I left, but the internet was a newish thing back then so I was able to leave him an email address. When he turned eighteen and left, he emailed me." He closed his eyes and smiled at the sky. "We still use that same email."

"It's good to keep connections to people who mean something to you."

"Yeah. Do you have siblings? I honestly can't remember if I ever asked."

"Two step-siblings, both older. Sister, Lily, and brother, Peter." Wyatt shrugged, his attention somewhere in the distance. "They're okay. We were never close but we didn't hate each other. I was young when our parents got married so I don't really remember a time without my stepfather around. I just...sometimes really want to know who my bio dad is. If I've got another family out there."

"I kind of envy you wanting to know that." Jackson bumped Wyatt's shoulder with his own. "And I'm not patronizing you. Guess I figured since both my parents didn't want me, there was no use in lookin' or hopin'. But it sounds like you had a mom who loved you. She kept you and raised you when your father couldn't be bothered, for whatever reason. Don't discount that on your quest to find the other half of yourself."

Wyatt's jaw twitched several times before he turned his head and looked at Jackson. An interesting mix of determination and acceptance floated in his green eyes, and Jackson wanted to know more about that. But he wasn't sure Wyatt would tell him, and he didn't want the young cowboy wannabe to shut down. Not when he'd been so open today.

"I'll keep that in mind," Wyatt said. "I do love the family I know, even if I don't always agree with them. I just...

can't explain why I need to know my father. And whatever family he might have."

"You don't have to explain it, not to me or anyone. Your reasons are yours." Something shot from the back of Jackson's mind directly into the forefront. "You got reason to think he lives around here?"

"In Claire County, yeah. I was headed in this direction the night we met, and I just happened to get the interview with Brand the day after. I didn't lie about not being exactly sure where I was heading." His lower body jerked and then he laughed. "Sorry, phone vibrated." He pulled it out and checked the message. "Ramie's checking on me because I didn't come home last night."

"Ramie's good people."

"I like her a lot. She's like a big sister." Wyatt thumbed out a text faster than anyone Jackson had ever seen. "Just told her I'm fine, crashed with a new friend." He looked up, eyes uncertain. "We are friends now, right? Real friends? I'm not just some dumb, inexperienced kid you're teaching to be a cowboy?"

"You might be inexperienced in some things, Wyatt, but you are far from dumb. Don't ever devalue yourself, okay? Everyone's got their own set of skills, and we all use them the best we can. Maybe you ain't so great at roping, but I bet you could run circles around me when it comes to anything besides basic math."

"Probably so, but math doesn't help me learn how to rope a steer any faster."

"Guess not. So you got any leads on who your old man might be?"

Wyatt turned his head, attention back on the vast land ahead of them and the broken road leading to a town far beyond the horizon. "I trust you, Jackson, but right now I don't want any help with that. I could be completely wrong about things."

"I respect that. But if you do need help, ask me. I've been around here a long time and know a lotta people."

"Thanks. I mean it, Jackson, thank you. It's nice having a friend nearby. My best friend Jared is supportive of me coming out here, but he doesn't get it. He thinks I should just let everything go and move on. But his bio parents are still together and happily married, so I can't really talk to him about it. Not knowing your roots. But you get it."

"On some level, I do. If finding your past is what will help you walk into the future with confidence, then find it. Even if it's not what you're hoping for, I do hope you get the answers you want."

"Me too." He flashed Jackson a familiar, flirty smile. "I'd be melodramatic and say if I don't find those answers, then I'll have just wasted my time. But I met you, so either way I got something great out of this whole experience."

"Yes, you did."

Wyatt swatted playfully at his ass. Jackson leaped off the tailgate and wandered a few feet toward the gulch. Plucked a long blade of grass and as he twirled it between his fingertips, an old trick Kirby taught him eons ago came back. It took Jackson a minute to get his thumbs and the grass positioned just right. He raised his hands to his mouth and blew. A reedy, high-pitched whistling sound came out and he smiled.

"Dude, what did you just do?" Wyatt asked.

"You ain't never whistled with a piece of grass?"

"No." He got up and walked over to Jackson. "Do it again."

Amused, Jackson did, pulling out a louder sound this time. "Want me to show you how?"

"Hell yeah. Sweet."

It took Wyatt a while to get the hang of it, but once Jackson taught him the right way to hold the grass and his thumbs, the kid managed a decent squawk of sound. They messed around for a while, trying to match the music still playing on the radio, and with different pieces of grass. Wyatt grinned and laughed like a kid without a care in the world and, in some ways, it reminded Jackson of the day he'd learned. Of the awe he'd felt watching Kirby make music out of something as simple as a blade of grass.

One of the few beautiful, magical moments of his childhood.

"This is so cool," Wyatt said. "I can't wait to show Jared. Do you know any other tricks?"

Jackson stuck the thumb and forefinger of his left hand into his mouth and whistled so loud Wyatt covered both ears with his hands. "How's that?"

"Fuck, dude, that's loud. Wow."

"It takes a lot of practice. Maybe I'll show you another day."

"Cool. You're a good teacher. Anything else you want to teach me today? Maybe back in your motel room?"

The heat in Wyatt's eyes obliterated Jackson's ability to say no, and he hustled them both back into the truck. Their second round lasted longer than the first had, with Wyatt taking more time exploring Jackson's body: his neck and pits and chest and groin, even his feet, which were ticklish. Wyatt fucked him with two fingers so slowly that Jackson's impatience won out. He flipped their positions, sat on Wyatt's chest and put his cock-warming skills to great use. Wyatt thrashed but had no real purchase to toss Jackson off. All he could do was take the torture.

And Jackson tortured him, dragging Wyatt to the edge of orgasm, then backing him off, until Wyatt was a blubbering mess demanding to come. When Jackson released him and moved to his hands and knees, Wyatt barely had the coordination or patience to get the condom on before shoving inside on a long, steady thrust that Jackson felt in the back of his throat.

It was fucking awesome.

Wyatt eventually came on a long, low moan, his chest collapsing onto Jackson's back. On the edge of coming himself, Jackson waited for Wyatt to slither onto his back, then crouched over him. When Wyatt opened his mouth, Jackson fucked shallowly inside, wanting the heat and pressure but not to choke the kid. Jackson warned him, but Wyatt swallowed his load with a lazy grin that made Jackson's belly squirm with something new and kind of scary. Affection.

After a quick cleanup, they both napped and Jackson woke with the sun setting. Almost dinnertime and time for their daylong maybe-date to end. The entire affair had lasted longer than Jackson had anticipated when he'd scraped Wyatt up off the parking lot and brought him home. It had been the best, oddest day Jackson had had in a long damned time and he didn't regret a thing.

He reluctantly drove Wyatt back to the Tavern and his car. Wyatt kissed him for a long time, making a silent promise that this wasn't over. That they'd do it again. And again.

Jackson waited, engine idling, until Wyatt had started his own car and turned onto the road that would eventually lead him back to Weston. He drove to the motel, already missing Wyatt's smiles and scent and body heat, and unsure how the hell he was going to stay hands-off at work tomorrow.

Getting involved with Wyatt was probably a very bad idea, but it was Jackson's mistake to make.

He just hoped the whole thing didn't blow up in their faces.

Chapter Eleven

Wyatt barely paid attention to the fact that Ramie's car was in the driveway when he stumbled into the house that night, doped up on endorphins and confusion. The living room and kitchen were empty, and he didn't see her until about fifteen minutes later. He'd nuked a frozen dinner and eaten it in the kitchen, and he was considering texting Jackson about their day together when she shuffled in.

"Welcome home," she said as she went right for the coffeepot. "Hot date?"

"Something like that. I didn't bring him home, though, so no problem, right?"

"Yeah, you're cool." She set about making a pot of coffee, which meant she was probably working tonight. They hadn't lived together that long but she never drank coffee at night if she was staying home.

"Ramie, can I ask you something kind of personal?"

"You can ask anything you want, but I don't guarantee I'll answer."

Same as the day he moved in. Consistency was a trait he liked in people. "Do you know who both your bio parents are?"

Ramie turned away from the counter slowly, her whole body pivoting as one unit, muscles tense in her neck and shoulders while her face remained blank. "Why?"

"I'm curious. I don't know my bio dad. One of the guys—this guy I met last night doesn't know either of his bio parents, because they gave him up to the system, and he doesn't seem to care. I guess I used to think that not knowing one of my parents was unusual, but I guess maybe not so much? It's why I'm asking. I'd hate to be that spoiled, sheltered brat who thought everyone else had great, nuclear-family parents and am just figuring out that's a lie, but I guess that's who I am."

"Hey, there's nothing wrong with that. There are hundreds of millions of people who grow up in a traditional nuclear family, and that's what's normal to them. A lot of us don't get that, and that's normal to us. Nothing better or worse about any of it, though, it's just different. We're different from what was considered the norm fifty years ago and that's fine. Times change. People change."

"I guess." He poked at the final bits of his frozen meal, mostly for something to do with his hand. "So you didn't have a traditional nuclear family?"

"Actually, I did. Bio mom and bio dad, but they had an awful marriage. Nuclear doesn't always mean good or healthy, and does not guarantee a happy or harmonious family. Only love does that. And love comes in a lot of shapes and sizes, as I'm sure you know."

"How's that?"

"The ranch. I mean, the Woods family is obviously the epitome of a solid nuclear family, that bullshit with Colt aside, of course. But you, Alan, Jackson, Hugo, you cowboys are like a little family of your own, right?"

"I guess." No way was Wyatt admitting to how close he and Jackson had gotten today. So far, she hadn't nosed her way into his personal business or which friend he'd spent the night with. "I haven't actually met Alan yet because he broke his hand the day before I was hired, but I understand what you mean." He stood and tossed the dinner tray into the trash can. "Guess I've been so focused on that traditional family dynamic that I never gave a lot of thought to all the other kinds of families that exist."

"Welcome to the real world, honey. And no offense, but you're still a baby in the grand scheme of things."

He understood her point of view but also resented being talked down to. "So if your parents were so toxic, who's your family now?"

Instead of getting annoyed and leaving him alone, she smiled. "The people I work with at the Roost. Brand. A few girlfriends I confide in over social media. Someone doesn't have to be physically in front of you to be your family."

"You really consider Brand family? I mean, I guess you're good friends if his word was enough for you to rent me a room." Yeah, he was digging, but after his conversation with Jackson today about Wyatt's reason for being in Claire County at all, he couldn't help himself.

"Brand is one of those guys you want at your back during a crisis. He's an amazing friend. If you have one of those kinds of friends in your back pocket? The kind who will step into traffic for you? Or just bring you a piece of pie when you're having a bad day? You're golden."

"You believe in him that much." Less a question than a statement based on her tone of voice.

"I do." She pulled a coffee mug out of a cabinet and set it by the brewing pot. "Brand and I share a similar thing in our pasts, things that happened long before we met and got to be friends. But it bonded us and before you even think of asking, I'm not telling what that thing is because it's hugely personal and a little painful. I know he's your boss but he's loyal. You hear what he and his family did for Josiah Sheridan last fall?"

"No." He knew the name Josiah in relation to dating fellow cowboy Michael but that was it.

"Josiah is a home-care nurse, and his roommate kicked him out without notice or any kinda warning, and he tried to keep all Josiah's stuff. When his now-boyfriend Michael heard about it, his dad called Wayne Woods, who collected his sons, plus Michael, and they went and got Josiah's stuff. They had Michael's back and by extension, Josiah's."

"But Josiah helped save Brand's life when he was stabbed, right?"

"Sure. Even if Josiah hadn't been there that night to help Brand, Brand still would have helped Josiah because he was a friend of Michael's, and Michael works for him. You don't get that kind of loyalty from your manager at a big box store or grocery outlet."

"I guess you're right." Wyatt's handful of managers from his college jobs hadn't cared about his personal life, only that he showed up, did his job, and clocked out on time so they didn't go over expected payroll hours.

"If you're gonna land somewhere, Wyatt, Woods Ranch is a good place to be. I hope things keep working out for you."

"Me too, thanks."

"No problem." The coffee maker spat out its final dregs. "So this guy you spent the night with. You gonna see him again?"

"Yep." He'd obviously see Jackson at work tomorrow, but he took her other meaning to heart. Wyatt absolutely wanted to see Jackson again socially. To fuck him again and maybe even swap positions. He was curious how it felt to be fucked, and he trusted Jackson to be careful with him. To not hurt him.

He got the impression Jackson had been hurt enough in the past to be careful with his current partners.

A weird jolt of annoyance wiggled down his spine at the word *partners*. He didn't like the idea of Jackson being with anyone else while he was doing this thing, whatever it was, with Wyatt. Was the jealousy irrational? Absolutely. Did he care? Not much. He'd never felt such a close connection to someone after only knowing them for a week, and it was as scary as it was intriguing.

And something he definitely wanted to keep exploring.

Wyatt was only twenty and a relationship at his age was unlikely to last, but by God, he'd have some fun with it while he could.

"This nameless dude must have made an impression," Ramie said. "You just drifted off to la-la land for a little while. Good lay?"

"He was a great lay, actually."

"That's good. But here's some unsolicited big-sisterly advice, okay? Try not to get too attached if you aren't sure you're sticking around the area. Make sure you're both clear on what this thing between you is so feelings don't get hurt. Yours or his."

"I will." They hadn't made any promises, other than to keep their fling off the ranch, and Wyatt was cool with that. The last thing he wanted to do was get fired for fucking in the hayloft. Then again, if he did get fired there was nothing stopping him from asking Brand point-blank if he'd given up his parental rights twenty years ago.

Not that there was anything stopping him now. He didn't like lying to Jackson. Mostly lying by omission, but lying was lying.

Then again, telling the truth only got you hurt. Bad things happened if you told. Keeping things to yourself was better.

"Thanks, Ramie," Wyatt said. "I appreciate the advice."

"Not a problem." She winked as she poured a mug of

steaming coffee. "I also don't want any drama landing on my doorstep if this fling goes sideways."

"Understood." He stood, put his fork in the dishwasher, and headed toward the kitchen door. "Get lots of tips at work tonight."

Ramie pulled the hem of her already low-cut red top down a quarter inch. "Count on it. Mama needs to fix her roof."

He laughed. "See you tomorrow." He really, really liked her, and as he walked down the short hall to his room, battled a pang of guilt for what he wasn't saying to his landlord and friend about Brand. He truly hoped that if—when—the truth came out, she was able to forgive him for lying to her.

Monday was nowhere near as awkward as Wyatt antici-pated and that was largely due to the fact that he and Jack-son spent most of the day riding the line. Getting Wyatt used to the different pastures, the places in each where cattle could occasionally get lost or stuck, checking for fence damage, and doing everything except being in close quarters with each other.

As much as he missed how it felt to rub his naked body all over Jackson's, Wyatt appreciated the man's profession-alism. He was doing exactly what he said he would do, which was leave their personal life off the ranch. Wyatt's libido wasn't happy about that, but his work ethic appre-ciated Jackson's restraint.

Tuesday, Wyatt was on barn duty by himself. Brand and Rem were both off for the day, because Wayne was hav-ing outpatient surgery on one of his hands. It was a fairly simple surgery, but because of his age and previous com-plications with anesthesia, the family was anxious, and none of the Woods kids wanted their mother to be alone in the waiting room. Plus, it was a fifty-minute drive to the surgery center, which meant a long day for everyone.

Wyatt didn't mind doing the grunt work of mucking stalls, feeding the horses, polishing saddles, and keeping everything as clean and organized as a barn could get. He ate his lunch alone, which kind of sucked after being used to eating with Jackson (even if all Jackson usually did was grunt in response to Wyatt's attempts to start conversation).

His shift ended at five thirty, but Wyatt hung around the bunkhouse porch with Jackson, Hugo, and Michael, waiting until the Woods family finally returned a little after six. Rose and Rem stuck close to Wayne as the trio went inside the main house. Brand headed straight for them and pulled Hugo into a hug.

"Everything went fine." Brand kissed Hugo's cheek, then took a step back to address all the men on the porch. "Had a slight reaction to the anesthetic, but the surgery went fine. He just needs to take it easy and let his hand heal, which means supervising only. He goes anywhere near a shovel or a bridle, y'all tell me so I can yell at his stubborn ass."

A round of acknowledgments went around their small circle of coworkers. Brand's protectiveness over his father struck an odd chord for Wyatt because it butted up against everything he'd been told his bio dad was—so maybe Brand wasn't his Maybe Daddy and his intelligence was all wrong. He could live with that.

He just couldn't empathize with Brand's protectiveness over his father, because he'd never experienced anything like it. Wyatt loved his stepfather in his own way, but he'd hardly been sick or injured a day in Wyatt's life, so he'd never really worried over his health or future. Not like Wyatt had worried over and pampered his mom during her final few painful months. Sitting by her side as she succumbed to the disease ravaging her body. Holding her hand as she took her last breath. Watching nameless people take her away.

The funeral had been a surreal kind of hell he still had few clear memories of. Mostly he remembered the emotions. The overwhelming grief and loneliness.

"Kid, you okay?" Jackson elbowed him in the ribs. "This is good news."

"Huh?" He must have spaced out, because Hugo and Brand were gone and Michael was heading toward his pickup, leaving Wyatt alone on the porch with Jackson. "What?"

"What what? You had this weird look on your face just now. You okay?"

"Sorry, I got lost in the past. Unhappy stuff."

"You always get maudlin over good news?"

Wyatt stared at him.

"Weepy and emotional," Jackson said. "Maudlin."

"Oh. Not really. I guess I've been thinking about my mom a lot today. I'm really glad Wayne got through everything just fine. Honest."

Jackson nodded and glanced over his shoulder, as if to make sure they were alone. "It's gotta be a mind fuck, huh? Being glad for someone else's dad bein' okay when you're out here lookin' for yours?"

"A little. But I honestly don't resent Brand having a good relationship with his father. Michael, either. It's just how the chips landed, you know?" And for all his swirling confusion about his Maybe Daddy, Wyatt truly didn't resent Brand for being close to Wayne. He was a little jealous maybe but not resentful.

"Why don't you go home and relax? I'd say have a beer to unwind but you're underage."

Wyatt tried on a flirty smile. "You could always buy me one."

"I could also stick my finger in my truck's cigarette lighter, but I ain't doing that, either. Get some rest and I'll see you Thursday."

They both had tomorrow off, and Wyatt didn't like the idea of a whole day passing between his Jackson times. "What if I said I'd be at the Tavern tonight around eight thirty looking for a drink of Tall, Dark and Handsome?"

Jackson's eyes narrowed. "Good night, Wyatt."

He stared at Jackson's ass as he strode to his truck and got in, unsure if Jackson had taken the bait or not. While Wyatt's neck and shoulders were sore from all the manual labor, and he didn't really feel like driving all the way out to the Tavern, Jackson was more likely to seek him out there than if Wyatt said he was going to the Roost for a burger. Jackson didn't strike him as the type to back down from a challenge or hide if he was interested in someone, but the Tavern was a much better hunting ground for a dude interested in another dude.

Wyatt hadn't forgotten the story of Brand and Hugo's two-in-one-night bar brawls at the Roost thanks to a couple of drunk locals, and he wasn't looking to re create the experience. Wyatt had never been in a fight in his life, and he'd probably get his ass kicked. Jackson, on the other hand, would make anyone who came at him cry.

"Good night," Wyatt said to Jackson's departing truck. And if Jackson did take the bait, he hoped it would end up being a *great* night.

Jackson was an idiot. A surefire fool with no common sense, because if he had any common sense, he would have stayed at home. Stayed home and avoided any and all temptation. Instead, he let his dick lead him into his truck and across the county to the Blue Tavern. Right onto a barstool with a beer in hand and a bowl of stale pretzels within reach.

He'd shown up at eight fifteen. At eight twenty-five, he fully intended to eat a few more pretzels, drain his beer bottle, and leave. This was stupid. He had more self-respect than to sit around and pant after a boy half his age—even if everything about Wyatt made his body sing and demand and want.

At eight twenty-nine, according to the clock above the bar, Wyatt strode into the Tavern. No coat, just tight jeans and a too-tight black button-up shirt that made his hair gleam like fire in the dim bar light. He didn't pause or look around—he sauntered straight to the bar, leaned forward on his elbows, and waited his turn to order. The bartender gave him something clear and fizzy from the soda gun so probably club soda.

Wyatt sipped his drink, seeming not to notice anyone else around him, not even the two guys who sidled up close and tried to chat with him. They didn't stay long. Jackson watched Wyatt, occasionally sipping his own beer, curious what this game was. Wyatt had practically solicited him earlier and now he was playing hard to get by ignoring Jackson completely?

Maybe that was the game. Maybe he wanted to be flirted with and picked up like a stranger might, taken somewhere and ravished, but he didn't have the stones to go with an actual stranger. Or he simply wanted Jackson and no one else. It had been a long time since Jackson had been anyone special to another guy. More than a hand to scratch an itch like he'd been for Brand.

The idea intrigued him as much as it terrified him. He was forty fucking years old. He should be able to do this. Whatever this was.

A third man tried his hand at picking up Wyatt. This guy was closer to Wyatt's age with slicked-back brown hair and a full beard. Wyatt gave a few one-word answers Jackson didn't catch, because he wasn't good at reading lips, before leaning into the stranger's personal space far enough to make Jackson sit up straighter. Wyatt ran his finger around the rim of his soda glass in a subtle, flirty way.

Jackson grunted, uncertain if Wyatt was deliberately baiting him or if he was actually interested in this guy. Had someone else stolen his attention from Jackson already?

Fuck that.

Irritated now, Jackson gulped the dregs of his semiflat beer, stopped himself from physically slamming the bottle down on the bar, and stood. His intention was to walk to the door, grab his coat, and leave empty-handed. What he actually did was walk over to Wyatt's stool and put his hand on the back of Wyatt's neck. Wyatt sat up straighter but didn't turn around.

The stranger looked up at Jackson and frowned. "Can we help you, pal?"

"He ain't goin' home with you tonight," Jackson said.

"Says who? Pretty sure Wilson here's got a mind of his own."

"Sure he does." He stroked his thumb up and down the knobs of Wyatt's spine. "Who you goin' home with tonight, firebrand?"

Goose bumps rose along the exposed skin of Wyatt's neck. He slowly turned around in his stool, eyes gleaming and cheeks flushed. "Now there's my drink of Tall, Dark and Handsome," Wyatt said in a seductive purr that sent blood to Jackson's groin.

The stranger grabbed his drink and left.

Jackson left his hand on Wyatt's neck and leaned down. "You're a pain in the ass."

"I know. You like it."

"Might need to give you a small pain in *your* ass, maybe from a good spanking."

Wyatt's lips parted. Nothing in his expression hinted at fear or dislike of the idea. Jackson wasn't really much for hard spanking and shit, but Wyatt could probably use a few good swats just to pink up his pale ass cheeks.

"You ready to get outta here?" Jackson asked.

"Soon." A sly smile twisted those pretty lips. "You need to dance with me first."

"I don't dance."

"Too bad." Wyatt grabbed his shirt and tugged Jackson lower. Put his mouth right by Jackson's ear and whispered, "One song if you want this dick tonight." Then he sucked on Jackson's earlobe, reminding him vividly of what that mouth felt like around his cock.

"Fine. One song."

Fortunately, this wasn't the hearts-and-flowers kind of place that put slow songs on in between the dance music. Jackson did not do slow dancing. The floor wasn't too crowded, which was typical for a random Tuesday in winter. Jackson didn't resist Wyatt leading him toward the small cluster of men gyrating to whatever techno stuff was currently being piped over the speakers. It was usually mixed with more traditional country music and pop songs, depending on whatever the manager was in the mood for that night.

Since Jackson had agreed to one song, he held Wyatt back until the current tune switched over to something new. Fortunately for him, it went from techno to country, and this was the kind of dancing he was actually good at. Fun footwork and timed spins, and he kind of liked that Wyatt was a little out of step when they started. Okay, a lot out of step. For all Wyatt's "let's dance" bravado, he didn't know actual dance moves too well. Thanks to his adopted mother, Jackson did.

He showed off a little, enjoying the way Wyatt let him spin him around the dance floor and manhandle him into the right positions. They got a bunch of wolf whistles and cheers from a gathered crowd of observers. It wasn't proper line dancing, and they'd never win any awards on reality shows, but Jackson put on a good show for the audience. And for Wyatt, in an expression of dominance he wasn't fully aware of making until the song ended.

The applause made him laugh out loud. It had been a long time since he'd let go like that, and Wyatt clung to him, red-faced and panting from the exertion. Another similar song came up, but Jackson was tapped out. He pulled Wyatt over to the bar and before he could ask for water, Darlin' passed them each a beer.

"You two dance like that every night," Darlin' said, "and you'll have folks creaming their jeans left and right. Great job, sugars."

Jackson shoved one of the beers away. "The kid will have water, thanks."

Wyatt sulked, then chugged from the water bottle offered. Jackson drank both beers, positive he'd be okay after all that exertion. But once he and Wyatt left the bar and were in the cold parking lot, he handed over his keys anyway. No sense in risking it. "If you remember the way to my place," Jackson said, "then you are getting very lucky tonight."

"Oh, I remember." Wyatt snatched up the keys and practically shoved Jackson into the passenger side. This slightly aggressive side made Jackson smile at the dash while Wyatt figured out his truck and how to drive it. It was at least twice the size of Wyatt's own car but he navigated the parking lot without much trouble.

Wyatt drove with an attractive amount of confidence, taking every correct turn like he'd done it a hundred times. Jackson stretched out on his side of the bench seat, half a mind to lean over and tease the kid. Maybe stroke his dick over his jeans or kiss his neck a few times. But holding back seemed to amp Wyatt up more, because he kept tossing eager looks at Jackson. Looks that said Wyatt would pounce if he wasn't responsible for getting them both safely back to the motel.

As much as he wanted to demand Wyatt pull off on the side of the road so they could get down to business, Jackson was old enough to restrain himself. He did stare, though, and he delighted every time Wyatt squirmed and adjusted himself. It took forever before Wyatt finally slammed on the brakes in front of Jackson's room. Tonight was the night to park in front of room seven for variety, but Jackson didn't really give a shit.

He was out of the truck and had Wyatt pinned against the hood in seconds, kissing the younger man with a hunger he'd never felt before. A hunger born of loneliness, chemistry, and flat-out need. He needed this man to kiss him, suck him, fuck him, and make him feel something real. Something more real than the chilly air against his skin, the dirt beneath his boots, and the moonlight streaming down on them.

Something real deep inside.

Wyatt kissed him back hard, licking into his mouth while his hands tugged at Jackson's belt, already getting down to business. Jackson yanked at the buttons on the front of Wyatt's shirt, not caring a few ripped off. He'd buy the guy a new shirt tomorrow if he had to, especially if it got them fucking faster. He raked his fingernails down Wyatt's bare chest, imagining the red marks he'd probably left behind. Wyatt bit his bottom lip hard enough that Jackson growled.

The odds of anyone happening down this dead-end road this late were close to zero, but the slight chance of it happening emboldened Jackson. He manhandled Wyatt around and turned them so Wyatt was bent over the hood of the truck, one hand on the back of his neck to keep him still just like at the bar. Wyatt stilled but his entire body thrummed with energy. They both knew he could break Jackson's hold with ease but he submitted instead, and that was an insane turn-on.

With his free hand, Jackson managed Wyatt's belt and fly, and he tugged those tight jeans down to his knees, baring his ass. A pale, freckled ass he wanted to explore more, but not right now. There were two things he wanted to do more. The first of which he did with his right hand while keeping his left firmly on the back of Wyatt's neck.

Jackson smacked Wyatt's right cheek, and Wyatt yelped. He didn't tense or fight or try to get away, though. He wriggled a bit but otherwise stayed in position, so Jackson smacked his left cheek. In the dim light, he could barely see the outline of his handprints on both ass cheeks, and the sight made Jackson grin. He pinched the very top of Wyatt's left thigh and earned another delicious yelp.

"Love seeing my handprints on your ass," Jackson said. "You like feelin' it?"

"Yes. Fuck yes. I like it but…not too hard?"

"I've got you. I go too far with anything, you pick a word. Say it and I stop."

"Like a safe word? How about Shirley Temple?"

Jackson chuckled, not sure if he was referring to the actress or the horse. "How about just Shirley?"

"Works for me."

"Good." He brought his palm down again, three more

times on each cheek, getting each one cherry-red. Wyatt squirmed a little but never fought him or tried to break free. "You done this before?"

"No. Never. But I like it."

A quick jerk of Wyatt's heavy erection proved that. "Yeah, you do, don't you? Getting your ass spanked like a spoiled child who got caught for keeping secrets." He slid a finger into Wyatt's crease. "You think liars deserve to be punished, Wilson?"

Wyatt shivered. "Yes."

He rubbed Wyatt's hole without breaching him. "Wouldn't mind seeing my dick sliding in and out of that red ass of yours." When Wyatt shivered again, Jackson squeezed the back of his neck. "Not today but one day."

"One day." Wyatt practically panted the words.

"Think you can come without me touching your dick?"

"Maybe. Close now." He thrust at Jackson's finger, but Jackson pulled his hand away. "You're a fucking tease."

"Not a tease. You'll come, you just have to work for it. Keep still."

"Make me."

"Don't make me truss you up, because I will have you down and roped up like a runaway steer before you know what hit you."

Wyatt released a long, low moan. "Promise?"

Fuck, but the kid was kinkier than Jackson had anticipated. As much as doing some of those things did appeal to Jackson, they didn't feel right for tonight. Not for this particular encounter. He wanted to ease Wyatt into the waters, not shove him into the deep end and hope he didn't drown. He wanted to give Wyatt all the things he never had. Make sure Wyatt knew how wonderful sex with the right person, for the right reasons, could be. To show Wyatt he was worth so much more than just his body.

"Maybe one day," Jackson said. "Not tonight. Need to make you come without a hand on your dick first."

"You think you can then go for it."

Cocky brat. "Oh, I can, Wyatt. I can." Jackson went to his knees in the grassy parking lot, pulled Wyatt's cheeks apart and licked from the top of his balls to the small of his back.

Wyatt hollered.

Chapter Twelve

Wyatt knew what rimming was thanks to the internet and porn, but he'd never had anyone lick his asshole before, much less make love to it like it was his mouth. And that's what Jackson seemed determined to do: make love to his hole with every lick and stab and swirl with his tongue. The hand on the back of his neck was the only thing keeping Wyatt semistill, when all he wanted to do was both clamber away and shove closer. It was too much and not enough, and he was going to lose his fucking mind.

But that hand. *That hand.* Something about it kept Wyatt still while his insides went insane with sensation and pleasure. Jackson's free hand occasionally pinched Wyatt's most sensitive places, from his ball sac to his upper thighs, and it staved off his looming orgasm, torturing Wyatt in the very best way. He never imagined being spanked would turn him on as much as it had, and Jackson's threat to tie him up?

Dead. Gone. Blown away.

His safe word lingered in the back of his mind, but Wyatt knew in his bones he wouldn't need to use it. Jackson had an eerily innate ability to know how far to push Wyatt without going too far. It made Wyatt curious about the mysterious past Jackson hinted at without real details,

but now—with Jackson's tongue burrowing halfway up his ass—was not the time to ask.

Now was the time to exist and experience.

Wyatt's fingers slid against the cold metal surface of the truck hood, and it finally penetrated his lust-clogged brain that they were doing this outdoors where anyone could see them. Not that anyone except maybe a coyote or an armadillo lived out here on a deserted, dead-end road, but still. His ass was bare to the world and stars, exposed to the January cold, and Wyatt had never been happier to be in such a bizarre position in his life.

A position he could get out of with a strong jerk of his body or by saying his safe word, but he didn't want to do either. Not while Jackson was playing his body so beautifully. And the deeper Jackson licked into his ass, the more Wyatt wondered what it would be like to have a dick in there, pounding inside him, stretching him and slamming into his prostate.

As if summoned to the spot by his thoughts, Jackson's finger worked inside with his tongue and bent, stroking over Wyatt's gland. Wyatt yelled again, uncaring how loud he was or that his voice was echoing off the long building behind him. Nothing mattered more than the orgasm teasing him from just beyond his reach.

He humped backward against Jackson's finger and tongue, needing more, not caring if Jackson decided to just shove his dick inside and get the job done. All he knew was the desperate need to come. He instinctively reached for his own dick. Jackson's hand squeezed his neck hard, and Wyatt slapped his palm down on the truck hood. The finger in his ass stroked harder and if Wyatt had been physically able to bite through steel, he probably would have. Instead, he keened and clenched around that amazing, wicked finger.

"Fuck, please!" Wyatt whined. "Need to come, please."

"You will."

"Now!"

"No."

"I hate you."

"I know you do." Jackson bit his left ass cheek hard and Wyatt yelped. "Come now, Wyatt. Now!"

The finger deep inside Wyatt's ass smashed against his prostate and Wyatt had no choice. He thrust his hips and yelled and came all over the truck's grille, not giving a shit where his spunk landed when his body was convulsing with the best orgasm of his entire twenty years. His voice echoed in the vast emptiness around them, and he rode wave after wave of sensation until Jackson's finger pulled out of his ass, giving him a moment to collect himself. The only contact between them was the constant, familiar weight of Jackson's hand on his neck, the only sound their combined heavy breathing.

"Fuuuuuuuck," Wyatt slurred. "Holy shiiiiit."

"You like being told what to do." Not a question.

"I guess I do. Don't have to think." While he'd had fun fooling around in college, he'd never imagined an experience like this, or that he'd be so turned on by commands and being held down. It seemed so...well, submissive, and Wyatt had never considered himself such in any aspect of his life. His refusal to back down and let things lie was why he was here at all, in Claire County, getting to know his Maybe Daddy in secret.

"Sometimes it's nice to let go and have someone else lead," Jackson said softly, just above a whisper. "To trust someone to take care of you. Trust can be hard to find."

"Yeah." Wyatt twisted his neck to get a partial view of Jackson's face. Jackson was staring past Wyatt, probably

at nothing in particular beyond a memory only he could see. "I trust you, Jackson. I hope you trust me."

"Gettin' there, firebrand." He took his hand off Wyatt's neck, and Wyatt immediately missed its heat and weight. "Come on, let's get inside and get you cleaned up."

Wyatt straightened, his belly a bit sore from where he'd been bent over for so long, and looked at Jackson's tented jeans. "You haven't come yet."

"I will."

"Do you, um, want to fuck me?"

Jackson's eyes narrowed. He leaned in and brushed his nose lightly against Wyatt's. "Yes, I do. But not tonight, not while you're high on endorphins and I've been drinking. We'll talk about it first, so we both know what we want."

"Okay." If Jackson had asked in that moment, Wyatt would have happily bent back over the truck and let Jackson pop that particular cherry. To let him fuck Wyatt the way Wyatt had fucked him last weekend. The older man's restraint made Wyatt fall for Jackson a little bit more, especially with Wyatt standing there with his bare ass hanging out, and Jackson's raging boner obvious to them both.

He pulled his jeans up far enough that he wouldn't trip as he walked and followed Jackson inside the motel room. He stood in the middle of the room, waiting for Jackson to approach him, shove him to the bed, to do something besides get a cup of water from that dispenser.

"Go ahead," Jackson said, gesturing at the bathroom. "If you don't want a full shower, there are washrags under the sink with the extra towels."

"Um, okay. You really want me to clean up before you get me messy again?"

"Might be a while before that happens." He winked. "One thing you learn as you get older is delayed gratification can be kind of awesome."

"If you say so."

Wyatt dropped his jeans and belt once he was in the bathroom, door shut, and began running water in the sink. He wasn't actually that messy, just a little sticky between his cheeks and the tip of his dick, because most of his come had landed on the truck. Jackson didn't seem bothered by the mess, so Wyatt cleaned and dried himself, then tucked his business back into his briefs and jeans. Wyatt rubbed the back of his neck, still able to feel Jackson's hand there and kind of wishing he'd left a bruise. But while Jackson's hold had been firm, it had never gone beyond that; he knew how not to leave a mark.

When he left the bathroom, Jackson was in one of the sitting chairs, legs spread-eagle in front of him, jeans open while he lazily jerked himself. Wyatt had an idea of what Jackson might ask him to do before Jackson spoke. "Put your mouth on it. Don't suck, just keep it warm."

Wyatt's spent cock gave an interested twitch as he crossed the small room and knelt between Jackson's long legs. Licked his lips, excited to taste the thick cock in front of him and just as eager to please Jackson after such an amazing orgasm earlier. "Not sure it'll all fit," Wyatt said, putting every ounce of seductive purr he possessed into the statement.

Jackson tapped his cockhead against Wyatt's cheek. "Take what you can. Don't choke yourself."

Wyatt nodded and opened his mouth. He went slow, taking in just the head first, savoring the taste of Jackson's skin. The heat and silk of him before traveling farther down. When Jackson's glans nudged at the back of his throat and threatened to upset his gag reflex, Wyatt paused. He held still, desperate to work the length in his mouth with his tongue, to do more than just kneel there, but this was all Jackson had asked him to do. Warm his cock.

"Your mouth feels amazing," Jackson said. He sifted his fingers through Wyatt's curls in a relaxing, petting way. "So hot and tight, just like your ass must be."

Wyatt moaned, his hole clenching, and he resisted the very real urge to take his pants off again so he could finger himself. Put on a show for Jackson. His dick started getting back into things—sometimes being twenty years old was truly awesome—and pressed against the zipper of his jeans.

"Fuck, you feel good." Jackson thrust.

His dick hit the back of Wyatt's throat too hard, and Wyatt pulled off, gasping and swallowing so he didn't do something embarrassing. The instant he regained control of his gag reflex, he took Jackson's cock back into his mouth, because he hadn't been told to stop. Drool coated his chin and he didn't care. All he could think about was pleasing Jackson and doing what he said. He trusted the man never to ask for something Wyatt could not or would not do.

Jackson continued to pet him, fingers stroking through his hair and occasionally across his temples or cheekbones. The simple touches expressed his pleasure at what Wyatt was doing, and it fueled Wyatt's need to do better. To be the best for this man, whatever that meant.

"So pretty," Jackson said. "Your lips are almost as red as your hair."

Wyatt wanted to thank him for the compliment, but his mouth was otherwise occupied, so he showed his appreciation by rubbing his tongue on the underside of Jackson's cock. Jackson inhaled sharply, his hand a new, wonderful weight on Wyatt's neck that stilled him. Wyatt's senses were full of the smell and taste of Jackson and he wanted more. Wanted Jackson to come down his throat. He also wanted to be told what to do, and those two things warred in his head.

It was why Wyatt balanced on one hand and sneaked a finger up to rub behind Jackson's balls. He didn't have much room to work because of the way Jackson was sitting down, but he managed and got a delightful moan out of Jackson.

"Keep acting out like this and you'll get another spanking," Jackson said.

Wyatt hummed around his mouthful of cock. Dude needed to work on his threats.

Both of Jackson's hands rested on the back of his head. "I'm gonna stand up now. Don't bite." Wyatt made an agreeable noise, so Jackson bent his legs and began to stand. The motions were so fluid Wyatt had no trouble extending his neck and repositioning his knees so he could keep his mouth around Jackson's dick. "You remember your safe word?"

Jackson pulled his head back and off his cock so Wyatt could answer. "Yes."

"I won't choke you, but if you can't say the word and need to, then pinch me hard on the thigh. It'll get my attention." He caressed Wyatt's cheek with one finger in an affectionate gesture that made Wyatt want to purr, before returning that hand to the back of his neck.

Wyatt opened his mouth and waited.

Jackson was all kinds of turned on by the easy way Wyatt was submitting to him. Wyatt wanted to be told what to do, to be given direction, and as much as it appealed to Jackson, it also worried him. The kid was out here searching for his father, and Jackson wasn't sure having a "daddy" ordering him around was what Wyatt really needed.

He'd think harder on that another time. Right now, he wanted to come down Wyatt's throat.

He slid his cock back into Wyatt's open mouth, loving the way Wyatt instinctively guarded his teeth with his lips. Jackson didn't have to hold Wyatt's head hard; he seemed to enjoy getting his face fucked and relaxed his throat muscles to accommodate Jackson's girth. Jackson went slow, enjoying the way Wyatt's cheeks puffed out and his throat worked each time Jackson pushed inside. Wyatt's eyes gleamed as he stared up at Jackson, taking his own pleasure while giving Jackson his in return.

The moment seemed to stretch out like pulled taffy, on and on, as Jackson sought his climax. His balls tightened and pure delight sizzled down his spine, and it took all his willpower to restrain himself when instinct said to drive into Wyatt's throat. But he refused to choke or scare the gorgeous young man giving him this gift. Submitting so beautifully to everything Jackson asked.

He wiped a stream of drool from Wyatt's cheek and smiled down at his boy. While Wyatt seemed willing to submit during sex, nothing about the obstinate younger man was submissive outside the bedroom. At work he was determined to prove himself, no matter how many scrapes and bruises he accumulated along the way, and Jackson admired that.

He also wanted to wrap Wyatt up in bubble wrap so he didn't hurt himself. To keep him safe from all enemies, especially ones who'd take advantage of him. He'd hurt anyone who tried taking advantage of Wyatt the way Jackson had been taken advantage of at the same age.

Jackson stroked one hand through Wyatt's soft, tangled curls, beating back a new wave of anger toward the men from last weekend. Over the thought of Wyatt being hurt like that, and he thrust a bit too hard. Wyatt choked, his eyes widening, and Jackson immediately pulled out of his mouth.

Wyatt held his gaze for several long seconds, then sucked Jackson back in. Jackson moaned and lost himself as Wyatt took over the blow job, sucking and licking and seducing with lips, tongue, and a little bit of teeth. Urging Jackson closer and closer to orgasm with every touch and stroke. And for as much as he loved everything about this, Jackson needed to come. He closed his eyes and existed in the moment and in Wyatt's very talented mouth. He shouted a warning once and then was coming hard. Hard enough that he doubled over and had to grab Wyatt's shoulders for support, while Wyatt milked him dry.

Once he got his sense back, Jackson dropped to his knees and captured Wyatt's mouth in a claiming kiss, licking inside to taste his own come combined with the essence of Wyatt himself—and he liked it. A lot. They kissed for a long time, fingers tangling in hair, chests pressed together, their breaths becoming one and the same.

It was perfect.

And terrifying.

Jackson tucked himself back into his pants, then pulled Wyatt to his feet and dragged him to the bed. Smothered him into the mattress so they could kiss more. As they kissed and rolled around, clothing came off until they were both naked beneath the covers. Jackson was half-hard again, and Wyatt was fully erect, but neither of them seemed to care all that much. It wasn't about the orgasm now; it was about the experience.

It was about their bodies and minds and existing together until exhausted.

Jackson woke at some point during the night because he needed to pee. Wyatt was curled up close to him, but not draped over in such a way that he couldn't slide out of bed and into the bathroom. After doing his business, he studied his reflection in the bathroom's yellowish light. For the first time, he didn't see exhaustion, confusion, or loneliness. All he saw was a well-fucked, tired guy who actually liked where he was.

Physically, emotionally, and spiritually, Jackson was content with his life. Romantically, would he like a long-term partner? Probably yes. Almost definitely yes. Was Wyatt that person? Unlikely. But as he watched the hot redhead sleeping in a sliver of light from the bathroom, Jackson liked the idea of exploring this thing between them. And of exploring the body in his bed for as long as Wyatt wanted to be with him.

Jackson returned to bed, and he loved the way Wyatt scooted closer to him without waking up. He inhaled Wyatt's scent and twirled one finger in his hair, way too happy and confused by it all. Joy was a foreign concept for him. Loneliness and confusion were far more familiar.

From the corner of the room, Dog raised her head once and whined. Jackson shushed her, and she put her chin back down on her paws. While his relationship with Wyatt was still new and ill-defined, he liked it, more than he'd liked anything or anyone in a long damned time. He didn't expect it to last, because everyone in Jackson's life eventually left.

But for right now, he'd enjoy this beautiful thing while he had it.

Wyatt woke with a sticky mouth, an intense thirst for water, and a hand possessively cupping his ass. The first two things bothered him while the third did not in the least. He still felt the phantom sensation of Jackson eating his ass last night, and he definitely wanted that to happen again. He'd redo the entire night, step by step, if he could.

He floundered for the side table and the cup of water Jackson had put there at some point and managed to sip some without spilling it. He lay on his stomach, so he was proud of not dribbling it anywhere. When he put the cup back he glanced to his left and looked right into Jackson's dark brown eyes. Sleepy, almost shy eyes.

The shyness after what they'd done last night was incredibly cute. "Hey," Wyatt said.

"Hey." Jackson did that adorable nose nuzzle thing. "Sleep okay?"

"Oh yeah, like a rock for a while. You wore me out."

"Same. I had a, uh, really great time last night."

"Me too." Wyatt humped his hips a little, and Jackson's fingers slid closer to his crease. He hadn't forgotten Jackson saying he wanted to fuck him, and Wyatt was more than down with finding out what that felt like. "Really loved you playing with me here."

"I loved that, too. You're so fucking responsive."

"No one's ever done that for me before. Rimmed me."

"I figured. Figure there's a lot of stuff you still don't know about your body. If you trust me, I'd like to keep helping you discover that stuff."

"I do trust you." Even though he kind of had to pee, Wyatt slid over so he was half draped on Jackson's body, their groins pressed together. He folded his hands on Jackson's chest and rested his own chin on them. The closeness made him slightly cross-eyed but he didn't care. "Can I, um, chill with you for a while today? Like, we can talk or not talk, or we can take a walk or whatever. We don't have to fuck again, but I'd like to if you're okay with it, and now I'm babbling like a twelve-year-old with his first crush."

Jackson grinned. "We can do whatever you want today. Only plans I had were to rest and maybe hike for a while with Dog."

She heard her name and yipped. Wyatt looked up and spotted her at attention by the door, probably eager to water a bush.

"I hear you," Jackson said. "Gotta let her out."

"I'll do it." Wyatt climbed out of bed. He shivered immediately in the cold room, dashed over to unlock the door and let Dog go outside, and then darted back under the covers. Cuddled up close to Jackson's hot, slightly hairy body. Jackson wrapped him up in his arms, and Wyatt settled against his chest. "I like this new side of you."

"What side?"

"The warm side. You're so businesslike at the ranch, and I get that. We're both there to do a job, and me being trained right is important. Totally get it. It's just nice seeing a human side and not just the cowboy robot."

Jackson snickered. "I guess I do kind of act like an emotionless jerk at work sometimes. I've got a long, bad habit of keepin' people at arm's length. Been hurt too much in the past, so it's hard to trust. Don't often feel right letting myself risk that trust bein' broken."

Wyatt traced a finger around the coarse hair on Jackson's chest, enjoying the way it tickled his skin. "Will you tell me a little about that? Your past? You don't say much ever."

"What do you wanna know about?"

"I don't know. When you did know you were gay?"

"Not until I was about eighteen and gettin' ready to go into the world on my own. I mean, I'd admired boys for a long time, since puberty really, but my parents were the type who preached hellfire and brimstone for gay folk and women who had sex before marriage, and don't get me started on what they thought about female politicians. So you can imagine I didn't examine my thoughts for boys or act on any of those urges until I got out of that place."

Something sad in Jackson's voice made Wyatt raise his

head. Jackson was staring up at the ceiling, his expression somewhat blank, as if caught up in something only he could see. Memories in his head that had stolen him briefly away. "Let me guess," Wyatt said gently. "You acted too much on those thoughts once you were free?"

"In a nutshell, and it took me to some pretty bad places. I had a little money saved up when I left but it didn't stretch as far as I hoped it would. Got a few minimum-wage jobs, but I was an eighteen-year-old virgin with no real skills outside of farming, trying to find his way in a city I could barely navigate or understand. Really long story short, I ended up working for a pimp."

Wyatt's stomach rolled unpleasantly. "Really?"

"Yeah." His gaze stayed on the ceiling. "I mean, I liked sex and was good at it, so it wasn't all bad. I made money. My boss, Cyrus, was fair with his boys. He didn't stand for us gettin' hurt too bad. It was okay for a while until I started gettin' requested by the same john, several nights a month. He got possessive."

Wyatt was still stuck on the whole "hurt too bad" part, like getting hurt even a little was acceptable. He tried to imagine being in the same position at his age as Jackson had been, and it blew his mind to think of what Jackson had experienced. Of all the hurts and bad memories he wasn't sharing that had to be taking up space in his head. "What happened?"

"Cyrus started hintin' around that the john wanted to, essentially, buy me from him. To be his exclusive property, to live with him, and at the time I wasn't opposed to the idea. I mean, the guy had a huge house, drove fancy cars, had a lot of money, and the thought of fucking one guy, instead of dozens, was kind of appealing. And it wasn't like I had any kind of legal contract with Cyrus, but we made a deal and I went to live with the john."

Jackson's face reddened and his mouth flattened. "Let Dog back in."

Pretty sure Jackson needed a moment to collect himself, Wyatt did as asked. Dog went straight to her empty food bowl, but she could wait for a little while longer. Wyatt went back to bed and wrapped himself around Jackson, hoping the older man wasn't done with his story. It hadn't concluded yet.

When Jackson didn't say anything, Wyatt prompted him. "Long story short?"

"It was good for a few weeks. Regular sex, good food, my own room, an allowance to buy clothes and shit." Jackson reversed their positions so he was now spooned up behind Wyatt, telling his truths to the back of Wyatt's head. "Then the john had a party, and I was the featured favor. They fed me drugs and alcohol, and I don't remember a lot of that night. Only wakin' up disoriented, naked, in agonizing pain, with the john's dead body next to me. His head was bashed in with a glass paperweight."

"Jesus fuck," Wyatt said. "Oh my God." He wanted to turn around and hug Jackson, but being the one doing the hugging seemed to be what Jackson needed right now. To spill these secrets without being looked at.

"I was obviously arrested after a brief stay in the hospital. The charges went up and down, and I didn't have anyone in my corner except a public defender. Because of my medical records from that night, I was convicted of manslaughter instead of murder."

"Manslaughter?" Wyatt sat up, the covers falling away but he didn't care. He stared down at Jackson, horrified. "You went to jail?"

"I went to prison for three years." Jackson still spoke to the pillow where Wyatt's head had been a moment ago. "I don't remember hittin' him in the head, but my prints were on the paperweight. My attorney tried to argue that it was circumstantial, because I'd been living in the house, but I was a hooker. That's what the prosecutor called me and it's all the jury saw, so I went away. I've spent the better part of twenty years tryin' to remember that night but I don't, and it's probably for the best, because I remember way too much about those three years in prison."

"I'm so sorry." Wyatt would never ask about those things. Not because he didn't care, but because he could guess and the pain in Jackson's one visible eye was too stark not to notice. Wyatt had seen way too much on TV and could easily imagine the things Jackson had survived.

"It's the past but it's what you wanted to know." He snorted, the sound part angry and part surprised. "You're only the second person I've ever told all that to."

Wyatt took a stab in the dark. "Wayne Woods?"

"No. When I interviewed for the job, I was honest with him about my time in prison, but he didn't ask for the details. He knows I was convicted and served time, and he hired me anyway. No, I told Brand about it a year or so ago."

Shock hit him in the chest, and it took Wyatt a few seconds to find his breath. "I didn't know you and Brand were that close."

"It's complicated and real simple." Jackson sat up, his face twisted into something kind of pained. "This is probably gonna make me sound like a giant hypocrite, but Brand and I had an arrangement these last couple of years that ended when he got together with Hugo. Before that, actually."

"An arrangement?"

"We fucked. It started before I got hired, if that helps, and it had nothing to do with me *being* hired. It was a casual thing for us both, and he was also fucking other people. So was I, when the mood struck."

Blood pulsed in Wyatt's temples as a headache threatened thanks to these new truth bombs. The guy he was... well, dating wasn't the right word, but seeing? The guy he was seeing had also fucked around with his Maybe Daddy? That was beyond weird to think about, so Wyatt shoved it into the back of his mind. That particular fact mattered less than something else. "So is that why you're all hands-off at work with me?" Wyatt asked. "Because you used to fuck your boss?"

"Yeah. Mostly, plus my time as a prostitute. I need to keep work and sex separate things, and that's not easy when you're fuckin' a coworker." Jackson sat up slowly and scooted a few inches away. "I'd also get it if you're weirded out by all this and wanna end things between us."

"Hell no. I mean, yeah, I'm a little weirded out by you fucking Brand, but your past is just...your past. I don't care about that shit. I mean, I care because it's obviously something that changed your life like crazy, but what I mean is I'm not judging you as a man for it. Hell, if I didn't have the savings I did before traveling out here, I might've had to make a similar decision about making money."

"Never." Jackson yanked him into a fierce, unexpected hug. "As long as I am alive and able to help, you will never end up in that kind of position. I am thankful every single day I was there last weekend when those guys took you outside."

Wyatt rested his chin on Jackson's shoulder. "Me too." He glanced to his left and smiled. "Not to interrupt the moment, but Dog is giving me some serious puppy eyes. I think she's hungry."

Laughter rumbled from Jackson's chest into his. "I bet.

How about I feed Dog, we both take a shower, and then we go get breakfast at the truck stop."

Wyatt pulled back just far enough to rub his nose against Jackson's. "Sounds like a plan, boss. Sounds like a plan."

Chapter Thirteen

After a leisurely breakfast at the truck stop, they bought a few bottles of water and some snacks, and then spent a few hours exploring the terrain around the motel with Dog as their constant companion. Jackson had not expected to spill so much of his personal past to Wyatt this morning, but something about Wyatt just made him comfortable. Urged him to open up and be honest about things he preferred not thinking about. Ever.

A few of his demons had tried to strangle him during his confessions, but Wyatt's constant presence and support kept them at bay, and Jackson was grateful for that. More grateful than he could say, so he tried to show it by buying Wyatt breakfast, and then showing him some of his favorite places to hike.

Dog loped around them, happy for the exercise, and her constant headbutting of Wyatt's leg spoke loudly to how much she liked Wyatt. And Wyatt seemed to like her right back, ruffling her soft ears and scratching her back whenever she was within reach. Fast friends. They paused several times to take pictures of the land, to sit on rocks and snack on beef jerky, or just to make out for a while. Jackson was quickly getting addicted to kissing Wyatt Gibson.

Sometimes Wyatt got super-quiet while they walked, and Jackson wasn't sure if Wyatt was mulling over everything Jackson told him this morning, or if Wyatt was thinking about his own past and reasons for being here. This mysterious search for his biological father that he refused to open up about. Jackson would help him if he asked, offer up his own limited resources, but Wyatt seemed determined to do this by himself.

But Jackson also valued honesty above all else, and he truly hoped Wyatt would open up. That they could both get to a place where they were comfortable sharing the hard parts of their pasts. Especially if they kept pursuing this thing sizzling between them.

Jackson wanted to pursue it for all the ways it made him feel alive inside; he was terrified of doing so for all the same reasons.

They returned to the motel midafternoon. Dog went straight for her water bowl, while Wyatt went straight for Jackson's dick. The blow job was spectacular, and Jackson eagerly returned the gesture. He had a couple of shelf-stable beef stew meals in his dresser that he nuked for an early dinner. They ate in their underwear, as comfortable as a couple who'd been dating for months, not just days.

If *dating* was the right word. He hoped so.

At one point they ended up lying in the bed of his pickup, legs dangling over the edge of the tailgate, as the sun sank lower on the horizon. It had been an amazing day, and Jackson plucked a blade of grass to whistle on, sending his music to the sky above. Wyatt seemed to take that as a challenge, picked his own piece of grass, and tried to remember what Jackson had taught him. He wasn't as good but he did his best, and it was a lot of fun. Whistling on grass in the January cold, with the gorgeous Texas land all around them.

Perfection in its own way.

And something Jackson didn't want to lose. But all good

things had an inevitable end and around five he drove Wyatt back to his car. The Tavern parking lot was pretty empty, with only a few early dinner stragglers coming in for cheap beer and greasy appetizers, so they kissed for a while. Jackson wasn't sure how he'd stop himself from kissing Wyatt at work tomorrow, but he'd manage. He was a grown-ass man, after all, and he'd learned his lesson about letting his libido guide him.

He waited until Wyatt drove away before moving to a different spot that gave him a better view of the bar's entrance. While he'd reported what he knew about the night Wyatt was drugged to the owner, Jackson couldn't help watching out for the two fuck-nuggets. He stayed for about two hours, watching for the guys, but didn't see them. Good. Even if they hadn't been the ones to roofie Wyatt, they'd definitely been planning to take advantage of his state. That made them predators in his book, period.

Work the next day was a challenge and a half, because Brand had him and Wyatt out riding the line again. Intellectually, Jackson knew it was to get Wyatt familiar with the pastures, the land borders, and comfortable riding Cobblepot so he could eventually be trusted out on his own, but it was still frustrating as hell, all alone with Wyatt and unable to touch him the way Jackson wanted. Wyatt seemed to be on his best behavior, though, only tossing him a handful of flirty smiles.

Then the kid somehow managed to cut the back of his hand while untacking his horse. It bled enough that instead of patching it with the first aid kid in the break room, Jackson sent him to see Rose in the main house. Wyatt came back twenty minutes later with a bandaged hand and a sugar cookie.

Michael, who'd been on barn duty that afternoon, snickered. "You sure know how to work a wound. You bring any cookies for the rest of us?"

Wyatt waved his bandaged hand in the air. "Trust me, this hurts like hell and was not done on purpose. If I want a home-baked cookie, I'll go to the store, buy a tube of premade dough, and bake them myself."

"That's not technically home-baked."

"Actually, it is. Baked at home. Just not homemade."

Michael opened and closed his mouth several times in an amusingly confused way. "Whatever. Enjoy the cookie and try not to harm yourself again today."

"Will definitely try not to do that. One injury per day is enough. I don't want to give Brand a reason to fire me." He shot Jackson a meaningful look that wasn't just about Wyatt's employment here.

Jackson winked and nodded in a way he hoped telegraphed what he couldn't say in front of Michael: that if Wyatt blew his trial period and wasn't hired on, Jackson would help. He'd help him stay in the area until he got the answers he was seeking. He'd help him stay so they could be together, because them together was so much better than alone.

For the first time in a long time, Jackson liked together a lot more than alone.

As January bled into February, the next few weeks took on a kind of routine, with Jackson and Wyatt as perfectly professional as possible during working hours, and then spending their shared days off holed up in Jackson's motel room having sex. All kinds of sex and really great sex. Jackson enjoyed bottoming for the eager younger man, and Wyatt never brought back up the idea of Wyatt switching things around, so Jackson didn't, either. They had fun, explored each other's body, and had some amazing orgasms.

The farm equipment consignment auction was the first

Saturday in February, and Hugo, Brand, and Rem had all
been active in preparing old Woods Ranch items for sale,
in between regular ranch duties. The whole thing was held
in a field adjacent to the Pearce property, and while Jackson was working that day and couldn't attend—not that he
was looking to buy a tractor or rototiller for himself—the
Woods family apparently made out well in selling their
stuff. Likewise, Wyatt passed the four-week mark of his
trial run without a single complaint to Jackson, so the
training was going well. Only four weeks left to prove he
could be a real horseman.

The only thing that bothered Jackson at all was Wyatt's
secret search for his birth father. They didn't talk about it
during their days off together, and they definitely didn't
discuss it at work. Jackson was crazy curious about Wyatt's
progress, and if he already had an idea of who the man was.
Between the combined populations of all the small towns
in Claire County, he had quite a few possibilities who'd be
the right age, which Jackson guessed to be forty and up.

Jackson knew with absolute certainty it wasn't him, because he hadn't grown up here or slept with any women
in his life.

Today, he'd met Wyatt at their favorite truck stop diner
for breakfast, and they'd left Wyatt's car there because
they planned on going back for a late lunch/early dinner
that afternoon. They were quickly becoming well-known
by the waitresses, which was fine. It was far enough from
Weston that they were unlikely to run into anyone they
knew. Both of them wanted to keep their relationship on
the down-low for right now. Ramie had a clue that Wyatt
was seeing someone, but so far she hadn't pressed him for
details. She just made the occasional joke to Wyatt about
him leaving home and sowing his wild oats.

Wyatt was definitely sowing some oats, but as far as

Jackson knew, he was only sowing them with him. They hadn't talked about exclusively dating each other, but Wyatt didn't have a whole lot of other free time to fuck around on him. Maybe he'd bring it up today.

One of their favorite things to do while chilling was spread a blanket out in the bed of Jackson's truck and park in different spots around the motel simply to talk and enjoy the view. Today a random rain burst ruined that plan, so they were lounging on the bed in just their jeans, their shirts and boots scattered around the floor. Wyatt's head rested in Jackson's lap, and Jackson was enjoying the soft tangle of Wyatt's hair in his fingers.

"We've been seeing each other a couple of weeks now," Jackson said, picking his words carefully so he didn't come across the wrong way. "You wanna keep doin' this, right?"

"Of course, I do." Wyatt gazed up at him, his lips pursed into an upside-down frown. "I love hanging out with you and the sex is fantastic. We get along. Do you want to keep seeing each other?"

"Definitely. I guess I can't help but wonder, because you're still so young and have never been in a serious relationship, if maybe you'll wanna explore...other options."

"Like see other people?" He shrugged, which wasn't very effective on his back. "Not really. I mean, yeah, I'm curious, but right now I really like what we're doing." A blush crept up his cheeks. "I really like you, Jackson."

"I like you, too." Jackson helped Wyatt sit up and face him. "So are we exclusively dating? Just you and me, until one of us says he's done?" Wyatt seemed briefly hurt by the idea that Jackson might dump him. "As things are right now, I have no intention of doing that. I don't trust easily, but so far you've earned it."

Wyatt smiled. "Then yeah, just you and me. I know I'm

young but I'm also incredibly stubborn when I set my mind on wanting something."

"Like finding your birth father?"

"Yes. And I'll tell you more about that at some point, I promise. I just…need more time before I confront him."

"So you think you know who he is?"

"Yes. I also really love my job at the ranch, and if confronting my Maybe Daddy hurts that in any way, or if I feel like I need to leave town, that'll really hurt me. I like it here, and Ramie's a dream roommate."

"You've got allies at the ranch, Wyatt. Me, Michael, Hugo, and the entire Woods family. We wouldn't let some stranger who dropped his sperm once upon a time and then disowned it run you out of town. You've got my word."

"Thank you."

The unfamiliar sound of an engine outside and gravel crunching sent Jackson's pulse racing. He never had visitors and definitely wasn't expecting anyone. He climbed off the bed and glanced out the window. One of the ranch pickups was pulling in beside Jackson's, and he quickly recognized Brand behind the wheel.

"It's Brand," he said.

"Shit, really?" Wyatt scrambled to his feet and yanked his shirt off the floor. "He can't find us together like this. Why's he even here?"

"How should I know? He's never been here before." Back during their arrangement, Brand never came over here for sex. They'd mostly fucked in the hayloft, occasionally in one of their trucks, because Jackson valued his privacy and solitude. His address was obviously in his personnel file, so it had to be serious for Brand to have hunted him down. Jackson didn't want to do something asshole-ish like ask Wyatt to hide in the closet, because he wasn't ashamed of their relationship. He just didn't want it mixed in with work.

Wyatt seemed to read his mind. He grabbed his boots and socks and bolted into the bathroom, closing the door quietly behind him. Jackson stared at the door until Brand knocking startled him back into his head. Brand stood on his stoop, hat in hand, an unfamiliar, tentative smile on his face.

"Hey, man, somethin' wrong?" Jackson asked.

"No, nothing's wrong. I just wanted to talk to you. About personal stuff."

"Oh, uh, come in then." He and Brand used to talk about personal stuff at work when no one else was around, usually in between stealing quickies in the barn. But when Brand ended their arrangement and asked to keep things professional at the ranch from now on, Jackson had taken that literally. Plus, Jackson knew from past experience, he wasn't the first person Brand turned to for advice. "Ramie busy?"

"Actually, this is only partly about me and I didn't want to spread your business to her, so I came here first."

"For the first time, too. A phone call would've been nice."

Brand seemed to notice his half-dressed state for the first time. "Shit, did I interrupt something? Were you, uh?" He made a jerking-off gesture.

"It's fine." Jackson gestured at the two sitting chairs. "So what's up, boss?"

"Well, first I was curious about you. You seem different at work recently. More upbeat, I guess."

"A good mood's a bad thing?"

"No, I guess I was wondering if you'd met someone? I know you'd rather have flings than serious relationships. You made that very clear while we were fucking around."

Jackson's heart skipped and it took all his self-control

not to glance at the bathroom door. He'd told Wyatt about his arrangement with Brand, but it was weird to be discussing it with Wyatt on the other side of the door. And Brand saying Jackson wasn't interested in serious relationships was a harsh slap at what he hoped to try to build with Wyatt.

Hiding in the bathroom like a teenager sneaking into a girl's room on a school night was a tacky thing to do, but Wyatt wasn't ready for Brand to know about him and Jackson. And there was no other explanation for two bare-chested men together in a motel room than they were fucking around. So he hid and tried not to eavesdrop, but the bathroom had a very thin door. When Brand dropped the "when we were fucking around," comment, Wyatt nearly dropped his boots.

He was so damned casual about saying it. Sure, Wyatt knew Jackson and Brand had been together and it ended a while ago, but it weirded Wyatt out now as much as it had when he first found out. Jackson used to sleep with Wyatt's Maybe—nope, not going there. He really didn't need those mental images in his head, especially after having just fucked Jackson.

"I'm not completely against a serious relationship," Jackson said. "But that wasn't what you wanted, so I never pushed for anything more than what we had. You threw me for a loop when you got serious with Hugo, but you two make each other happy. I see it every day. I'm happy for you guys."

"I know, and thank you. And if you happen to find someone who makes you happy, I'll be just as happy for you, too. Hand to God, no jealousy or anything."

"Thanks, Brand." He said something else too softly for Wyatt to make out, and as shitty as he felt for listening in, he couldn't stop now. Several long moments passed before their voices returned to normal levels. "So you said that was the first thing? Is there a second thing for me, or is that one for Ramie?"

Brand laughed. "I already know what Ramie will say. I wanted to get your opinion on something. I know it's going to seem really fast to some, because we haven't even been together a full year yet, but I want to give Hugo one of these."

"Holy shit, boss, are you proposing to Hugo?"

Wyatt nearly dropped his boots a second time. He hadn't even "met" his father officially yet, and he was getting another stepfather?

"No," Brand said. "Yes? Kind of? I want to promise him forever with this gesture, but I also don't want to push him into getting married if he isn't ready. It doesn't even have to be an official engagement."

"Do you think Hugo will go for that? He always struck me as the romantic type. I mean, the guy pined after you for ten years, and then he came back and won you."

"Yeah, he did. And we haven't brought up marriage or anything yet, I just want him to know I'm serious about us. I don't say 'I love you' a lot, because that's just not me."

"So you want to show him with a grand gesture."

"I do. And you know what? If Hugo says he wants to go straight to town hall for a marriage license and do it this weekend? I will in a heartbeat. The ranch is doing well, so there's no money issues to worry about. I just…" He made a noise, maybe a sigh, and Wyatt pressed his ear to the door. "I just want Hugo to be happy."

"I know and so does he. Congrats, boss, I mean it."

"Thank you."

No one spoke for long enough that Wyatt wondered if they were hugging, and he couldn't help a tiny pang of jealousy. Jealousy that made no sense. Sure, Wyatt and Jackson were now exclusively dating each other, but a hug was just a hug between boss and employee. And friends. And ex-lovers.

Not going there.

"So is there a third thing?" Jackson asked in a joking tone. "Or can I get back to what I was doing?"

"No, man, that was it. Thanks for listening. Again, I'm sorry for ambushing you. I really needed to talk this out away from the ranch."

"S'okay."

"See you at work tomorrow. And don't wear out that wrist."

They both laughed. Wyatt had been confused about a comment Brand made earlier, and now it hit him that Brand probably thought Jackson was sitting around jerking off. Wyatt smiled at the door. Jackson had definitely *gotten* off today. It sounded like a door opened and shut, but Wyatt still waited for Jackson to open the bathroom door.

He blinked hard against the bright light. "Um, hi. Come here often?"

Jackson snorted and kissed him. "You didn't have to hide, but I understand why you did. Hard to keep this a secret at the ranch if the boss finds us together like this. I guess you probably heard us talking."

"Yeah." Wyatt flinched, then followed Jackson into the main room. Dumped his stuff on a chair and sat on the bed beside Jackson. "So you and my May—my boss used to hook up here, I assume, so that's why he knows where you live?" Lame statement since he remembered too late Jackson saying Brand had never been here before, but Wyatt was still coming down off the adrenaline spike of nearly being caught in bed with Jackson.

"When we hooked up, Brand was still keepin' the fact

that he's bisexual a secret, so we used each other to scratch that itch, but not here. This was my place away from work, and even though what Brand and I did was personal, I didn't wanna mix my place with anyone who reminded me of work. So we mostly fucked in the barn. I was a little disappointed when he ended things, but I knew what we had was temporary. We'd both said it from the start." Jackson squeezed his knee. "I know I asked once before, but does knowing that bother you? Honestly?"

Yeah, but probably not for the reason you think, because I'm too stubborn to tell you who I think Brand really is. "Because you were fucking the boss but don't want the boss to know you're fucking a coworker? Not really. You said you try to keep work and sex separate because of your past, but you brought me here."

"You're different."

"I still remind you of work."

"You're not my boss."

Wyatt could accept that for now, and he liked knowing he was different, maybe *more* special for Jackson to break his own rules. "So we've both got our reasons for keeping this thing private."

"Right. And this is still new, so how about we give it a few weeks? Later on, if one of us starts feelin' different, maybe wants other people to know, we'll sit down and talk about it like grown-ups."

"Yes. Like grown-ups."

He didn't always feel like a grown-up. Some days he still felt like a kid seeking his parents' approval. Other days, he felt way too old for his age and life experience. Jackson made him feel mature, because he didn't treat Wyatt like he was a kid, didn't look down on his age or act superior because of his own. No one had ever treated Wyatt so carefully, like an equal, and he fell for the older man a little bit more that afternoon.

He still felt weird after hearing straight from Brand's mouth that Jackson and Brand used to fuck but had no way of explaining it to Jackson without revealing the truth of what he suspected. So he kept it to himself for now, grabbed Jackson by the shoulders and kissed him. A hard kiss full of intent, and Jackson got on board quickly. They shed their jeans, got back into bed, and that was all that mattered for a long time.

Chapter Fourteen

"Hey, man, who pissed in your boot this afternoon?" Michael leaned against the break room's doorway, both hands tucked into his jeans pockets, his expression mild but curious.

"No one, why?" Jackson asked. He stood at the coffeepot, waiting for some fresh coffee to brew while in between chores. His plan to spend the afternoon riding the fence line with Wyatt had been shot to hell a few hours ago, so why not tar his insides with the strong coffee blend Brand bought for the barn.

"You just seemed, I don't know, gruffer than usual. Are you mad at Wyatt for getting himself hurt again?"

Jackson grunted.

That morning, he'd taken Wyatt out on their horses to a quiet pasture so Wyatt could practice his roping skills. Mostly how to throw while mounted, and then throw while riding at different speeds, and it had all gone well. Wyatt said he liked it because some element of math was involved: speed, wind force, the speed of the animal he was trying to rope, plus how hard he could throw. It made sense to Jackson in an abstract way, because he just went with his gut when he roped.

They'd gone back to the barn for lunch, both smiling and exhausted from the work. As he dismounted, Wyatt turned his ankle and instead of grabbing the saddle for balance, he flailed and crashed backward into the wall elbow-first and jammed his funny bone. Brand had heard the commotion and helped Jackson get Wyatt settled on a chair in the break room with his ankle up. Rose came down from the house to inspect him. The ankle had been sore but not swollen.

Either way, Brand had sent Wyatt home with orders to elevate and ice that ankle, and to see a doctor right away if it started to swell.

Wyatt had looked so embarrassed and defeated over being sent home from tripping. Jackson had wanted so badly to hug him, to offer him some kind of comfort. All he did was stand outside and watch Wyatt drive away. Then he'd gone into one of the empty barn stalls and sent Wyatt a text: Rest easy, firebrand.

It wasn't a lot but it was all he could think to say.

Since Cobblepot was saddled, Michael rode her out with Jackson to check the line. The herd was in the west pasture right now, and it had rockier terrain, more places for a steer to get stuck or lost from the rest of them. Michael tried to initiate conversation several times, but Jackson's litany of one-word responses shut that down fast. Jackson wasn't trying to be rude, but it had been a week since Brand nearly found him and Wyatt together, and something about it still bothered him.

He just couldn't put his finger on what.

"I'm not mad at Wyatt," Jackson said. A little worried but not mad. If Wyatt had busted his ankle for real, that would have been a quick end to his brief employment contract. "We've all turned our ankle before. Brand's just bein' careful. The last thing the ranch's insurance needs is a worker's comp claim from some clumsy kid who keeps hurtin' himself on the land."

"Yeah, I'm a little surprised Brand hired such a walking disaster, but at least they've all been minor injuries so far."

"So far." Jackson grabbed one of the dozen assorted mugs kept on hand for staff and set it on the small counter too hard. The handle broke off in his hand. "Shit." He glared at his hand, annoyance level rising.

"You cut yourself?"

"No. Just clumsy today too, I guess." He dropped the broken mug in the trash and reached for another, much gentler this time.

Michael moved closer. "You can tell me to fuck off and mind my business, but if you need to vent about anything, Josiah says I'm a good listener."

"He's your boyfriend. You'd better be a good listener with him."

"Not all men are, not even with their partners." Something in Michael's eyes flickered, probably his own past and being taken to the cleaners by his cheating ex-husband.

Jackson wasn't much for discussing his personal business at work, but he decided to take a chance here. "Even when you were in Austin and thought you were happy with your life and career, did you ever get lonely?"

"All the time. It's very easy to be lonely in a crowd of people. You second-guessing some of your life choices?"

"Not second-guessing so much as reexamining. I love my life here, and I love this job, but living in such a small town can be, well, stifling. All I really know are small towns, though, and I'd rather be in one than a big city, but it's hard to…"

"Meet people out here?"

"Yeah." And when he did meet someone he could care a lot about, he couldn't tell anyone because of a semi-inappropriate work relationship, a huge age gap, and because his boyfriend wanted to keep it a secret, at least until his probation period was up. Maybe in a few more weeks, when Wyatt was officially a cowboy, he'd want to come out.

Jackson sure hoped so. He was falling for Wyatt a little bit at a time, and maybe it was nowhere close to love yet, but Jackson could almost see it one day.

"Uh-oh, I know that look," Michael said, grinning now. "Is there someone?"

"Kind of, but it's complicated."

"Like 'fucking around with Brand' complicated?"

Jackson stared, the hand holding his hot coffee trembling once. "What?"

"I'm sorry, man, I don't know the details. I happened to overhear Brand and Hugo talking about it once in the barn, and I didn't stop to eavesdrop when I realized it was a personal conversation and not about work. It wasn't my business."

With a grunt of annoyance, Jackson put the coffee down. "Not 'sleeping with the boss' complicated, no, but he's not out and has his reasons. We both have our reasons for bein' discreet about things, I just…" He crossed his arms. "Until recently, I never used to feel lonely when I was alone. I liked the solitude. Craved it most of the time, because I spent too many years forced to be around other people and do what I was told. I like the freedom of my life, but sometimes the other side of the bed feels real empty."

"I get that. You talk to him about your feelings?"

"Not yet. We both agreed to give it some time, and I don't wanna pressure him if he isn't ready to be out."

"Which is perfectly reasonable and very kind of you, man. But you have to consider your own feelings, too. Maybe this one is just the guy for now, and not the guy forever."

Jackson held Michael's gaze. "You think Josiah is your forever guy?"

Michael's smile was his answer even before Michael said, "I think so. I hope so. It's still pretty new, but we love each other and we're trying to make it work every single day. That's all any of us really can do, right?"

"Right."

"Anyway, I'll stop bugging you. But if you need a friend to talk to, you can come to me. I didn't really get to know my coworkers all that well in my old life, because that life was all about coding and the programs, not the people. I want to change that here."

"I think I do, too." Jackson held out his hand, and they shook. "Thanks for the chat."

"Anytime."

After Michael left, Jackson took his coffee to the break room table and sat for a minute, his thoughts dancing all around each other. Everything he'd said to Michael about being lonely was true. Loneliness was an emotion he never expected to feel again, not after the first half of his life, but here he was. On a ranch in northern Texas, working with a guy he really liked, and unable to show the world how amazing he was. Or how great Jackson felt about himself when he was around Wyatt. But coming out as a couple was bigger than just Jackson's feelings. Wyatt also got a say.

He knew their arrangement wouldn't last forever. Wyatt would either get bored with him or find someone new (and younger) and move on, either from Jackson, the ranch, or both at once. And Jackson could live with that, as long as Wyatt found what truly made him happy. If discovering his birth father made Wyatt happy, Jackson would do whatever he could to help him do exactly that.

Wyatt felt like a dumbass fool for twisting his ankle this morning, and he grumped his way through the afternoon by bingeing a TV show Jared had been begging him to watch. It was entertaining, with funny dialogue, and some good eye candy. Ice packs and ibuprofen kept his ankle from swelling, thank God, so he'd be good to work tomorrow. What he really wanted was a cold beer, but Ramie kept count of the ones she brought home like a good big sister would. He didn't mind the coddling. In some ways, she reminded him of his mom, with her kindness and bright smile—both things Mom had lost as cancer slowly stole her away.

A little after seven, Jackson texted him: How's your ankle?

It's fine, not swollen. Barely hurts anymore.

Good news. Ramie at work?

Yeah, I think she's on until two. Bored by TV.

Want some company?

Wyatt hesitated, fingers hovering over the keyboard. He did want company, and he wanted it to be Jackson's company. Someone could see you.

I'll park one block over and walk. But if you're uncomfortable, it's okay.

Part of him *was* uncomfortable, but the idea of them being caught was a little thrill all its own. They'd be done "hanging out" long before Ramie got home. Bring beer?

Jackson sent back a laughing emoji. See you in a bit.

That wasn't a yes or no on the beer, so Wyatt didn't anticipate anything. He did pop into the bathroom to brush his teeth and clean up a little, though he was unsure why. Jackson had kissed him with morning breath before without complaint. But this was Wyatt's place and he wanted to make a good impression. He also had no idea if Jackson had ever been here before, but he was guessing probably yes, since Jackson hadn't asked for the address.

The house was tidy, so he didn't have much to do except wait. They hadn't agreed this was a booty call, a quiet movie night, or a combination of both, and Wyatt was definitely down for both. He missed Jackson's quiet touches and sweet smiles that he only shared when they were alone. He also missed the harsh way Jackson kissed him mixed with the tender brushes of lips and tongue. Revving him up and then slowing him down. Taming him like any good cowboy would with a wild colt.

Jackson knocked on the door a little before eight, and he held up a six-pack of beer. Nonalcoholic beer.

"Really?" Wyatt asked as he ushered him inside.

"What? I'm not gonna contribute to the delinquency of a minor. Beer taste and no alcohol."

"Thank God I'll be twenty-one in a few months. I can drink like a normal person."

"You just got too used to drinkin' in college."

"Probably." Wyatt put the six-pack on the coffee table, then leaned in to properly kiss his boyfriend. "Hey, you. Want to make out?"

"Absolutely. But first, I was wondering if you wanted to do somethin' we haven't done together yet."

"Oh yeah? Like what?"

"Watch a movie."

Wyatt's lips parted, and he started to say they had, but no, they hadn't. Jackson had a TV, but no cable or internet, only an old VHS player. Wyatt had always been more interested in hanging out or fooling around when at his place, and none of the library tapes had looked all that exciting. They occasionally watched short videos on Wyatt's phone, especially if he found something he thought Jackson might find particularly funny.

But no, they'd never sat down together to watch a whole movie.

"Okay, let's do that," Wyatt said.

"Great."

Jackson seemed a touch befuddled by Ramie's streaming setup, which was kind of adorable in its own way, especially for a guy who was only forty. Wyatt navigated them to an app he liked. "So what's your pleasure? We've got all genres, all kinds of things to choose from, even live sports."

"Never been much into sports, but I'll support our Texas teams when I need to. You didn't seem keen on the tapes I'd rented from the library, so what's something you like?"

"Honestly, I used to play a lot more video games than I watched movies, but most of those games were about zombies or science fiction adventures, so I guess stuff like that." Wyatt clicked through until he found a recent zombie thriller that looked good. "How about this?"

"Go for it."

"Want popcorn first?"

"Sure."

Wyatt threw a bag of popcorn into the microwave, and in less than three minutes they were settled close together on the couch with their fake beer and popcorn. The movie was pretty good, but Wyatt found himself paying closer attention to Jackson. The way he'd tense at a suspenseful part or cringe when someone got hurt, like he actually cared about the characters on-screen. He liked seeing this emotional side of Jackson. A lot.

Their fingers brushed constantly in the popcorn bowl,

and they each drank two beers. It tasted fine but lacked the slight buzz of real beer.

Why did I have to date a responsible older man?

He kind of liked it, though. Jackson looked out for him. Ramie looked out for him. His coworkers at the ranch did the same in their own ways. After leaving his entire family behind in Glasbury, it was nice to have found one again. One that accepted him. And one he'd hurt if the truth came out about why he'd come here in the first place. As the days and weeks passed, and he settled in with the people around him, he feared telling them the truth.

What if I give up the search, say nah to Maybe Daddy, and just live my life?

Giving up on proving Brand was his father would only prove his stepfather right, that this had been a waste of time. Only it hadn't, because Wyatt had found something very special here with these people. Especially with Jackson. What more did he need to prove to his stepfather? Nothing, not really.

He leaned his head against Jackson's shoulder and smiled through the rest of the movie. Wyatt barely registered the ending. It was a few minutes after ten, so not super-late. Jackson stood and stretched, and several vertebrae popped. "Listen to you snap-crackling, old man," Wyatt teased.

"Old man? I would pick you up and sling you over my shoulder for that if I didn't have to piss so bad."

"Sure, likely story. Bathroom's down the hall."

"I know."

Wyatt bit back on the urgent need to ask how he knew until Jackson returned. "You've been here before?"

"One time, yeah." He stood near the TV, hands in his pockets. "Might not be my place to say it, but Brand and Ramie used to have a sex-only arrangement, too. One night

the pair of them got wasted, and Brand called me for a ride.
I brought them back here and tucked them in."

"Oh. Okay." It shouldn't surprise him that Brand probably had former fuck buddies all over the county, but hadn't
someone said Ramie was Brand's best friend? Seemed
weird to Wyatt, but okay. Maybe some people were able
to fuck and still be friends? Or maybe they were friends
first? Whatever, that wasn't his business.

"You really have so much to learn about how complicated adult relationships can be," Jackson said.

His gentle smile was the only thing that kept Wyatt from
taking offense at the statement. "I know more than you
think. My family is plenty fucking complicated. Maybe
that's part of the reason I decided to come out here and
look for something new. Get away from the drama and
expectations and letdowns."

"Letdowns like what?"

"Like my grandparents knowing who my bio family is
and refusing to contact them. Refusing to tell me when my
mother was dying so I could reach out to them. She needed
a liver transplant and was on a list, and a lot of folks we
knew got tested. I thought more options might help her.
But my family was always like that. Keep your secrets
and don't tell, no matter how much it hurts other people."

Jackson took a few steps closer, hands falling to his
sides. "Is that why you don't want my help finding your
bio dad?"

"That's a huge part of it. I grew up learning how to keep
things secret. Telling is bad, and that became a huge life
lesson after my stepbrother was arrested."

Jackson's eyebrows went up but he didn't comment.

His quiet encouragement helped Wyatt sit on the couch
and keep talking, glad when Jackson sat beside him. "I was
just a kid when it happened, because he's older than me.

When he was fourteen, Peter and a friend of his did something that led to the harm of another person, but at first no one knew it was them. But his friend's conscience got the better of him, so he told what they'd done."

"His friend told the truth."

"Yeah. But my stepfather was furious, not just at Peter for what he'd done, but at his friend for narcing on them and getting them both arrested. Both boys got probation and community service but the damage was done. My stepfather sat me and my stepsister, Lily, down and basically said if we ever told on a friend like that, he'd use a horse whip on us until we couldn't sit for a month."

Wyatt had seen his stepfather wield that leather whip, often at county fair demonstrations, sometimes on real horses. The cracking sound still made him jump from absolute fright. He glanced over at Jackson, whose face was flushed, his eyes narrowed. Anger wafted off him like a bad smell that initially frightened Wyatt.

And then it hit him: Jackson wasn't furious at him. He was furious on his behalf for something that happened half a lifetime ago.

"Did your stepfather ever beat you?" Jackson asked with a snarl in his voice.

"Spanked me twice when I was younger. Once for breaking Mom's favorite vase, and the other time for stealing some jumbo syringes from his clinic to use as mini water guns. But that's what put the fear of God in me about telling secrets, especially if it's a secret that'll get someone else hurt."

Jackson took his hand and squeezed, eyes glittering with emotion. "I can understand that. But sometimes secrets can eat away at you. Sometimes it's okay to tell."

"Maybe." Wyatt still wasn't convinced but he did accept Jackson's point of view.

"You said that was part of the reason you don't want help?"

Since he was spilling all kinds of truths tonight, he might as well go all in with this one. "I'm afraid of being disappointed in who my bio dad is, of him slamming the door in my face." Unlikely, if it was Brand, but Wyatt had a feeling that finding out why Brand abandoned him before he was even born was going to hurt just as much as being dismissed like an unwanted salesman. "I'm scared of confronting him."

"So you know who he is?"

Time to choose his words carefully. "I know who I suspect he is, but my grandparents spent my whole life telling me that my bio father and his family were awful people, and my mom never defended him. They were like the Manson family or those cannibals from the Leatherface movies, so for a long time I didn't want to know who he was."

"But then your mother died."

"Yeah." Wyatt pressed his shoulder against Jackson's, grateful for how well Jackson seemed to understand him. "They could have tried harder to help her but they didn't because *secrets*, you know?"

"I understand secrets. My adoptive parents were awful people at home, but to the rest of the town? We were a Sunday service–attending, God-fearing, loving family who worked hard and supported each other. None of us were allowed to talk about what happened behind closed doors. When you're taught not to trust and to keep secrets, especially as a kid, it sticks with you."

"Yeah." He didn't mean for his voice to be so hoarse. So many emotions were rattling around inside and he couldn't stop a few from getting out.

Jackson kissed his temple. "Where's your room?"

"My room?"

"It's not what you think, I promise. Show me?"

"Sure." Wyatt was not in a sexy mood but he trusted Jackson not to force anything tonight. He led him down the short hall to his room, which was still decorated exactly the way Ramie had left it, with the slight additions of Wyatt's phone charger and a framed photo of his mom.

Jackson, naturally, zeroed in on that picture. "You look like her, and not just the red hair. You have her eyes, too."

"A lot of people say that. About my eyes, I mean. The hair color is kind of obvious."

"Just a little."

Wyatt didn't protest when Jackson led him over to the bed, or when he gently arranged them on their sides, Jackson curled up behind him. Strong, warm arms wrapped around his chest, and they wiggled a bit until they comfortably shared a pillow. Wyatt closed his eyes, leaned into Jackson, and inhaled Jackson's familiar scent. He hadn't showered so he smelled of sweat and horse and a hard day's work, and Wyatt couldn't think of anything sexier.

Not that his dick cared right then. All he wanted to do was exist for a while.

Which he did, until the sound of Ramie shouting his name startled him awake so hard and fast he nearly rolled off the bed.

Chapter Fifteen

Wyatt hadn't meant to fall asleep, and he really didn't expect to be woken up by Ramie yelling for him from elsewhere in the house. He was half sitting on the edge of the bed, his room only lit by a light in the hall and streetlight from outside, and he couldn't quite figure out what was happening.

"Wyatt! Where are you?"

"In here!" It wasn't until the bedspread rustled behind him and the bed bounced that he remembered Jackson. Crap.

Ramie raced into the room, cell phone in one hand and some kind of long wrench in the other. "Are you okay?" She stopped short. "Oh, hey."

"I'm fine, why?" He ignored her acknowledgment of Jackson for now, because he'd never seen her frantic like this before. "What happened?"

"As I was coming home, I saw someone trying to break into your car. I don't think they know I saw them right away, because they tried to hide, but I parked across the street, grabbed my wrench, and called the police. They took off while I was talking, and the front door wasn't completely shut, and I got worried."

It took him a few seconds to absorb all that. "Someone was breaking into my car?"

"Yeah."

"Fuck."

Wyatt bolted out of the room. While he didn't have much of value to steal other than the car itself, why would anyone around here want to steal it? Somehow Jackson beat him to the front door and blocked Wyatt from going outside.

"Are you sure you wanna go out there?" Jackson asked. "Maybe you should wait until the law shows up."

"Whoever did it is probably long gone."

"Probably, but I need you safe."

The plea in Jackson's voice kept Wyatt inside. He stared at his car through the screen door, unable to see it clearly where it was parked by the curb. He didn't want to have to deal with repairs, especially with all the information under Jared's name, so hopefully there wasn't any damage. Although he'd still have to deal with the cops and explain why he was driving a car not registered to him.

Jared was going to be pissed.

Ramie had relaxed a lot by the time a sheriff's cruiser pulled up next to Wyatt's car. She hadn't spoken a word about finding Jackson in Wyatt's bed, and he adored her for her discretion—although he'd probably get questions later. A short man in uniform climbed out of the car and put his hat on before striding up the driveway to the house.

"I'm Acting County Sheriff Bloomberg," he said from the porch. "I'm responding to a report of a possible break-in."

"Right," Ramie replied. She described what had happened in slightly more detail than she'd given Wyatt, because Wyatt knew where she worked, why she got home so late, and that Wyatt was her roommate, so she knew his car. She simply introduced Jackson as a friend of Wyatt's. "He ran that way and into the neighbor's yard." She pointed.

"Can you give me any sort of physical description?"

"Not really. Average height, I guess. Probably male from the body shape but they were wearing a black ski mask or something. Black clothes. I couldn't see much of anything."

"Were they carrying anything? A weapon?"

"Something long and slender, like maybe one of those things locksmiths use to break into a car when you lock your keys in, but I can't be sure."

"Anything about the way they ran? A limp or particular way they moved?"

"No, not that I noticed."

Bloomberg asked Ramie a few more questions before turning his attention to Wyatt, who stood near the couch with Jackson an arm's reach away, a silent protector. "And you are the owner of the vehicle in question?"

"Actually, no, it belongs to my best friend Jared. He's letting me borrow it for a while."

"I'm going to need his contact information."

"Okay. I can give you that. He, uh, did sign a letter giving me permission to drive the car. We've shared it for like two years, so I keep that in the glove box just in case."

"That's good to know, thank you."

He asked a few more random questions, before asking them to stay inside while he inspected the car. Wyatt watched from the door, unsure what was happening or the next step. He should probably call Jared himself with a heads-up but didn't want to get in trouble if Bloomberg needed to do it first. He really wanted to be able to tell Jared there was no damage to the car. Not that it was an amazing, new-model sports car or anything, but it was Jared's car.

Bloomberg finally came back inside. "There's evidence of damage to the trunk area, but I'll need Mr. Gibson to verify if it was already there or if it's fresh."

"Okay. That was the only place?"

"Only obvious place I saw, but I'm going to contact the state police and have someone come over and dust for prints, take a few samples. Might not find anything, and it could be as simple as some neighborhood kid playing a prank."

"I just don't know why anyone would break into my trunk."

"Hard to say. I haven't heard about a rash of car break-ins around town, so it's possible this was a onetime thing."

"Or a first attempt by an inept thief," Jackson said.

Bloomberg's gaze zeroed in on Jackson. "I know you, I think. You work out at Woods Ranch. Seen you around a bit."

"Yes, sir, I do. Work out there with Wyatt."

"And you were here at two in the morning because?"

Wyatt's heart thudded, but Jackson's cool expression never wavered. "Wyatt twisted his ankle at work today on my watch. I came over to chill and watch a movie. It got late and we both fell asleep."

All completely true, and Bloomberg seemed to buy it. "Come on with me, Mr. Gibson."

Wyatt followed him to the car and verified the scrapes in the paint had not been there before tonight. They weren't awful but they were noticeable. Fantastic. He also opened the car and showed Bloomberg all the paperwork, including his own license.

"You're a long way from Glasbury," Bloomberg said as he wrote things down in his notebook.

"I wanted a new start and to try my hand at being a cowboy. Woods Ranch happened to be hiring right when I was looking, and I was lucky enough to get the job. I'm sure when I've got more saved up I'll be able to get my own car and give Jared his back."

"Of course. I remember what it was like to be your age and struggling."

He was struggling a bit but not in the way Bloomberg probably meant. Wyatt was okay financially. No, he was struggling emotionally, and tonight's conversation with Jackson had him doubting so many of his decisions. It challenged the child in him who refused to tell secrets because he feared his stepfather's horse whip.

A state police officer arrived not long after, along with a CSI person, and a whole new conversation began. Wyatt was exhausted by the time the entire production was over and grateful they didn't have to impound his car as evidence or any such shit. The officer didn't seem very interested or hopeful they'd ever find the person, because Ramie had no real description and the neighborhood had no traffic cameras. He seemed to agree with Bloomberg it was likely a teenager responding to a dare, but that they should still keep an eye out.

Wyatt did one better. As soon as everyone left, he asked Jackson to help him take everything out of the car except the spare tire and jack. Everything else went into his bedroom, including some loose change and the emergency roadside kit. The kit wouldn't do him much good in the house, but Jared had seemed worried about it the last time he called so better safe than sorry.

He felt a tiny bit better when they were finished. Ramie asked him if he wanted to start parking in the driveway for a while, but he said no. If someone was pulling pranks, he didn't want Ramie's car damaged, too.

Then their trio was standing awkwardly in the living room, no one speaking. Wyatt had no clue what to say, Ramie seemed to have too much she wanted to say, and Jackson simply looked uncomfortable.

"Okay, look," Ramie finally said, "I don't care what

you guys were actually up to tonight, because it's not my business. I won't say anything to anyone about you being in bed together."

"We really did just fall asleep," Wyatt replied.

"In your bed."

"He was comforting me after an intense conversation."

"And you're just friends."

"Mm-hmm."

She sighed. "Like I said, not my business. You two do you. Or do each other, I don't care, I'm going to bed. Lock up after he leaves. Night, Jackson."

"Night, Ramie," Jackson said to her departing back.

Once her bedroom door closed, Wyatt could breathe a bit more easily, but his stomach was still an angry ball of acid. "Well, that was a clusterfuck if I ever saw one," Wyatt said.

"I'm real sorry someone tried to break into your car. There ain't a lotta crime around here because most folks know each other."

"Yeah, well, maybe it really was some stupid teenage prank." He allowed Jackson to fold him into a warm, firm hug that helped ease some of the acid in his gut. He pressed his face into the side of Jackson's neck and breathed. "This is nice."

"It is. I didn't mean for us to fall asleep but I'm glad I was here for all this."

"Even though Ramie knows?"

"Ramie is very discreet. I trust her to keep us bein' in bed together to herself."

"Me too." If Jackson, who was incredibly slow to trust, trusted Ramie about this then Wyatt would, too. "And I'm glad you were here. Jared's going to kill me."

"Why? You didn't do anything wrong."

"I don't know." He pulled back far enough to look Jackson in the eyes. "Things were a little off between us when

I left. Like, he supported my choice to come here and do this, but he also didn't approve. Does that make sense?"

"It does." A new kind of protectiveness and affection simmered in the depths of Jackson's dark brown eyes, and Wyatt soaked it in. He hoped his own eyes reflected something similar. "I should probably go."

As much as Wyatt wanted to ask him to stay, he knew Jackson wouldn't. Not only to keep their secret, but because he had Dog waiting for him at home. Wyatt was incredibly fond of the cute mutt, and she was probably missing her daddy like crazy. "See you at work tomorrow," Wyatt said. "Give Dog a kiss for me."

Jackson laughed. "Kiss her yourself next time. Try to get some sleep, okay? And if you want, we can look into installing an alarm system in your car."

We. "Maybe. Thank you." He kissed his boyfriend at the front door, then watched him disappear down the semi-lit street. A tiny flash of worry over this mysterious car thief wiggled down his spine, but it disappeared quickly. Jackson was more than capable of taking care of himself.

Still. He pulled out his phone.

Wyatt: Text me when you get home. Please.

He was lying in bed, in the dark, trying not to fall asleep when his phone pinged with a reply.

Jackson: Home. Sleep now.

Wyatt smiled and closed his eyes, then welcomed sleep with open arms.

Jackson was dragging a bit when he arrived at the ranch for work, despite having drank about an entire pot of coffee before leaving the motel. He'd been exhausted when he arrived home but his brain was still full of Wyatt, the confessions from last night, how much he loved falling asleep with Wyatt in his arms, and then the drama of the car thief. He was so grateful to have been there for Wyatt, even if he'd mostly stood by and offered silent support. Wyatt's thanks had been sincere, and Jackson only wished he could have done more. He'd had half a mind to whisk Wyatt away to the motel for the night, but that would have just complicated things even more.

Not that they weren't already complicated with Ramie basically in on their secret relationship, and now the acting sheriff knew Jackson and Wyatt had a friendship beyond the ranch. Not that Jackson expected the news to get back to Brand or anyone else at the ranch, because why would it? Weston was a small town, but he didn't see many folks gossiping about an interrupted car theft. Or interrupted theft of its contents, since the only damage was to the trunk and not one of the doors.

Knowing that made Jackson lean more toward teenage prank. Pop the trunk open and run! Or get in and steal the spare tire! Something bored, idiot teens would dare their friend to do just to post on social media and prove how brave he was. Still, it irritated him that of all the cars on the road, they'd picked Wyatt's to break into. If the cops actually caught whoever it was, Jackson would relish the chance to scare the holy hell out of them to keep them from doing anything so stupid again.

He had to piss like crazy when he got to the ranch, so he headed toward the bunkhouse. Hands used to use the downstairs bathroom of the main house, until the bunkhouse was cleaned up and converted back into a livable space. Brand and Hugo didn't mind the hands using that bathroom, because they were all respectful of the fact that the pair lived there. No one went into their shared bedroom, or into Brand's office without permission.

He opened the bunkhouse door in time to see Hugo and Brand in the midst of what looked like a pretty passionate kiss near their bedroom door. Not wanting to interrupt, Jackson backed up a few steps until they broke apart. Hugo spotted him first and flashed an "oops" smile in Jackson's direction.

"Mornin'," Jackson said. "Sorry, drank too much coffee."

"No worries," Hugo replied. "I'm heading out. See you in the barn."

"Yeah."

Hugo darted past him. Brand nodded in his direction without saying anything, so Jackson went to the can. Did his business. Brand was in the same spot when he came out, watching him with an indecipherable expression. "You need somethin', boss?" Jackson asked.

"Huh?" Brand blinked dumbly several times. "Oh, sorry. I got lost in thought, is all."

"Thinking about that thing we talked about last week?"

"Kind of. Hugo and I had a long talk last night about a lot of stuff, mostly our commitment to each other and to making this work for the long haul. Getting married one day down the road, when we're both ready. I didn't give him the ring yet, but now…" He grinned. "When I do it'll be a real proposal. Even if it's a long-term engagement, I wanna marry him."

"I'm glad. You two make sense together."

"We do. More than I ever thought possible. You find somebody who makes you feel that way, Jackson, you hold on tight."

"I'll do my best." Wyatt was someone Jackson could see himself with for a long time, but the fact that Wyatt still had one big secret he was keeping from Jackson worried him.

Wyatt's age also kept him from going all in with the kid this soon into them dating. Yes, they were exclusive. Yes, Jackson was incredibly happy with him. Yes, he wanted things to last far into the future.

No, he wasn't one hundred percent positive they would.

"There's that look again," Brand said. "You get it every once in a while. You sniffing around someone?"

He didn't want to lie to his boss, who'd asked a direct question this time, so he skated around the truth as best he could. "There's someone who makes me happy, yes. But it's real fresh and not somethin' we're tellin' people right now."

"Understood, and I won't push. I wasn't exactly open and honest about being with Hugo when we first got together, so if things are complicated with this person, I'll back off until you're ready to talk about it."

"Thanks." If Jackson were the only one involved here, he might have spilled his guts to Brand about his feelings for Wyatt, if for nothing else than to get his friend's opinion on the situation. But Wyatt wasn't out, and it was not Jackson's place to out him, especially not to his boss. Not that Brand would care, but it was the principle of the thing. He and Wyatt made an agreement, and Jackson wouldn't break it.

Maybe he could get Ramie's advice? Since she was already somewhat in the know after last night's incident.

"I should get to work," Jackson said. "Me and Wyatt are workin' on his ropin' skills again this morning."

"Then get to it. He still has some things to learn, but Wyatt is working out a lot better than I honestly expected. Hiring someone with no experience is always a risk, but you've been an excellent teacher."

In more ways than you know. "Thanks, boss."

Jackson left the bunkhouse and headed for the barn.

Wyatt's car was there, as was Rem's truck. Pretty sure today was Michael's day off. They could run the ranch well with the number of hands they had, but calving season was coming up, and they always needed extra help then. Part of the herd would be ready for slaughter soon, too, and separating the steer they wanted to butcher from the ones that needed to continue growing could get tricky. Wyatt might not be ready for that, but Alan would probably be back and working when the time rolled around.

None of that was really for Jackson to worry about. Running those things was Brand's job, with input from Wayne. Jackson knew Wayne hoped to retire soon and step back from daily operations, but he also imagined it was difficult to let go of something that had been part of his life since he could walk. Generations of Woodses had grown up here, run the land, and been buried both here and in nearby church graveyards.

Jackson had no idea where his own roots were buried. Sometimes, when he thought about Wyatt's search for his biological father, he did give serious thought to his own past. The people who'd created him, why they'd given him up when he was three, and if he had biological family out there somewhere who remembered he existed. Other times, he told himself it didn't matter, because his family was here in Weston and on Woods Ranch. Dog was his family. Wyatt was his family. He didn't need more than that.

The next few days passed much as the previous few weeks. He kept training Wyatt during the day, whipping (metaphorically) the accident-prone younger man into a proper cowboy during paid hours, and exploring their sizzling chemistry off-hours. Wyatt had been grumpy after his conversation with Jared over the car issue, but Jackson had cheered him up quickly with a blow job. Even Dog seemed to anticipate Wyatt's visits to the motel.

For the first time in a long damned time, Jackson was content. Not just happy and enjoying his life, but content in the things and people around him. He had a boyfriend he adored, a job he loved, plenty of open space around him to explore, and enough money in his pocket to feed himself and his four-legged best friend. He really didn't need much more than that—except maybe the support of the people around him regarding his relationship.

With each day that passed, Jackson found himself wanting more and more for others to know he was dating a pretty terrific guy and that they were happy. But they'd agreed to wait a few weeks, give them both time to settle into things, before discussing it again.

Doubt began creeping in around the edges the closer they drew to the end of Wyatt's probation period. Had Jackson simply been a distraction? A mistake? Someone fun to fuck around with while he got his Cowboy Degree?

Jackson hated second-guessing himself so much, but Wyatt fucked with his head in all kinds of ways. He both loved it and hated it. Loved because he'd never been with someone who challenged him so much; hated because Jackson liked being in charge and fully aware at all times. He had no idea what to do, so he existed in this strange, nebulous space between the comfort of his old life and the excitement of something new just on the horizon but still out of reach. And for a while, it was enough.

Chapter Sixteen

Wyatt's plan had been to put off talking to Jared for as long as possible—which turned out to be about eighteen hours, since Bloomberg had to contact him about the police report and attempted break-in. The conversation hadn't been great.

"Someone tried to steal my car?" Jared had asked over the phone, his voice bizarrely shrill. It wasn't as if the car was worth that much. Hell, Jared might have gotten more back on insurance if it *had* been stolen.

"It was probably just kids playing a prank," Wyatt replied, doing his best to soothe his friend. "They tried to break into the trunk, not the actual car, and nothing was stolen. I put pretty much everything in the house, so it's cool."

"Yeah, so cool. Damn, man, maybe you should just forget this cowboy crap and come home."

Wyatt glared at his bedroom wall. He'd just gotten home from work when Jared called. "It's not crap. I really love what I do at the ranch, okay? When was the last time you really loved your job?"

"I'm getting there, I just need to find what I love to do."

Other than sit on your ass and play video games. Wyatt kept that thought to himself. "I'm not going to forget it. I like my job, I'm keeping an eye on the car, and I think I'm getting close to finally confronting my Maybe Daddy."

"Really?"

"Yeah." Okay, so not really. Wyatt was still caught between his need to know for sure if Brand was his bio dad and his desire to protect the small, precious family he'd found here in Weston. Confronting Brand would blow everything up, and Wyatt had no idea if the pieces would fall in any reparable way. But continuing to keep this secret from Jackson only increased the odds of Jackson finding out from someone else and feeling betrayed. He never wanted Jackson, with his big heart and cargo ship's worth of personal baggage, to ever feel like Wyatt had betrayed him. Jackson was too fucking special, and Wyatt cared about him too damned much.

Wyatt had a huge choice to make in the next few weeks. And a serious conversation to have with Jackson before his boyfriend had a chance to feel even remotely betrayed by the secret Wyatt had kept this entire time.

"So once you have this confrontation with Maybe Daddy," Jared said, "does that mean you'll pack up and come home?"

"I don't know, okay? I have no idea how this confrontation or conversation, or whatever you want to call it, is going to go. I might be run out of town and head straight back to Glasbury. I might get an acceptable explanation and decide to stay, I just don't know."

"Well, then can you figure out some other way to drive around? I need the car back with all my stuff that was in it."

Wyatt frowned at no one in particular. "Dude, I said I was sorry about the trunk. I'll pay to fix the paint if you want, but nothing was stolen."

"That's not the point, man."

"So does that mean you got a job and can afford to pay the loan and insurance?" Silence. "Didn't think so. It's stupid for you to take a car you can't drive."

"Okay, fine. Shit. Then can you mail me back the road-side kit?"

"The what?" Had Jared lost his fucking mind? "You want a roadside kit for a car you don't have? Are you high, dude?"

"The kit was a present from my grandma, okay? It's sentimental. Buy your own."

"Yeah, whatever." And Wyatt thought his own deal was strange. Jared was about to win a prize for bizarre requests. "I'll mail it back when I get a chance, fuck."

"Tomorrow."

Not a chance, since he worked all day and the Weston post office was only open from nine to one every week-day. "I'll mail it. Talk to you later." Wyatt had ended the call and flopped onto the bed on his back, exhausted by the brief conversation.

He lay there, gazing up at the popcorn ceiling, confused by the bizarre way Jared was acting. At first, he'd been to-tally fine with Wyatt taking the car for an extended road trip. Maybe Wyatt hadn't said he could be gone for as long as two months, but he was here now, with the car, and that was that. Not like Jared was going to go the fourth-grade route of reporting the car stolen just to get back at him. Jared would just have to deal with it for now, until Wyatt knew for sure what he was going to do.

One thing he was not going to do was go out of his way to mail a damned emergency roadside kit you could buy at any Walmart in the state. He'd never known Jared to be incredibly sentimental, so he could wait for his package.

Ramie's headlights flashed in his window, and he checked the time on his phone. A little after seven. Must have had a day shift if she was home already. Wyatt didn't always pay attention to her schedule, even though she posted it on the fridge. He lounged there for a while, his thoughts muddled by his conversation with Jared, and listened to the vague creaks of Ramie moving around in the kitchen. Then a long period of silence.

She hadn't gone to her room. The television was off. Even if she was eating a late dinner in the kitchen, she usually played music or something. She said once that she didn't like total silence; silence was too loud, so she filled it with background noise as often as possible. The complete silence roused his curiosity enough to get him onto his feet and down the short hall. The living room was dark, the only light coming from the kitchen.

Curious about this change of habit and slightly alarmed after last night's scare with his car, Wyatt took slow, careful steps toward the kitchen. Paused in the entry and peered inside. Ramie sat at the small table in the one of the chairs that gave him her profile. A bottle of whiskey, a full shot glass, and a single cupcake rested on the table in front of her, all of it untouched, and her head was angled as if staring at the trio of objects.

Did I miss her birthday? Crap.

But if it was her birthday, wouldn't Brand or one of her other friends have taken her out? Maybe she was the kind of woman who didn't like to celebrate birthdays after a certain age. Lily liked to say that once she hit twenty-nine, she would forever celebrate the anniversary of that age.

Women made little sense to Wyatt on the best of days.

He shifted his weight, which made a floorboard creak. Ramie looked at him, her eyes wide and startled, as if she'd forgotten she had a roommate. "Hey," Wyatt said. "I didn't mean to interrupt."

"It's okay, I was lost in my own head. It's your kitchen too."

"I just, uh, is it your birthday or something? Did I miss the notice?"

"No, it's not mine."

Her particular choice of words suggested it was someone's birthday. Parent? Distant relative she loved and missed? On the occasional night they shared dinner or watched a movie together, they didn't talk about deeply personal things. They stuck to surface stuff like work, social media, and the weather.

"Do you want me to leave you alone?" Wyatt asked.

"Actually, no. Grab a shot glass, kid."

Wyatt frowned but did as asked. It no longer irritated him on the rare occasion Jackson let "kid" slip out, but it still did a bit with other people. But Ramie wasn't being the big sister right now, so he poured himself a shot of the brown liquor and sat across the table from her. "Are we toasting someone?"

"Yep." She held up her glass, so Wyatt tapped his rim to hers. "To my daughter's birthday. Cheers." She tossed back the shot.

He stared at her a beat before knocking his back, too. The strong liquor burned down his throat and into his belly, and he fought back the urge to cough, a tad out of practice with straight shots of booze. "Your daughter?"

She poured herself a second shot. Swiped her finger through the blue icing on her cupcake and licked it off. "Yep. She'll be thirteen today. Wherever she is."

"You don't know where she is?"

"Nope. I gave her up for adoption when she was born. I didn't want kids before I got pregnant and I don't want them now, but I couldn't..." She drank the second shot, her dark eyes gleaming. "So I had her and gave her up. Closed adoption. I don't think about her a lot, but every year on her birthday I send up a little prayer that whoever adopted her gave her an incredible life."

Wyatt's brain flashed to Jackson's description of his

own adoptive parents and rocky childhood, and he hoped the same thing. He was lucky to have grown up with a very loving mother and supportive extended family. Well, mostly supportive. "That's a brave thing to do, Ramie. Have a baby and give them up to parents who desperately want a child. I'm sure they've had an amazing life."

"I hope so. Not all of us are meant to be parents, and popping out a kid doesn't guarantee you'll be a good one. I knew I wouldn't be and I am at peace with that. I just wish Brand had gotten a say in the matter."

Something odd and kind of cold crept up Wyatt's spine. Ramie didn't seem fully aware of what she'd said, her gaze back on that cupcake, half-lost in her own thoughts again. He wasn't used to seeing her so distracted. Ramie was always put together, in charge, and a force to be reckoned with. This uncertain side made him want to get up and hug her, to offer some measure of comfort while she was upset.

Then it really hit him what she'd said and what it implied. "Wait, Brand was the father?"

"The what?" She looked at him, lips slightly parted. "Oh God, no, Brand isn't the father of my baby. This all happened before we met. Although we did bond over the fact."

You bonded over the fact that you both had kids you gave up?

Wyatt tried to order his thoughts and words so his racing brain didn't short-circuit and cause him to blurt out the wrong thing. "Then why would Brand get a say in you putting your baby up for adoption?"

"That's not what I meant." Her cheeks darkened. "Shit, I don't like spreading people's personal business around. I shouldn't have said anything."

He pretended to ponder over it for a second and reach a conclusion any reasonable person, not already in the know, would come to. "Brand gave up a baby for adoption, too?"

She looked at the table, which was as good as a verbal yes.

Wyatt poured and drank a second shot, grateful for the alcohol now. Ramie had gotten pregnant when she hadn't wanted to be pregnant, so she'd given the baby up. Women did it all the time, and it had been her decision. He didn't judge her for it at all.

What if Brand had a similar explanation for why he'd given Wyatt up? It was as simple as Brand being a teenager and not wanting to be a father or saddled with paying child support for the next eighteen years, so he'd given Mom the freedom to move forward and live her life, unburdened by a deadbeat dad. As a simple answer it made sense, but it still didn't explain his maternal grandparents' collective hatred of Wyatt's bio dad, and their complete unwillingness to color in the unshaded parts of Wyatt's past. He didn't know the full story but he was positive Brand was not now and had never been a cruel man or the type to abuse his girlfriend.

"I can't imagine making that kind of decision," Wyatt said. "Giving up part of yourself so that they could be happy somewhere else. It must have been hard. For you and for Brand, in your own ways."

"Please don't tell him I said anything." She reached across the table to squeeze his wrist, eyes wide and fearful in a way he'd never seen her before. "It's a family secret that only a handful of people know."

"I won't tell a soul." At least now he had confirmation of his suspicions. "Um, how old would Brand's kid be now?"

"I guess around your age. Twenty or so." Her lips twitched. "Maybe that's why he agreed to hire on an accidental cowboy with no real experience. You remind him of something he lost a long time ago."

Wyatt's heart sped up. "Do you think he regrets giving up his kid?"

"No."

Ouch.

"No, I don't think he regrets the decision," she continued. "Not so much giving them up as why he had to. He was sixteen going on seventeen. His oldest brother, Colt, had just run away to chase his own dreams, and Brand was suddenly burdened with inheriting the ranch one day. Making it a success. He was a kid himself with too much on his shoulders, so he probably would have agreed to the adoption route, if that's what the mother and her family had agreed to."

"They didn't want to adopt out?"

She shook her head. "According to Brand, Ginny wanted to keep the baby but her parents had some huge issue with the Woodses and refused to let Brand be part of her life."

Ramie knew his mother's name. She had no idea she was telling Wyatt his own origin story. Holy crap.

"They wanted to move away, start over," she continued. "Brand tried to fight it but her parents threatened to bring statutory rape charges if he didn't back off and sign away all rights to his kid."

"What the fuck? Rape?"

"It wasn't like that, Wyatt. Brand was a few days over seventeen when the shit hit the fan, but Ginny was still sixteen." And seventeen was the age of consent in Texas. "Even though they were both underage when they made the baby, Ginny's parents made a lot of noise about charges, and Brand was scared of ruining his parents' legacy with the ranch. So he conceded and signed away his rights. He gave up his kid for his family, which I know he'd do again in a heartbeat. But sometimes I think he regrets being bullied into that choice. He had no real say."

Wyatt's eyes burned with unnamed emotions, and he would not cry, damn it. For all the stories he'd been spun about how horrible his father's family was, about how Wyatt had been given up and abandoned by them, his entire body ached with grief for these new truths. Ramie had no reason to lie to him. Brand had no reason to lie to Ramie about his own motivations, especially given Ramie's history with adoption. If this was true...

"But why?" he asked. "Why would her parents do that?"

"I don't know. I guess you'd have to find them and ask them."

"But he never—I mean, he knew her name. Why didn't he ever look for his kid?"

Ramie shrugged, fingering the whiskey bottle as if pondering another shot. "Honor, I guess. He gave his word to stay out of their lives, and he's done his best to move forward. I know he thinks about it once in a while, but he was also a teenager facing a huge familial burden, and he did his best. Made his best choices and lives hoping his kid is happy wherever they are, whatever they are doing. Knowing they'll probably never come looking for him."

"Why wouldn't they?"

Her eyebrows seemed to suggest he was an idiot. "If Ginny's parents hated Brand so much that they'd threaten rape charges, do you really think Brand's kid grew up believing his bio dad was a good person? Or do you think he or she was told all sorts of awful things so they never bothered to come looking? Or maybe they never said anything about Brand at all and the kid grew up thinking someone else was their dad? Whatever was or wasn't said, it's been twenty years and no one has shown up claiming to be Brand's child."

Wyatt swallowed back a rush of acid, because everything she said sounded like his grandparents. Trash-talking his bio dad's family, calling the man a terrible person, that Wyatt would only be disappointed if he ever met him. Mom refusing to say anything one way or the other. But why? Why hold a decades-long grudge against Brand Woods? It made no fucking sense.

"I don't know," Wyatt said, which was the gods' honest truth. He felt like he'd been dropped into the middle of some sort of Greek tragedy and had no idea what his role was, or how to negotiate his way safely out of the narrative. He finally had confirmation that his Maybe Daddy had given up his rights to a kid twenty years ago, and he'd never sought out that child. Why? Because of an obligation to his blood family, never mind his own kid growing up without knowing his heritage.

"Sorry," Ramie replied. "I'm not taking this out on you, I promise. I just get testy when I think about people trash-talking Brand, because I know what a good person he is. I know how big his heart is, even if a lot of folks don't."

"It's okay. I know this isn't about me at all, and I won't tell anyone. I am stupidly good at keeping secrets. Family tradition, actually." He eyeballed the liquor bottle but too much lubrication might spill way more than he was willing to admit to tonight. "Can I ask you a hypothetical question?"

"Go for it."

"If your daughter showed up on your stoop and wanted to get to know you, would you talk to her?"

"I would." A single tear left an uneven path down Ramie's left cheek and stopped on her chin without falling. "I'd answer her questions as best I could. I'd just want to know she was safe and happy."

"Do you think Brand would do the same if his son showed up and wanted to talk to him?"

"Yeah, I do. I think Brand would want to explain his

side of things. That it wasn't as simple as just signing away his parental rights. He was a teenager forced to make a choice, and his choice was made. Just like I made my choice with my daughter. We can't take those decisions back, but we can attempt to explain the things that might not make sense."

"Not a lot makes sense to a kid who's been given away." As soon as the words passed his lips, Wyatt regretted them. But Ramie seemed a touch drunker than him, probably fueled by her depression over tonight's anniversary. "I hope you don't thump me for this, but I wish your daughter a happy birthday. And I wish her birth mother a good night's rest and the best of luck going forward. You are a terrific landlord and roommate, Ramie. Thank you for that."

"No problem." She offered him a watery smile, and if she really started to cry he might, too. "You're a pretty great roommate, too, Wyatt. Thanks for listening to me ramble."

"You're welcome. You gave me a lot to think about."

"Son."

Wyatt blinked. "What?"

"You said if his son showed up. What makes you think it was a boy?"

"Just a guess. Probably me projecting, since I don't know who my birth father is."

"Oh, right. Man, what a fluster-cluck we are, huh?"

He chuckled at her slight mangling of the phrase. "Yeah, we're a fluster-cluck. At least we keep things interesting, though, right?"

"Yeah, we do. Fuck, I'm tired. You want this?" She shoved the cupcake at him.

"Um, sure. Take some water to bed with you."

"Yes, Dad." She winked as she stood.

Wyatt sat quietly while she poured a glass of water and

left the kitchen. Vanilla from the cupcake scented the air, but he couldn't bring himself to eat the sweet treat. He was now ninety-nine-point-nine percent sure that Brand Woods was his Maybe Daddy. Everything in Ramie's story about Brand's teenage years tracked perfectly with what little Wyatt knew about his mother's past. She'd even known Mom's name.

The biggest question he had now was why? Why had his grandparents forced the separation? What had the Woods family done to his own to create such a huge rift? He could call his grandparents, tell them everything he'd learned and demand answers, but he was unlikely to get them. He'd probably get a lecture about leaving the past in the past and coming home to his real family.

No, if he was going to get answers, it would be from Brand himself. Brand was the man he'd come here to find and get to know. Brand had taken a chance on an accident-prone newbie who'd lied to his face and to whom Wyatt owed the truth. But Wyatt loved his life here too much to risk blowing it to pieces if that conversation went poorly. He adored Jackson and the time they spent together, and Jackson would be furious when he found out the huge secret Wyatt had been keeping this entire time. He enjoyed his job at the ranch, despite the frequency with which he needed bandages or fielded jokes about his tetanus booster, and he didn't want to lose it. Didn't want to lose his friendships with Brand and Hugo and Rem.

He didn't want to lose everything he'd built, but what chance did he have of a certain future when what he'd built was on a foundation of lies and deceit? He owed it to the people he'd come to care about, like Ramie and Jackson, to be honest with them, even if he lost everything in the process.

"T'was a foolish man who built his house upon the

sand," Wyatt said softly to the cupcake. "I can see the wave coming. I just hope it doesn't wreck everything when it hits shore."

Chapter Seventeen

Nothing gold can stay was a line from Jackson's favorite Robert Frost poem, one he'd memorized back in high school thanks to doing stage crew for a senior-year play production of *The Outsiders*. All he'd really done was run a few props on and offstage in between light cues, but he'd been there for the rehearsals, listened to the story, and memorized the poem. He'd even read the entire book the play was based on, which was pretty amazing, since at the time Jackson was only allowed to read the Bible and a handful of books preapproved by his parents.

The story of the Curtis brothers and their struggles had hit home in a unique way for Jackson. Ponyboy's effort to be part of the gang he'd been born into versus his desire for something bigger, and his realization that violence wasn't the answer. Jackson had gone through his own battle to claim his identity in a world that wanted to define it for him. Ponyboy wasn't a Greaser or a Soc; Jackson wasn't a prostitute or a felon. Both young men were simply themselves, and they had to learn what being "himself" truly meant.

The poem's line *Nothing gold can stay* stuck with him through the weekend, and Jackson wasn't sure why. His secret relationship with Wyatt was going strong, work was good, and yet in the very back of his mind, this bizarre gong of doom lingered, waiting to be rung. He didn't want it to ever ring, obviously, but what if it did? Something undefinable about Wyatt's secret search for his bio dad kept niggling at the back of Jackson's mind, but he couldn't put his finger on it.

So he worked and loved on Wyatt every chance he got, and he did his best to ignore the feeling entirely.

They did, however, get an alarm system installed in Wyatt's car to ease their peace of mind in case the neighborhood prankster decided to go at it again. So far, though, the police had no leads and no new reports of attempted trunk theft in the area. Hopefully, it had been a one-off prank and was over with.

Sundays were fairly casual at the ranch, thanks to generations-old beliefs that Sunday was for big family dinners, not work. Which was fine in theory, but on a ranch like this the cattle still needed tending, the horses still needed feeding, and nothing ever truly stopped moving. He and Wyatt were on line duty that morning, and when they found a breach in the fencing on the south pasture, he let Wyatt do the repair. Naturally, Wyatt cut his wrist on the barbed wire, which required a quick bandage fix, but the kid was pretty much 0-30 in terms of getting some sort of cut, scrape, or bruise.

Around four in the afternoon, the parking area by the main house began filling with vehicles as the Woods clan descended upon the house for a big family dinner. Jackson knew all the in-laws and various kids, and he greeted the handful he saw as they went inside. His best guess was that tonight was the night that Brand gave Hugo the commitment ring and/or asked Hugo to marry him. Either was an option at this point. A grand, romantic gesture at the end of a big family meal sounded like something Brand would do, and Jackson was kind of sorry he'd miss it. But he'd probably hear all about it at some point, if not from Brand directly then for sure from Rem. Rem was a huge gossip no matter the subject matter.

The only dark cloud over his day was Wyatt, who'd kept an emotional distance from him for the past few days. Jackson couldn't put his finger on exactly what was different. Since they'd both worked, they didn't have any real time off together to talk about whatever was bothering Wyatt, and Jackson didn't like that. He was very much close to breaking his own "no relationships stuff at the ranch" rule just so he could find out what was bothering Wyatt and fix it.

He hadn't managed a private moment with Wyatt today, despite being out on the line together for three hours, and it was ten minutes past quitting time when he finally gave up and headed for his truck. Wyatt's car was still there but the guy was nowhere to be found. At his truck's door, two figures on the bunkhouse porch captured his attention: Brand and Hugo. They weren't up at the big house yet with the rest of the family.

While Jackson wasn't much for eavesdropping on private business, neither man looked happy. So he stopped and watched, curiosity overtaking his manners.

Brand pointed at the family home and said something Jackson couldn't hear. Hugo waved two hands in the air in a gesture Jackson couldn't interpret. He felt a little douche-y for observing what was probably a private moment (and apparently not a happy one) but he couldn't seem to move. Less to see what was going on and more so he didn't startle or interrupt them.

He caught "told me sooner" from Hugo, followed by "telling you now" from Brand.

What on earth?

Hugo said something else too low to hear, then turned

away from Brand. At this angle, Jackson wasn't sure if he heard the words or just saw Hugo's lips move to say, "Apologize to your mom for me." Then he stormed off toward the garage. Brand watched him go, shoulders slumped, entire body radiating his upset.

He finally noticed Jackson and frowned. Instead of approaching or attempting to explain the fight, Brand pivoted and strode toward the main house. Unsure what was happening but pretty certain there wouldn't be a proposal tonight, Jackson followed Hugo to the garage. He found his friend standing next to a workbench with a hammer in his hand, simply staring at it like he wasn't sure what to do with it.

"Hey," Jackson said. "You okay, bud?"

Hugo looked at him, not startled exactly, but probably confused why Jackson had chased after him instead of his boyfriend. "No, not really. I just, uh, needed some time alone."

"Sorry. I can leave you alone."

"It's okay." He put the hammer down, then picked up a screwdriver. Turned it over in his fingers a few times before he put it back, too. "Did you know?"

Jackson blinked. "Know what?"

"It's just you were with Brand for a lot of years, so he had to have said something to you about it, right? But he waited almost a whole year before he told me about it."

"Okay, you need to back up a minute. What do you think I knew about but Brand didn't tell you?" While he and Brand had talked a lot during their interludes while "seeing each other," they never had heavy heart-to-hearts, and if Brand had some sort of life-changing secret he hadn't told Hugo about, Jackson couldn't guess what it was.

"About the baby."

"The what now?" He took a few steps closer to Hugo

in case someone else wandered into the garage. No need to blare this conversation to the entire ranch. "What baby? Brand's having a baby?"

"No, he had a baby. I mean, obviously he didn't have the baby, but back in high school he apparently got his girlfriend pregnant, her parents forced him to sign away all his rights, and they moved away."

Something began poking at the back of Jackson's mind like the first hints of a migraine, warning him of devastating pain ahead. "Brand has a kid out there?"

"Yes. And I'm not mad about the fact that he's got a kid, that's not important. It all happened before I was even friends with Rem, so I never knew about it when it went down. But we've been together for a while and Brand just now told me. That he's never looked for the kid because he wanted to put that part of his life away and live in the now, but he wanted me to know this part of him. His last big secret."

"Wow." Jackson braced his hand on the edge of the workbench, all turned around by this. Not just the shock of finding out Brand had a kid out there somewhere that no one knew about (except his family, obviously), but also that this new fact was clashing with Wyatt's Maybe Daddy search out here in Weston. Clashing in an alarming way. The math was way too similar, the coincidence too freaking huge. "How old would his kid be now?"

"Twenty."

Fuck. Fuuuuuck.

"I, um." Jackson's tongue stuck to the roof of his mouth and words weren't coming out. "Sorry."

"I guess you really didn't know, huh? Shit, I probably shouldn't have said anything, I'm just so turned around by all this. You don't expect the person you love to keep such a big secret for so long."

"No, you don't." But Brand had kept it, just like Wyatt was keeping a big fucking secret of his own. There was no way that Brand just happened to have a mysterious kid out there the same age as Wyatt, and Wyatt just happened to end up working here at Woods Ranch. Which meant Wyatt had been lying to him for weeks while Jackson laid bare his worst secrets.

He'd lied while Jackson had slowly fallen in love with the feisty, accident-prone cowboy wannabe.

"I don't mean to fuck up your Sunday night," Hugo said. "I'm all right, I just need some time to sit with this before I face Brand's family for supper. Obviously his parents know what went down, but I don't know which of his siblings know about it. I didn't want to say the wrong thing."

"Take your time with it, bud, and you know Brand would say the same thing. This is pretty big news to learn about someone you love and trust." He hated that he wasn't just talking about Hugo right now. He needed to find Wyatt as soon as possible, so Wyatt could tell him this was all some huge cosmic coincidence, and that Brand Woods was not the Maybe Daddy he'd come to Weston to find.

Wyatt *had* to tell him that. Coincidence. Yep. Had to be.

Anything else would break his heart.

Wyatt kind of hated that he'd kept an emotional distance from Jackson for the past few days, ever since his conversation with Ramie about the child she'd given up. He hadn't brought it up with her again, and she hadn't either when they saw each other in passing at the house, so he assumed the subject between them was closed. It wasn't closed for Wyatt, though. Not really. He needed to confront Brand with everything he knew and hope the truth didn't get him fired. He also needed to talk to Jackson but he flat-out wasn't ready to have either conversation. Not yet.

He was too scared of losing a family he was beginning to love and of imploding the best, healthiest relationship of his entire life.

So he stayed as professional as possible every day at work, even though he could see Jackson was chomping at the bit to talk to him about something. They'd both agreed to keep things completely professional while on the clock, and neither of them seemed willing to break that promise first, for which Wyatt was grateful. In some ways, it also made him a coward, because he was hiding behind this façade of professionalism when it was really fear keeping his mouth shut.

They both had Monday off, and Wyatt had spent the better part of his work shift Sunday talking himself into telling Jackson the truth tomorrow. He owed Jackson that truth if they were truly going to move forward, and Wyatt wanted to move forward. He was falling in love with Jackson, already had strong feelings for the man, and he didn't want to be yet another reason why Jackson distrusted people or kept them at arm's length.

Wyatt needed to be fucking honest with Jackson and Brand both about why, out of all the places in the entire ginormous state of Texas, he'd landed in Weston. At Woods Ranch.

So yeah, he'd avoided Brand all day, and then hidden in the barn like a coward hoping that Jackson would head home without cornering him for a conversation. He'd seen Jackson heading toward the garage at one point, which gave him a chance to make his getaway, and he did. Straight back to Ramie's house. She wasn't home because she was working a midshift. State laws required bars to close earlier on Sundays than other weekdays, so she'd be home around ten.

As much as he wanted to settle down and chill with

a movie or something, Wyatt couldn't sit still. He paced the living room for a while with music blasting from his phone, but it wasn't enough. He was unsettled and upset and nervous as hell about what he needed to tell Jackson tomorrow. They hadn't made any specific plans but their joint days off almost always began with a late breakfast at the truck stop.

He palmed his phone, intending to text Jackson and make sure they were still doing that tomorrow morning, when a familiar truck engine rumbled outside. He ran to the front window and peered out. Jackson was parking on the street behind Wyatt's car. Surprise jolted through him, followed quickly by a terrible combination of delight and trepidation. Had his moment to confess this final secret just jumped up by more than twelve hours? Seemed likely. He really should talk to Brand first, but now that he'd made the choice to come clean about his Maybe Daddy, Wyatt couldn't not say anything to Jackson tonight. Could he?

Jackson didn't even knock; he yanked open the door and came inside like a tsunami, big and foreboding, and Wyatt's heart sank to the floor before Jackson asked, "Did you come here to Claire County because you think Brand Woods is your biological father?"

Wyatt's brain stuttered and his mouth fell open, shocked to his core by the blunt question and at how neatly Jackson had flayed open Wyatt's exact reason for being here. How the hell had he found out? And how was Wyatt supposed to explain this in a way that didn't make Jackson dump him for hiding the—

"I need the truth," Jackson said. His red face and blazing eyes betrayed his hurt and confusion, and both things scorched Wyatt to his core. Wyatt had done that, put that pain in Jackson's eyes. "I deserve the truth."

"Yes." Wyatt didn't know what else to say so he went

with the God's honest truth for once. Even though everything inside of him rebelled against being confronted like
this, before he talked to Brand, Jackson had somehow
found out on his own and he deserved the truth. "I came
here suspecting Brand was my biological father."

Jackson stared at him from the doorway, his big body
seeming to vibrate with anger and confusion and so many
things that hurt Wyatt's soul to see. "So you knew and
you lied."

"No, I suspected. What little I knew about my mother's
past led me here, and a little digging pointed me toward
Brand, but I wasn't sure about anything until a few days
ago."

"What happened a few days ago?"

"I talked to Ramie. She told me about Brand giving up
a baby twenty years ago. Until that moment I wasn't sure,
Jackson, I swear. I didn't want to say anything to you until
I was sure, because it was all a theory. It was only a theory for a long time, and then Ramie had a birthday and
she was really depressed, and we talked about the baby
she gave up thirteen years ago, but she also let slip about
Brand's baby with a woman named Ginny and that was it.
It was the proof I needed about what I'd only suspected."

"You suspected Brand's your father and now you've got
the proof, but you never said anything to me."

"I didn't know how. I knew I needed to talk to Brand
but I kept putting it off because I didn't know *how* to tell
you or him."

"You just say it, Wyatt. You tell the fucking truth. And
the truth is you came here with a suspicion about Brand.
You applied to the ranch with that suspicion. You took the
job and flirted with me and fucked me with that suspicion,
without ever once admitting to it. And when you got proof
your suspicion was right you never said a goddamn word."

"I'm sorry." The fact that he'd planned to come clean very soon, had basically talked himself into doing it tomorrow, didn't seem to matter anymore. Not under the glare of Jackson's obvious hurt.

"That's it? You're sorry for lying to me for weeks? For breaking my trust when you know how hard it is for me to extend that trust? I asked you so many times if I could help with this search for your father and you brushed it off. Not because you didn't want my help but because you didn't need it, because you knew who you were looking for the entire fucking time."

Wyatt's face crumpled, more devastated by the quiet fury in Jackson's voice than if he'd actually hollered at him. "I wasn't positive who I was looking for until recently, I swear. All I had were hints and ideas but no proof until the other night."

"The other night. You've known for days, Wyatt. *Days.* I honestly don't know what to do with that. Our entire relationship has been built around a lie."

"No it wasn't. Maybe our work relationship was built on a few fibs, but I was always myself with you. What we feel for each other isn't a lie. I care about you so much, Jackson. I think I'm in love with you, but I've never been in love before so I'm not totally sure what it feels like, but it's there. We can fix this."

"Can we?" The absolute grief in those two words made Wyatt want to cry. "How can I ever trust you again? I only ever asked you for one thing. And I get that you have your reasons, but I have mine, too. And I can't do this."

"Jackson."

"Don't call me." He turned and strode toward the door. Put his hand on it, then looked over his shoulder. "You have until work starts Tuesday morning to come clean with Brand, or I'll tell him."

Wyatt's insides shriveled into a cold, tight ball as Jackson left. Walked away from what they'd briefly had and stalked to his truck. Wyatt's ingrained habit of keeping secrets had just imploded the best thing in his life. He was only vaguely aware of sitting on the couch and of the house getting dark all around him. His stomach growled once but he couldn't imagine putting food in it.

At some point, he curled up around a pillow, his body shaking, as if crying for him because his dry eyes wouldn't. The life he'd built here was going to crash and burn, and he wasn't ready to say goodbye to it. Not to Jackson, Brand, Ramie, and everyone else at the ranch. But somehow Jackson had found out Brand had a kid once. And for the first time since landing in Weston, Wyatt had been completely honest. He could hear his stepfather's voice in the back of his mind, berating him for sharing a secret, demanding he look at all the hurt he'd caused, and threatening him with the horse whip if Wyatt ever did it again.

Where do I go once this is over?

Home was out of the question. He'd never live this down. Sure, he'd succeeded in his goal of finding his biological father, but he'd also failed at so much more. He was still a clumsy cowboy with a lot to learn, and he'd completely obliterated the first romantic relationship of his life. And Ramie? Would she kick him out once she learned the truth?

He had no idea.

Time passed, and too soon Ramie let herself inside. She gave a startled yelp at the sight of him on the couch, simply lying there and doing nothing in the semidark. "Hey, are you sick?"

"No." Heartsick, but that didn't count.

"Then what's wrong? It's not like you to sit around in the dark like a bridge troll."

"I lied."

She perched on the edge of the couch by his feet, eyebrows furrowed. "You lied about not being sick?"

"I lied about why I came here."

"Home from work?"

Man, she really gave people the benefit of the doubt, and he adored it about her. He'd also hate losing such a genuine friend. "No, Ramie." He dragged himself upright, his entire body aching with grief, and he couldn't look higher than her chin when he said, "I lied about why I came to Weston. I mean, I did want to learn the cowboy life, that was true. But I applied to Woods Ranch for a very specific reason."

She tilted her head, wariness coloring over some of her confusion. "They were hiring."

"Yes, they were, but that was an actual coincidence. They were hiring exactly when I planned to apply. To Woods Ranch specifically, because I wanted to get to know the family. Brand, in particular."

"Why Brand in particular?" All the tumblers clicked into place quickly, and Wyatt saw the moment she understood what he hadn't yet said. She paled considerably, her lips parting in a shocked O. "You are shitting me right now."

"I'm not." Something thick clogged his throat; it didn't get any easier to say, and he had no idea how he'd get the words out when he confronted Brand. "I suspected Brand was my birth father. It's why I came to Weston."

"Wow." She made several different faces he had no hope of understanding. "So you came here to what? Pull some kind of long-con on Brand and his family?"

"No, I didn't come here to con anyone. Ramie, my whole life my grandparents have told me how horrible my father's family is. That my father was selfish and didn't want me, and I believed that because why would they lie? I needed to see for myself what kind of man he was and that's what I've been doing. Brand is nothing like the monster I was told about. I really like him and his family. They've been nothing but amazing to me, especially Rose."

"So when I told you about my daughter and about Brand having a kid, that's when you knew for sure?"

"Yes. I've been waffling over what to do for days. I know I need to tell Brand the truth, but then Jackson found out about Brand's baby somehow, and he put it together with my story about being here, and we had a fight tonight. I think I lost him." His voice cracked.

Ramie scooted closer and pulled him into a tight hug. He melted against her chest, grateful for the silent support when his body seemed ready to shake apart and leave his entire world in jagged pieces on the ground.

"Just so we're clear," she said after a few minutes, "I *am* mad at you for lying to me about why you're here. But I also understand why you did it. Sometimes we don't make rational decisions when family is concerned."

"We really don't." He told her a bit more about his upbringing and the ways he was taught to keep secrets at all costs. They moved apart while he spoke, but she kept hold of one of his hands the entire time and he adored her for that single point of contact. Her dark eyes glittered with tears but she never cried. "I was so fucking turned around when I got here. I wanted to be honest but I was scared of getting in trouble, and I kept talking myself out of telling Brand."

"Why do you think you'd get in trouble? Family means everything to Brand. He'll probably be upset that you were under his nose for two months, but he's not going to fire you or run you out of town."

"You don't think?"

"No, I don't."

"Do you think he'll want to get to know me? Not just as his employee but, you know, as his kid?" She was Brand's best friend, and if Wyatt was going to trust anyone's opinion on that, it was hers.

Ramie smiled. "Yes, I do. He really did regret being forced out of your life. Don't be scared to tell him."

"I will. I knew I needed to be honest with him and Jackson."

"But Jackson found out before you could tell either of them."

"Yeah. I was working my way up to doing it tomorrow. Me and Jackson both have the day off. I could sit him down and explain it all from the start. He knows a lot of it. I told him about the keeping secrets thing, and he knows I'm looking for my bio dad. I was going to tell him I thought it was Brand, I was just waiting."

"You kept finding excuses to put it off instead of biting the bullet and taking the pain."

"I don't know. I don't understand who told Jackson. Would Brand just blurt it out right before a big family dinner?" He'd seen the vehicles of the extended Woods siblings parked by the family home.

"To Jackson? Unlikely, especially now that they aren't together. If Brand was going to tell Jackson it would have been before." She pressed her lips together. "The only person I can imagine him confessing it to is Hugo, but I'd be really surprised if Hugo didn't already know. They've been together for a while."

Hugo kind of made sense as the person Brand might have confessed this baby secret to, but Ramie also made a good point about how long Brand and Hugo had been together. Maybe Brand had taken a mental step forward in how serious their relationship was and decided to share the secret tonight. But why on earth would Hugo have told Jackson about it?

So many questions and Wyatt had no answers.

"However it happened," Wyatt said, "Jackson found out before I could tell him and he's so hurt. I never meant to hurt him, I swear. I have crazy strong feelings for him."

"Do you love him?"

"I think so. I've never felt real romantic love before, so I'm not sure, but I think I do. Not like it matters now, though, not if I've completely broken his trust. He's been through hell, Ramie, and I knew that his one big thing was being able to trust me. I don't know if I'll ever get him back."

"I don't know, either. Jackson and I are only casual friends. I don't know him the way you and Brand do, so I can't speak on it. All I can do is give you the best advice I can muster right now, and that is to be honest going forward. One hundred percent honest about your feelings, your actions, and your intentions."

"He said if I didn't tell Brand the truth by Tuesday morning then he would."

She nodded slowly. "Then I guess you've got to have a very important conversation with your boss by tomorrow night."

"Yeah."

"I'm going to be mad at you for a while longer yet for lying to me, but I'm not going to get dramatic and kick you out. You're so young, and you're trying to find your footing in a very fucked-up world. We all make mistakes at every age, but especially when we're twenty. Learn from those mistakes. Grow. If you and Jackson are meant to be, you'll figure it out. If not, then he was a stepping stone on your path toward being a human adult navigating relationships."

I don't want him to be a step. I want him back. Period.

"Thanks," he said instead. "I'll, um, disappear for a while so you don't have to look at me while you're mad."

"Much appreciated. And believe you'll have a good conversation with Brand tomorrow. I do."

"I'll do my best."

Wyatt hauled his exhausted body off the couch and trudged to his bedroom. Shut the door and spread out on top of the covers. A gaping maw of uncertainty loomed in front of him, dark and dreadful, and he had no idea if he'd be able to pass by, or if that terrifying, lonely darkness would swallow him whole.

Chapter Eighteen

Jackson stared at the bubbles rising from the depths of his beer glass, mesmerized by their constant dance from where they formed at the bottom, to the top of the glass, where they broke and released their tantalizing aroma. He'd fucked around once with a guy who was a professional bartender, and he'd once waxed poetic about beer, temperatures, carbonation, and the way your sense of smell worked in tandem with your tongue to create the best beer flavor experience. Or something.

Bubbles were bubbles.

He'd left Ramie's place and headed straight for Blue Tavern to drown his confusion, anger, and grief in beer and free popcorn. He hadn't eaten dinner and while the place had a meager selection of bar food, he wasn't in the mood to eat. Just to drown in booze for a while. Dog will have probably peed on the carpet by the time he got home but he didn't care. His fault for going from work to see Wyatt to here.

The beer wasn't giving him the buzz he wanted, so when the place's lone waiter came by Jackson ordered two whiskey shooters. The waiter gave the order to Darlin', who shot him a curious look from across the bar, but didn't come over or inquire about Jackson's bad mood. Jackson was grateful for that. While he appreciated the staff looking out for their patrons and considered Darlin' an almost-friend, Jackson didn't want to be consoled or questioned.

He wanted to wallow, damn it. He deserved to wallow. Maybe wallowing at home with a bottle of whiskey was a better idea than getting drunk and having to drive later, but here he was. Part of him didn't want to be alone, even if the rest of him did not want company of any sort. He missed Wyatt, despite being furious and hurt, and he didn't know what to do.

Over the course of several more beers, a handful of guys stopped by his table. Jackson refused all offers of company because as much as he'd love to fuck his frustration away, he couldn't do that to Wyatt. Not until they'd both officially declared this thing between them over and done with. Jackson might be a lot of things, but he didn't cheat.

Right around the time Darlin' announced last call, a familiar body landed in the chair across the table from him. Brand stared at him, head tilted to the side in an assessing, curious way.

"What the fuck are you doin' here?" Jackson asked. He wasn't slurring his words so he wasn't drunk enough to be imagining Brand.

"I got a text from Darlin'," Brand replied. "He said you were about one beer away from him confiscating your truck keys. Asked if I knew why you were out here tying one on."

"And?"

"I said I had no idea but I'd swing by and check on you. Last time we talked outside of work you seemed happy. Like you were really looking forward to something. Did the thing you had with that guy not work out?"

Jackson snorted so hard it hurt his nose. "He lied to me, Brand. Lied about somethin' huge and for the whole time we've known each other."

"Hell. I'm sorry."

"It's okay. Can't build a relationship on a lie."

Brand flinched. "Yeah. No matter why you keep something from someone you love, it's gonna hurt when it comes out."

"Like Hugo and the baby?"

"Like…what?" Brand's confused frown melted into wide-eyed surprise. "How the hell did you find out?"

"Hugo. Saw you guys fight today, and I followed Hugo into the garage. He vented."

"He vented? To you?"

"Don't be mad at Hugo. He thought I knew because of our history. Yours and mine, I mean, not me and his because we don't have any history, and he kind of let it all out. I didn't tell anybody else." And technically, he hadn't. Jackson had not told Wyatt how he knew Brand had a child who'd be twenty years old now, and Wyatt hadn't asked. As angry and semi-drunk as Jackson was, he also couldn't bring himself to tell Brand what he knew about Wyatt.

It wasn't his secret to share and Wyatt knew when the deadline was.

"I'm glad Hugo had someone to vent to, I guess," Brand said. "So he told you that I gave up my parental rights when I was seventeen. I've got a kid out there somewhere I've never bothered to look for, because I want to put that part of my life to bed. And I figured if he or she wanted to know me they'd come looking, so I'm never gonna force the issue."

If only you knew, boss.

"Sounds like you made a hard, deeply personal choice back then," Jackson said. "Couldn't have been easy tellin' Hugo."

"It was and it wasn't. I didn't want us to fully commit to a future together without coming completely clean about my past. I mean, I guess I could have never said anything, considering it was half a lifetime ago, but what if by some chance that kid does come around later on? I don't want Hugo to find out that way and be blindsided. So I told him."

"Probably for the best you did. Never know what'll happen tomorrow." Jackson couldn't help wondering how pissed Brand would be at him when he realized Jackson was sitting across the table from him, half-drunk and fully aware that Brand's lost-lost kid was his employee. But Jackson could handle Brand's temper just fine. He had no idea what would happen when Wyatt came clean. It worried him a little, but again, even as pickled as his brain was right then, it still wasn't Jackson's secret to tell.

"You're right, we don't know." The lights in the bar came up and the music went off, signaling the end of the evening.

Definitely sooner than Jackson would have liked but it was Sunday. Everything closed too soon on Sunday because of stupid, outdated laws. "Gotta settle my tab."

"Okay."

Jackson paid Darlin' what he owed, plus a tip, grateful to the guy for looking out for him, despite them not being what he'd call friends. Maybe he should fix that in the future. Darlin' seemed like a pretty decent guy and probably had an interesting story. Jackson signed the tablet with his finger and waved off any kind of receipt. He was a little surprised to turn and see Brand waiting for him at the door.

They went outside together. The night air had a bitter bite to it that sometimes suggested snow, but the sky was clear. No clouds, just a blanket of stars winking down at them. Almost mocking Jackson with their beauty and vastness.

"You want me to give you a ride home?" Brand asked. "I don't mind."

"Nah, no way to get back here for my truck in the mornin'."

"Then how about I follow you home, just in case."

"Fine." If Brand wanted to mother-hen him he wasn't going to complain.

"First, let's do a field sobriety test. Recite the alphabet backward."

"Fuck you, I can't do that when I'm sober."

Brand snickered. "Walk five paces heel to toe."

Jackson did and nailed it, not a single wobble in his steps. "Want me to close my eyes and touch my finger to my nose, too, Officer Woods?"

"Nah. But if you so much as swerve onto the shoulder on the way back, I'll blind you with my high beams until you pull over."

"Understood." He started to turn and walk to his truck, then paused. Brand had been a terrific friend tonight and Jackson hadn't even asked. "Did you and Hugo talk about things yet?"

"A little bit, but then I got the call to come check on you. We'll talk again when I go home. One thing I learned from my parents and their marriage is never go to bed angry or upset. We'll get through this once the shock wears off."

"I'm glad. Thank you, boss."

"It's what friends are for, Jackson." Brand offered his hand and Jackson shook it.

He blasted the radio on the drive back home, using the noise and the chill from a half-open window to keep him awake. Dog was barking up a storm when he finally parked and got out of the truck. Brand idled nearby, and Jackson didn't hear the engine moving away until after Dog raced outside and Jackson shut the door.

He inspected the room but didn't see any wet spots on the carpet. When he let Dog back inside, he gave her a handful of treats from her special stash to say sorry. Sat on the carpet and scratched her ears the way she liked while she panted and watched him with soulful eyes that seemed to say she knew her daddy was upset.

Animals know.

"At least I've got you, girl," he said. "Don't ever change."

Dog licked his hand. Jackson continued to pet her and tried not to think for a long time.

Wyatt was a hot mess and then some on Monday morning, and he tried to contain himself to his room so he didn't irritate Ramie too much. His days off had taken on a beautiful routine of a late breakfast with Jackson, and today he wasn't doing that. He was sipping coffee he probably didn't need and practicing what he'd eventually say to Brand later today, when he finally talked himself into driving to the ranch.

As much as he wanted to put this off, to simply ignore it and hope it went away, he couldn't. Jackson had given him an ultimatum last night: tell Brand today or Jackson would tell him tomorrow. And while the idea of telling Brand still scared him a little, the thought of Jackson being the one to do it scared him more. Wyatt wasn't that sort of coward; he wouldn't let someone else tell his truths for him.

He did waffle for hours on when exactly to do it, until Ramie said his pacing was driving her nuts. After a quick "shit or get off the pot" pep talk from her, he finally called Brand.

"Hey, what's up?" Brand asked, answering after only two rings.

"Hi, um, are you around the ranch right now or out in the pastures?"

"Doing some office stuff today so I'm around. Everything okay?"

"Yeah." *No, not at all.* "I was just, uh, hoping to have

a chat with you in private this afternoon. About my progress and stuff."

"Sure, if you want. We can talk tomorrow, too, when you're on the schedule."

"No, today is better. Um, one o'clock?"

"Yeah, that's fine, I'll be in my office. Is everything okay, Wyatt? You aren't quitting, are you? Because Alan isn't supposed to be back for another week or so." The touch of humor in Brand's tone kept Wyatt from overreacting to the comments.

"No, not quitting. See you at one." He hung up without giving Brand a moment to reply. Wyatt stared at his phone. Part of him wanted to call Jared for advice about all this, but they hadn't exactly been on the best of terms since the whole car break-in thing, and Wyatt still needed to mail that stupid roadside kit back to him. Whatever, it could wait until Wyatt figured out his private life and career.

Two things he was about to blow up in a few hours.

He typed and deleted several texts to Jackson composed of every possible combination of apologies and pleas for forgiveness. Nothing sounded right or like enough to properly express how he felt. He'd hurt Jackson on a soul-deep level, and Wyatt didn't know how to apologize or atone for such a thing. Not in a way he thought Jackson would truly appreciate and embrace. If Wyatt didn't do this right, he'd lose Jackson forever.

Jackson's comments about Wyatt still being young, about relationships at his age not necessarily lasting filtered through his mind over and over while he waited. Wyatt sneered at the idea that this couldn't last, that just because Wyatt was young he didn't know his heart. He knew his heart. He loved Jackson, and he wouldn't let the older man go without a fight. Maybe Wyatt was a kid compared to some of the men he worked with but he was no child.

Wyatt knew who and what he wanted. He just had to confess to his bio dad first.

His stomach was too knotted up to take more than a few plain crackers for lunch, and he barely managed choking those down with some ginger ale. Ramie had already left, whether for work, shopping or lunch with a girlfriend, he didn't remember if she'd told him. He kept staring at the time on his phone, watching the minutes tick down. He didn't want to show up too early for their appointment, and he definitely didn't want to be late. He also kind of didn't want to go at all.

In the end, he drove to the ranch and idled just past the entrance with music blasting until it was closer to one. He pulled up in front of the bunkhouse and barely managed to get the keys back out of the ignition with his trembling hand. Somehow he got the keys into his pocket, climbed out of the car, and made sure his phone was on him. Not that he planned on calling anyone. After this conversation, he might not have anyone close by to call for help or commiseration.

In that moment, Wyatt really wanted to talk to his mom. To get her advice, her blessing, her confession, anything. But he couldn't. She was gone and he missed her more than anything in the world—except for Jackson. Jackson was still alive but he might as well be on a different continent for as far apart as Wyatt felt from him right now.

Brand opened the bunkhouse door before Wyatt could knock, and he gave Wyatt a familiar smile. Too fucking familiar and not because he'd seen it a lot these last two months. He saw it in the mirror when he smiled at himself.

"Hey, come on into my office," Brand said. So calm

and patient that Wyatt wanted to punch him and scream his secret to the sky.

Instead, Wyatt followed Brand across the living room and into his office. Brand left the door open, so Wyatt assumed Hugo wasn't home and about to bear witness to this. To the moment when Wyatt went against everything his family had ever taught him and confessed to a huge, life-altering secret. Witness to the implosion of the wonderful life Wyatt had created here at Woods Ranch. Despite Ramie's reassurances, Wyatt wouldn't believe in a positive outcome until it happened.

Now or never.

"So you wanted to talk about your work progress, right?" Brand asked as he sat behind his desk. "I admit I'm not overly fond of your record of minor injuries, but some folk can't help being clumsy."

"Yeah, I do my best." Wyatt stood behind one of the chairs, unable to sit himself, positive his entire body would vibrate apart at any moment and break the chair along with it. "Not to get hurt but to not get hurt. Um."

"Well, apart from that I think you're making great progress. Jackson has nothing but good reports as you learn new skills, and he thinks with time you'll be a great asset to us here at Woods Ranch. Actually, with Alan coming back soon and on light duty, I might pair you two up for a while. He's been in the life a long time like Jackson."

"Right." Even if Brand didn't fire him after this conversation, it was unlikely Jackson would want to continue mentoring Wyatt.

"Is everything okay, Wyatt? You seem really nervous about something. You're not thinking of quitting, are you?"

"No. No, I don't want to quit, not at all. I just…um."

Brand stood and circled the desk, lips pursed and eyebrows slanted. He urged Wyatt to sit and then perched on the chair beside him. "If you're having some kind of personal issue, you can talk to me. I'm your boss but I can still be a friend if you need one."

"You might not feel that way in a few minutes."

"Why? You didn't do anything illegal, did you?"

"No." At least, he was pretty sure lying the way he had wasn't illegal. He'd been honest on his application forms.

"Then what's going on? If you're in trouble we can help."

"I'm not in trouble. There's just something I lied about when I moved here, and after Jackson talked to Hugo last night, Jackson figured out my secret, and he's really mad at me for lying, and I told Ramie after she saw how upset I was that Jackson hates me, and I have to come clean about it. With you."

Brand's concern had shifted into utter confusion. "Okay, Hugo mentioned he'd spoken to Jackson last night, but how does what they talked about relate to you?"

Relate *is the most perfect word ever for this situation.*

"Because I moved to Weston to get to know you," Wyatt said, the words burbling up like acid in his throat. "To see if the stories I'd been told about you and your family were true or false."

"Me? But why would—?" Brand's entire face went pale and blank, and Wyatt saw the understanding forming in his eyes. Eyes that seemed to really look at Wyatt, to take in his green eyes and red hair, and all the things he'd inherited from Ginny Foster. "You're fucking with me right now."

"I'm not." Wyatt wasn't sure if he wanted to throw up, burst into tears, or scream at the sky. "Ginny Foster was my mother. I'm her only child and I never knew my biological father. Not his name, not where he was from, not until these last few years when I started digging. That digging led me to you."

"Ginny." He said the name softly, almost reverently, his own eyes glistening. "She's your mother."

"Yes."

"And you're twenty years old."

"Yes." Brand was still scarily pale and seemed likely to topple right out of his own chair if he wasn't careful. "You think you're my son." Not a question.

"Yes. It all fits. My mother was born here, moved away when she was sixteen. Gave birth to me when she was seventeen. She married my stepfather when I was just a kid. My grandparents never talked about their life before I was born, and all I was ever told about my father was that he was selfish. That he gave me up, signed away his rights, and never wanted a thing to do with me. That his whole family was mean and selfish and to forget that side of my family tree."

"Why didn't you forget it?"

The only reason Wyatt responded instead of fleeing the office was because Brand sounded more curious than angry. "Because Mom died when I was sixteen."

"Fuck, I'm sorry. She was a special girl."

"Yeah. She was an amazing mom." Part of him didn't want to share this with Brand, but Brand was paying attention, not getting mad and demanding he leave. "It was liver cancer, and she might have survived if she'd matched for a transplant, but she didn't. I had a huge argument with her parents about biology. Asked what I was supposed to do if I ever got sick like that and needed a transplant. That I wanted to know my biological father, and not just as a backup for potential illness, but because he was half of me. I thought I deserved to know who he was, even if he was a bad person."

Brand rubbed his eyes with one hand. "I knew Ginny's parents hated me but I never imagined they would try to poison you against me and my family. Not that I'm all that surprised. Not after how everything went down."

"Ramie told me a little about that."

"Ramie did?" His eyes flashed with anger. "Why?"

"It wasn't really her fault. Last week was the birthday of the baby she gave up and she was really down about it, and she blurted out the thing you two had in common. Giving up a kid. Told me a little about it, like how my grandparents threatened to bring rape charges if you didn't sign away your rights."

"Yeah, that definitely happened." More anger brightened his cheeks and blazed in his eyes. "I would have done my part. Stuck by you and Ginny, but her parents were too embarrassed by the whole thing. They wanted to move away and leave behind the stigma of a teen pregnancy. I always wondered if Ginny kept the baby or gave it up for adoption, and if this is real then I guess I know the answer."

"If this is real? Do you think I'd be here baring my soul to you if I thought it wasn't? Everything fucking fits. And now I hate that I lied, because I really like this job, and I really like Jackson, and I don't want to lose everything I've built here."

"Wait, what does Jackson have to do with all this?"

He'd already laid down the dynamite and connected the fuse. Might as well press the button on the detonator. "Because we've been secretly dating almost since I was hired, and he knew I'd come here to Claire County to find my biological father, and after he talked to Hugo last night and learned your secret, he put it all together. We had a fight, and I'm pretty sure he dumped me, and I had to confess to you, so if I'm fired now that you know the whole truth I will go."

Brand blinked hard. "You think I'm gonna fire you because you might be my kid and are dating my friend?"

"Aren't you?"

"Wyatt, I am trying to process this. Honestly, I don't know what I think or what I want to do. It's just all so surreal."

"Tell me about it." He picked at a loose thread on the inseam of his jeans. "For what it's worth, I am sorry for deceiving you. Maybe another guy would have just knocked on your door and told you what I suspected, but my family is all about secrets. Keeping secrets. Not telling, or else. And I also wanted to see if the stories about you were true before I said anything."

"Are they? True?"

"No. No, you're a pretty cool guy, and your family is awesome. You aren't the Manson family. You're the Woods family and I like you guys. Especially Rose. Her kindness reminds me of Mom sometimes."

"My mom loves her kids and grandkids without condition. Doesn't surprise me Ginny was like that. I'm glad to know she kept the baby. Raised you. You're a pretty decent person."

"When I'm not lying about my reasons for being here? Or at least leaving out part of the truth. I did want to learn how to live this life, be a cowboy. That wasn't a lie."

Brand frowned. "You just left out the whole part of you suspecting I was your bio dad."

"Yeah."

He stood and moved to the window behind his desk, arms crossed, expression flat now. "I wanna believe you about all this and just accept it as truth."

"But I've lied already and you don't trust me."

"I'm sorry."

"It's okay, I deserve that. We can do any kind of DNA test you want. We can confirm it for both of us."

"Okay. You good with doing it right now?"

Wyatt stared dumbly for a beat. "Right now?"

"Yeah. I'll drive us to the hospital. I mean, you can get those DNA test kits and mail them in, but I'd rather go to a real lab and do it that way. Plus, we'll get the results in days rather than weeks."

"That's fine." He was still a touch stunned Brand was being so calm about all this, instead of running him off the land with a shotgun.

Stop it, that's your grandparents talking. Brand isn't the villain.

There was no real villain here, only a tangled web of lies that Wyatt had both been born into and constructed on his own. Time to do his best to tear the web apart and set himself free to be whoever he was truly meant to be. Even if he had to leave Texas behind for good.

Brand picked his phone up from the desk. "I'm texting Hugo and Michael that I'm going off the land for a while. Today was an office day for me anyway."

"Okay. Um, are you going to tell Hugo about me?"

"I have to tell him. After our fight last night, I can't keep this from him, but I don't plan on telling the rest of my family anything until the DNA test confirms it. I won't do that to them."

"You won't dangle a grandson in front of your parents without proof?"

"Exactly." Brand leaned against the wall by the window, arms still crossed, definitely on the defensive now. "I wish I could do better by you, Wyatt. I wish I could believe you, walk over there, and hug you as my son but I can't. This is all so sudden."

"And surreal, I get it, I really do." Wyatt didn't know if he wanted to laugh, cry, or both, so he settled on clearing his throat really hard. "I guess we should go."

"Yeah. Meet me in the parking lot of the Roost. We'll

leave your car there and both go in my truck. That way you don't have to come all the way back out here when we're done."

The requirement surprised him more than it probably should have. Not so much Brand wanting to escort Wyatt to the hospital to make sure he went, but that Brand didn't want him back on this property anytime soon. "Okay. Am I fired?"

"No. Until this DNA test is back the regular schedule will be worked as posted. However, tomorrow I'll have you shadowing Rem instead of Jackson."

"That's fair." Jackson would probably appreciate it, too, and Wyatt's insides ached at the thought. "I, uh, guess we should go. Meet at the Roost, I mean."

"Yeah. You go first. I'll be a few minutes behind you."

"Okay."

Wyatt stood and left the bunkhouse, walking to his car on autopilot. Nothing about his life right now felt tangible, as if he was sleepwalking through it all. Or insanely drunk and unaware of his own actual movements. Deep in his heart he knew what the DNA test would prove, but they both needed it to be sure. To have that document in their hands that said they were father and son. Then they could begin to process things and move forward.

Maybe.

He hoped.

Chapter Nineteen

Brand was such a tangled mess when he returned from the hospital that he didn't bother trying to do any more work in the office. He nearly went inside the main house so he could vent all of this to Mom and get her advice. But he couldn't give her the joyous fantasy that she had a grandson out there, only to potentially yank that happy news away. So he walked into the bunkhouse, which was dark and quiet. Not a surprise since it was only four o'clock.

The lab at the hospital had been a tad backed up when they arrived, so they'd had to wait for their turn. Wyatt had seemed a touch green at the idea of a needle and blood draw, but Brand didn't trust those cheek swab tests. Plus, the kid had seen enough of his own blood these past couple of weeks that it amazed Brand he might be squeamish.

They hadn't spoken much, and Brand had found himself studying Wyatt's profile while pretending to do something on his phone. The more he looked, the more of Ginny he saw in Wyatt—and more of himself, too. Wyatt definitely had the Woods family nose, inherited by each of them from Dad's side.

Brand went for the cupboard above the mini-fridge and hot plate. He kept a bottle of bourbon up there for nights when he had trouble sleeping and wanted to knock a few back. Less of those since he and Hugo had moved in together, so the bottle was mostly full. He didn't have a proper snifter for it—broke his only one moving from the house to here, which was pretty stupid since the distance was less than twenty yards—so he used a coffee mug. Poured some and took the mug to the kitchen table.

Wyatt could be my kid. Wyatt could be my kid.

The words had been stuck on repeat in his head ever since Wyatt confessed, and they only got louder while he sat alone in the dimming room. The sun didn't set quite as early in February as it did in January, but it was still dark outside when Hugo walked in. Brand had sipped his way through one pour of bourbon and was nursing his second.

Hugo jumped and let out a startled yelp when he flipped on the main overhead light and spotted Brand. "Christ, give a guy a heart attack, why don't you?"

"Sorry," Brand said. "Just sat down and got lost in thought."

He eyeballed Brand's mug, then sniffed the air. "No coffee left?"

"I didn't brew any." Brand tilted his head at the bottle. "I found something out today that's fucking with my mind a little, and I need to tell you about it."

"This isn't another secret kid, is it?"

"No, this is actually about the same secret kid."

Hugo frowned as he hung his hat on a peg by the door. Pulled off his boots and left them on a mat before joining Brand at the table. "Am I going to need a mug of that, too?"

"Guess we'll find out." Sitting there with his boyfriend and lover across from him buoyed his courage a bit. Might as well rip the damned bandage off and see how bad things bled. "It's Wyatt."

"What's Wyatt? Did he hurt himself again?"

"No, shockingly no. Wyatt came to me today and told me something he's been keeping from me, keeping from all of us really, since the day I hired him." When Hugo simply stared at him with raised eyebrows, Brand added, "Ginny had red hair and green eyes just like his."

"Okay." Hugo's gaze went briefly distant and Brand saw the moment his partner understood. He made the most peculiar "What the actual fuck?" face Brand had ever seen in his life, complete with bugging eyes and a wide-open mouth. "You are fucking with me."

"No. He came here specifically to get to know me, because his grandparents told him stories all his life about what a horrible, selfish person I am, and I guess he needed to see if that was true before he told me anything. We talked about it a bit and then went to the hospital to have DNA tests done. I need to see it in black and white before I can truly believe it."

"Jesus, Brand, that's huge. I can't believe your long-lost kid is back."

"*Maybe* back, if it's true." But something deep inside of Brand believed it was. He'd instantly liked Wyatt from their first interview, had seen something special in the kid, and now he better understood why.

"But why say anything now? After all this time?"

"Because Jackson knew Wyatt was out here searching for his bio dad but not who Wyatt suspected of being him. And when you told Jackson about my kid, he put it together and confronted Wyatt."

"Oh shit, my bad."

"It's fine. You needed to vent and, to be honest, this secret needed to come out. We have to deal with it. If the DNA says he's my son, then my family is gonna have a lot to process in the next coming weeks." He waited until Hugo made eye contact. "How do you feel about being a stepfather?"

Hugo made a noise, half laugh and half choke. "A little

weird considering he's only eight years younger than me, but if he's your kid, Brand…we'll figure this out. Sure, I was mad last night that you never told me you had a child out in the world, but it was your secret to tell in your time. I get that now. And thank you for telling me about Wyatt right away."

"I owed you this truth. But I don't wanna tell the rest of my family yet, not until I know for sure. If Wyatt's wrong, they never have to know. If he's right, then they deserve a chance to get to know him as part of the family."

"How do you think your parents will react if Wyatt is yours?"

"Mom will be over the moon. My parents were furious with Ginny's when they threatened me with rape charges. Furious that they forced me out of any of the decision-making process. When they moved away, I could only imagine what happened. Had she carried to term and kept it? Given it up for adoption? Miscarried and never had the baby at all? I actually got really depressed for a while, and I finally had to make a clean break from it all in my mind. To imagine the best for her and our kid and to move on."

"That sounds like the healthiest thing you could have done. You were a kid doing the best you could in an awful situation that was not helped by some of the adults involved. But I think you've shown Wyatt that you are a kind, fair person. He wouldn't still be working here if he believed you were any sort of threat, to him or to others."

"Thank you." Brand reached out and clasped their hands together, grateful for Hugo's unwavering love and support. "I'd never admit this to anyone else, but I'm kind of terrified right now."

"Tell me why."

"Because I don't know how to be a parent. Sure, mine were loving and supportive, except for that thing with Colt.

And Dad was pretty strict when we were growing up, but this is a working ranch and we were expected to complete our chores on time, or something could go wrong."

"The good news is that Wyatt is an adult, not a child who needs raising. He needs love and support and probably advice from time to time, and he needs to know he has that love and support from you. We still need our parents no matter how old we get."

Brand raised Hugo's hand to his mouth and kissed the knuckles. Hugo still struggled with his estrangement from his mother. Less so with his stepfather, because they'd never been close, but Hugo missed his mom. But she had chosen her husband over her son, so Hugo had made his choice, too. No contact.

"You've got my parents," Brand said, "and you know you've been family since you and Rem got to be best friends back in high school."

"Thanks, and you know I adore your parents. But I want to ask you a question, and if you don't know for sure right now then think about it and get back to me."

"Okay."

"If Wyatt is your son, do you want him to *be* your son?"

Brand stared, not understanding. "What? If he's my son, he's my son."

"Biologically, yes. I'm talking about emotionally and, I guess, how you'll treat him. Think about him. Knowing he's your son and changing how you think about him as your son and not just an employee is a big shift. Mentally and emotionally. You told me you never tried to find him because you wanted to shelve that part of your life and move on. Is that still true?"

"I don't know. It was true as of a few hours ago."

"That's fair. You got hit over the head with a mallet today, Brand, you're going to be spinning for a while. Like

I said, if you don't know, then think on it. Up until a few hours ago, your child was a distant memory. Now he's possibly a living, breathing guy we've worked with for almost two months. Take your time with it."

"Well, I've got at least two to three business days to try and figure this out." Brand turned their hands so he could stroke Hugo's palm with his thumb, a soothing gesture he often used when Hugo begged for a hand massage after a long day mucking stalls. "If it turns out Wyatt isn't mine, would you be angry if I decided I did want to find my kid?"

"No. I know what family means to you, Brand. You know I'll support whatever you want to do."

"I do know that." Maybe it was a combination of the gigantic emotional drop-kick he'd taken today, plus the bourbon, but Brand nearly went to his knee and offered Hugo the ring. Nearly. He didn't want Hugo to think Brand was doing this as a reaction to Wyatt's revelation today. Brand would wait and do it when it felt absolutely right. "I know I don't say it a lot, but I love you."

"I love you, too. And I will be there to love and support you through this entire journey."

"Thank you."

"Of course. You eat dinner yet?"

"Nah. I think Mom said something about everyone helping themselves to whatever leftovers are in the fridge, so she can clean it out and go shopping. Wanna walk over?"

"Give me ten minutes to shower?"

"Sure."

Brand reluctantly released Hugo's hand. Once his partner had disappeared into the bathroom he pulled his phone out and called Jackson.

"Hey, man," Jackson said with an edge of caution in his voice.

"Wyatt told me."

Jackson didn't speak for long enough that Brand checked to make sure they hadn't been disconnected. "I see."

"I wanna believe him but we went and had DNA tests done. We'll know in a few days."

"I'm real sorry, boss. I had no idea he was here lookin' for you specifically."

"I believe you. And I don't hold any of this against you, especially since I never did tell you I had a child out there."

"That wasn't my business. Maybe we slept together off and on for a lotta years, but you never owed me that kinda secret."

"Thanks." He was all kinds of glad Jackson didn't hold any of this against him, because he valued the older man's friendship. "So I guess the guy you said you were happy about being with was Wyatt, huh?"

"Yeah. I didn't wanna say anything to anyone, because I needed to keep my personal and professional lives separate after what happened with us. Not that we were bad together or anything, but I didn't want that complication again, even though it wasn't technically boss and employee this time. I was still his trainer, though."

"I get that. And Wyatt?"

"Can't really speak for him. He had his reasons."

"Of course. Reasons he told you." For the first time in the past couple of hours, it struck Brand that if Wyatt was truly his son, then that meant Jackson had been screwing around with his son. A guy who was literally half his age! If they'd simply both been employees the age gap wouldn't have bothered Brand in the least, but they weren't simply employees. Wyatt might be *his kid*.

A protective streak Brand had never felt before bubbled up from deep inside, and he tamped down on it before he growled at one of his dearest friends.

"Yes, reasons he told me," Jackson said, a new edge

in his voice now. "I respected the fact that he wanted to check out this potential bio father without revealing himself. And after he told me more about his childhood and stepfather, I understood his reasons for keeping things close to the chest."

Brand sat up straighter. "What did his stepfather do to him?"

"Sorry, boss, still not gonna speak for him. It doesn't affect his ability to work at the ranch so if he chooses to tell you about his past, that's his choice."

"Fair." Frustrating but fair, and it dropped a cold ball of worry into Brand's gut. He'd missed the first twenty years of his son's life. A son who'd left his hometown and family behind not only to try his hand at the cowboy life but to discover his birth father. There was so damned much Brand still didn't know. So much he wanted to find out about Wyatt, even if he didn't end up being Brand's son.

Odds of that are pretty fucking low. Everything fits too perfectly.

"You mad at me?" Jackson asked.

"I don't know. I mean, I'm not really mad at you. Frustrated and resentful, I think. But you also had no real way of putting everything together until last night when Hugo told you I had a kid out there. I'm frustrated you didn't call me right away."

"Wasn't my secret to tell."

"But it was your secret to keep?"

"It was my choice to keep it, and it was Wyatt's obligation to be the one to tell you. Not me. I did say if he didn't, I would, and I'm proud of him for sucking it up and doing the hard thing."

The pride was clear in Jackson's voice, as was his lingering grief. Brand knew him too well not to notice. "But how Wyatt went about things still hurt you." Brand didn't know all the gritty details of Jackson's past, but he knew enough to understand how much Jackson valued honesty.

"Yeah, I'm...workin' through how I feel about all that. I think can forgive him, I just don't know..."

"If you can trust him again?"

"Yeah."

"Do you love him?"

"I'm not sure answering that question is appropriate right now, especially since I don't know if you're asking as my friend, his friend, or his father."

"Might be asking as his boss, too."

That got a brief snort of laughter from Jackson. "I think this is a conversation I need to have with Wyatt before I do with you in any capacity, Brand."

"Point taken. I just needed to talk some of this out with you so I could parse it all myself. I'm not mad at you for keeping Wyatt's confidence. The circumstances are all fucked up on both sides. But man, you've been boning my kid and you're twice his age and I am not okay with that. Even if Wyatt wasn't maybe my kid, I'd be weirded out by the age difference."

"Why?"

Brand blinked at the wall in the same instant the shower shut off. Hugo was almost finished. "Twenty years, dude. I mean, Wyatt was born when we were still figuring out how to text by hitting the same button three times to get one letter. All he knows are touch screens and apps and probably can't even read cursive."

"When was the last time you wrote anything besides your signature in cursive?"

"Not the point."

"Well, your point is made, taken, and considered. But my relationship with Wyatt is between me and him. If you are his biological father, Brand, I will respect that relationship. So long as you respect mine, whatever it ends up being. Whether Wyatt and I stay together, or we break up and go back to just work acquaintances, it's for him and me to figure out. Not him, me, and you."

Brand wanted to argue the point but didn't. Jackson was one of the most stubborn people he'd ever met and Brand wasn't going to change his mind. All Brand could do was move forward, trust Jackson, and hope they all made the best choices possible for their futures.

"I won't interfere," Brand said. "But if you hurt my kid, you'll answer to me."

He swore he heard Jackson smile when he replied, "I wouldn't have it any other way, boss. I do have one request and you know it's not something I ever ask for unless it's important."

"I'm already gonna reassign Wyatt's final week of training to Rem."

"Not the request, but that's fine. Wyatt's done real good so far and shouldn't frustrate Rem too much."

Brand resisted laughing. Everyone knew Rem wasn't the most patient person. Rem had been a mess when Susie was a baby and he was still figuring out how to be a dad. "Name what you need."

"The day off tomorrow. You can swap me a day with Michael if you have to, I just need the day to myself to think. I don't think I can do my job right knowing I could run into Wyatt at any moment."

"I get it and you've got the day. I don't have much to do in the office tomorrow, so Hugo and I will be out and about, too. We'll be fine."

"Thanks. I mean it. See you Wednesday."

"Yeah, see you."

He ended the call just as Hugo left the bathroom with a towel around his waist. Hugo strode across the room, his lean torso still lightly glistening with moisture, and went into the bedroom. If they hadn't committed to dinner with his family soon, Brand might have followed his boyfriend right in there, shut the door, and made good use of his nearly naked state.

Instead, he waited patiently for Hugo to dress and did his best not to think about that damned DNA test.

Chapter Twenty

Wyatt wasn't surprised when he got to the ranch Tuesday and found out Jackson had taken a personal day. It didn't surprise him, no, but it still felt like he'd been punched in the nuts. Jackson was so hurt by this that he couldn't even see Wyatt today?

It was his own fault, though. He'd kept his secret even after Jackson was so open with him about his past and his need for trust, and Wyatt had blown up the best thing in his life. If Jackson couldn't stand to work beside him anymore, much less maybe forgive him and take him back, it was Wyatt's own fault.

Rem was a lot of fun to work with and talked way more than Jackson, or even Michael. His favorite subjects were his wife and daughter, naturally, but he probably overshared a little with how much he and Shelby were trying for another baby. Hugo shot Wyatt the occasional sympathetic smile, while Brand was all professional and shit, the whole day. Wyatt wasn't sure how he felt about that so he did his best to work and not dwell on it.

Ramie had been at work last night when Wyatt got home from the DNA test, and he'd gone to bed early, exhausted from grief and fear. When he got home tonight, she was there, eating leftovers in front of the television. While Wyatt didn't mind leftover food, he was always a little weirded out by her habit of eating it cold straight from the fridge. Cold pizza was fine, sure, but cold egg rolls? Cold mac and cheese? Who did that?

"You look like you got kicked in the nuts," she said.

"Metaphorically, I guess I did." He sank onto the couch beside her. "I told Brand the truth yesterday and we took a paternity test. Just waiting on the results. But all day long, Brand acted like not a thing had changed, and then Jackson called out, and I hate thinking they're mad at me. I miss Jackson so much."

"I bet he misses you, too. This isn't easy for anyone, especially him and Brand."

Wyatt flinched. "I know, but it isn't easy for me, either. I didn't come here to hurt anyone. All I wanted was answers."

"I know. But the way you went about getting those answers had some pretty awful consequences. Now you have to navigate these choppy waters and hope you find shore in a place you can live with."

"Guess we'll start to see in a few days when the DNA results come back."

"Do you want Brand to be your father?"

"I do." He didn't have to think about it at all. "My whole life my bio dad was built up as this cartoon villain with his villainous family right beside him. But Brand and the Woodses are nothing like what I imagined. They are warm and accepting and generous, and I would really love to have one side of my family who's like that."

"So would I." Ramie bumped his ankle with hers and smiled. "A lot of people would, so I hope you get what you want."

"Thanks. And I hope you get whatever it is you're looking for in life, too. You're, like, the best big sister who isn't related to me ever."

"Thanks, dude. You're a pretty cool not-really little brother. You work tomorrow?"

"Yeah. I hope Jackson is there. Even if he won't talk to me beyond a few work-related grunts, I just want to see him. Until I met him I never realized it could physically hurt to be apart from someone."

"I'll have to take your word on that."

"You've never been in love?"

"No. Had a few aesthetic crushes over the years and regular sex with Brand was nice while it lasted, but I've never had that driving desire to be part of a couple. Which goes against everything society and Hollywood and everyone else tells us is normal, but there it is."

She spoke matter-of-factly, perfectly comfortable with this part of herself, and Wyatt kind of envied her. He wasn't comfortable with most things about himself, and that was probably because he still didn't truly know who he was. He'd hidden his sexuality most of his life; he'd grown up not knowing half of his background or family; he'd come here and settled in Weston on a lie that was breaking what he'd thought was a solid foundation.

A foundation built on a lie never stood the test of time, though. A foundation needed to be built on truth. If he got a chance to start over with Jackson, he'd be truthful always.

"I'm glad you know yourself and what you want," Wyatt said. "Maybe I'll get there someday."

"I know it's trite and you're probably sick of hearing it, but you're still young, Wyatt. These are the years when you figure things out. Don't be too hard on yourself when you make mistakes, even mistakes as epic as this one. People might be mad for a while because we're human beings with complex emotions. Just give it time."

"I will. One thing I do know for sure with Jackson is

pushing him won't help. He'll hunker down and push back and it won't do either of us any good."

"Good." She offered him the white carton in her hand. "Beef and broccoli?"

"Not unless you nuke it."

"Fancy pants. Go get your own food, then." She winked. Wyatt laughed and did exactly that.

Jackson spent the better parts of Monday (his day off) and Tuesday (his requested personal day) wandering the land around the motel with Dog. She was excited to have his undivided attention again during those long hours. Hours he used to devote to Wyatt, but that wasn't happening for a while. He couldn't say ever again, because he just didn't know. No matter what the DNA test showed, Wyatt had lied. For weeks.

That was a tough bit to chew through, and Jackson still didn't know what he wanted to do when he arrived for work on Wednesday morning. The wide-open spaces around the motel hadn't provided any answers, but they had kept the memories of the worst years of his life at bay for a while. He couldn't hide forever, though, and he had to face Wyatt. Even if they didn't speak beyond work stuff, he had to face the younger, fiery ginger who'd stolen and then broken his heart.

His first glimpse of Wyatt in the barn made Jackson's heart race in a familiar way, as if his body knew they'd been apart for too long. Instead of going over and claiming his guy, Jackson put his lunch away and hid in the break room for ten minutes, until he heard the clomping of two horses being led out. Rem was off today, so Wyatt was probably out with Michael.

Good. Wyatt knew the basic skills. All he needed to do was hone them, and being around guys other than Jackson would help. And he was perfectly safe out in the pastures with Michael, who was both a great horseman and also happily in love with someone else. Jackson's possessiveness over Wyatt annoyed him, but he and Wyatt hadn't officially broken up. They were in this weird holding pattern.

A holding pattern Jackson needed time to get out of, and Wyatt was giving him both time and space to figure things out. To understand why Wyatt had done things the way he had instead of trusting Jackson enough to be honest about his intentions.

Jackson worked in the barn most of the day, taking his lunch break early and in his truck to avoid Wyatt. He somehow managed to not speak with Brand or Hugo all day, too, and when Jackson clocked out for the day he kind of regretted how distant he'd been with all his coworkers. But no one in the know was pushing him. He'd just have to be a little less standoffish tomorrow so Michael or Rem didn't start to suspect anything was wrong.

A lot was wrong but Jackson didn't want to talk about it. Not yet.

Not in the mood to be alone, Jackson went to the Roost for a beer and a burger. Dog was content to chill on the front seat with a piece of beef jerky to keep her company. He didn't normally like leaving her in the truck, but it was a chilly night and with both windows cracked, she'd be fine.

Jackson wasn't at all surprised when Ramie came out from behind the bar to deliver his burger personally. "Look, I know we aren't exactly friends," she said softly, "and the only thing we really have in common is we both used to fuck Brand and we love this place's bleu cheese and bacon burger, but if you ever need to talk about what's going on, you can vent to me."

Jackson stared at her, surprised by the offer. "As his roommate, aren't you on Wyatt's side?"

"No, I'm not. I get where he's coming from, but his subterfuge hurt Brand and that hurts me. He hurt you the most, though, judging by the sad-face emoji hanging in the air over your head."

"I guess more sad-face than angry-face is an improvement. Thanks, Ramie. I appreciate the offer but I just gotta work through this on my own."

"Heard and understood, but my door is always open. So to speak. Enjoy the burger." She went back behind the bar and straight to the guy holding up a twenty-dollar bill. Ramie moved with such confidence and grace that he kind of envied her and her comfortable place in the world. Jackson had never possessed that sort of peace and comfort.

Except when he'd been with Wyatt, who'd accepted everything about Jackson and cared about him anyway. If Wyatt could accept Jackson killing a man, then maybe Jackson could work through Wyatt lying to him.

Maybe.

The burger was perfection and it hit the spot in terms of hunger. Not so much with his emotions, so he indulged in a second beer before driving home. It only vaguely struck him that Ramie hadn't been behind the bar when he paid his tab because he would have thanked her again for trying to be his friend, but even the best bartenders got breaks.

He had a few minutes before they closed to buy some lunch fixings at the general store, mostly lunchmeat and bread, and then he headed home. He put his groceries away, filled Dog's food dish, then paced for a while, unable to settle. His instincts were bouncing all over the place, telling him something wasn't right. He put a leash on Dog and walked the perimeter of the motel with her, but all the doors were locked, no windows broken. Nothing wrong around this place.

But he couldn't shake the sense that something was wrong elsewhere. And the feeling left him restless for a long time.

Wyatt poked at the plate of chicken-fried steak and mashed potatoes he'd ordered for dinner, less interested in actually eating it than in turning it into impressionist art. He hadn't wanted to go home and sit around alone tonight, so he'd first driven over to the Roost, but as soon as he saw Jackson's truck, he'd changed plans and headed over to the diner instead. He recognized Shelby Woods immediately from all the pictures Rem had shown him, but she wasn't working his sections tonight.

Work today had been fine, even though it stung that Jackson had done everything possible to avoid being near him. Wyatt just wanted a word, one single word spoken in his direction, even if it was as simple as a "Hey." He hadn't even gotten that out of the angry older cowboy.

A body moved past his table, then backtracked and stopped. Wyatt looked up, curious if it was the bus-person trying to claim his plate before he mashed it further into oblivion. Instead, a guy around his age, probably older, smiled down at him. He held a plastic take-out bag in one hand and a paper tray with three drinks in the other.

"Hi," the man said. "We haven't met, but I'm going to take a stab that you're Wyatt Gibson?"

"Yeah, I am." Random strangers knowing who he was put his hackles up. "You are?"

"Josiah Sheridan, Michael's boyfriend." He hefted the bag. "I was picking up dinner for me, him, and his dad when I spotted you. Michael has mentioned you and I wanted to say hello. Welcome to town."

"Thanks, it's nice to meet you." There was something soothing about Josiah, and he tried to remember—oh yeah, Josiah was an in-home care nurse. "You guys have the camper I was supposed to rent when I first got here."

"That's us. Thankfully, we fixed the problem and it's available again if you're ever in need. I lived in it for a while before I began dating and eventually moved in with Michael."

"I appreciate that. I think I'm good where I am right now, but I'll keep it in mind." Even though the conversation about his first eight weeks was closing in fast, Ramie hadn't said a thing about him finding a new place to stay. He liked having a roommate and he liked Ramie's quirky decorating tastes. He liked Jackson's motel room and remote location a hell of a lot more, though. Plenty of room for two people, plus Dog.

"Well, it was nice to meet you, Wyatt. I won't keep interrupting your dinner."

"It was great meeting you too, Josiah."

Josiah made his way out of the diner, and Wyatt stared blankly at the door for a few seconds, before remembering his own food. He ate a couple more bites of steak and shoveled in some potatoes, mostly so he didn't waste it all. Not that Ramie wouldn't eat it cold out of the doggie bag if he took his leftovers home, which he decided to do about five minutes later. Sitting alone in the booth had lost its appeal, so he got his remnants wrapped up.

Time to go home.

For most of his life, going home meant back to the house shared by him, Mom, his stepfather and two step-siblings. It was a small two-story house with three bedrooms they'd moved into when Wyatt was eight, so Wyatt had shared with Peter for a few years until Peter moved away for college. A cramped space with a lot of people had been normal, until it was suddenly just Wyatt and his stepfather. Then he had craved his own space, which he'd sort of gotten with college.

He adored the space he had living with Ramie, because she was hardly ever home and she didn't try to mother him. She gave him his freedom, only a few small rules, and they both lived their separate lives. It was the perfect living arrangement for two single people. He only hoped his dating status didn't drop from "in a relationship" back into "single." Somehow he had to win back Jackson's trust and his love.

More than anything else in his life, Jackson's love— whether either of them had said the words or not—gave Wyatt something he'd been missing in his life since Mom died. It gave him security, confidence, and hope. Three things he desperately needed to keep hold of, because right now everything was up for grabs.

Ramie's car was in the driveway, which surprised him because she had a closing shift tonight. Worried his surrogate big sister was sick, he left his doggie bag on the front seat and sprinted across the small front lawn. Burst through the unlocked front door and froze about three steps inside the house, unsure what he was seeing at first.

Ramie sat on the couch facing the TV, ramrod straight with both hands in her lap, staring ahead at nothing in particular. She didn't move when he walked in. The second thing he noticed was some dude with shaggy brown hair, a goatee and a bored glare sitting in the chair catty-corner to the couch, mostly facing the door. The third thing was the black object in the stranger's hand, and its aim shifted from Ramie to Wyatt.

Gun. That's a gun. Why does this guy have a fucking gun?

"Should I come back later?" It was the first thing that slipped out of Wyatt's stunned mouth.

"No, please join us," the stranger said. He waved the gun at the other end of the couch. "Put your cell phone on the floor and kick it over to me."

Unsure what the hell was going on and pretty positive that gun was real, Wyatt did as told, perching on the edge of the far cushion. He hated kicking his phone because the screen had enough cracks, but he'd deal with that later. Ramie barely moved, her face expressing nothing except mild boredom. If she was afraid of whatever this was, she hid it well. Wyatt, meanwhile, was pretty sure he was thirty seconds away from wetting himself.

He glanced at Ramie. "Friend of yours?"

"Nope," she snapped without looking at him. "You?"

"No."

"No, none of us have ever met," the stranger said. "We never should have met like this, but I need my property back, and I wasn't having any luck hiring locals."

"What? What property?" Fear was overriding his good sense, and Wyatt couldn't help blurting out to Ramie, "Why are you even home?"

"I needed a tampon," she replied.

"There isn't a machine in the bathroom?"

"It's a dive bar, not a convenience store."

"Okay, ladies, that's enough," the stranger said with a sharper bite to his voice. He also had an odd accent, something like West Texas by way of Brooklyn, and it made him less menacing and more comical. Not that Wyatt dared laugh. "Wyatt, you are in possession of something I need back."

"I'm pretty sure I'm not in possession of anything of yours." Maybe back-talking a guy with a gun was a stupid move, but Wyatt wasn't used to having one pointed at him and it was fucking with his sense of self-preservation. Everything he'd brought with him from home had been his—except the car. "Shit, man, Jared said he bought the car from a legit dealer. It wasn't stolen, was it?"

"No, this isn't about the car specifically, it's about something Jared was holding for me in the car. The car you left town with two days earlier than he expected, so he was unable to retrieve my property beforehand."

What in the holy blue hell was this guy— The roadside kit. The one Jared had bugged him about a few weeks ago and insisted Wyatt mail back. "You came all this way for a roadside kit? He said it was a sentimental gift from his grandmother."

The stranger sighed. "Jared was my mistake, and he's learned his lesson about disappointing me."

A chill zinged down his spine. "What did you do to him?" He hated the tremor in his voice, but Wyatt had seen way too many cop movies not to immediately jump to the visual of Jared's body being dumped in a dry gulch somewhere.

"He's gonna have a limp, but he'll live."

That did not make Wyatt feel any better, because he still didn't understand what the stranger wanted from him. Granted, Jared could have stashed anything from drugs to a money roll in the kit and Wyatt wouldn't have known. He hadn't gone through the thing when he left or looked inside it since he got here. Not even when he boxed it up last week and stashed it in the car for whenever he managed to get to the post office.

Uh-oh. Oh shit.

"Wait a minute, did you try breaking into my car trunk a few weeks ago?" Wyatt asked.

"Like hell. But it's amazing the idiot teens you can find online and pay fifty bucks to go get something for you. He thought he was playing a harmless prank by stealing it for me, but we all know he fucked that up. For two hundred, I paid a man to break in here and find my shit."

"Someone was in my house last week?" Ramie asked, a flash of fury in her voice and eyes.

The stranger smirked. "Yes. He sent pictures to prove he'd poked around, and he was worth the price, since you obviously never noticed he broke into the place." He frowned at Wyatt. "But you had apparently put it someplace else. Where is it?"

"Um…at the, uh, post office," Wyatt said.

"You mailed it?"

"No, my, ah, boss mailed it. It had been in my car for like a week and when he mentioned he needed to make a post office run for stamps and to mail a package, I asked if he could take my box, too, because I hadn't mailed it yet, so yeah, I don't have it." The stranger glared in his general direction, and Wyatt's gut clenched with terror. "But he went at lunchtime and the office closes at one, because it's a small town, so maybe it hasn't been sent out yet."

Encouraging a guy with a gun to break into the post office. Real smart, Gibson, real smart.

"Who'd you address the box to?" the guy asked.

"Jared. He wanted it." And now Wyatt knew why, even if he didn't actually know anything. Only that something valuable was in it, and this guy with the gun really wanted it back if he'd paid two people to try to retrieve it, and then come himself. Wyatt hated knowing whatever his idiot best friend had gotten mixed up in had brought danger right to Ramie's doorstep. She did not deserve this.

Maybe I do, though, after hurting everyone with my secrets.

The stranger raised the gun, and Wyatt momentarily forgot to breathe. All the stranger did was use the pinkie of that hand to scratch his cheek, and if he thought that was intimidating…he was half-right. "This is a wrinkle I did not expect. Getting it from Jared in two or three days is too complicated, because of you two. I can't exactly leave you here to tell the police about me."

"Then take me with you," Wyatt said without thinking.

"What?" Ramie squawked.

"Take me with you," he repeated, ignoring her for now. "We can go to the post office and break in, you know, see if the package is still there. And if not, take me with you back to Jared's house. Ramie won't say anything about this to the cops, because she knows I'll be your hostage and you could hurt me or whatever. She's really good at secrets."

"You are not going with him."

Wyatt met and held her angry gaze, trying to tell her without words that this was a good plan. It didn't sound like this guy was going to kill them if he didn't have to, so going with him back to Glasbury meant neither of them being shot if he didn't get his property back from the post office. Her own eyes seemed to yell at him in a big-sisterly way that he needed to stop trying to be a hero. He'd lied and broken her trust; he needed to do this. To try to atone for his sins somehow.

Plus, Ramie had to be late coming back from her break by now, so maybe if he got this guy to leave her behind, someone from the Roost would come looking for her. She'd be okay no matter what.

"I think the man with the gun gets to make all the decisions here," the stranger said. "You both look like trustworthy people, but I don't trust no one no more, not after this shit Jared pulled with my stash. So what I'm gonna do is tie the little miss up and stash her in a bedroom. Then you and me, Wyatt? We're gonna go get my package. We don't get it from the post office? All three of us is going on a road trip."

The menace in the stranger's voice sent a fresh bolt of terror through Wyatt's gut, and he resisted the urge to retch. He had to keep it together, be strong for Ramie, and get them out of this.

"No complaints? Good." He stood. "Both of you, into the bedroom."

"Which one?" Wyatt asked.

"Like I care. Go."

He and Ramie stood at the same time. She reached out, and Wyatt took her hand, hating the faint tremble he felt from her. He squeezed tight, trying to show confidence he didn't feel. They went to her room, the stranger behind them the entire way, and once inside he produced a roll of duct tape. Wyatt had never stepped foot inside Ramie's room before, only peeked in from the hall.

The stranger told Ramie to sit on the bed by the headboard and get comfortable. Wyatt watched with ice in his stomach as he wrapped her wrists and ankles in the duct tape, then used more to tape her to the corner of the four-poster bed. She endured the whole thing with sharp fury in her eyes and flushed cheeks. He imagined she despised being so helpless in such a dangerous situation, but it got that gun out of her house.

All Wyatt could do now was pray they broke into the post office and found that fucking package. If not… Nah, not going there. One step at a time.

"Be careful," Ramie said to him seconds before the stranger put a piece of tape over her mouth. The sight of her like that broke Wyatt's heart, but she was safer here than with them.

Wyatt winked.

"Let's go," the stranger said. He closed the bedroom door behind them.

Wyatt walked slowly into the living room, back straight

and shoulders squared, hoping to display more confidence than he felt. "So, uh, should I call you something other than Scary Guy with the Gun?"

The guy snorted. "How about John Smith? Now let's go, you're driving."

Fabulous.

Chapter Twenty-One

Brand had just finished cleaning up from his and Hugo's dinner while Hugo searched for something for them to watch tonight when his phone rang with an unassigned ringtone. He preferred specific ones for people who called him a lot so he knew who it was as soon as it rang or chimed or made whatever sound or song he'd given that person. He'd left his phone in the office and had half a mind to ignore it until tomorrow, but sometimes businesses called after hours.

Annoyed at the interruption, he swiped the phone off his desk. The Roost's main line. Weird. "Hello?"

"Hey, is this Brand?" a deep male voice asked.

"Yeah, is this George?" George was one of the bar's owners, and the only time Brand recalled ever getting a call from the man was when Ramie got real sick on her shift and needed a ride home.

"It's George. Listen, have you heard from Ramie in the last half hour?"

"No, why?" His skin prickled. "Is something wrong?"

"I'm not sure. Davy said she asked for a fifteen-minute break to run home for personal reasons, and that was almost an hour ago. She's never late coming back."

"I haven't talked to her since yesterday, but if you don't

have any spare help, I can drive over to her house and check on her."

"I'd really appreciate it. It's just me and Davy here right now, and we're running a Wednesday-night drink special that's got us hopping."

"Not a problem. I'll call if I find her."

"Same."

Brand ended the call and stared at his phone's lock screen, anxious about this brief disappearing act. Ramie loved her job and wouldn't just not go back to work after a break. Even though he knew it was fruitless, he still tried calling her. Straight to voice mail so her phone was off for some reason.

"Hey, H, we need to hold off on the movie," Brand said as he strode back into the living space. "I need to run out for a few."

Hugo frowned at him from the couch. "What's wrong?"

"Maybe something, maybe nothing. Ramie didn't go back to work after her break, and George is a little worried. I'm gonna go check her house, see if everything is okay."

"You want me to come with you?"

He adored Hugo's instant desire to help, but if something was wrong he didn't want Hugo anywhere near it. Not after last summer's drama with Buck. "No, it's okay. It's probably nothing. I'll call you when I know something so don't sit around and worry. Catch up on that show you like but keep putting off watching because you're addicted to bingeing things."

Hugo blew a raspberry at him. "Fine, go play hero. Hopefully it's just a dead phone battery and a flat tire."

From your mouth to God's ears, my heart.

Brand kissed Hugo on the mouth, shrugged into his coat, checked he had his wallet and phone, and headed for the pickup. He always left the keys inside, since he didn't lock the bunkhouse, and he'd recently switched the office door lock to a digital keypad. He knew the dirt road down to the state road by heart and sped up when it was safe, avoided the worst of the ruts they needed to fill when the weather warmed up, and made it out to the main road.

He blasted music to distract himself on the drive into town, probably too damned fast but no one pulled him over. His phone chimed once with an email alert but he ignored it. Work could definitely wait for a while longer, until he knew Ramie was safe. Halfway there, it occurred to him to try calling Wyatt, since the guy was her roommate.

Wyatt's phone went straight to voice mail, too. Brand's guts churned with unease. After so many people he knew being hurt by others in the past year or so, he wasn't taking anything for granted in this situation. He wished he'd thought to grab the shotgun he kept in the bunkhouse but too late now.

Ramie's truck was in the driveway when Brand pulled up to the curb. The house was dark, no lights on that he could see from the street, which wasn't like Ramie. She always left a living room light on when she worked a late shift, and as far as he knew she hadn't quit the habit just because she had a roommate.

He strode up the short path to the porch and didn't even try the knob; he just used his key to open the door. The living room was dark and quiet. He switched on the floor lamp and looked around. No sign of a disturbance, nothing that immediately alarmed him. "Ramie! You home?"

An odd, muffled banging sound from the bedroom yanked him in that direction. He shoved open the door and flipped the light switch on. For a split second, he thought he'd lost his fucking mind, but no, there was Ramie duct-taped to the bed. The relief in her wide, red-rimmed eyes punched him in the chest, and he carefully peeled the tape off her mouth.

"Oh thank fuck you're here," she said. "We're in trouble. He's got Wyatt."

"What? Who's got Wyatt?"

"This guy. Get me loose, please, before I pee on my bed."

"Okay, okay." He pulled a Swiss Army knife from his pocket and cut through the layers of tape. As soon as she was free, Ramie bolted across the hall to the bathroom.

She didn't shut the door, and they'd seen each other in more intimate positions before, so he followed her, angled away to give her some amount of privacy, and asked, "Who has Wyatt? What happened tonight?"

"I came home on a break and there was this guy here with a gun, and he told me to sit until Wyatt got here, so I did. Apparently, Wyatt's friend who owns their car put something in the car that this guy wants back, but Wyatt just mailed the thing back to his friend at home, and now they're at the post office trying to break in."

Brand closed his eyes, willing any of that to make sense. "What was in the car?"

"No idea, but the friend stashed it in the emergency roadside kit. Wyatt was supposed to mail it back a while ago and didn't do it until today."

"Shit, was it the box he asked me to take this morning?"

"Yeah, Wyatt said his boss mailed it." The toilet flushed. Ramie washed her hands and appeared in front of him. "It was Wyatt's idea to try and get the package from the post office, but I'm pretty sure it's been picked up to go to the sorting center. He got the guy out of the house, though, Brand. He protected me, and now he's out there with this guy and a gun."

The idea of his son out there, basically held hostage by

some criminal with a gun, incensed Brand on a brand-new level he'd never felt before. Every instinct in his body demanded he protect Wyatt somehow. He had to solve this and bring him home safely. "We need to go someplace safe and then call the police."

"We can't. What if this guy hurts Wyatt?"

"Ramie, we can't fix this ourselves. We're a cowboy and a bartender, not exactly special forces here. How long ago did they leave?"

"I don't know. It was around six thirty that I took my break, and we sat here for a while until Wyatt got home."

Brand looked at his phone. Almost eight. If he was guessing correctly, this kidnapper was probably casing the post office right now. "What if the package was sent out already?"

She blinked hard several times, a sure sign she was fighting back a rare wash of tears. "Then they were going to come back, get me, and we were all going back to Glasbury to wait for the package. It sounded like killing us was a last resort, but people do crazy things when they're stressed out and cornered."

"No kidding." Brand had the scar on his belly to prove it. "Look, first step is getting the fuck out of this house and to someplace safe the bad guy wouldn't think to look for you. Then we call the police."

"Okay." She coughed once. "He protected me, Brand. I think he feels like he owes me for lying. He's such a good kid."

"Yeah. And he's going to be fine. Believe in that."

"Right."

Brand led her out of the house and to his truck, then drove them to the diner's parking lot. It was right on Main Street, fairly busy all the time, and the kidnapper dude had no idea what Brand's truck looked like, so they were safe enough here. He called 911 and reported what he knew, where it had happened, where he suspected Wyatt and the kidnapper were now, and where he and Ramie currently were. The dispatcher promised to send cars and officers to all three locations.

He briefly entertained the idea of calling Jackson and giving him a heads-up on what was happening, but what could Jackson do? Nothing except get in the way or pace his motel room and worry. No, he'd wait until he actually knew something.

All any of them could do now was wait.

Wait and wonder and hope beyond hope that Wyatt was okay.

Wyatt was doing his very best not to piss his pants from fright. At the time, suggesting Smith try to break into the post office had seemed like a genius way to get him away from Ramie—and that part had worked. But the post office was in a brick municipal building that also housed town hall and two other businesses. Everything was closed for the night, but the parking lot was well-lit and traffic went steadily past on Main Street. Not exactly ideal break-in conditions, even for seemingly seasoned criminals like Smith.

Definitely not for unseasoned criminals like Wyatt.

Wyatt had been instructed to park around back and, after securing his hands with duct tape, Smith spent time testing windows and doors for an entry point. He'd left Wyatt alone in the car, behind the wheel, but Smith had taken the keys, Wyatt didn't have his phone, and he was terrified that if he blasted the horn or tried to run he'd get shot in the back. So far Smith had been calm and rational. That could all change on a dime, though. He needed to keep Smith away from Ramie's house until help arrived, or Wyatt came up with some genius plan to rescue himself.

Yeah, right. He couldn't even muck a stall without getting a splinter. How the fuck was he supposed to get himself out of this mess? A mess completely of Jared's making, and his anger at his best friend was tempered by knowing the poor guy was in pain right now, if not still in the hospital after whatever Smith did to him.

What the fuck kind of mess did you get yourself into, Jared?

The rear area of the municipal building was basically an alley with a tall wooden fence behind it, and residential homes on the other side of that. The fence was too tall for Wyatt to climb, and even if he could do it and got away, he might not make it back to Ramie's house before Smith. God knew what Smith might do to her if he was pissed off. No, Wyatt had to keep Smith's attention firmly on him. He'd brought this mess into her life, so he'd do his best to clean it the fuck up.

Smith never went out of sight of the car, so Wyatt didn't have a lot of time to act any particular way. His only advantage was that Wyatt knew his car. He'd shared it with Jared for years, and he'd had it solely to himself for almost two months. The cigarette lighter insert was long gone so no help there. He'd removed everything of value after that first attempted robbery of his trunk, so the handful of tools and random shit that had accumulated was in a bag under his bed.

The only useful thing he'd left in the trunk was the tire jack and the iron bar needed to crank the thing, but could he get into the trunk before Smith shot him? Probably not, and he'd have trouble wielding it with his hands secured with too many layers of tape to bite through.

As discreetly as he could in the dim alley light, Wyatt

leaned over and opened the glove compartment. Rooted around. Registration and insurance cards and a maintenance book? Not useful unless Smith was susceptible to infected paper cuts.

"What do I do? What do I do?" he asked the empty car.

Smith had disappeared from sight, so Wyatt took a chance on bending over and feeling as best he could beneath his seat, then the passenger seat. His fingertips brushed over a slender piece of cold metal and he grabbed it. An old box cutter from one of his college retail jobs. They were skinny and flat, and he'd frequently forgotten one was in his jeans pocket when he went home. The blade was small and not super-sharp anymore, so it didn't make a great weapon, but it was useful. It had to be—he just had to think.

A scene from a movie he'd liked as a kid, because it had been one of Mom's favorites, flashed in his mind. But he couldn't count on Smith not putting on his seat belt. Back in the eighties, seat belts were pretty much voluntary but nowadays cops would ticket you for anything. Still no sign of Smith anywhere, so maybe he had managed to break into the post office after all.

Didn't matter right now. Wyatt grabbed the passenger seat belt and tugged it over, then began sawing at the nylon fabric with the dull box cutter. He hacked through it more than halfway in one spot, then chose another place. If he had any kind of luck not related to his own clumsiness (because God knew he had no luck there), Smith wouldn't notice the cuts.

A shadow moved, and Wyatt let go of the belt. Dropped the box cutter in the space between the two seats without meaning to, and there went his only weapon. Smith flung himself into the passenger seat, his face a thundercloud. "The box isn't there," he snarled. "Must have been picked up. Damn it."

Uh-oh.

"Back to your house, kid. You, me, and your girlfriend are going on a little trip."

No way. No fucking way is he going to put Ramie in danger again.

Smith unwrapped his hands so Wyatt could drive. He eased his car back onto a quieter Main Street and turned in the direction of home. In the rearview mirror, he swore he saw flashing red and blue lights in the distance, and as he drove farther away, he also swore they stopped at the municipal building. Either Smith had tripped an alarm or Ramie had told someone what was going on.

His tiny flash of hope dimmed fast. If cops were heading to the post office, then surely there would be cops at the house, and that was going to piss Smith off royally. Wyatt discreetly tightened his own seat belt. His adrenaline spiked as he committed to the plan.

Don't tense up or it'll hurt worse later.

Wyatt pressed on the accelerator, surpassing Main Street's conservative twenty-five miles per hour through most of town, increasing the speed slowly enough that Smith didn't notice until they were almost going forty.

"Slow down, kid, before someone flags you," Smith said.

The fact that Smith wasn't actively holding the gun in his hand gave Wyatt the courage to continue speeding up. He blew past the road he should have turned on, destination clear in his mind. One of the oldest homes in Weston had a fancy, waist-height stone fence around the property, rather than a simple wood one. Jackson had once joked how fancy-pants it was when the house it guarded was made of weather-worn logs that were constantly needing repair. But it was a county historical landmark so the town took care of it.

Hopefully, Wyatt wouldn't get into too much trouble if he damaged the fence with his next act.

"Kid! Slow the fuck down." He pulled out the gun but didn't aim it at Wyatt. Not directly, though its existence was terrifying enough.

The house came into view ahead and Wyatt didn't think about it anymore. He had to do this so Smith didn't get away or hurt Ramie. He had to make all this up to her. He had to.

Wyatt closed his eyes, hit the accelerator, and swerved to the left.

Smith screamed.

After speaking with both Sheriff Bloomberg and a state trooper about everything they'd heard and experienced tonight, Bloomberg asked Brand and Ramie to wait back at the county sheriff's office. For their safety and so he didn't have his witnesses running around town getting in the way, Bloomberg had said.

Brand had argued, because the office was back in Daisy, which was too far away for his liking, especially if something bad happened. He couldn't be so far away from his friends. Bloomberg had compromised and told them to park across the street from the municipal building. Officers were on the scene, the street was well-lit, and they would be easily available for further questions.

Brand drove himself and Ramie there in his pickup, both of them squirrely with nerves and adrenaline. He hated not knowing what was going on or where Wyatt was. Ramie sipped at a bottle of water she'd brought from home with trembling fingers. She'd already called the Roost and let them know what was going on—mostly. They got the gist that she wasn't coming back in tonight.

Brand kept glancing at his phone, silently begging it to

ring, and at one point an email notification popped up right when he looked. A quick flash of the subject line made his insides tighten. A hot flush spread through his chest. The DNA results were back. Did he look? Did he wait and do it with Wyatt? Did he need to know this right now with everything else going on?

Two state police cruisers zoomed by, lights flashing and sirens wailing, startling Brand into almost dropping his phone. Something was happening. He climbed out of the truck but this end of Main Street was quiet, other than the car still positioned by the post office entrance. They were in the middle of town and to the east. Ramie's house was to the southwest from here with access to the highway to Amarillo due west.

Brand despised not being in the middle of all this. Waiting for information was not his strong suit. When Dad had his hand surgery back in January, Brand had been a stoic mess the whole time, silently worrying, despite it being a fairly routine procedure. He hadn't truly calmed down until Dad was home safe, sound and still a touch loopy from the anesthesia.

Ramie came out and hugged him from the side. Brand draped an arm across her shoulders, so grateful to know his best friend was out of harm's way tonight. But still insanely anxious to find out about Wyatt.

My maybe kid. Please be mine.

He squeezed his phone tighter. "I got the DNA results."

"What? Have you looked?"

"Not yet. It won't help what's happening right now."

"No, it won't get Wyatt back safely, but it's still the truth. You deserve to know it."

Brand didn't like showing weakness in front of others, but Ramie had been his best friend for years, and she was the first person outside his immediate family he'd ever confided in about his and Ginny's baby. "Can you look? Please?" He shoved his phone at her.

Ramie took the phone, kissed his cheek, then started tapping the screen. It might have been a minute or ten hours that passed before Ramie let out a soft gasp. "You're a match, Brand. Wyatt's your son."

"Fuck." Something he couldn't describe fled his body in that moment. Twenty years of wondering and regret. Two days of stress and the unknown. He felt lighter for a few seconds, until a new feeling blasted through him. An instinctive need to protect his son from the dangerous man who had him. "Fuck, I need to find Wyatt."

"You can't." Ramie held him still with a fierce grip on his arm. "Let the police do their job. I know it's hard, but you need to wait."

"He's my kid."

"I know. And that is exactly why the police need to handle this. You are emotionally involved and that's how people get hurt."

He hated that she was right but couldn't come up with a good counterargument. "I feel like I should call someone." Jackson. Jackson deserved to know the results of the DNA test. But shouldn't he get that truth from Wyatt? Hell, Jackson probably had no idea Wyatt was even in danger right now, and how would telling him help?

It's the truth.

Brand couldn't imagine being completely in the dark if Hugo had been in Wyatt's current position. He would be furious to know after the fact. Unsure if this was the right thing to do or not, Brand called him.

"Hey, boss, what's up?" Jackson asked after only two rings.

"Are you home?"

"Yeah, why?"

"Are you sitting down?"

"I am now. What's going on? Is it about Wyatt?"

"Yeah. Yeah, it's definitely about Wyatt."

Jackson stalked into the Claire County Hospital emergency room in the most mixed-up emotional state of his life, and he hated being so out of control. He hadn't felt this way since getting out of prison, and he wasn't sure he'd ever find his balance again. Not until he saw Wyatt with his own two eyes. Saw him, touched him, and knew for sure he was safe.

He immediately spotted Ramie in one of the chairs, and she stood to meet him as he crossed to her. "Brand is with him," she said. "He isn't alone."

"How is he?" When Brand had called earlier and told him first that yes, he was Wyatt's biological father, and then about the whole house invasion/kidnapping thing, Jackson had temporarily lost his mind. Then Brand had put him on hold for an excruciatingly long amount of time before coming back and telling Jackson to get to the ER. All Brand had known was that Wyatt had been in a car accident—not how badly he was injured.

"They think the air bag broke his nose," she replied, both hands on his forearms in a grounding touch. "He'll probably have a hell of a bruise from the seat belt, but other than that, he's okay. From what little we heard, it sounds like Wyatt saved himself from the bad guy."

"Where is the son of a bitch? Not Wyatt, the other guy."

"In his own room with cops watching him. Apparently, his seat belt broke and he smashed his head into the windshield when they crashed."

Jackson blinked. "But you said… Wait, Wyatt crashed the car on purpose?"

"Yeah."

"Jesus Christ. That was such a stupid thing to do. He could've been killed."

"But he wasn't. He protected me tonight, Jackson, and I will never forget that. Wyatt was a hero."

"Yeah. I can't believe all this happened while I was sitting pretty in my place."

"You mean both the kidnapping and the DNA results? Yeah, it's been a roller coaster for sure. Go see him." She told him the room number.

After getting buzzed through, Jackson navigated the confusing ER halls until he found Wyatt's room. Wyatt was sitting mostly upright in his bed with thick, blood-stained bandages over his nose. He had a bruise on his forehead but seemed perfectly alert, and he brightened when he saw Jackson. Brand sat in a chair in the corner of the room, tense and stone-faced, and he stood when Jackson walked in.

"Hey," Wyatt said. "Didn't expect you."

"I called him," Brand replied. "Figured you needed all the support you could get. Driving into a rock wall is likely to create some aches and pains."

"No shit. Thanks."

"Sure thing." To Jackson he said, "They just took some X-rays of his face. May or may not have to reset the nose, not sure yet. Someone will be by in a bit."

In hospitals, "in a bit" could be five minutes or five hours. Jackson didn't care. For as angry as he was at Wyatt for the big lie, he couldn't deny the way his heart responded to his nearness. Or the relief he felt at seeing Wyatt was alive and safe with his own two eyes. "Thank you, Brand. I mean it."

"I know." He looked back to Wyatt, his expression softening a touch. "Do you want me to bring you anything? A soda?"

"Nah, I'm fine," Wyatt replied. "Thanks for staying."

"Of course. See you guys in a while." Brand walked out.

Jackson shut the door and took a few steps closer to Wyatt's bed. "I can't believe what you went through tonight. Brand gave me the bare bones when he called. Do you even know what that guy was looking for?"

"No idea," Wyatt replied with a grunt. The poor guy sounded like he had a head cold because of his busted nose. "Small enough to put in a roadside kit. I honestly don't give a shit as long as he stays away from me and the people I care about. Tonight was fucking scary as hell."

"I can't imagine." He kind of could, given his own history, but Wyatt wasn't used to being around criminals who threatened bodily harm if you didn't comply. And he never wanted Wyatt back in that position again. "I bet you're relieved now."

"To be here and away from him? Fuck yes, I am."

"No, I mean about Brand."

Wyatt frowned. "What? That he was nice to me tonight? Definitely."

Crap, he'd stepped in it.

"You're talking about something else, aren't you?" Wyatt asked. "What?"

"I'm surprised he didn't tell you." Jackson sat on the edge of the bed and rested one hand on Wyatt's blanket-covered thigh. "Brand got the DNA results back tonight. You're a match. He's your father."

Wyatt did an impressive imitation of a goldfish with the way he opened and shut his mouth over and over. Jackson disliked breaking the news like this, but Wyatt deserved to know the truth. And if Jackson was the one to tell him? So be it. Wyatt's bright green eyes filled with tears and they broke Jackson's heart.

"He stayed with me," Wyatt said, voice low and raspy. "Once he got here, he stayed. Like a dad would."

"Yeah." He squeezed Wyatt's thigh, his own eyes burning with emotion. "He stayed. Do you want him to come back? I can go."

"No, don't go." One of those tears spilled down Wyatt's left cheek. "I know it's only been a few days but I've missed you. I am so fucking sorry I lied. I can never apologize enough for how I handled everything since I came to town, and I will do anything I can to make it up to you."

Jackson scooted closer and wrapped gentle arms around Wyatt, holding him as close as he dared after Wyatt's accident, mindful of his damaged face. "Stop. We don't have to talk about that right now. Yes, we need a long conversation at some point in the near future, but definitely not tonight. I can't imagine how scared you were."

Wyatt sobbed into his shoulder. "I was terrified, but I couldn't let him hurt Ramie. Couldn't let her suffer for my bad decisions."

"You had no way of knowing your friend let a criminal stash something in your car. That's not on you." For the first time, Jackson wished he was taller than Wyatt so he could hug the younger man the way he needed to be hugged. To completely wrap him up in Jackson's body. He did his best while his boyfriend trembled in his arms and hoped it was enough.

Jackson still hadn't processed everything himself. Wyatt's life had been in real danger tonight, and he could have easily killed himself by crashing the car on purpose. But Wyatt had done it to protect a friend. Wyatt was also Brand's son, and that was still a little too big to truly wrap his brain around, so he pushed it aside for later. And Jackson did know one thing for certain—he loved Wyatt and couldn't imagine his life without the accident-prone cowboy in it.

"We'll get through this," Jackson whispered, lips close to Wyatt's ear. "We just need time. And patience."

"Time I've got. Patience? Not so great at that."

He ruffled the red curls he loved so much. "We'll work on it. Together."

"Yeah." Wyatt sighed softly. "Together."

Chapter Twenty-Two

Wyatt had zero mental energy left after he finally got home to Ramie's place a little before sunrise. The sky was just starting to lighten in the east. He didn't care what time it was, that his car was police evidence, and he still didn't know what Smith (whose real name was Antonio Walters) had hidden in the emergency kit. Whatever. It could wait until he'd slept for a few days.

Jackson had sat with him throughout the entire hospital ordeal, from having his nose set and rebandaged, to more interviews with cops, to the long, slow process of finally getting released from the damned ER. For all that Jackson was still angry with him, he also obviously cared, and that gave Wyatt hope that he hadn't lost his cowboy for good.

He also managed to have one private conversation with Brand when Jackson tagged out for a bathroom and snack machine break. Brand had been so tentative as he stood at the foot of Wyatt's bed, hands in his jeans pockets, unsure of himself for the first time since Wyatt had met the man.

"So you know about the results," Brand had said.

"Yeah." For the first time, Wyatt had found himself looking at Brand through the lens of a son's eyes, rather than a potentially related employee's. He admired Brand and his ambition for the ranch, his love for his family, and his loyalty to the people around him. People who'd earned it. "Are you mad?"

"That you're my son? The child I gave up any thought of ever knowing, because I wanted it to be their choice? Never. You chose to find me. I might not agree with how you went about things, keeping who you thought I was a secret all this time, but I am starting to understand it better. And I would like to have a relationship with you outside of just boss and employee. For my family to know who you are to me. If you want that."

Wyatt's eyes burned. "I wouldn't have come here if I didn't want that. My grandparents built you up to be this bogeyman and you're not. Ramie told me about how my grandparents forced you to give up all your rights, and you did your best to move on. You're as flawed as anyone else and that's okay. But you are definitely a person I want in my life. Even if I'm not sure about calling you Dad just yet."

Brand smiled warmly and circled to the side of the bed. Rested a firm hand on Wyatt's shoulder. "Call me anything you want except a cuss word."

"Deal," Wyatt said on a snort of laughter that hurt his already tender nose. "Ugh. Wish they'd give me the good drugs instead of super-strength ibuprofen."

"I'll try not to make you laugh anymore. At least until your nose heals."

"Thanks." Wyatt gazed at his father, and a pang of gratitude slammed into him. Gratitude that his gamble in coming here had paid off, that Brand was a great person he genuinely wanted to know, and that they'd all gotten through his insane ordeal alive and mostly well. "Thank you, honest. How, uh, do you want to go about telling people?"

"I'm not sure. Ramie knows because she was there when I read the report, and I told Jackson because I thought he should know, since he's involved. For now, we can wait on telling my family until after you've had a chance to rest. Let's deal with this whole Antonio Walters situation first before we subject you to my family's scrutiny."

"I like that idea."

"What about telling your stepfather and grandparents?"

As much as Wyatt craved the satisfaction of telling his stepfather that this wasn't a waste of time, and that his bio dad was a great guy after all, he had no energy to gloat right now. "I'll wait on that, too. All I really want to do is sleep for a month."

"I don't blame you. After I got stabbed last year, the couch was my best friend for a long time."

"I keep forgetting that happened to you."

"Feels like a lifetime ago. And like you protected Ramie tonight, I was protecting Hugo. I wonder if hero complexes are hereditary?"

Wyatt grunted, which saved his sore nose from another amused snort. "Maybe. Brand, when I'm feeling better, I'd really like to talk to you about my mom. She never wanted to talk about her past, about my father. She didn't bad-mouth you the way my grandparents did, but she just... didn't say anything. I'd love your perspective on that time of your lives."

"We can do that. I don't hold any grudges against your mother. She was doing what her parents told her to do. I am just grateful we've gotten a chance to know each other."

"Me too."

"Hugo knows a bit about what happened tonight," Brand said. "I didn't need him panicking when I didn't come home, but I didn't tell him about us or the test results. I mean, he knows we took the test but...yeah."

"Tell him," Wyatt replied. "He's your partner, he deserves to know."

"Thank you. I'll tell him in person tomorrow."

"Okay."

They'd sat together in silence for a while, until Jackson returned and took over. Wyatt told Brand to take Ramie home, that he'd be okay until he was released. Jackson stayed, no matter how many times Wyatt insinuated he should go home, too. That Wyatt would call a taxi or something when he was released. Jackson's truck was outside the entrance ready to pick him up when the time came, and Wyatt relaxed into the familiar passenger seat.

Wyatt wasn't surprised to find Brand asleep on the living room couch when they got back. A quick peek into Ramie's room showed her snoring softly in her bed. Wyatt trudged into his own room and nearly fell face-first onto the mattress before remembering his nose. Breaking it again so soon was a terrible idea, so he eased onto his back on one side of the bed. Patted the other side so Jackson knew it was okay to stay.

"I could have lost you last night," Jackson said. "As if I'd go anywhere."

They curled together on top of the covers, facing each other, their hands tangled together beneath their chins. Existing in the quiet of the morning before others on the block began to wake and go about their days. Before more intrusive phone calls would inevitably begin. Before Wyatt had to face the entire Woods family as one of them and not just a rustler.

Wyatt dozed and woke with a dry throat and intense thirst, probably because he couldn't breathe well through his nose right now. Jackson had rolled onto his back but one hand still rested possessively over Wyatt's forearm. More than realizing what he could have lost if things had gone badly last night, he understood everything he'd gained since he'd been here in Weston. He loved Jackson more than he'd ever loved another human being. Even if Jackson didn't love him back anymore, Wyatt would do his best to prove he was worth a second chance.

His chest was sore as hell from the seat belt and air bag collision, but he also really needed to pee so movement was necessary. The second he tried to roll to his side and to sit up, Jackson came awake with a start. "What's wrong?" Jackson asked.

"Nothing's wrong, I just need to pee. I'm a little stiff and not in the fun way."

Jackson snorted. "I bet. Give me a second." He wriggled around until he was sitting next to Wyatt and able to help Wyatt lever into an upright position. "Better?"

"Yeah. Fuck, I never thought driving into a wall would hurt so much. Not that I ever really gave it that much thought until last night, and that was a pretty last-minute decision."

"Hopefully, you'll never do it again. Come on, let's get you up."

"Yes, please." Sitting up hurt like hell and made it a touch hard to breathe for a few seconds, but Wyatt managed. Jackson grasped his forearm and helped him stand. Wyatt wobbled a few times as he regained his balance, and then he was good. Jackson still followed him to the bedroom door and waited there while Wyatt did his business. Then Jackson took his turn.

Together, they investigated the living room. Ramie's funky frying pan wall clock told him it was a little after one o'clock, so he hadn't slept as long as he'd hoped. No one was in sight, but Brand's boots were over by the door. They found Brand and Ramie in the kitchen, drinking coffee and sharing the last of the cinnamon buns she'd bought from the diner yesterday morning.

Seeing them side by side like that, now that he knew

they used to be a thing, helped him see why Brand might have been attracted to her. They'd have been a cute couple if Brand wasn't deeply in love with Hugo.

Shit, am I going to have another stepfather one day if they get married?

"Afternoon," Brand said. "Coffee?"

"Definitely," Jackson replied. "Wyatt?"

"Actually, water would be great," Wyatt replied. "I don't really want the caffeine, I'm just thirsty as hell."

"On it." Jackson poured him a glass of water from the filtered pitcher in the fridge, then got himself a mug of black coffee. Wyatt didn't know how anyone drank that stuff black, but at least he didn't have to. He tried not to gulp the cold water so he didn't upset his empty stomach.

"The next couple days are gonna be crazy for you," Brand said to Wyatt. "Take as much time off as you need. The rest of the week, at least. You don't need to be moving around too much with your nose and chest like they are."

"Thank you," Wyatt replied. The dull throb in his face thanked him, too. "I should eat something so I can take another pill or six."

"I'll make you toast," Ramie said. "Anyone else?"

In the end, their quartet had the most bizarre (and yet also fun) toast-making lunch Wyatt had ever experienced. She used up the last of a loaf of white bread and put every possible topping on the table, from peanut butter to hazelnut spread to cheddar cheese. Wyatt put a little bit of margarine on his so it wouldn't be dry. Jackson made a sticky sandwich with peanut butter and the remnants of a jar of whipped marshmallow Wyatt hadn't even realized was in the cupboard.

It was the most unique family meal of his life, and Wyatt loved every second of it.

Brand fielded a few texts while they ate, and around

one forty said, "I should be heading back to the ranch. Michael needs to leave two hours early today because he has to drive his father to a checkup, so it's just Hugo and Dad."

"What about Rem?" Jackson asked.

"Took the afternoon off because of something at Susie's school. Parents get to sit in on the class or something."

That was a thing? Who wanted to go back to school as an adult to see what little kids learned about?

"Do you need me to fill in?"

Brand shook his head. "Nah, you're fine to take the rest of the day, too. And tomorrow if you need it. Wyatt there might need some looking after. Playing hero takes a lot out of you." He jacked his thumb at Ramie. "Maybe keep an eye on this one for me, too? She had a good scare last night."

"Can do, boss."

Ramie scowled but didn't contradict him. The mother henning was simply part of who Brand was as a person; he took care of his family.

"We'll talk later, yeah?" Brand said to Wyatt as he stood.

"Yeah." Wyatt had a lot more to say to the man but nothing that was urgent. "Later." After Brand left the house, Wyatt pinched himself on the arm. "Is it me, or have the last twenty-odd hours been the most surreal ever?"

"Totally," Ramie replied. "If you'll excuse me, I'm going to take a shower and then go back to bed for a while. I've got a shift that starts at five."

"You're going to work tonight?"

"Honestly? Right now, I'd feel way safer in a bar full of people I mostly know than sitting around this house alone."

"Why do you think you'll be alone?"

She quirked an eyebrow. "I just assumed you and Jackson would head back to his place to chill, instead of knocking around here."

"We can hang here if you want company," Jackson said. "I just need to run home soon and let Dog out. She's well-trained but her bladder can only hold out for so long. Poor thing is probably running circles around my room."

"You can bring her over if you want."

"Yeah?"

"Sure. I like dogs. Never had one because I didn't trust myself to handle the responsibility, but yeah. Bring Dog back."

"Okay. Thanks."

Wyatt's heart trilled. "If you want to go get Dog, I'm going to shower after Ramie and then go back to bed. In between what I'm sure will be a lot of phone calls this afternoon. If the cops haven't already picked up Jared, they probably will soon. It's going to be a long day." And he probably had missed calls and messages on his phone, which he really didn't want to look at yet.

"I bet." Jackson kissed his temple. "Be back in a while. Lock the door behind me."

"Yes, sir."

Wyatt did exactly that, then stood at the living room window and watched Jackson walk to his truck. Get in and drive away. The creaking of floorboards told him Ramie was behind him before her arm went around his waist. "You're lucky to have him," she said softly.

"I know. I'm lucky he's still here and I didn't totally fuck everything up with my lies. I think I love him."

"Then tell him. When things are a little less stressful, tell him your truth. All he can do is give you his truth in return."

"Yeah."

One day soon, Wyatt would say the words to Jackson he'd only ever said to relatives. Words that he'd never felt so acutely in his heart and soul about another person. Words that would either cement their relationship or tear them apart for good.

Please, God, don't let me fuck this up.

As soon as he got home, Brand took a shower. Partly to wake him up and partly to clear his head a little bit about everything that had happened, not just last night, but ever since his conversation with Wyatt on Monday. He still couldn't comprehend the complete way his world had shifted since finding out Wyatt was his son. He shouldn't be as surprised as he was. Brand had noticed something about Wyatt the day they met, a familiarity he couldn't put his finger on, and not just from Wyatt's flaming red hair.

Maybe he had known, deep down, but old hurt had kept him from examining those feelings until they were dropped right in his lap.

Hugo was, as expected, on the couch when Brand emerged from the bathroom in his robe. Hugo thought his preference to wear a robe from the bathroom to the bedroom to get dressed was fussy and adorable, but that living space was chilly in winter, damn it. No sense in being cold indoors when he spent plenty of time cold outdoors.

"So you had a busy night," Hugo drawled.

"More than you can imagine." He dropped down next to Hugo and kissed his boyfriend. "I'm just glad we all got through it safe and mostly sound. Told Wyatt to take it easy for a few days before he thinks of coming back to work."

"Good call. He's probably stubborn enough to try and come back with a broken nose. God knows he's worked through all kinds of other injuries."

"He probably gets that stubbornness from me."

Hugo's eyes widened. "What?"

"I got the test results last night while everything was happening. Ramie encouraged me to look, so I'd know if

I was praying for my employee or my son. We're a match, Hugo."

"Wow." Hugo pulled him into a tight hug that released the last of Brand's anxiety over this. More than telling his parents and siblings that his kid had been under his nose for nearly two months, he'd stressed about Hugo's feelings over it. Granted, it wasn't as serious a commitment as if Wyatt had been a small child they had to raise; Wyatt was a grown man with dreams, aspirations, and a lot of raw talent that needed to be honed.

Still, Brand needed to know his partner was okay with this whole insta-kid situation.

"I take it he knows, too," Hugo asked as he sat back, hands still gripping Brand's tight.

"Yeah, I told him. Ramie and Jackson know, and now you, but no one else. Wyatt and I need a little time to process it before we bring the whole family in on things."

"I understand and completely agree. You need to tell other people in your own time. This is big news."

"It is, and I am so grateful that you're with me on this."

"Of course I am. Even if some mystery ex dropped an infant in our laps and said 'here, he's yours,' and left, I'd be with you. I have never been more grateful to be part of a family than I am to be part of yours, Brand Woods. No matter what gets dumped in our laps, I'm with you."

"I hope you mean that." Brand reached for a jeans pocket that wasn't there, because his jeans were on the bed. He'd been carrying the ring around with him ever since his individual chats with Jackson and Ramie two weeks ago, and now seemed like the perfect time to offer it to Hugo. "Come with me."

Brand stood and pulled Hugo up. Led him to their bedroom and nudged Hugo until he sat on the bed. The spark in his eyes suggested Hugo anticipated sexy times—and

Brand was on board with that in a little while—but it wasn't the first thing on Brand's mind. He got the ring out of his jeans, went to one knee in front of Hugo, and held it out. Hugo's lips parted and his cheeks pinked up.

"I've been waiting for the right time to give you this," Brand said, grateful neither his voice nor his hand was trembling. "I know it's not even been a year, but in some ways it's been ten years. I wanna commit to our life together, Hugo Turner. It doesn't have to happen tomorrow or even five years from now, but I love you. Will you marry me?"

"Yes." Hugo's eyes glistened. "Of course, yes. My God, I've been dreaming of this moment since I was a teenager. Yes."

Brand blinked hard as his own tears rose, and he slid the ring onto Hugo's waiting finger. "You are my family."

"And you're mine." Hugo yanked him up and into a hard kiss that sealed their promise of a life together. Their commitment to love and cherish each other far into the future, and to always be each other's family.

For as long as they both shall live.

some takeout to eat whenever they were hungry. The toast lunch had been fun but not exactly filling.

And now Wyatt was Brand's son from a high school girlfriend. That had kicked him right in the nuts, and yet it didn't completely surprise him. The more Jackson thought back, the more he could see bits of Brand in Wyatt. His height (not so much his build, because Wyatt was slender, while Brand was on the bulkier side), the way Wyatt smiled, and sometimes the way he walked when he was confident in what he was doing. Revisiting those memories, it was so much easier to see the pair was related.

Jackson was also too exhausted to go through the mental gymnastics of trying to reconcile the fact that he'd slept with both men, so he ignored that little factoid for now. Mostly, he focused on how he'd felt these past twelve or so hours. Panic and fear. Relief and gratitude. Love. Anger and confusion. Love.

But love continued to hit the hardest, and Jackson knew that he would be able to forgive Wyatt for his betrayal. It wouldn't be overnight and it wouldn't be easy, but his heart told him that coming to terms with things, talking long and hard with Wyatt about why this hurt so much, would be worth it.

They were worth it.

He took a slow walk around the entire perimeter of the motel to center himself before collecting Dog and heading back to Weston. Shelby greeted him when he walked into the diner, and he went to the counter to order two BLTs and a turkey club, unsure what Ramie might like but he didn't want to not offer her a sandwich if she was hungry. Dog sniffed eagerly at the bag of food on the drive over to Ramie's, but she obediently listened when he told her no.

He adored his dog and was forever grateful she'd wandered into his campsite that day and stuck around. All his

Chapter Twenty-Three

Jackson must have gotten back to his home just in time. Dog bolted out into the yard on a soft yelp and even though he adored and trusted his pup, he still sniffed around for any sign she hadn't held it. Then he sat quietly in the middle of the floor with Dog beside him, absently stroking her head while, now that he had some time alone to think, he let his thoughts tumble all over themselves.

Deep down, he was still furious with Wyatt for his lies, and that was going to take more time to process. But when Brand had called to tell him what was happening, that Wyatt had been taken hostage by a criminal, crashed his car, and was on his way to the ER, all those bad feelings had been squashed down by fear. Real fear that he could lose Wyatt without them having a chance to talk and process things.

For Jackson to say he loved him. Because he did. For all Jackson's anger, he *did* love Wyatt and *hadn't* lost him tonight. They still had a chance to work things out.

Sleeping beside Wyatt, holding him close, had both warmed Jackson inside and woken those old hurts again, and he was grateful for a chance to distance himself. Even if only for an hour with the excuse of getting Dog. He'd probably swing by the town diner, too, and grab them all good luck seemed to happen around that time, with both the room at the motel and his job at Woods Ranch. Things had just fallen into place, and he'd never taken that luck for granted. He wouldn't take his luck at meeting and falling for Wyatt for granted, either.

They could work through this.

When he got back, the front door was locked, so he assumed Ramie and Wyatt were both asleep. He rang the bell and waited. A rumpled Wyatt let him in, then brightened when he saw both Dog and the bag of food.

Wyatt knelt to ruffle her ears and cheeks, and then gave her a hug. "Great to see you again, girl." She licked his hand.

"Brought food." Obvious statement was obvious, but whatever. Jackson carried it into the kitchen to unbag and organize. Wyatt immediately grabbed one of the BLTs. And why not? Everyone Jackson knew loved bacon. "What do you think Ramie will want?"

"What are my choices?" Ramie asked as she walked into the kitchen, dressed in familiar jeans and a tight, low-cut blouse.

"BLT or turkey club."

"Ooh, BLT please, and thank you."

Jackson handed her the container, then took the club to the table and sat beside Wyatt. They didn't talk as they ate, everyone occasionally sneaking Dog bits of meat from their respective sandwiches. Jackson gave her a few of the kettle-cooked potato chips that came with the meal. The way Wyatt tried to navigate his thick sandwich without wrinkling his broken nose too much was kind of adorable and also a little sad. He hadn't thought through the sandwich thing and probably should have gotten Wyatt soup.

Wyatt didn't complain once, and when Ramie offered

him a beer, he looked to Jackson for approval. "Go ahead," Jackson said. "You had a rough night."

"Awesome, thank you," he replied to both him and Ramie, then took the beer.

Jackson turned down a beer in favor of a cola.

After Ramie left for work, Jackson cleaned up the kitchen and gave a few more scraps to Dog, since he'd stupidly forgot to bring some of her food. He and Wyatt settled on the couch together, and Jackson pulled a surprise out of his pocket. Held it up.

Wyatt stared at it dumbly. "What is that?"

"It's called a lot of different things, but I call it a mouth harp. I remembered how fascinated you were about whistling on a blade of grass, so I thought I'd show you this. It's an old-fashioned thing not a lot of folks still play, but my adopted father did and it was somethin' he actually taught us besides farm work and bedtime prayers." Jackson held no affection for the man who'd passed on a few years ago, but he did have fond memories of playing the harp in the barn with Kirby.

"Father encouraged us to play and enjoy music if we had a talent," Jackson continued. "One of my younger brothers, Donnie, had a real affinity for the classical guitar and was good. I hope he kept at it."

"Do you ever regret not keeping in touch with more of your siblings?"

"No. No, I needed to leave as much of that life behind so I could build my own future, and I did. Hit some rough patches for sure, but I'm here now. Happy. Well, mostly happy but that's something we need to work on together."

Wyatt's green eyes widened with hope. "Yeah?"

"Yes. I love you, Wyatt. Been falling this whole time, even though I didn't realize it at first, and then I wanted to ignore it, because of us workin' together, but I don't wanna ignore it anymore. I wanna work on it, not throw it away because I'm hurt and angry."

"I think I love you, too, Jackson." Wyatt squeezed both of Jackson's hands. "I feel good when I'm with you and I don't just mean sex. Even if all we're doing is staring out at the wilderness, I am happy and settled in a way I never have been before. I want to be with you all the time. You make me so happy, and I will do whatever it takes to earn your trust back, I promise."

"I believe you." Jackson pulled their joined hands into his own lap and held them there. "I'm just gonna need time and your patience, okay? We gotta build from the ground back up again."

"You've got both. Promise." In a surprise move, Wyatt let go of his hands and stood. "Hi there, sir. I'm Wyatt Gibson, and I'm here in town because I want to get a job working at Woods Ranch and maybe become a decent cowboy, even though I have no experience in the life. I also suspect that the ranch foreman, Brand Woods, might be the biological father who abandoned me and my mom twenty years ago, but I want to check out him and his family before I say anything to anyone about it. Nice to meet you."

Jackson chuckled at Wyatt's adorable combination of sincerity and dorkishness with that ramble. He held out his hand. "Nice to meet you. Jackson Sumner, professional cowboy with trust issues, a dog named Dog, and I live in a motel."

"Great to meet you." Wyatt shook his hand in a firm grip, before plopping back down on the cushion beside him. "So how about you show me how to play that mouth harp thingie."

"We can do that. One thing first?"

"Sure."

Jackson leaned in and kissed him softly. Not the hard

kiss he wanted, because of Wyatt's nose, but it was a quiet promise to persevere through this latest hardship. To re-create things with a solid foundation and come out solid on the other side. To say "I love you" again without words. Wyatt seemed to say it back, and they settled in for a while, Dog at their feet, to play beautiful music together.

After a long dinnertime conversation the next day with Brand, Hugo, Jackson, and Wyatt at Ramie's house, they all agreed to tell Brand's parents first about Wyatt's parentage. His parents had known and liked Ginny a lot before their families went to war over the pregnancy. Wyatt also said he wanted to come out to them, too, so they knew it all up front, no secrets.

Brand was a touch nervous about Dad's reaction, though not necessarily to Wyatt being gay. As time passed, Dad was becoming more openly accepting of both Colt and Brand being queer, rather than silently tolerating it. No, Brand was worried about the age gap between Jackson and Wyatt, and how his parents might perceive that: Jackson taking advantage of a young kid on a quest to find himself.

But if coming out right away was Wyatt's choice, Brand wouldn't talk him out of it, and Jackson seemed completely on board.

So Saturday evening, once chores were done for the day, Wyatt, Jackson, and Hugo sat down with Brand and his parents for a clean-out supper. Mom liked to use Saturday as an excuse to use up leftovers and get the fridge ready for the food she'd make tomorrow night for the bigger family dinner. With six of them at the table, there wasn't a Pyrex container left in the fridge that hadn't been reheated.

Mom asked about Wyatt's nose, and he told them all a bit more about those few hours he'd spent with Antonio Walters and the dramatic ending. His car was at Murphy's shop and should be finished Monday. He'd worked a half day today to test the waters as his nose healed, and Jackson had run out to pick him up.

Dad talked a bit about the county fair coming up in April. It was back to being hosted at the regular fairgrounds this year, and he was eager to once again show off their organic beef, which had gotten a decent launch at last year's fair. Brand was excited too, because their first two slaughters had sold well, and they now had a contract with the Grove Point CSA to offer their beef as an option in the subscription boxes.

It meant doing business with Hugo's estranged stepfather, but that was part of being an adult.

By the end of the meal, Mom began fidgeting in her seat and tossing Brand meaningful looks, like she knew he had something to tell her. It wasn't as if he invited two employees into the house for supper all that often, but she couldn't have a single possible clue what Brand had to tell her tonight.

"Boys," Dad said after a long gulp of his lemonade, attention on both Brand and Hugo. "Did you have something you wanted to share tonight?"

Wyatt frowned.

Hugo glanced at Brand quizzically, then down to his own left hand, which rested on the table by his empty plate. Gold glinted. Brand's chest heated. Oops. While working out in the barn or riding, especially in winter, Hugo had always worn gloves around Dad. Until tonight. Hugo dropped his hands to his lap.

"Well, uh, there is something I need to tell you both," Brand said, a little thrown now because he and Hugo had wanted to wait. "We were going to announce this to the whole family tomorrow. We just, um, forgot about the ring."

Mom squeaked. "You're engaged?"

"We are. I proposed and Hugo said yes."

"Oh, honey!" She rose and circled the table to hug him hard, already sniffling back tears. "I'm so happy for you both. I've never seen you as happy as since you and Hugo got together."

"Thanks, Mom." He took a moment to study Dad while Mom strangled Hugo with a hug. Dad's face was calm, his eyes giving away nothing. But he hadn't stormed off or done anything rude. He was simply…listening. Absorbing. "Dad?"

"Seems soon," Dad said. "It's not been a year yet."

"You proposed to Mom after four months."

"That's diff—" He caught himself, which contained Brand's temper. "No, I suppose it's not different. What's your catchphrase? 'Love is love'?"

Hugo bit his lip and looked like he wanted to burst into tears—happy tears. Brand's own throat tightened and he swallowed hard before he could speak. "Yeah. Love is love. Hugo's been family a long time, and soon he'll officially be part of it."

"How soon?" Mom asked. She still stood between Hugo's and Brand's chairs, one hand on each man's shoulder.

"Not that soon," Hugo said. "We haven't even talked about setting a date or plans or anything. We had something else to deal with first, and that's actually why we're all here for supper tonight." He angled toward Brand, deferring to him.

"Mom, you might wanna sit back down," Brand said. "Trust me."

She flashed him a curious smile and did as asked.

"Hugo and I learned something a few nights ago, and we've been taking our time processing it. We agreed to tell you both first, before we tell the rest of the family."

"Something else besides the proposal?" Mom asked. Then her face went fierce. "Is it about Wyatt's kidnapping? Did that awful man do something we don't know about?"

"No, he didn't. I mean, we found this out the same night, but it has nothing to do with Walters or the gems." The police had finally gotten their hands on the emergency kit package and arrested Jared for his part in hiding what turned out to be a collection of rare, uncut gemstones worth mid-six-figures. Wyatt had been dumbfounded to realize he'd been driving around with a small fortune in his trunk.

"Then what's this about, son?" Dad asked.

"It's about Wyatt."

"Oh?"

All sets of eyes in the room landed on Wyatt, who squirmed and blushed bright red. "First off, ma'am and sir, I never meant to hurt anyone," Wyatt began, a slight tremor in his voice. Jackson looked like he was restraining himself from leaning over and hugging Wyatt. "When I moved here, it was to apply specifically to your ranch for work. I wanted to get to know your family. Brand, in particular."

Dad went stiffer in his chair. "And why's that?"

"Because my mother's name was Ginny Foster before she married my stepfather and took the name Gibson."

Mom let out a small gasp, hands flying up to cover her mouth. "You look like her. Such a sweet girl."

"I've been told that I look like her. And I'm starting to see the ways I look like my father."

Mom seemed confused but Brand saw the moment Dad put it together. He pushed his chair back and stood slowly, making no sudden movements. He simply stared at Wyatt as so many unnamable emotions flashed across his face. Then Mom understood and released a sharp cry. If Jackson hadn't been seated between her and Wyatt, Brand suspected she'd have snatched him right into her arms.

"We did a DNA test," Brand said when Wyatt seemed too overwhelmed to continue. "I'm Wyatt's biological father. He's the baby I signed away my rights to twenty years ago."

For the first time in a very long time, Dad looked like he might burst into tears. The last time Dad had gotten this emotional in front of his children had been when Colt walked back into their home after sixteen years away. Brand thought Dad might cry back then, and he almost expected it now.

"We didn't want to give you up," Dad said in a harsh whisper. "Didn't want Brand to, but her family threatened ours. Threatened Brand."

"I know, sir," Wyatt replied. "Brand and I have had a few long talks this week. I don't blame him or you. I blame my maternal grandparents. They told me my whole life I was better off not knowing you guys, that my father's family was cruel and selfish, but as I got older I still wanted to know where I came from. I begged my mom to tell me who my father was, but even on her deathbed, she refused. So I did my own digging and it led me here. To your ranch."

"I'm so sorry about your mother, sweetheart," Mom said. She seemed to be climbing on board the acceptance train a lot faster. The trickier reaction so far was Dad's.

Wyatt's insides were shaking apart and he kind of wished he'd eaten less supper, because his stomach was threatening to empty itself all over Rose's dining room floor. He couldn't tear his eyes off Wayne. As the patriarch of the Woods family, his reaction to this news mattered most. His children would take their cues from him. Brand too, but mostly Wayne.

"Thank you, ma'am," Wyatt said to Rose without taking his eyes off Wayne.

Wayne slowly circled the table to stand behind Wyatt's chair, his face still a bizarre mix of emotions, and Wyatt didn't know the man well enough to understand any of them. His eyes glistened brightly and his posture was more relaxed, though, so Wyatt didn't immediately panic.

"Please, stand up, son," Wayne said.

Wyatt swallowed, mouth too dry, and he cast a seeking look at Jackson. Jackson smiled and nodded his head ever so slightly, so Wyatt did as asked. Carefully rising from his chair and scooting out from behind it to face Wayne. Wyatt held himself as stiffly as possible, realizing for the first time that he was actually taller than Wayne, too.

Wayne rested both hands on Wyatt's shoulders. "I told Colton something once when he came back into my life four years ago," he said. "I told him I never thought I'd become a man who'd drive his own child off without a word. I can't imagine ever doing that to a grandson, either."

Something warm and wonderful squeezed Wyatt's chest so tight he was sure he needed to cry or scream with joy, or do something else to release the pressure. Wayne helped him out by gently wrapping his arms around Wyatt's shoulders and hugging him. When Wyatt began this journey, he never expected to find himself here: being hugged and accepted by his father and grandparents. The rest of the family was still up in the air, but for right now, this was everything in the world to Wyatt.

He tried to hug Wayne back, but Wyatt wasn't used to casual hugs from his extended family. And then he was transferred over to Rose, who hugged the life out of him while she seemed to be holding in sobs. When she pulled back, a few tears had tracked down her cheeks but her eyes blazed with joy.

She cupped his cheeks in both hands, fingers lightly trembling. "I never dreamed I'd get to meet you. My very first grandbaby."

That did it. Wyatt couldn't stop a few tears of his own from falling, overwhelmed by all the instant acceptance and affection, not used to such open displays of emotion from his own family. The Gibsons weren't huggers or criers, or very big on family traditions outside of Christmas morning and Easter dinner. This was brand-new territory for him.

"It's a true pleasure to meet you both, too," Wyatt said once he could speak. "As your grandson."

The floor creaked, and Wyatt wasn't surprised to see Brand get a big hug from Wayne, plus a slap on the back. Hugo was grinning at no one in particular. Wyatt couldn't see Jackson's face, because his back was to Wyatt. He knew Jackson was happy for him, though. Now that Wyatt was part of the Woods family, so was Jackson.

Something they still hadn't dropped on the elder Woodses.

"Oh my goodness," Rose said to Brand as she fluttered to his side of the table. "I can't wait to tell your brothers and sisters. What a surprise!" She threw her arms around Brand. "Oh, sweetheart. You must have been so shocked to learn the news."

"*Shocked* is a very small word for how I felt, Mom." Brand smiled at Wyatt over her shoulder. "But after I sat with it, I realized how wonderful of a shock it was. I gave up on living an authentic life *and* being a dad a long time ago. But Hugo helped me be me. And now I've got my son back. I couldn't ask for a bigger miracle."

"Good man," Wayne said. "Our children are blessings, no matter how long we're estranged from them." And since Wayne apparently missed nothing at his dining table, added, "I'm so grateful to know this exciting family news, but I have to admit I'm a touch surprised Jackson doesn't seem shocked at all."

"Because Jackson helped unravel the whole thing," Brand replied. "And he's become someone very special to Wyatt. We all wanted Jackson here tonight."

"Someone very special." Wayne's sharp gaze landed on Jackson. "How special exactly?"

Wyatt held his breath.

Jackson had fought against a familiar pang of wistfulness as Wayne and Rose Woods came together to easily welcome Wyatt into their family, embracing him with love and joy. The kind of love and joy every child deserved from their parents. The kind he'd only ever observed from a distance until now. While he hadn't been included in the celebration, he was bearing witness to it and that was enough.

Until he was suddenly the direct focus of everyone in the room, especially Wayne, whose joy was slowly disappearing under a cloud of suspicion. Wyatt was still behind Jackson, so he had no idea how to respond to Wayne's question. And since everyone else involved except Hugo was standing, Jackson stood, too. Moved around his chair to Wyatt, close enough their arms brushed. Rose and Wayne stood together by Brand, all three watching.

Then Wyatt slipped his hand into Jackson's and said, "Jackson's extra-special to me because I'm falling in love with him. And he loves me. And I needed you both to know that so you know exactly who I am."

"You're in love," Wayne repeated. "Are you outta your mind, Jackson? You're twice that boy's age. You're older than his own damned father!"

"Age is just a number when it comes to love," Wyatt said. His voice was softer, a young man intimidated by an elder, and Jackson didn't like that.

"That's easy enough to say when you're only twenty years old and have hardly any life experience."

Wyatt bristled.

Jackson squeezed his hand tighter, working to keep his own temper at a low sizzle. They both knew this wouldn't be easy. "With all due respect, Mr. Woods, Wyatt has been through a lot. I've gotten to know him pretty well these last two months, and I can tell you he's a man who knows his mind. He did the pursuing here, not the other way around."

"I'd hope you'd be mature enough to stop things before they started."

Brand opened his mouth but Jackson held up his hand. This wasn't Brand's fight. "I understand that you're still battling with some old, ingrained beliefs about men loving men, and I'm not here to fight with you about that, or about our age difference. Only to say that I love and respect your grandson, and while we've had our differences, we're working through them like mature adults. Wyatt isn't a child. He's a grown man who's actively reaching for what he wants. He came here to find his father and he did. Neither of us expected this when we first met, but we wanted it and have made it work."

Jackson had said his piece now, so he didn't object again when Brand spoke up. "I know this is a surprise, Dad, and I admit I was a lot taken aback when I found out. But I've seen them together this week. I saw the way Jackson watched over Wyatt in the hospital. I support them."

Those words shouldn't have surprised Jackson as much as they did, and he sent Brand a silent thank-you with his eyes. Brand nodded.

"Well, this is all a touch unusual," Rose spoke up. "I think it's something your father and I will have to sit with and think about. But who you date, Wyatt, does not change the fact that you're part of this family. I lost one of my boys for far too long, and I won't lose anyone else." She side-eyed her husband, who didn't respond. He simply put his hands in his pockets and looked off to the side.

Jackson got the feeling Rose demurred to her husband in most things, but not when it came to her children and grandchildren.

"And just think, Mr. Woods," Hugo said in a charming, almost teasing tone. "You've got that grandson you always used to talk about."

Brand groaned. "Oh Lord, don't go there yet. Wyatt needs to go at least three days in a row without scraping, slicing, bruising, or tripping himself before there is any discussion of that. He'll burn down the barn."

"You know, now that we know they're related, the clumsiness really reminds me of Rem."

Wyatt smiled and seemed to relax as the tension levels in the room dropped. Wayne looked more thoughtful and less wound up, and Rose seemed pleased to have kept the peace. Hugo and Brand were both smiling. Jackson was still a touch miffed at Wayne for insinuating he'd taken advantage of Wyatt in some way, but he also understood the man's POV a little.

"Now, boys," Rose said, "do we have any other major announcements before I serve the carrot cake I made this afternoon?"

Their younger quartet let out a chorus of *no*s.

As the men returned to their seats, Rose went off to get the cake. Jackson pulled Wyatt's chair out for him before sitting himself, slowly losing the sense of tension he'd felt all day long. Everything was finally out in the open with the elder Woodses, and the rest of the family would find out the news tomorrow. Everything from their new family member to Brand and Hugo's engagement. He imagined it would be a pretty chaotic dinner.

Wyatt squeezed his thigh, and when Jackson looked at him, his green eyes swam with so much affection and thanks that Jackson nearly lost himself in them. He loved looking into Wyatt's eyes. He loved teaching Wyatt new things, from how to tie a proper sheet bend double knot to holding a mouth harp right so he didn't hurt his teeth. There were so many things he wanted to teach and show Wyatt, for them to explore together.

It would be messy and sometimes hard, and there were a lot of new family members about to get tossed into the already complicated mix. But they'd get through it. Jackson truly believed that.

For the first time in his whole life, Jackson knew he was finally home.

Epilogue

Wyatt leaned against the picnic table with a beer in hand, legs spread out in front of him on the trodden earth at this end of the fairgrounds, and soaked in the family all around him. Tonight was the final night of the Claire County Fair, and while the majority of the regular fair activities were over for the year, attendees had gathered under the table-filled pavilion to listen to a local country band cover favorite songs from Johnny Cash to Blake Shelton.

Most of the food stalls were closed, so families had packed coolers and were picnicking together to celebrate the end of the fair and the successes of the blue ribbon winners in all categories. Woods Ranch had won for their organic steer, and Rose proudly showed off blue ribbons for both her peach pie ("I beat that Shirley Johnson two years in a row!" she'd crowed this morning), and her celery relish.

Leanne and Sage had provided the picnic food for the extended Woods clan, who had overtaken two picnic tables close together, farthest from the band so they could talk more easily. They'd even brought a small cake for Wyatt to celebrate his twenty-first birthday, which wasn't technically for three more days, but they'd insisted since everyone was together. Wyatt's beer was also hidden inside a cozy, a gift from Jackson, in case anyone looked too close.

Jackson sat beside him and sipped at his own beer, the most relaxed he'd been all weekend. And the most Wyatt had seen his boyfriend all weekend. Even though Wayne had said he'd give Jackson the weekend off to spend at the fair with the family, Jackson insisted on working alongside Alan and Michael to keep the ranch going while the Woodses were away. And while Wyatt had enjoyed the novelty of spending the night in the park's barns with Brand and their cattle, he'd missed Jackson.

He planned on showing Jackson how much he'd missed him later at the motel.

Wyatt loved spending the night there with Jackson and Dog, not only because he loved the pair, but because it gave them a lot more privacy than at Ramie's house. They usually only went to Ramie's house to take advantage of her kitchen and big TV, but Jackson rarely slept over. As serious as Wyatt and Jackson were about their relationship—a hard-won relationship that they'd worked very carefully on these past two months—they'd agreed they weren't quite ready to move in together yet.

Plus, the secluded motel gave them a lot more space to continue exploring Wyatt's blossoming kinky side.

"Does anyone want more pasta salad before I put it away?" Rose asked. "Don't want the mayonnaise to get too warm."

Wyatt was stuffed full, and it seemed like everyone else was, too. The family was split between the two tables, many still snacking off their plates or out of bags of chips. Michael, Josiah, Michael's father, Elmer, and their dog Rosco had joined their family, too, and they sat at the same table with Wyatt, Jackson, Brand and Hugo, and Colt and Avery, who'd flown in for the weekend. Rose and Wayne moved between the various groups, sharing their time with all of their friends, kids, and grandkids.

Grandkid.

It was still a bit surreal for Wyatt to consider himself a Woods, even after two months of wrapping his brain around it. Rem and Shelby had been wholly accepting of him and Jackson. Leanne and Sage had welcomed Wyatt into the family as their nephew, and while their husbands were accepting of Wyatt in general, they were not happy about his relationship with Jackson.

Oh well, they could stuff it. Wyatt was thrilled with his relationship with Jackson.

Little Susie walked over to him, the spitting image of her mama. "Are we gonna have cake soon?" she asked.

"Pretty soon, I think," he replied to the adorable little girl. "Probably when everyone's dinner has had a chance to settle."

"I'm settled."

"No doubt. What did you have for dinner, Susie-bo-boosie?"

She giggled at the nickname he'd bestowed upon her last month. "A chicken leg and corn bread."

"Hmm. Sounds like you definitely have some room left to fill. Why don't you go see if Aunt Sage has any more of that fresh-cut fruit?"

"Okay." She wandered off toward her aunt and various cousins at the other table.

"You're charming with kids, you know," Jackson said.

"Not sure how, since I never had any younger siblings." Wyatt had actually invited his two older step-siblings, Peter and Lily, out for the fair, but they'd both cited work.

After the drama of Jared's arrest and the plea deals both he and Walters made had settled a bit in the papers, Wyatt had gone home to see his family in Glasbury. It had been a long, hard trip, and it had taken every bit of his courage to tell Jackson no, he could do this on his own. And he had done it, coming out to his stepfather, step-siblings, and both sets of grandparents. He'd also admitted to having a great relationship with Brand and the Woods family.

While Mom's parents had been furious that Wyatt had secretly gone looking for his father, they'd eventually parted on good terms, and Wyatt had come home to his job, his boyfriend, and his father. A father he still couldn't call Dad, and he might never, which was okay. They had a long time yet to figure things out between them. And even though Brand and Hugo were planning on a long engagement, Brand had already asked Wyatt to stand up for him as his best man. Wyatt had given him a resounding yes.

Wyatt planned on asking Brand to do the same for him one day if (When? If?) he and Jackson ever got married. It was too far ahead to think of, though, as anything but an intangible maybe. Right now, Wyatt was content to live his life with Jackson in the here and now, not in maybes.

Dog came over and put her chin right in Jackson's lap, looking up with those soulful blue eyes that always reminded Wyatt of a husky, even though she was definitely a mutt. "Did you not get enough table scraps, girl?" Jackson asked. He reached behind him and snagged a crust of bread off his plate. Held it out. She didn't move until he clucked his tongue, then she snapped it up.

"I still can't believe how well-trained she is," Wyatt said.

"I didn't do much of it. She came to me knowing a lot of basic commands. All I can think is some asshole who got tired of the responsibility dumped her on the side of the road, and she happened to find me that night. Just wish she would tell me her name."

Wyatt ruffled her fuzzy ears. "Maybe she's waiting for you to tell her what her name is."

"You think?"

"Sure. I mean, unless you teach her how to bark her ABCs, I don't think she's going to be able to tell you herself. Is there a name that's special to you?"

Jackson tilted his head to the side, his expression thoughtful for several long moments. "Not really, no. I've honestly never thought about it. She's just been this cute, furry blessing in my life. What about you? Any special names?"

"My mom's name, but you don't want to name your dog after her."

"Why not? I think Ginny's a good name."

Dog's ears perked up.

"I'm not sure Brand would want to hear us calling out Ginny at random on the ranch, that's all," Wyatt said. "Even though she refused to tell me the name of my birth father on her deathbed, I still loved Mom to bits. She was a fantastic mother for the first sixteen years of my life, and I'll always miss her."

Jackson squeezed his thigh. "It's okay to love someone and still be a little mad at them. God knows we've gone through our share of that these last few months, and we're still here, together and happy."

"True." He covered Jackson's hand with his. "So Ginny?"

"Ginny. Might take her a bit to get used to being called by it, though."

"It's okay. We've got time to work with her." Wyatt scratched her ear again. "Right, Ginny?"

She woofed. Wyatt grinned.

Jackson chuckled as he leaned down until his face was close to her muzzle. "Hey there, Ginny. It's nice to finally meet you." Ginny licked his cheek.

Wyatt wrapped one arm around Jackson's waist and bent over to receive his own kiss from Ginny. "Hey, lady." Ginny blinked, and in those soulful eyes, Wyatt swore he saw his mom smiling back at him.

"Come on!" Susie's high-pitched voice broke the moment. She bounced over and petted Ginny's back as she announced, "Grandma says it's time for cake!"

"Just as long as no one sings," Wyatt said.

"But it's your birthday, we gotta sing. Please?"

How was he supposed to resist his adorable little cousin? "Okay, fine. I'll endure it for the sake of cake."

"Yay!" She ran over to her parents, cheering the entire time.

Rose called for the family to gather around Wyatt's table as she presented the white frosted cake with two big wax candles representing 21. Wyatt stood with Jackson, and leaned into him while his new family sang, his face flaming with embarrassment at being the center of attention. But beyond the embarrassment was joy. So much joy his heart wanted to burst.

When he first came to Weston four months ago, he'd never dreamed of having this one day. A happy, loving (even if not always completely accepting) family that had tucked him and Jackson right under their wings. It hadn't been easy and he'd made a lot of mistakes. He'd probably make a lot more mistakes going forward, and he was okay with that. It was all part of growing up and of falling in love.

And as Wyatt blew out his birthday candles that evening, with Jackson and his father by his side, Wyatt wished for this happiness they'd all found to last.

Always.

* * * * *

*Welcome to Clean Slate Ranch: home of tight jeans,
cowboy boots, and rough trails. For some men,
it's a fantasy come true.*

Keep reading for an excerpt from
Wild Trail *by A.M. Arthur.*

Chapter One

"How come you look like you stepped barefoot on a horse pie?"

"Dunno, how come you smell like one?" Mack Garrett replied to his best friend. He raised his head, not at all surprised to see Reyes Caldero standing in the open doorway of Mack's small office. Reyes wore heavy boots and stomped around in them in a way that told you the man was coming long before he appeared.

"Looking over the roster for this week's guests." Mack held up the tablet with said roster on it, then pulled a face. He opened his mouth, but Reyes cut him off.

"Oh no, you're not," Reyes said. He stalked over to the desk. "I know you've got more responsibilities now, but don't you dare say you aren't coming out tonight."

Mack sighed, unsurprised Reyes had read him so well. Mack and their other best friend, Colt, had a tradition of going clubbing in San Francisco on Saturday night, looking for fast and dirty hookups. Reyes accompanied them on occasion, usually to drink and dance and let off steam. "I really shouldn't go into the city."

"Yes, you should, especially since you're the one who convinced me to go with you and Colt this time." He knuckled Mack hard in the shoulder. "You are not leaving me alone to go clubbing with that man."

Mack couldn't help chuckling at the mental image of the more reserved, introverted Reyes clubbing alone with their excitable, flirts-with-everyone friend Colt Woods. "I need to make sure everything is ready for the new guests tomorrow."

"You've got hours to do that, my friend. Besides, maybe you'll run into your last hookup, the guy you said had a cowboy fetish and knew how to deep throat."

"Not interested in repeats, you know that." As much as Mack had enjoyed that particular encounter, he wasn't looking to date. And he absolutely wasn't interested in a new relationship, not after his last one ended with Mack's heart shattered.

Reyes nodded with understanding. "No repeats, but at least come out to dance. Saturday night is the only time we're not on call for guests and are allowed off the ranch grounds for fun and thrills."

"Says the guy who'd rather spend his Saturday reading a book."

"I like books better than people."

True enough. Reyes only occasionally dated—both men and women—and he'd never been a big fan of random hookups. He'd never come out and identified as bi, but Reyes also wasn't a big fan of labels. He seemed content enough in his solitary lifestyle, and that was good enough for Mack.

"What if I help you finish your work?" Reyes asked. "Tell me about the new guests."

"We've got a bridal party."

Reyes let out an exaggerated groan as he leaned against the doorframe. He was one of the most easygoing cowboys on the ranch, and even he found them stressful. Bridal parties at the dude ranch were rare, but they often tended to be the neediest and most disruptive because of their size.

"You think I can still switch my week off with Slater?" Reyes asked.

Mack grunted. "Doubtful. Slater bolted the second it hit three o'clock, and he's had an hour to make his getaway. He's probably in San Jose by now."

"Damn it."

"Chill out, pal, it's not that bad. This one is only five people."

"Really? Seems small. Our last bridal party was eighteen people."

"Trust me, I haven't forgotten." While Mack had enjoyed the novelty of the couple being gay, their friends had been high-strung and extremely anti-dirt. And dirt was impossible to avoid on a ranch in Northern California. "Maybe it's going to be a small wedding."

Mack glanced at his tablet and the list of names. "One woman and four guys. The reservation was placed by the Best Person to the bride, a Wes Bentley."

Reyes frowned. "Like the actor Wes Bentley?"

"Who?"

"Seriously? *American Beauty.* How can you not remember his eyes?"

Mack thought back to the film in question, which he'd seen once, in the theater. "The daughter's creepy boyfriend who filmed plastic bags blowing in the wind?"

Reyes rolled his eyes. "You have absolutely no taste in movies."

"Yes, I know, you've been telling me that since we were fourteen."

"You said *Pulp Fiction* was terrible and overrated."

"It is." Mack had wanted to set fire to that VHS after Reyes forced him through the film.

Reyes grunted. "You were mad that *D2: The Mighty*

Ducks didn't get an Oscar nomination. Your film taste carries no weight with me. Ever."

Mack laughed at the familiar rebuttal. At fourteen, he'd been too busy obsessing over the male cast of a teen hockey comedy to really care about art films or cinematic story-telling breakthroughs. He'd wanted to watch Joshua Jackson ice skate. He still kind of did. The actor had barely aged a day since *Dawson's Creek*.

"Anyway," Mack said, "no, I doubt the Wes Bentley who made the reservation is the actor, but I guess we'll find out in the morning."

"True. How many guests total?"

"Sixteen, so almost a full house, and one of them's a family."

Figuring out the rooming arrangements wasn't usually Mack's job, but he'd been taking more responsibilities to help his aging grandfather work less and enjoy his ranch a little bit more. Arthur Garrett was a proud man, and even though he'd never admit out loud that he was slowing down as he neared his seventy-eighth birthday, his age and new-found forgetfulness worried Mack. After all, Arthur was the only blood family Mack had left.

Reyes had been family ever since they were twelve years old and jointly put cherry bombs in the girl's bath-room toilets at school. Mack's other best friend, Colt, had been in his life far fewer years, but he was family, too. Within the same six-month time period, each man had quit his previous career and moved to the ranch to find... something. Something new.

And to start over, away from the pain in their pasts.

Mack was still getting used to figuring out the sleeping arrangements for guests. He was in charge of overseeing the horses, guest interaction with horses and the camping trips. Simple things. Putting warm bodies into rooms in a way that made sense didn't come naturally to him, so he waved Reyes over.

"Tell me how this looks," he said, handing him the tablet.

Reyes scanned the rooms and the names attached, which was linked to the guest registration information that asked: Are you comfortable sharing a room with a stranger of the same or opposite sex? Other variations of the question gave Mack enough information to guess. The second floor of the guesthouse had four four-bunk rooms, each with a private bathroom. Sometimes strangers ended up bunking together—which also meant every other week, someone had an issue on arrival day and bunks had to be switched around.

Arthur had always rolled his eyes and muttered about tourists being coddled.

"No, this looks good," Reyes replied. "The bride said she didn't mind sharing with strangers, so putting her into a four-bunk room with the three single ladies is good. It all looks good."

"Always looks good on paper."

"Or pixels."

"Whatever." Mack took the tablet back. "Food delivery here yet?"

"Truck pulled up a few minutes ago. It's actually what I came to tell you. Arthur, uh, put the order in wrong."

Mack groaned. "Shit, what are we missing?"

"We're light on flour, eggs and bacon."

All breakfast staples for the guesthouse kitchen. "Great."

Every week, Arthur placed a food order for the next week's guests, and the food was trucked over Saturday afternoon. Arthur had been placing the order for years, and it was another weekly ranch task he was hanging on to tightly with his wrinkled, arthritic fingers. But this was the third mistake in four months.

He followed Reyes out of the barn and into bright May sunshine that had him squinting the whole hundred yard walk to the guesthouse. Their usual delivery guy, Juno, was standing by his truck talking to their cook, Patrice, and they both went perfectly still at Mack's approach. Mack was well aware that his squint made him look perpetually pissed off, but there wasn't much he could do. It was the only face he had.

"I'm so sorry," Juno said as soon as he was within earshot.

"It's not your fault," Mack replied, trying to put the guy at ease. He looked like he was ready to jump out of his skin. "Give me your list."

Juno handed over a paper printout from the grocery store that handled their business. Arthur preferred dealing locally, so Mack had to be nice and fix this without accusing anyone—not his best act. Mack logged into the business records and found their copy of Arthur's order. They matched.

"Our mistake," Mack said, handing the list back. "Go ahead and accept the delivery, Patrice. Figure out the difference. I'll run into town and buy what you need."

"Bless you," Patrice said. A genuinely sweet lady, Patrice had been on the ranch for decades. She prepared every meal, kept the rooms clean, and generally doted over the guests, especially the children.

Juno and Patrice went off to restock the kitchen pantry.

Mack pivoted one-eighty to stare at the main house. The last original building on the property, the hundred-and-fifty-year-old single-story ranch home looked pretty good under a new coat of paint. Its wide front porch no longer sagged, thanks to Colt's handiness with a hammer and nails.

"You gonna tell Arthur?" Reyes asked.

"I have to. He'll wonder about the in-town credit card purchase if I don't."

"How do you think he'll react?"

"He'll brush it off as a one-time problem, like he always does."

"You think Arthur would be more receptive to it coming from Judson?" Reyes asked, spookily following along on Mack's silent train of thought. Twenty-four years of friendship did that.

"I doubt it matters who tells him. Once is a mistake. Twice is something to watch. Three times is a pattern and potentially a problem."

"Yeah."

"You gonna come into town with me for the extra supplies?"

Reyes shrugged. "Why not? We'll get it done so you don't have an excuse not to come into San Francisco with me and Colt."

Patrice came outside with a handwritten list. "Here you go, hon."

"Thanks." Mack stuffed it in his pocket. "I'll text Judson about the grocery trip, and then we'll get going. I can talk to Arthur later."

"Good luck with that chat," Reyes said.

Mack felt kind of bad about buying out the store's entire stock of bacon, but it was a breakfast staple at Patrice's table—both the one she set in the main dining room for guests, and the smaller buffet she provided for the ranch hands in the back room. This was why they ordered ahead of time: so the store's owner could fill their needs without depriving his own customers.

Oh well.

One of the stock boys brought boxes out of the backroom to use for the groceries, instead of wasting a bunch of plastic bags. Reyes bought himself a bag of barbecue potato chips, which had been a favorite of his since forever. Mack studiously avoided the ice cream aisle. Ice cream always reminded him of Geoff, and he didn't need to get depressed on his Saturday night off.

He and Reyes packed up the bed of the ranch's pickup truck with their supplies, then puttered back through town. Garrett had a meager population of five thousand, give or take, and had been settled during the gold rush.

Mack hadn't even known the town existed until about ten years ago, and now he couldn't imagine leaving. He loved knowing more about his roots, and he loved this old, dilapidated town.

The truck ambled through the worn downtown, past town limits, to where Mack could safely press on the gas. Their police force was tiny, but they gave out tickets for anything they could in order to keep funding their own jobs. Their town barely kept afloat year after year, as the population continued to dwindle. Arthur had long lamented he couldn't do more to drive tourists into Garrett itself.

"Stop it," Reyes said.

"Stop what?" Mack retorted. "Driving? We don't want the bacon to cook in the sun."

"Jackass. It isn't your job to save this town, and you know it."

"Maybe, maybe not. There's a lot of my family history here, buried on this land."

"Even so, worry about the ranch first. You still gotta talk to Arthur about the supply order snafu."

Mack grunted. A small part of him hoped Judson had taken care of that chore, but he'd yet to get a text about it. Mack would probably end up confronting his grandfather himself, and that would suck. He wasn't afraid of confrontation. Hell, Mack had been Los Angeles County SWAT for four years. No, he was more afraid of the emotional damage this might do. Reminding an old man he was just getting older.

He parked in front of the guesthouse. Reyes and Patrice helped him unload the truck and store the supplies in the kitchen's industrial walk-in. When they finished, Reyes took the empty boxes over to the garbage shed—the place they hid their garbage and recycling containers so they didn't kill the feel of the ranch, or attract unwanted pests. Behind the shed was also a compost pile for food scraps. The ranch made extra cash for the horse rescue by turning the compost into a nice fertilizer to sell to town residents. The smell stayed downwind of the guesthouse, so it had never been an issue. Not that it should be. It was a ranch. The place smelled like horses and dirt.

Mack would never forget the guest two summers ago who'd carried a bottle of air freshener with him everywhere the first day, until he tried spraying it around the horses. After that, Mack banned its use to the guesthouse.

He moved the pickup to its usual spot east of the main house, next to Judson's personal vehicle, and the garage that housed four ATVs that the staff had free range to use.

"Mack!" Arthur's voice dragged his attention to the front porch. He stood at the top step in his ever-present denim overalls, the purple undershirt making his white hair and beard stand out even more.

A widower from a young age, Arthur had served in the Army for a lot of years, before turning a struggling cattle ranch into a successful vacation spot and horse rescue. And while no one was getting rich working here, he took care of his staff. But he was also aging, and sooner or later, he'd have to retire from the business end of things and turn control over to his general manager and foreman, Judson Marvel.

"Yes, sir." Mack strode over to the porch, shoulders straight.

"You got the sleeping arrangements done for tomorrow?"

"A while ago. I posted it so you could take a peek, but Reyes double-checked me. It's good."

"Excellent. Food delivery come okay?"

Mack stifled a sigh; Judson hadn't talked to him. "It came, but we had a slight hiccup. You under-ordered again. Three staples."

"Well, shit." Arthur frowned. "You checked—"

"I checked your original order against the one Juno had on him. They matched. Reyes and I went into town a bit ago to get what extra Patrice needed. You'll see the charge on the business card."

"I'm sorry about that. Honest mistake."

"On flour, bacon and eggs that you've been ordering for ten years?"

Arthur's shoulders slumped. Mack loved his grandfather and hated seeing him upset, but this was about the business. Arthur's business, and they both had to protect it.

"We fixed it, but this is the third incident in four months," Mack said. "This coming week, just let me or Judson double-check you before you send the order over. We all need a second set of eyes sometimes. Just like I had Reyes double-check me today."

"Makes good sense. Better for business."

"And I think the store will appreciate it. I bought out all of their bacon."

Arthur's eyes lit up with silent laughter. "Hopefully no one in town wants a BLT for dinner tonight."

"They would be shit out of luck."

"How's our new batch of guests look?" Arthur descended the four wood steps to stand next to Mack. They had similar heights and builds, and some folks swore they saw Arthur in Mack, but Mack never could.

"Not too bad. Married couple, small family, two groups of friends and a bridal party. Sixteen total."

"Good, good. You and Colt going out tonight?"

The abrupt conversation shift startled Mack. He'd come out to Arthur years ago, right after Arthur came out to him—gay his entire life, but hiding it for decades until he said fuck it, I'm out. Hence his purple T-shirts and the rainbow flag proudly displayed on their flagpoles each day next to the American flag and the California state flag. The Clean Slate Ranch was gay-friendly and proud of it.

"Yeah," Mack replied. "Reyes is coming out for a change."

"You're never going to meet someone if all you ever do is visit bars and dance clubs."

Mack shrugged. "I don't want to meet anyone right now."

"Hmm. Maybe, maybe not. Why don't you try those dating apps on your phone?"

"What's with the sudden urge to marry me off?" That came out with more anger than necessary. "Sorry, I just... I'm not ready."

"It's been nearly five years, son."

"I know how long it's been, believe me." Long enough that he could think about Geoff without his heart breaking wide-open, but not long enough that he was ready to risk his heart a second time. Losing Geoff had hurt too damned much.

Arthur sighed. "Why don't you come have dinner at the house with me and Judson tonight? Reyes and Colt, too." Also a widower, Judson was the only person who lived in the main house with Arthur. A row of two-man cabins fifty yards north of the house was where the hands lived.

Mack could have had a cabin to himself, but he genuinely didn't mind sharing with Reyes. He was quiet, tidy, and he'd seemed to really need the companionship when he first moved to the ranch, only a few months after Mack. "Sure, why not?" he replied. "You cooking?" Silly question, because if Arthur loved anything more than his horses, it was cooking. Even if his recipes were pretty basic.

"Certainly. I've had a roast in the slow cooker all day."

Mack sniffed the air, but couldn't detect the scent of cooking meat over the rest of the odors of the ranch. "Mashed potatoes?"

"Of course. What kind of monster do you think I am?"

"Just checking." And teasing. Arthur was a tried-and-true meat and potatoes man. Where there was one, there was the other. "I'll see you around six, then?"

"Six it is."

"Cool. I have to get a few more things ready for tomorrow's check-in. See you in a while."

Mack strode toward the tourist barn and his office. Most of his work for tomorrow was finished, so he bypassed the office and walked down two stalls to his personal horse, Tude. A paint mare with several ugly scars on her flanks, thanks to a brutal previous owner, she'd come into Arthur's care around the same time as Mack. Mack had fallen in love with the high-strung horse, renamed her Attitude, Tude for short, and Arthur had helped him retrain her.

She nickered at his presence, her big head rising over the stall's gate. Mack held up a cube of sugar that she greedily picked up with her lips. He rubbed a hand over her smooth nose, up her long forehead. She had big brown eyes that simultaneously said "I like you" and "I dare you." Attitude.

"What do I need a boyfriend for when I've got you, lady?" Mack asked softly, the only sounds in the barn the quiet movements of the other horses.

Tude didn't have an answer for him.

Don't miss Wild Trail, *available now*
wherever ebooks are sold.
www.CarinaPress.com